Also by Julia London
and Canary Street Press

A Royal Match

Last Duke Standing
The Duke Not Taken
The Viscount Who Vexed Me

A Royal Wedding

The Princess Plan
A Royal Kiss & Tell
A Princess by Christmas

The Cabot Sisters

The Trouble with Honor
The Devil Takes a Bride
The Scoundrel and the Debutante

The Highland Grooms

Wild Wicked Scot
Sinful Scottish Laird
Hard-Hearted Highlander
Devil in Tartan
Tempting the Laird
Seduced by a Scot

For additional books by Julia London,
visit her website, julialondon.com.

THE
VISCOUNT
WHO VEXED ME

JULIA LONDON

CANARY STREET PRESS

CANARY STREET PRESS™

Recycling programs
for this product may
not exist in your area.

ISBN-13: 978-1-335-49822-9

The Viscount Who Vexed Me

Copyright © 2023 by Dinah Dinwiddie

For questions and comments about the quality of this book, please contact us at CustomerService@Harlequin.com.

Canary Street Press
22 Adelaide St. West, 41st Floor
Toronto, Ontario M5H 4E3, Canada
CanaryStPress.com

Printed in Lithuania

MIX
Paper | Supporting
responsible forestry
FSC® C021394

"Life isn't fair, it's just fairer than death, that's all."
—William Goldman, *The Princess Bride*

THE
VISCOUNT
WHO VEXED ME

CHAPTER ONE

London, England
1870

IT BECAME NECESSARY, the spring the Santiavan duke came to London, that every woman, no matter her age or place in society, should have a friend who could be trusted to tell her what no one else would.

For Miss Harriet Woodchurch, that person was Miss Flora Raney, the daughter of the venerable Viscount Raney. Not only was she Hattie's dearest friend, she was also Hattie's employer of sorts, as her father paid Hattie a modest fee to accompany Flora as she flitted about town.

Flora would explain what Hattie could not see for herself. Something terrible, something that Hattie could neither forgive nor forget...at least to begin.

She did, in fact, put it completely out of her mind in the weeks that followed. But on that particular day, forgetting seemed impossible, as not only was the news heartbreaking, but it was wrapped up in the sighting of the most talked about bachelor in all of London.

Hattie and Flora, and Flora's oldest friend, Queenie, were shopping. The three women had attended the Iddesleigh School for Exceptional Girls at the same time. Flora and Queenie had come to the school as daughters of titles and wealth, which automatically set them apart from the other girls. Hattie had come on scholarship, which distinguished her in an entirely different and not complimentary way. But she and Flora had shared a room for a term and had become friends.

They were in a millinery shop, standing at the large store window, examining the gloves for sale. Or rather, Flora and Queenie were. Hattie had no money for things like gloves or petticoats or hats.

"But why haven't you any money?" Queenie had inquired earlier. "Your father has the largest public transport company in all of London."

That was true—Mr. Hugh Woodchurch proudly provided hansom cabs, Clarence cabs, and horse busses to the masses of London around the clock. It was a lucrative business. But he did not believe in sharing that fortune with his daughter. What she needed, he said, she had at home. Money spent on gloves and hats and clothes was unnecessary when a young woman had two serviceable day gowns, a morning gown, and one evening gown. Never mind that the evening gown was handed down from her mother and was the style of a different era. Hattie's father said if she wanted more, she ought to see herself married.

Hattie would like nothing better than to see herself married and was looking forward to the day that she and her fiancé, Mr. Rupert Masterson, would settle in the rooms above his shop. But because her engagement was not yet official—although he'd promised to speak to her father any day now—she'd sought work to pay for the few things she would like to have. She now had four serviceable day gowns, one evening gown, and two morning gowns, thank you.

Flora and Queenie had decided they must have eight-button gloves made of silk and linen in the event they were invited to a country house weekend this coming summer. Hattie had exactly two pairs of gloves, also handed down to her by her mother, with only three buttons. There was no room in her meager budget for new ones, so she followed along, refolding the gloves that Flora and Queenie handed to her without thought when they'd lost interest and moved on to the next pair.

Suddenly, a woman entered the shop in such a hurry that she set all the bells above the door clanging. "Mrs. Perkins!"

Mrs. Perkins, the shopkeeper, burst forth from the curtains covering the entrance to a back room like she thought the shop might be on fire. "What is it? What's happened?"

The woman rushed to the front window where Flora and Queenie were, forcing them aside. "What in heaven!" Queenie cried.

"He's there!"

"Who's there?" Queenie demanded—she'd never been shy about seeking answers.

"Here?" Mrs. Perkins gasped and sprang to the window like a gazelle. "Where?"

The woman pointed across the street, and Queenie grabbed Flora's arm. *"Look!"*

"You're hurting me," Flora said.

"For once, will you do as I ask?" Queenie demanded. "Look!"

Hattie watched the four ladies in the shop window, leaning forward and peering out over the glove displays, confused about what was happening. "Oh my. Oh *my*," Flora said, then gestured wildly for Hattie. "Come here, come *here*, you have to see!"

There was not enough room for the five of them, and Hattie had to stand on her tiptoes to see over Flora's shoulder. "I can't really see," Hattie said.

The rest of them ignored her. *"Where?"* Mrs. Perkins demanded, sounding panicked.

Mrs. Perkins's friend pointed.

Hattie tried to make herself taller. The only thing she could see was a haberdashery across the street. Three gentlemen stood before it, chatting. "Is that it?" Hattie asked and sank down onto her feet again.

"Not *them*," the woman said. "The viscount."

There had to be at least a dozen viscounts on Regent Street on any given day. "Which one?"

"Which one?" Flora repeated, and shot a disapproving look over her shoulder at Hattie. "Viscount Abbott, of course."

"Of course," Hattie muttered. She didn't know of any Viscount Abbott. Or why any of these women were interested in him.

"Who is also the Duke of Santiava," Queenie said. Hattie blinked. Queenie rolled her eyes. "Why do you never know these things, Hattie? It's as if you live in a cave."

She never knew these things because she didn't know anything. How could she? She didn't exactly exist in the same social circles as Flora and Queenie. She knew what they told her, and they had not told her about this viscount.

Just then, Flora grabbed Hattie's hand and gripped it so tightly that Hattie winced. Queenie pushed a display of gloves out of the way, and the four women surged forward, Flora dragging Hattie with her.

A man emerged from the shop, holding his hat in his hand. He was tall, with sun-drenched skin. His clothing fit him snugly, and it was apparent that he was trim with an athletic build. His dark hair brushed his collar, and when he looked up at something one of the other gentlemen said, he smiled. Only a little, but it was a smile that sparked through

Hattie. That gentleman was quite possibly the most beautiful man she'd ever seen in her life—elegant, strong, and astonishingly agreeable in looks.

No one spoke for a moment.

A carriage rolled in between the shops and stopped, blocking their view of the haberdashery. When it rolled away, the gentlemen were gone.

The ladies settled back. Queenie sighed and stepped away from the window, leaving the display of gloves knocked onto its side. The woman who had rushed in to announce the viscount sighting retreated to the back room with Mrs. Perkins. Hattie picked up the display and righted it in the window.

"You will be at the top of that list, Flora," Queenie said with certainty.

Queenie was short and round, with soft gold curls that fell around her shoulders. She carried herself like a queen and acted like one on occasion, too. Flora was tall and lithe, her hair auburn. She was pretty by any standard. When Hattie was with the two of them, she often felt like the plain cousin come to town from the village. Her hair was a dull brown, her figure unremarkable.

Flora gave Queenie's remark a high-pitched, breathy laugh that Hattie had never heard her make. "Don't be silly!"

"Don't be coy," Queenie said. "You know that you will."

"The list is quite long, I'm certain. What about Hattie? She might be at the top."

"The top of what?" Hattie asked.

"Really, Hattie!" Queenie said, sounding annoyed. "How can you be so ignorant of all the news around town? The list of potential brides for the viscount, obviously."

Hattie laughed. Loudly.

"I agree, it's hardly a possibility," Queenie said. "I don't mean to offend, but he is the Duke of Santiava, and now he's Viscount Abbott, as he is his English grandfather's only living male heir. He'll marry someone with a large dowry and from a titled family. Someone with proper connections."

Santiava? Hattie vaguely recalled something about it. A duchy, she believed, on the Mediterranean Sea. Once a colony of Wesloria if memory served.

"He's the sovereign duke, and *quite* rich," Queenie continued. "But they say he's a recluse. One must always be wary of the recluse."

One must? Hattie hadn't heard that rule.

"And unmarried, obviously," Flora added as the three of them departed the shop.

"Won't he choose a wife from Santiava?" Hattie asked as they walked toward Hyde Park.

"No!" Queenie scoffed, and Hattie was once again left wondering how her education could be so lacking. "He's come here to claim his title and his fortune and, as everyone knows, be fitted with an English wife. It serves a small duchy to have an English or Weslorian duchess, you know, if they were ever to need the backing of a larger country in times of war or economic hardship. This would practically guarantee it."

Queenie spoke with such authority about him that Hattie had to wonder if she'd consulted with the man himself. She was dubious that a marriage to Flora could guarantee anything of the sort. But she kept silent.

"Imagine, Hattie," Flora said, "if you were the link to the might of the Royal Navy should that duchy need it."

All Hattie could imagine was herself on a leaking, rickety boat. "I won't be the link to anything, because I'm already engaged." She smiled.

Flora and Queenie exchanged a look. "You haven't told her?" Queenie said to Flora.

"Told me what?" Hattie asked, confused.

"*Tell* her. She can't walk around without knowing," Queenie said.

Hattie's heart dropped. "Knowing what? What are you talking about?"

"Oh, Hattie… Mr. Masterson paid me a call," Flora blurted. "I was going to tell you. I was waiting for the right time."

"Well, this is hardly it," Queenie drawled, seemingly oblivious to the fact that she'd just urged Flora to tell her.

But tell her what, exactly? That Rupert had called on Flora? How odd—they weren't so well acquainted. "Mr. Rupert Masterson called on you," Hattie repeated, to make sure they were indeed speaking of *her* Mr. Masterson, the owner and proprietor of the Masterson Dry Goods and Sundries Shop.

"He…he came to me in confidence." Flora punctuated that remark with a look of sympathy.

Hattie's gut began to do a strange bit of swirling. "Why?"

"He said…that he thought it best if you and he…" She paused, as if trying to find the words.

Elope? That was it! What other reason could he have for needing to speak in confidence to Flora? He must have sought her help. *"Elope?"* she asked at the same moment Flora said, "Should not pursue things further."

No one said a word for a moment. Even Queenie kept her mouth shut. *"What?"* Hattie asked and stopped walking. This was stunningly incomprehensible. She pressed a fist to her abdomen to keep down the sudden swell of nausea. "What…what did…he…or you…say?"

"Oh, Hattie, dearest." They'd come to the park's entrance, and Flora pulled her to a bench and sat her down. She took both of Hattie's hands in hers. "I'm so very sorry, but there is no other way to say it, is there? He would like you to cry off your engagement. End it, I mean. He has come to the unfortunate conclusion that it must be done. But because he has the utmost consideration for you, he means to protect your reputation by having you write him and end it."

This didn't feel considerate of her at all—she felt she'd been run over by a team of four. She didn't even have enough air in her lungs to ask why. There had to be some mistake! She and Rupert were marching headlong into connubial bliss. *Weren't they?* He'd recently met her family and, on that very night, had promised he would formally call on her father within the week. And then he'd gone to *Flora* instead of coming to her? No, this couldn't be.

Hattie stood up. "I think you've misunderstood, Flora."

"Oh, darling," Flora said sadly.

"But you must have! It makes no sense!"

"It makes *some* sense," Queenie said with a bit of a shrug.

"No, it doesn't," Flora said quickly with a glare for Queenie. "Perhaps only a tad."

"He dined at our home on Sunday!" Hattie exclaimed. "Today is Wednesday! What could possibly have happened between then and now?"

"Mmm," Queenie said, and wandered off to pretend to look at some roses.

"I think," Flora said, "that if you were to carefully consider your Sunday dinner, you might imagine at least one reason why. Probably more than one. Probably many."

Hattie's heart wanted to leap from her chest. Heat crept up the nape of her neck as she thought back to Sunday dinner at her family home on Blandford Street, near the fashionable Portman Square...or, as Flora had once pointed out, on the less fashionable side of the square, where no one wanted to be.

But Rupert had said it was a fine house. He'd come with a box of chocolates for her mother, and Hattie had been so charmed by that. "But I thought the evening went so well."

Flora patted her arm. "Well...to begin, he worried about a smell in your house that he believes might be peculiar to cats."

Hattie looked at Flora with surprise. Yes, her mother had an unreasonable affinity for cats, but she had explained that to him. "He said he *liked* cats! He said he didn't know what he would do in his shop without Bobo."

Flora gave her that sympathetic smile again. "But I think it is not the same to have one cat and... How many are there now?"

Hattie swallowed. "Eight." Or maybe...ten? Frankly, she'd lost count. And Rupert had seemed a little taken aback when he'd entered the foyer and the cats had all come running at once, collectively expecting a treat.

"There's a bit more," Flora said.

It turned out that Rupert also found her mother's collection of tea services disagreeable. And the grandfather clocks. And the dress forms. Granted there were probably more than one hundred tea services, which probably wouldn't have been quite so noticeable had it not been for the clocks and dress forms. All right, it was the truth—Theodora Woodchurch was overly enthusiastic in her collecting, and a large residence such as the Woodchurch house could be made to look small when cluttered with so many collections.

Her mother's habits were a source of constant squabbling between her parents, because while her mother was a spendthrift, her father was a miserly king.

And apparently, though Hattie had been so pleased that her father had not asked how little Mr. Masterson would accept in a dowry, she'd missed what terrible taste it was that her father should ask how much profit Mr. Masterson turned every month. According to Flora, Mr. Masterson had been dismayed by it, had thought perhaps such conversations were better had between men in the privacy of a study. Not at the dinner table.

In Hattie's family, no topic was considered impolite at the dining table. None.

Her sudden heartbreak began to turn to sudden anger. She and Rupert had never shared a cross word—she had no idea he felt so strongly about such things. She knew her family was unusual, but she'd explained it to him, and he'd assured her that eccentricity in families made life more interesting.

Furthermore, she was humiliated that he had shared all these opinions with *Flora*. Flora was her friend! Even worse, Flora had clearly shared his opinions with Queenie.

Hattie squared her shoulders in search of a tiny bit of dignity. "Is there more? Or is the fact that my mother has too many cats and teapots—"

"He did mention your brothers," Flora interjected.

Oh no. "Which ones?"

Flora blinked. "*All* of them," she said, as if that could even be a question.

Hattie's heart sank. That was it, then.

"He said the younger ones argued loudly about a particular cut of meat at the dining table." Her brows rose, as if she couldn't believe this was possibly true.

It was not only possible, it was a regular occurrence.

The twins, Peter and Perry, ten years younger than Hattie, were, for lack of a better word, uncivilized. They thought nothing of wrestling in the main salon or using their cricket sticks to chase each other about. "Leave your brothers be," her mother had said when Hattie complained about their rambunctiousness. "They're children yet." But they were nearly fourteen years old, certainly old enough to exhibit proper manners. *Certainly* old enough not to argue over a turkey leg like two medieval warlords.

The heat was spreading to her cheeks.

"And your brother Mr. Daniel Woodchurch." Flora glanced uneasily toward Queenie, who was standing to the side, under a tree, patiently waiting. She whispered quickly, "I wouldn't say it if you weren't my dearest friend in all the world, you know I wouldn't, but his rakish reputation precedes him! Mr. Masterson said he sauntered in quite late to dinner, and who could say where he'd been, but that he smelled like perfume and whisky, and then your brother went on to say he couldn't imagine the hours one must devote to the operation of a dry goods store and didn't see why one would want to do it."

Hattie was feeling a little nauseated. Her brothers were ridiculous, she would not deny it. But she was beginning to wonder if Rupert wasn't even more ridiculous. He didn't have the courage to say these things to her face.

She knew better than anyone that her family was hard to understand. But she'd been very honest with Rupert about them. She'd told him the twins were wild, and Daniel wilder in a different sort of way. She'd told him that her mother had a habit of collecting things and her father was very tight with his purse. And really, wasn't the important thing that *she* wasn't any of those things?

"Are you all right?" Flora asked. "You've lost all your color and look as if you might be ill."

"I feel as if I might," Hattie weakly agreed. She couldn't believe this was happening. She'd already planned her trousseau.

"I'm *so* sorry. I didn't want to be the one to tell you, and I said to Mr. Masterson that surely there was a way he could convey this to you himself, but he insisted he'd not give even the slightest illusion of scandal where you were concerned, as he holds you in the highest esteem."

Hattie choked on a sob.

"We really should be going," Queenie called from her place beneath the tree.

Flora smiled sadly at Hattie. "When you've had a moment to think, you'll see that this isn't really such a loss. I know that Mr. Masterson has been very attentive to you. But he *is* a merchant, darling."

Hattie choked on another sob. She didn't care what he was. She esteemed him, and she was not in a position in life to demand that a gentleman have a certain occupation. She wasn't pretty like Flora, or rich like Queenie, or accomplished or well-connected. She considered herself lucky that Rupert had even noticed her the day she'd entered his shop.

"What I mean is, you're too good for a merchant. You should marry a duke!"

"Flora—"

"Come on, now," Flora said, sounding a bit impatient. "You'll write your letter crying off the engagement, then buy a new frock or two for the Season."

A new frock? Surely Flora had noticed she wore the same gowns over and over.

"Shouldn't we carry on now?" Queenie asked impatiently.

"Buck up, love," Flora said to Hattie and smiled. "We'll attend all the Season's parties and have a look at the Santiavan duke. Won't that cheer you up?"

"No," Hattie said, appalled at how easily Flora could brush off the end of her engagement.

And what did she have to do with a Santiavan duke, anyway?

CHAPTER TWO

THERE WERE TOO many people in London.

There were too many people in his *house*.

Was it even his house? Honestly, Mateo Vincente wasn't entirely certain. He didn't want to appear to be a half-wit for not knowing, but he'd not yet gone through all the properties and holdings of the late Viscount Abbott. There was quite a lot to learn about the estate that had belonged to his English grandfather—it was a vast network of investments and partial ownerships. And he was utterly baffled with the strange business about the purchase of some sheep that seemed mired in complete confusion between the viscount's estate and the shepherd.

Mateo had been in England a little more than a fortnight, and knew only two things with certainty: one, that this very large house was in the middle of London, situated near the excellent Hyde Park, and boasting a fine, but diminutive, garden, where he was just now, trying to escape the noise in his house.

And two, he wished every day he was home in the Duchy of Santiava, at Castillo Estrella, the mountain castle where he'd lived since he'd become duke six years ago.

The newspapers called him *ermitaño*. A hermit. Some called him mad. One gentleman, a prolific contributor to the Santiavan presses, said he was a simpleton, and his mother kept him hidden away so that she could rule.

None of those things were true. But it was true he preferred his own company to that of the world.

England felt foreign to him. His mother was English, but England itself had always seemed far away and inconsequential to the quiet life he led in Santiava. His grandfather had died without a male heir, and his estate and title had passed to Mateo through his mother. Which meant this house, presumably, and the rest of the estate, presumably, and anything else, presumably, in the ledger provided by the very helpful and rotund Mr. Callum belonged to him now.

Viscount Abbott. A very English name and title for a man who was not remotely English.

His mother, Elizabeth Abbott Vincente, *la duquesa viuda de Santiava,* had married his father at the age of seventeen, had borne him at the age of eighteen, his brother, Roberto, and sister, Sofia, shortly thereafter, and had lived most of her married life in Santiava. While she'd periodically returned to England to look after her parents, she'd brought her children only on occasion. Mateo remembered when he was twelve or so, his grandfather had been honored by Queen Victoria with the Order of the Garter. What he remembered about that visit was not the august ceremony, but the terrible row his mother had had with her father, in English, at a pace so frightening that he could hardly follow. The duchess and her children had left England shortly thereafter.

He'd seen his grandfather only once after that.

His mother, as far as he knew, had never mended her relationship with her father. *Like mother, like son.* Mateo's relationship with his father had been fraught with misunderstandings and resentments, too. He imagined he knew a bit how his mother felt now that her father was gone. Not that she cared to speak of it. "The past is dead and buried, Teo," she would say.

He wished he felt the same. His father had died six years ago, but unfortunately, that past still lived on in him.

His mother wasn't much help to him. At forty-six years, her memory of the Abbott estate was foggy. But even if she'd remembered every last detail since they'd arrived in England, she'd been too occupied with entertaining and being entertained to be of any help to him. Oh, she popped into the study now and again to chastise him for not eating properly (he did) or having refused an invitation (a few). Mostly, she spent her time receiving what seemed like cartloads of ladies in colorful gowns and expensive hats and left all the business of settling her late father's estate to him.

Even now, he could hear voices drifting out of the windows of her sitting room, reaching him in the garden. Gay, twittering voices. *Dios ayúdame.*

The small garden was exemplary. The path from the house was lined with dozens of rose bushes. The shrubbery that blocked the rest of London from this tiny patch of paradise had been meticulously shaped. And if one were to walk through an arch cut into the shrubbery, one would find a smaller, private garden, and a bench near a small fountain where one might read or close his eyes for a few moments.

Or enjoy a few pastries. He had a plate with him today.

He'd baked them himself. Another small part of his past that lived on in him. His father had insisted that no self-respecting duke or English viscount would ever bake *pastries*. It was ironic that Mateo's interest in baking was his father's doing—he had to give the old man credit for having left him and his siblings alone so much in their youth.

More practically, Mateo had learned how to bake from

Rosa—more formally known as Señora de Leon—who had been with Mateo's family all his life. When his parents flitted off to Madrid or Seville or Paris, Rosa would gather Mateo and his siblings like chicks to her. She would read them stories of Santiavan knights and ladies, of pirates and heroic sea captains. She would encourage them to imagine a life beyond the palace or castle walls.

Mateo's imagination in those years had run wild. He'd fished in the mountain streams and hunted in the forests. He and his brother had built a fort deep in the woods, fashioned like the infamous *Fuerta del Monte Parson*, the fort atop a great ocean cliff where the small Santiavan army had held the Weslorian navy during the War of Independence.

Mateo liked military history and had collected books about it over the years. His father had believed this hobby to be a waste of time, too. "The study might have had utility in an earlier era, but it's useless now," he would say. "We've been free for more than fifty years. Study trade, study politics. Anything but old war tales."

On the contrary, Mateo thought his study had more utility now than ever—there was something to be learned from the history of great battles waged and won, and those lost. For a small duchy like Santiava there had been a certain amount of cunning required to protect against threats from much larger countries like Spain, France, and Wesloria. Who knew when it might come in handy again?

His father felt equally annoyed with Mateo's interest in astronomy. When an uncle had given Mateo the gift of a telescope when he was nine years old, Mateo was so enthralled that he'd made his own charts of the sky and pinned them to the wall.

"Head in the clouds," his father would say dismissively.

The Santiavan newspapers could sense a father's disappointment in his heir, and that had added to the pressure to be perfect. They wrote about Mateo's appearance—as a boy, he'd been thin. They said he looked weak. On those occasions he'd been forced to make public remarks, he was so fearful of his father's disapproval that he would inevitably stumble over his words, and the newspapers wondered if he was a simpleton. So Mateo had learned to say as little as possible in public.

He'd spent a childhood seeking a way to be right in his father's eyes and never finding it. Rosa was the only adult in his life who had always seemed to accept him as he was.

He and Rosa were currently perfecting the art of crafting *miguelitos*, which required the layering of a dozen thin sheets of unleavened dough to form delicate pillows into which chocolate could be stuffed. *Delicioso*. Naturally, Mateo had insisted that Rosa accompany the entourage to England. He didn't intend to give up his hobby just because he was an English viscount now.

He picked up a small pastry from his plate and bit into it. He closed his eyes, savoring the taste. The layers of buttery leaf-thin filo settled nicely on his tongue, and the chocolate melted. This was his best batch yet. Mateo opened his eyes and was deciding which one to choose for his next sampling when he was startled half out of his wits by his mother's voice and fumbled the plate, dropping it to the grass at his feet. It landed upside down. He stared at the disaster, then lifted his gaze to his mother, who had come into his little patch of private paradise quite unannounced.

She looked at the plate, then at him. "You're not doing *that* again."

"Is there something you need?" he asked.

"I need *you*, darling. I've been looking everywhere for you. Even Señor Pacheco had no idea where you'd gone!"

She sounded agitated with his manservant, but Pacheco was a wise man and often claimed ignorance where the duchess was concerned.

"I was seeking a moment of peace and quiet, Mami," Mateo said, and bent over to return the pastries to the plate. "It's sometimes difficult to think with all the laughing and singing from your drawing room." He set the plate aside on the bench and turned to his mother, towering over her. "Is everything all right?"

"Everything is fine, Teo, but we haven't much time."

"For?"

"You know that Señora Martinez and I are leaving for Paris soon."

"Sí." Not only did he know it, he was counting the days.

"And here you are still muddling through this estate business!"

Muddling through. It was an odd complaint for something as tedious as his work was. Mateo spoke Spanish, French, and English fluently. But his competency in reading and writing the three languages was not equal, with English being the weakest. He found the written word terribly confusing, what with *there* and *their* and *where* and *wear*, and so forth. That, coupled with his grandfather's handwriting, which was so tiny as to require the use of a magnifying glass, had slowed his progress considerably. What was it he'd been reading this morning? *To consider some additions to be made to the* magnam bibliothecam, *and of matters relating thereto; that the gentleman be pleased to lay prints of his case on his lordship's table...* He'd puzzled over the tiny writing for an hour before deciphering that. And it meant nothing to him.

"I am not muddling. Perhaps you have forgotten, but the Abbott estate is quite large and involved."

"Yes, yes…but if you don't finish your review and make some decisions, they will have robbed us blind, if they haven't already."

"Qué?" What was she talking about? "Who? Mr. Callum?" he asked, referring to the estate agent.

"I almost forgot why I came for you," she said, gliding over that baseless and nebulous accusation. "I'm hosting a dinner party."

This was not news—she seemed to host one every other day. On rare occasions, she could force him to attend, but he generally preferred to take his meals in his rooms without having to play the part of society's latest find. "What has that to do with—"

"And I have someone for you to meet."

Mateo groaned. He stared at his mother with her dark hair and stark blue eyes and trim figure with all due suspicion. She had a habit of doing this to him, of throwing a lot of things at him at once. Disconnected things. Things that would give him pause, all so that she could slip in something particularly disagreeable.

"You've got that sour look, Teo. It's only Lady Lila Aleksander from Denmark."

"Perdóname," rumbled a male voice.

Mateo and his mother both turned toward the arch, where the family butler, Borerro, had appeared. He bowed. "Your guests have arrived, *señora*."

"What, *now*?" Mateo glowered at his mother.

"Oh, Mateo," she said with a sigh full of disappointment. He was nearly twenty-nine years old, head of the duchy, and it amazed him that his mother could still find reasons to be disappointed in him. "You must be more confident."

What in the hell was she talking about? His problem was not a lack of confidence, it was—

"Elizabeth? Where have you gotten off to?" A middle-aged woman and a gentleman ambled through the arch, squeezing into the small walled area beside Borerro.

"Thank you, Borerro," his mother said, and to her guests, "Come in, come in! Our gardens are small but pleasant."

"It's beautiful," the woman said. She looked to be in her fifth or sixth decade. She had a full figure, and her dark hair was lightly streaked with gray. Her smile was full of warmth, as if she was seeing a long-lost cousin. The gentleman was also middle-aged, with a thick mustache, as was the current fashion. Mateo remembered him—he'd been at a reception that the English prime minister, Mr. Gladstone, had hosted in Mateo's honor.

What had these two to do with him? He guessed his mother probably wanted him to grant a patronage.

"Your grace!" the woman trilled, turning her attention to him. "What an absolute pleasure to make your acquaintance. Or should I call you Don Santiava? I don't know which is proper."

"Teo," his mother said, and placed a hand on his arm. "May I introduce Lady Lila Aleksander of Denmark."

Mateo's body stiffened. This was beginning to feel like an ambush.

"And the Earl of Iddesleigh," his mother continued.

"Beck," the gentleman said, and strode forward, hand extended. "Everyone calls me Beck. I suppose Iddesleigh does not trip off the tongue. Please do call me Beck." He smiled. "A pleasure to see you again, my lord."

Mateo reluctantly stepped forward to shake the man's hand.

"I think, my lord, if I may offer an opinion," Beck continued as he shook his hand, "that as you are in England to assume the title of viscount, perhaps you ought to be styled *my lord*. What do you think?"

What he thought was that he didn't care how they addressed him, and in that moment, he was naive to think he would never see them again after this brief interlude. "Pardon, but will you excuse us a moment?" He took his mother by the elbow and pulled her away from the two visitors to a distance where their guests could not hear.

"Mami—"

"Lady Aleksander has come to help us," his mother whispered before Mateo could speak.

"I don't care if she's come to shine my shoes—"

"Teo, *mi amor*," his mother said, and pressed her palm against his cheek. "You're the sovereign duke of Santiava, and now you are a viscount."

"What has that—"

"And as you'll be in London several weeks—perhaps even longer, given how slowly you work—now is the time."

"Tiempo para qué?" he asked, unthinkingly slipping into Spanish.

"To find a match! It's the beginning of the social Season, the ideal time."

Mateo was stunned. It was not possible that his mother was broaching the subject of his bachelorhood in his garden. He glanced over his shoulder at their "guests," who, apparently, had discovered the *miguelitos* he'd dropped on the ground and had helped themselves. He looked back at his mother. He could feel thunder in his chest, the fury of being pushed by her. "You've no right—"

"I have every right. I am your mother. Teo, you need a *wife*," she said, speaking quickly, her gaze darting past him to their guests. "It must be obvious to even you that your lack of an heir begs for your attention."

The fury ignited. "I am aware of my responsibilities," he bit out.

"*Are* you? Because you won't meet your future bride locked away in your study. Now, Lady Aleksander will help you sort it out. She's an old friend of mine and quite good with this sort of thing."

His body felt as tightly wound as a clock. Without the slightest provocation, it was possible he might explode all over this garden. His mother had always been meddlesome, but this was outrageous. "I don't—"

His mother suddenly stepped away from him. "Lady Aleksander! Would you be so kind as to explain the service you offer to my son?"

"Certainly!" Lady Aleksander dusted her hands of pastry crumbs as she strolled forward. "My service is to bring people together. Men and women, as it were. I help a very specific clientele find their future spouse, and I must say, I've had quite a lot of success, particularly with the royal and aristocratic families of Europe. Is that not so, Beck?"

"Absolutely," he said, his mouth full of pastry. He swallowed. "The queen of Wesloria, her sister, the Duchess of Marley. My own sister is married to a prince of Alucia. Shall I go on?"

His mother had ambushed him. If Mateo wasn't so furious, he might even admire that she'd outflanked and outgunned him on this burning topic between them. Of course, this wasn't the first time she'd raised the issue—she talked about it all the time. But he thought he might be allowed to do what he needed to do in England before she continued her assault.

She'd caught him flat-footed. And what did military strategists recommend when ambushed? Fall back.

He fell back into silence. He'd learned that as a boy—it

was better to remain silent than to open one's mouth and find that every thought he had was the wrong one. He'd learned then that the wrong thought was to be ridiculed, especially in public.

"You can't disagree that the time has come," his mother continued gaily, without even a whiff of shame. "Now Teo, I—"

He held up his hand to stop his mother from saying another word.

Every time they'd had this conversation, he'd told her she didn't need to tell him to get on with the business of procreation. He knew very well he ought to, and honestly, he wouldn't mind it. Sometimes he was lonely in his title and in his house. But between what could sometimes be debilitating shyness and an inability to be charming, he hadn't had much luck. He knew that he was awkward around people. He felt oddly out of place at parties when everyone was looking for an introduction to him. He was exceptionally bad at small talk, preferred quiet evenings to raucous gatherings, and would like to meet a future spouse on his own damn terms.

Unfortunately, the young women he'd met so far—the ones deemed suitable matches—never seemed to like him much. And the women he'd met for baser pursuits didn't care if he talked or not.

In short, he'd never met a woman who seemed to know what to do with him, including his own mother.

He tried to think of how to end this deplorable conversation, but his mother was ahead of him, executing her plan. "Shall we go in for tea?" She linked her arm through his. "We can discuss it further."

"I hope you have more of those delicious pastries," Lady Aleksander said.

Mateo might have told them that they'd been picked up off the lawn, but he was too busy turning inward, pushing his fury with his mother into a deep hole and dreading a conversation he didn't know how to navigate.

CHAPTER THREE

HATTIE HAD LONG suspected that her father was trying all her life to drive her to madness, and today, he might very well succeed. Right now, he was stomping about the house, scattering cats and knocking over dress forms in search of his favorite walking stick. "The one with the carved hawk's head made of whalebone," he shouted to his wife, who was diligently searching through the piles of things scattered about.

Hattie consulted the watch pinned to her gown. "We will be late," she warned him. Which to her seemed an unpardonable sin—it wasn't every day the Earl of Iddesleigh invited one to tea, and if he did, one surely would not be so rude as to arrive late. "He doesn't care about your walking stick!" she called after her father. A cat rubbed against her skirt. She nudged it away.

"Ah, here we are." Her father reappeared carrying the walking stick and held it up to Hattie to inspect. "The earl will like this. I assure you he's not seen finer."

Hattie refused to look at it. "May we please go now?"

She was angry with her father for insisting he accompany her today—her chance encounter with Lord Iddesleigh was the best thing to have happened to her in the fortnight since she'd handed Rupert Masterson his freedom, and she didn't want her father to spoil it.

He would most definitely spoil it.

When she'd sent Rupert the letter he'd asked Flora to arrange, he'd responded immediately, assuring her it was the right thing to do and wishing her all the best. That was all he said. Nothing about the months they'd been courting or the times Hattie had helped him in his shop. Not a word about the plans they'd made, or how he could so easily step away from their commitment to each other. Why was it so simple for him, and so hard for her?

The initial shock had drained out of her. There were days when the end of her engagement seemed like a dream, but most days she was enraged that Rupert had turned out to be such a coward—and that her family had turned into such a glaring problem for her.

More than once, she'd found herself standing across the street from Masterson Dry Goods and Sundries Shop. She had a very strong desire to confront him and knock him in the mouth, just like she'd seen the boxers do in the gymnasium that Daniel had insisted taking her to see. But mostly, she stewed.

And she stewed.

And she stewed.

What had her so bloody angry at the world was that she had done everything she was supposed to do to gain a good offer of marriage. She'd been demure and accomplished. She'd been helpful and never argumentative. She'd held her tongue on those rare occasions that Rupert said something so inconceivably stupid as to make her eyes water. She'd helped him in his shop! That he'd so easily discarded her left her feeling like an old dog and very, very distrusting of men in general.

But Hattie was certain of one thing: she would never again conform herself to some social ideal of how she was to conduct herself. Or some social ideal of how she was to think. Or what she was to say. Or who she was to be. If Rupert Masterson could so easily cry off, her prospects for marriage were rather bleak, and she didn't see the point in being anything other than herself.

She had happened to be standing across the street from Rupert's shop envisioning how she would swing her arm and hit him right in the kisser when the Earl of Iddesleigh saved her from making a terrible mistake. Hattie had one foot in the street, having summoned the courage to confront the coward, when she heard her name called. She turned. She saw Lord Iddesleigh and his eldest daughter, Lady Mathilda, walking toward her. And in that moment, the earl breezily changed the course of her life.

For a *second* time.

If one believed in guardian angels, then the Earl of Iddesleigh was hers. The first time he'd saved her, she'd been fourteen years old. She'd been so angry at her father's unreasonable grip on his purse that she'd gone out looking for work. She had in mind an occupation as a bookkeeper, or a secretary. Something respectable but that did not involve children. She'd knocked on the door of the Duke of Marley's London residence because she'd heard he was rich, and certainly the house in Mayfair backed that up. She'd figured it was better to beg a rich man for work than a poor man.

How naive she'd been! There was no work for a fourteen-year-old girl that didn't involve chamber pots or scrubbing floors or children. But Lady Marley and her friend Lord Iddesleigh happened to be with the duke that day and both took a keen interest in Hattie. Lord Iddesleigh knew her father, and somehow, he'd convinced the notorious Hugh Woodchurch to send his daughter to the Iddesleigh School for Exceptional Girls in Devonshire.

On a scholarship, she would later learn. Funded by Lady Marley.

That school had changed Hattie's life. She'd learned about the world beyond her overstuffed house. She'd learned about math and science and art. And useful skills, the sort of skills she could use for employment. She'd learned confidence and how to stand up for herself—in a school stuffed to the rafters with girls, it often felt like survival of the fittest. Hattie was determined not to lose her spot at the school and return to her home until it was absolutely necessary.

It became necessary when she'd graduated and had nowhere else to go.

It had been a few years since Hattie had seen his lordship, but he seemed truly delighted to see her and inquired about her life, and asked after her family. And then he'd looked at her curiously and asked, "Is your penmanship still as pristine as it was when you were at school?"

Hattie had laughed. "How odd that you would remember," she said. "But yes, I think it is."

"I know someone who is in need of excellent penmanship."

"Someone needs *penmanship*?" Lady Mathilda asked. "How can one need penmanship?"

"When one's own penmanship is sorely lacking, which, my love, I would think you could appreciate."

Lady Mathilda groaned and looked away.

Hattie had never heard of such a thing, either, but a few days later, the earl sent round a note inviting her to tea. He said that he had an opportunity that might interest her. The note had been addressed to her only, but in her delight, Hattie had made the mistake of telling her parents. Would she never learn?

Her father—a short, wiry man with eyes like a hawk—

had sat up so abruptly that he'd startled a pair of sleeping cats, who then leaped off the back of the chair and knocked a pile of darning onto the floor.

"Tea with an earl!" her mother had cried. "I will know at once what mischief you've been about to garner such an invitation!"

"Mischief?" Hattie had repeated. "It's tea, Mama."

Her mother was plump and often lethargic, particularly in the afternoons after she'd had her sherry. She was stretched on a chaise, three cats nestled in beside her. But the news enlivened her, and she'd carelessly brushed the cats aside. "You'll not go to tea without someone to accompany you, Harriet. I won't have it."

"I'll go," her father said instantly. "I'd like to see Iddesleigh's house. They say he's a rich man, but I'd like to see if that's true."

"They *always* say the earls are rich," her mother said with another wave of her hand. "*I've* heard that most of them are poor as church mice, really."

"This isn't… That's not…" Hattie gave up. She knew from experience there was no argument she could make to dissuade her father. And now that the walking stick had been found, off they marched on foot to Upper Brook Street, despite her father owning most of the public transportation in London. "Why spend a shilling when it's not necessary?" he would ask every time she or Daniel asked to take a conveyance across town. But the cab seemed necessary to Hattie, as a light rain was falling. They arrived a quarter of an hour late and bedraggled.

The butler kindly showed them into a small parlor where the earl was waiting, all smiles…until he saw Hattie's father. "Ah, Mr. Woodchurch—I wasn't expecting you."

"Quite obvious, my good man," her father snapped. "I've come all the same to keep my daughter safe."

"Safe…from what?" his lordship asked, and genuinely seemed confused. But then he shook his head and waved them in. "No matter. You are most welcome, sir," he said graciously. "Miss Woodchurch, it is always a pleasure."

"Thank you." Hattie curtsied. She felt anxious, aware that her father was looking around the room, his gaze narrowed, as if he was assessing each individual furnishing.

"May I offer you some tea?"

Hattie's father said in response, "What is it you want with my daughter?"

"Oh, Papa—" Hattie tried, mortified at her father's manners.

"I do appreciate anyone who can come straight to the point. I live with six women in this house and finding the point of any given conversation is beyond my mental capacity at times. I have invited you, Miss Woodchurch, because as I have said, I think I have an opportunity that is perfectly suited for you. Please, have a seat."

"An opportunity, eh?" her father asked snidely, as Hattie took a seat on the settee his lordship had indicated.

Lord Iddesleigh ignored him and continued to smile at Hattie. "I believe I mentioned to you that I've an acquaintance in London who has need for assistance with correspondence. It must be someone with impeccable penmanship and spelling. The work would be three to four afternoons a week and would involve taking down notes and turning them into letters, responding to invitations, and so forth."

Hattie's father snorted. "Not a very important gentleman if he doesn't have a secretary, is he?"

Lord Iddesleigh's warm smile cooled. "The gentleman

is a visitor to London from another country. As such, he doesn't have a secretary at his disposal."

"A visitor—" Hattie started, but her father interrupted her. "It's paid work, is it? How much?"

"Oh no," Hattie murmured, and died another thousand deaths. "Papa, *please*."

Lord Iddesleigh looked almost stricken by the question. "The work is indeed remunerated, but I should like to ascertain if Miss Woodchurch is interested in the work before—"

"She's interested," her father said flatly.

"Father!" Hattie said sternly. "Please do allow me to answer his lordship's questions myself."

Her father clenched his jaw and reluctantly made a grand gesture with his hand indicating Hattie should continue.

Hattie turned back to the earl. "May I ask…is the gentleman married?"

The earl looked confused by her question. "No, he's… Why do you ask?"

"I think it would be highly inappropriate for me, an unmarried woman, to be in the employ of a bachelor—"

"Don't be ridiculous, girl," her father said sharply. "How much does it pay?" he asked again.

Lord Iddesleigh suddenly walked to the door of the study and opened it. "As I am offering the position to only Miss Woodchurch, and not you, sir, perhaps you will be so kind as to allow us a bit of privacy so that we may speak freely."

Her father looked like he meant to argue. Hattie added quickly, "I'll only be a moment. Thank you."

Her father fixed a glare on the earl with a sigh of irritation. "Very well," he said crisply. "Make it quick." And with that, he reluctantly left the room, still taking in the furnishings as he went.

The moment he was gone, Lord Iddesleigh turned to Hattie.

"I am so sorry—"

"I think we haven't much time," he said quickly. He sat next to her on the settee. "Allow me to go straight to the heart of the matter. This is a great opportunity for you, Miss Woodchurch. The gentleman is the Duke of Santiava, and now, Viscount Abbott. You may have heard that the viscount's title passed to a foreigner?"

Hattie was stunned into silence. She couldn't form a coherent thought, which was just as well, as her tongue felt thick in her mouth.

The earl continued to talk, but she didn't hear some of what he said. He frowned. "Miss Woodchurch? Do you know of whom I am speaking?"

Only the most sought-after bachelor in all of London. Only the most gorgeous man she'd ever seen. "Yes, my lord."

"His spoken English is impeccable," the earl continued. "You'd not suspect for a moment that anything was amiss. Unfortunately, his ability to write and read English is not as impeccable and he needs some help in that regard."

Help. He needed help. From *her*? Hattie couldn't grasp how this was happening. Lord Iddesleigh wanted her to write things for that beautiful man?

The earl leaned forward and looked her directly in the eye. "I don't think I'm getting through to you. This position could open doors for you. Doors that might not otherwise open, if you take my meaning."

She did not take his meaning. She could hardly even think.

He sighed. "Miss Woodchurch. What do you want in life?"

"Pardon?" She didn't know what she wanted in life since Rupert had rejected her. The visions she'd held of her future had disappeared like smoke. "I… A cottage of my own. Perhaps a dog or two. Maybe even a cow."

Iddesleigh frowned. "I think you should know that owning a cow is more trouble than you think. Nevertheless, if that's what you want, then you're even more perfect for this position than I first thought."

She wanted to ask what cows had to do with anything, and really, she hadn't meant she would rush out and buy one straightaway. But as it was, she sat numbly, trying to make sense of it.

And then the earl told her what the viscount would pay for her services, and everything the earl had been trying to say was clear. It was an amount that Hattie could hardly grasp. An amount that could be the start of endless possibilities. Her uncertainty about being alone with a beautiful bachelor still raged, but so did the want for that money. It truly was a way out of her father's house. "I accept," she said, her voice clear.

On the way home, Hattie's father demanded to know what the position would pay. When she told him, her father's thin eyebrows rose almost as high as his receding hairline. "That much? Well, Harriet, I'll make you a deal. I'll take only fifteen percent."

She looked at him aghast. "What?"

"It's only fair. You're an adult now, and you should have been married and out of my house long ago. Fifteen percent is a bargain compared to what you might pay for room and board."

She couldn't believe what she was hearing. "I would have been out of your house long ago were it not for *you*, Papa," she said. "You and our house and my brothers!"

"Nevertheless," he said with a shrug.

Yes, Hattie would do whatever it took to get out of her father's house. Whatever it took.

CHAPTER FOUR

MATEO THOUGHT THE viscount's house on Grosvenor Square looked rather plain from the street. Pale brick, a dark green door with brass knockers. A boot scrape to remove the mud off one's boots, a hitching post for horses. It was a fine, respectable home, he supposed, but unremarkable. But he did like that he could stand at the window of his sitting room and look down to see who stood on his doorstep.

Today, it was the Earl of Iddesleigh, or Beck, as he'd reminded Mateo more than once. He was with a woman who wore a bonnet that obscured her face, but she looked to be average in bearing and height. As unremarkable as this house. Not that her appearance mattered to Mateo—she was a clerk, come to write his English correspondence for him. And there was a lot that needed to be written.

On the afternoon his mother had brought the matchmaker into his life, she'd also managed, over tea, to complain about the slow pace of Mateo's work. He'd been mortified for a second time by her, but before he could explain himself, before he tried to describe how indecipherable his grandfather's writing was, Beck had seized on the complaint as a problem he could solve. He said he knew of a woman from his school in need of a position.

Lady Aleksander had pointed out what Mateo had been thinking—that it would be frowned upon to have an unchaperoned, unmarried woman work alone with the viscount, who was a bachelor.

"No reason to fret," Beck had said confidently. "She'll be no temptation to the viscount."

That remark had landed with a thud. "I beg your pardon, sir?" Mateo's mother had snapped.

"My apologies for misspeaking. I would not presume to know. What I mean is that the young lady is accustomed to work," Beck quickly amended. "And her family is accustomed to her working. Instead of thinking of her as an unmarried young woman, ripe for the plucking—"

"Good God," Lady Aleksander complained.

"Think of her more like a spinster aunt who comes for tea. No one would think twice about that, would they? Furthermore, if she comes and leaves through the servants' entrance, who can speculate what job she has come to do?"

It did not sit well with Mateo. The discussion was cold—whoever the woman was, she was a person. "Regardless of the door she uses, she is still a woman whose reputation deserves to be respected."

"Yes, of course, of course," Beck said quickly. "But she also deserves an opportunity to earn a wage. She is good and decent and possesses the skills necessary to help you. And…she needs the position."

"What do you mean, she needs it?" his mother asked before Mateo could open his mouth.

"She needs the money," Beck said flatly. "I imagine you will all think me crude for mentioning it, but her family is… They are…" He paused, screwing his face up as if he were trying to solve a riddle. "Unconventional," he said at last.

"Meaning?" Lady Aleksander asked.

"Nothing criminal."

Mateo's mother laughed. "That's hardly reassuring."

"I am trying to say that her situation in this world would be greatly eased if she could earn a bit of money on her own. I won't say more, I won't speculate, but I've known her since she was a student at my school. She is dependable and trustworthy, and acts with integrity. If you don't believe me, perhaps you might at least make her acquaintance and judge for yourself."

Later, Mateo would consider that he most likely would have said no to the arrangement, but his mother chose that moment to scoff at Beck and thereby sealed his decision. "I don't care if she's an angel, it's inappropriate."

"By all means, Beck. Bring her round," Mateo said.

His mother's teacup clattered in its saucer. "Teo!"

"Thank you, madam, but I've decided," he said quietly. And for once in his blessed life, his mother didn't argue.

He did need help. And something Beck had said resonated with him—that her life would be greatly eased if she could earn a wage. So he agreed—he would meet her and judge for himself.

Well, the day was here. He felt a bit uncomfortable; he always did with people he hardly knew. His longtime servants—Rosa and Pacheco and Borerro—were like family to him. But others? It did not come easily to him. He was a grown man now, not the boy who had feared the judgment of strangers. But he was not a charming man. He wished he was—how much easier life would be if he had the casual charm of his brother, Roberto, or the ease of hospitality, like his sister, Sofia. His siblings could walk into any room, with any number of people, and emerge laughing with new friends and invitations to dine. But he'd been cut from a different cloth. Making friends didn't come naturally to him. He couldn't seem to make people feel at ease.

Generally, he came through meeting strangers feeling exhausted and empty and doubting himself.

Be that as it may, he had too many pressing issues to worry how he was perceived. He had a stack of invitations needing replies, letters to business partners and estate agents that should be written, and some documents that he sincerely hoped the woman could read and interpret for him.

And, lest he forget—which would be impossible at this point—he had the curious problem of a misdelivery of goats instead of the sheep he'd bought, which he felt certain had to be the result of mistranslation of his English.

He needed a scribe, and he needed one now.

He heard the knock on the door, heard Borerro invite them in. He straightened his cuffs, again and again, until Borerro came for him. Then he straightened them one last time and went down to the study to meet his guests.

THE STUDY WAS on the eastern side of the house, darkly paneled, overlooking the garden and the street. On one wall were floor-to-ceiling bookshelves, stuffed with books about agriculture, history, and philosophy. The windows were opened to allow for more light, and through them, Mateo could hear the faint sounds of carts and horses and people moving about.

His grandfather's mahogany desk dominated one end of the room and was stacked with papers and ledgers, and behind it was a thickly padded leather chair. The room was very masculine, and he instantly tried to imagine a young woman fluttering about, touching the drapes, sitting on the furnishings, filling the space with her presence. At the other end of the room was a small writing table he'd had brought from one of the bedrooms.

"My lord," Beck said, bowing his head, and drawing Mateo's attention to him.

"Beck. Welcome." He folded one arm behind his back and gripped his hand into a fist, then shifted his gaze to the woman. It was an old habit he'd adopted as a boy when his parents would thrust him to the front of the stage. *Behold your heir, Santiava.* The crowd would behold, and later, his father would belittle his nerves, how he'd appeared and, if he'd said anything, how ridiculous he'd sounded.

He couldn't see but a few wisps of the woman's hair beneath her bonnet, but thought it was brown. She had wide, clear blue eyes, and she looked a bit surprised. There was a light in them, a bit of a sparkle that intrigued him. Was she excited? Happy to be here? And why did she clutch her reticule so tightly?

"Lord Abbott, may I present Miss Harriet Woodchurch," Beck said, and on cue, Miss Woodchurch stepped forward and dipped into a perfect curtsy.

"She comes to you with excellent credentials, having graduated from the Iddesleigh School for Exceptional Girls. She is currently occupied with bookkeeping for Mrs. O'Malley and her sweets shop, as well as serving as a lady's companion to the daughter of a viscount. In addition to her many talents, her penmanship is perfection." Beck smiled at Miss Woodchurch.

"Good afternoon, my lord," she said. "It is my great pleasure to make your acquaintance. I am grateful for your consideration."

She was looking at him so intently, Mateo was a bit unnerved. She reminded him of someone who believed they'd met a person before but couldn't place when or where.

"I've brought an example of my writing if you'd like to see it."

He didn't need to see her writing. He trusted Beck on this point—he would not have brought a woman to him whose penmanship was illegible. All he cared to know was the strength of her spelling and if she knew how to properly construct an English sentence. He had a terrible habit of translating what he wanted to say from Spanish to English in his head and was inevitably incorrect.

Miss Woodchurch apparently mistook his silence for a desire to see her sample and fumbled with the clasp of her reticule. He noticed her gown was the color of the plums that hung from the trees around the palace terrace in Valdonia. The fabric had a sheen to it that suggested it was both inexpensive and new.

She withdrew a paper from her reticule and walked forward, holding it out to him. Her hand, he noted, had a slight tremor. "It's a letter. It's not to a real person. I wrote it so that you might see my penmanship and spelling. I'm very good at both." She moved one step closer to him, and looked as if she might stuff the letter in his pocket if he didn't take it. So he did—he opened it, looked at it, folded it, and handed it back to her.

"As you can see, Miss Woodchurch has come prepared. A good sign of her abilities, I'm sure you agree."

Mateo nodded stupidly. He felt awkward—was he to congratulate the woman on her penmanship? Remark on the neatness of it?

"You probably have some questions for her?" Beck said. He was clearly the one most at ease in this room and reminded Mateo of his brother, Roberto. Like him, Beck probably never met a stranger. All Mateo ever met were strangers.

He looked again at Miss Woodchurch, his gaze quickly skimming her, down to the tips of her soiled shoes and up again. She was young. Too young? "His lordship has explained the work to you?"

"He has, my lord. You need someone to write for you."

"And you are confident in your ability to take down what I say and put it to paper properly?"

"Very confident, my lord. At my former school, I was often said to have the best penmanship."

How had she come to be standing here? She seemed so...*ordinary*. She wasn't as unremarkable as he'd first thought—she had a pleasant face, stunning blue eyes, and her hands were very elegant. That was it, he realized—she didn't have a vaunted title or riches beyond imagination, or beauty to stun him. She seemed practical, intent on earning the position. It was something of a relief to him that he sensed no other motive than to work.

Interestingly, he thought he might like ordinary. *He* was ordinary, save the circumstances of his birth.

"You must think it peculiar to be remarked for penmanship, and not something a bit more important, like the ability to do sums in one's head. But we all have our strengths."

"Pardon?"

"I was pointing out that while math might be someone else's strength, writing is mine."

He held her gaze.

"You must have a strength, too, my lord, wouldn't you say?"

Was this her attempt at conversing with him? He wasn't certain what his strengths had to do with her employment.

"Oh, I think his lordship must have many," Beck interjected. "More questions, my lord?"

More every moment she stood before him. "Why do you seek employment?"

Something in her expression changed. The light in her

eyes dimmed a little, and her ready smile faded. "I should think the same reason anyone seeks employment, my lord—a desire to earn a living."

He could think of only one or two instances of where a woman might need to earn a living. "Are you a widow?"

She blinked. "I've never been married."

"Perhaps it is not the same in England, but in Santiava, a woman who enjoys a certain privilege in life does not pursue work. It is considered..." He couldn't think of an appropriate word in English. *"Déclassé,"* he said in French.

Miss Woodchurch's brows dipped into a dark vee. "How unfortunate for Santiavan women. I think it's laudable that a woman of any class might want to provide for herself."

"Very laudable indeed, Miss Woodchurch," Beck quickly interjected. "I admire your motivation. But I think we might agree that in England, not everyone shares your opinion."

"I suppose not," she said primly.

Mateo already didn't understand this woman.

"My lord, have you any other questions?" Beck prompted again.

He had one hundred questions now if he had one. He was intrigued that she spoke to him as if they were somehow on equal footing. But practically, there was more to this position than simply taking notes and writing. Mateo stepped closer to her. *"Señorita...*do you understand this work is confidential? I should not like my private affairs talked about in drawing rooms and coffee houses around London, *sí?"*

A bit of color rose in her cheeks. "I beg your pardon, but I do *not* frequent coffee houses," she said, and sounded, he thought, a bit insulted. "You may depend on my discretion in all things."

"In *all* things?"

Her cheeks colored a little more. "As I said," she confirmed, and interestingly, sounded a bit defiant. If his mother had been here, she would have taken great offense, but he liked that she spoke with conviction. He liked that she was confident in her abilities. He studied her a moment longer.

"You are very young."

She actually laughed at that. "Four and twenty."

Twenty-four years? Only four years younger than him? She ought to be married and have a child or two by now. Why hadn't she? Was she in some sort of trouble? Perhaps an unwanted pregnancy?

"Now that we've established Miss Woodchurch has excellent credentials, and has taken a vow of discretion, and believes in the rights of women to seek employment, when would you like her to begin?" Beck asked jovially. "By the look of it, you have quite a lot of work to be done," he added breezily, and gestured toward the desk.

Mateo didn't have to look to know how much work remained. He gazed at Miss Woodchurch, she of the clear blue eyes. He didn't know why he hesitated, why he was being fussy about it. Her situation was nothing to him. The sooner he completed this work here, the sooner he could return to Santiava. "Tomorrow," he said flatly. "Two o'clock, if that suits Miss Woodchurch."

Miss Woodchurch suddenly smiled, and the effect was very pleasing. That was not an ordinary smile. "It suits me perfectly. Thank you." She put her paper back in her reticule, dipped a curtsy and said, "I won't take any more of your time," as if she was the person in this room to end the interview.

But end it, she did. Mateo looked at Beck.

Beck smiled. "We like to instill confidence in our girls at the Iddesleigh School for Exceptional Girls."

"I would say you have succeeded in Miss Woodchurch."

"Thank you!" Miss Woodchurch said.

CHAPTER FIVE

HATTIE WAS AWARE that she was striding along beside Lord Iddesleigh. Her arms and legs appeared to be functioning as they were intended, but it felt as if all the blood had drained from her limbs. She had no breath in her lungs and her heart was beating so fast she thought she might possibly be in danger of fainting.

Somehow, she'd managed to walk out of that house and carry on down the street with the earl all while newly-but-gainfully employed by the most beautiful man she'd ever seen.

God help her, he was even more stunning up close. She could hardly absorb the perfection of him—from his elegant fingers to the shape of his muscular arms in his tailored coat. From his trim waist and the thin gold chain of his pocket watch to his clean-shaven face. *And his eyes!* They'd mesmerized her—the lashes so dark that his eyes appeared to be lined in kohl, and his irises a beautiful shade of hazel—glittering gold and green and brown. His voice, quietly deep. His accent melodious, particularly in the way he rolled his *r*'s.

But it was more than that. Standing in his study, Hattie had begun to realize what a gift the position was. If she worked hard and proved herself an asset to him, the wages would provide her a path to real independence. One that could actually exist outside of her imagination.

At the corner where she and the earl would part, Hattie managed to thank Lord Iddesleigh both profusely and coherently. He said he was happy to be of service, and that he hoped she joined him and his family for tea very soon. "I shall like to hear how your employment progresses."

Yes, yes, tea and all that. Hattie could hardly think of anything else but the viscount and the opportunity. She couldn't wait to start.

"Miss Woodchurch," his lordship said, and Hattie glanced up.

He put his hands on her shoulders. "Be exactly who you are. I meant what I said—this is an opportunity for you, but you must approach it confidently, with enthusiasm and a willingness to speak...much like you did today."

"Did I speak out of turn?"

"No. You were perfect," he assured her. "But in my experience, sometimes gentlemen need to be reminded that we are all God's children, and not just the male sex."

She didn't understand him, but she swore she would do exactly as he advised before they parted ways.

THERE WAS A new grandfather clock in the foyer when Hattie arrived home, crowded in beside two more and leaving only a narrow lane to pass through. She shook her head as she slipped past and made her way to the drawing room.

Her parents were within. They were always within.

"Well?" her mother demanded, pushing cats from her lap when Hattie entered.

"He has employed me!" Hattie exclaimed happily.

"How much?" her father asked.

"I've already told you, Papa."

"No, you told me what Iddesleigh said he'd offer. You didn't take up the matter with the viscount directly? For heaven's sake, Harriet, always inquire how much the work pays! You might have negotiated a better wage."

She didn't need a better wage. She would do the work for free. For the mere chance to look at him again, to be in the company of a gentleman, to wander around a fine house.

"A better wage for what?"

Hattie's older brother, Daniel, strolled in. His hair was mussed, as if he'd been in a wind. His collar was open at the throat and Hattie could smell the drink on him from a distance of several feet.

"I have a new position," Hattie said brightly. "As a correspondent."

Daniel frowned as he went to the sideboard. "A what?"

"Someone who corresponds in writing."

"Thank you, Hat, I know what a correspondent is. What I mean is, why you think *you* are one." He reached for a crystal decanter and pulled the stopper free.

"Because I've been hired by the new viscount to do precisely that."

This news caused Daniel to pause momentarily before he poured brandy into a glass. "The new viscount... Do you mean Abbott? The Spaniard?"

"He's Santiavan, but yes. Him." She was beaming, she realized. She really had to learn to contain that. It wouldn't do to walk around grinning like a fool because she would be looking at a very handsome man several times a week.

Daniel put down the glass without taking a sip. He turned a dark look to his father. "What, and now everyone will think my sister must seek employment like a beggar?"

"A beggar!" Hattie exclaimed.

Daniel pointed at their father. "This is your doing," he said accusingly. "I told you, buy the lass a frock now and then."

"*My* doing!" her father sputtered. "It's all *her* doing! It's not my fault she can't find anyone to marry her! I shouldn't be expected to provide for her all my life."

"That is exactly what you should expect when you bear children," Daniel shot back.

"All right," Hattie said, throwing up her hands between them before her father and Daniel started an argument in earnest. "Please, I—"

She was interrupted by Peter and Perry bursting through the door, loudly and recklessly, the way they entered every day of their lives. They were dressed in plain shirts and trousers. Peter had a quiver on his back and a bow and arrow in his hands, and Perry appeared to be running from him—he leaped over the back of the divan and landed with a crash on the other side of it.

"What are you doing in here with that?" Hattie's mother shouted. "You frightened Mr. White and— Perry! Have a care!" she screeched when the white cat leaped from the back of the settee and nearly collided with the miniature tea service Perry knocked over. The sound of breaking china and a howling cat startled everyone. Perry peered down at the mess, making no move to pick up the pieces. All the cats scattered, darting out the open door.

"Look what you've done!" their mother cried, and hauled herself up off the chaise, stalking to the spot of the crime to inspect the carnage. Which made Peter laugh. Which in turn made Perry lunge at him. Daniel tried to step between the twins to put a stop to their brawling but ended up receiving a fist that Peter had clearly intended for Perry. Which prompted Daniel to toss Peter to the floor while Perry shouted his encouragement.

"All right," Hattie sighed, and slipped out of the melee.

She stepped over tea services and dodged boxes and cats and dress forms and clocks on the way upstairs to her room.

Once safely inside, she quietly closed the door and turned the lock. And then opened it again, shooed one of the cats out, then closed and locked it again.

She lived in a bloody madhouse. Her room was her sanctuary, but it was increasingly impossible to exist here. She couldn't wait to start her work, to save her money and escape this house of horrors.

She slipped out of the gown she'd splurged on for this very interview. She'd bought it at a dress shop in Battersea, where gowns were more affordable than the places Flora liked to shop. Much to Hattie's dismay, she noticed that the cheap fabric gave off a peculiar smell. She donned a simple gray-and-white gown that had once been her mother's, refashioned to fit her and the current trends. Oh, how she longed for new dresses. *Proper* dresses, like Flora and Queenie wore.

She went to the washstand to clean up. She was due at Flora's soon—she was to accompany her to her cousin's house. Moses Raney was significantly older than Flora, was unmarried or widowed—Hattie had never been very clear—and he loved to host soirees and musicales. His salon was always full, and Flora liked to go at least twice a week. As it was across town, Hattie was engaged to accompany her.

She couldn't wait to tell Flora about her new occupation. She would simply expire with excitement for Hattie.

FLORA DIDN'T EXPIRE, but she screamed so loud in her rooms that two servants came running. She shooed them away then pulled Hattie down onto her chaise longue. "This is perfect, you realize. Simply *perfect*. Hattie...you will be the one to capture his attention!"

"I won't!" Hattie laughed.

"No, you won't, but, Hattie…you can tell us *everything* about him!"

Hattie didn't know who she meant by *us*, but she had given her word everything would remain confidential. "I promised—"

"It won't be difficult to determine who he fancies, will it?" Flora suddenly surged to her feet. "I wouldn't be surprised if he confides in you. You're really the perfect sort for confiding secrets, you know. Always present, but a bit like a fly on the wall, aren't you? You'll know before anyone else who he fancies!"

Hattie realized her mistake at having told Flora and desperately tried to send the horse back to the stable. "No, that's… He wouldn't. Why would he ever confide in me?"

"I wonder if you can find out who is on the list of potential brides. I've heard the list is quite short." She clapped her hands with glee. "I can't wait to tell Moses about this!"

Alarm surged through Hattie. She'd only wanted Flora to be happy for her—but she hadn't anticipated this. "You can't tell him," she begged.

"Why not?"

"Because I swore my discretion, and really…" She drew a breath. "People will not view my employment with any charity, will they? Can you imagine what would be said of me if anyone knew my occupation?"

"Oh." Flora paused. She frowned thoughtfully. And then she sighed wearily. "You're right, of course. What was I thinking? They'll say you're a fallen woman."

"They will?" Hattie asked, slightly startled. "I was thinking more that working was inappropriate, not that I—"

"And then they'll imagine what sorts of salacious things

you're doing with him," Flora added ominously, her eyes widening with alarm.

"Good God, Flora."

"Hattie—we can't tell *anyone* about this," Flora said, as if Hattie had been threatening to expose herself. "Except Queenie. We *must* tell Queenie. Please don't look at me like that—Queenie wouldn't breathe a word."

"Really? Because Queenie is very good at breathing the words of any number of rumors, you may have noticed."

"But not this," Flora said confidently. "You are our dear friend. She would never."

She was not Queenie's dear friend, but before Hattie could gather her thoughts to object, Flora had rushed into her dressing room to find a gown to wear this evening, chattering about the many unmarried women she was certain would consider themselves at the very top of the viscount's list.

"Not I!" she called from the dressing room. "I'm certain I'm not even *on* the list." She popped her head out. "I don't think I could bear it if I was, Hattie. I don't. There are too many people watching. But did I tell you? I've been invited to dine at the Forsythes' soon, and the viscount is the honored guest."

Hattie gasped. "That must mean you are *on* the list!"

Flora returned from her dressing room, her expression suddenly somber. She sank down on the chaise next to Hattie. "Between you and me, I fear that I am. I wouldn't know what to say, Hattie. You know how I am—I'd be so tongue-tied as to make a cake of myself. And it's even worse when someone is as handsome and important as he is."

Hattie had never seen Flora tongue-tied. This uncertainty in her friend was surprising—she'd always seemed self-assured.

"And when I think of every woman who will have an introduction? I couldn't possibly compete."

"Flora!" Hattie took her hand in hers. "You're so beautiful. And kind. And *smart*. They must all compete with *you*."

Flora's smile was a little thin. "Thank you for trying to reassure me, darling, but never mind me. *You* will know who catches his eye and can tell us! Won't it be delicious to know before everyone else who he intends to offer for?"

As Flora rattled on, Hattie privately chastised herself. She'd been so careless! She would have to be very careful what she said from here on—she was not about to lose this work before she'd even begun.

She needed this position to escape her life.

CHAPTER SIX

THE NEXT AFTERNOON, at five to two, Hattie was standing at the servants' entrance of the viscount's house on Grosvenor Square. She carried a small leather satchel, a surprising gift from her brother, Daniel, upon her graduation from the Iddesleigh School for Exceptional Girls many years ago. He was not one to give gifts.

Inside the bag she had two pencils, notepaper, an apple, and a bit of bread tucked inside a cheesecloth. Lord Iddesleigh said she would spend only a couple of hours on those afternoons she worked, but one must always be prepared for contingencies. Mrs. O'Malley, the proprietor of the sweets shop, had taught her that. "Always have a bit of something in your reticule in the event you are a little peckish," she'd said, and had wrapped a few hard candies for Hattie. "Just a little something to keep you going."

Hattie knocked on the door of the servants' entrance, but no one came. She checked the watch pinned to her chest. She could have waited patiently at home and arrived at the requested hour, but her parents were arguing about a purchase her mother had made and, well, Hattie would rather take her chances waiting on a stoop, thank you.

The door suddenly swung open, and someone threw a bucketful of mop water out. Hattie shrieked and jumped back, but the mop water caught the hem of her gown.

An elderly woman with a thick pile of silver hair atop

her head came out on the stoop and looked Hattie up and down. *"Puedo ayudarla, señorita?"*

"I'm terribly sorry, I don't speak Spanish."

The woman held up a finger. *"Un momento."* She disappeared back inside.

A few moments later, a round man came out to the stoop and peered down at her. "Oh," he said, a twinge of disdain in his voice. "You must be the hired help."

"I am Miss Woodchurch, the correspondent," she said, shaking out her hem. Not that it did any good.

"The *correspondent*," he repeated snidely. "Of course you are. Come with me." He turned and disappeared inside. He didn't bother to introduce himself or hold the door for Hattie, forcing her to catch it before it swung shut on her.

"I know all about you," the man was saying over his shoulder as she hurried to catch up to him. "I'm Mr. Callum, the majordomo of the viscount's estate. I don't expect you to know what that is." He glanced back over his shoulder, presumably to judge her reaction to his condescension, but was distracted by the fact that she was a few feet behind him. "Mind you keep up."

"I am doing my level best," she said, as he strode down a long tiled hallway. They practically sprinted through the kitchen, then past the servants' dining room, where she spotted two footmen smoking and reading a paper. Then up some narrow servants' stairs. Another footman hurried down, forcing them to squeeze against the wall so he could pass. He glanced at Hattie and smiled. She smiled back and almost tripped up the stairs.

"Keep up!" Callum commanded again.

They were in another long hallway, this one carpeted, moving so fast and taking so many turns that Hattie was becoming disoriented. During her first visit, she hadn't noticed all the art and antiques that filled this home. She hadn't noticed anything but the viscount.

Mr. Callum turned abruptly into the study she'd stood in yesterday. This time, she noticed that the room was darkly paneled. The furnishings were covered with chintz, the draperies made of heavy velvet. It was a moment before Hattie realized that the viscount was there, seated on a sofa. He was wearing only his shirtsleeves, his coat and waistcoat draped over one of the sofa arms. He had one leg crossed over the other, and on his lap, a thick leather document case that held a sheath of papers. He glanced up. "Miss Woodchurch." He took a moment to glance at the pocket watch he pulled from his trousers. "You are prompt."

His accent was still divine. "My lord." She curtsied.

His gaze had already returned to his papers.

"Where shall I direct her, my lord?" Mr. Callum asked.

"She'll remain with me," the viscount said quietly. He looked up. "Thank you, Mr. Callum."

Mr. Callum glared at Hattie on his way out, as if she'd offended him. It was entirely possible that she had, by virtue of being one, a female, and two, an employee. He could very well be one of those men who believed a woman's place was only in the home as a wife and mother, which she had clearly failed to be.

"Miss Woodchurch?"

Hattie started and turned to the viscount. He motioned to a chair near the sofa, and then his attention went back to his papers.

She looked at the chair. "Am I to sit?"

He looked up, his gaze moving over her. She was desperately tempted to look down and make sure nothing was amiss.

"Of course. In the chair."

Not of course, she would argue, as he had merely gestured in that direction, and hadn't invited her in so many words to take a seat. But…he didn't seem to be interested in her explanation, so Hattie sat, very gingerly, just on the edge where she could hop up in the event he needed something.

She waited. He continued to read. She gazed at him, taking in the strong line of his jaw, the way his muscles were evident beneath his shirt. She thought about striking up a conversation, but his brow was furrowed, as if he was concentrating.

He turned a page; she reached into her bag and took out her pencil and paper. Her movement caught his attention; he looked at the paper in her lap, then lifted his very fine hazel eyes to hers, and a tiny whisper of sensation slipped down her spine. "What is that?"

Her breath scraped against her lungs, as if she couldn't get quite enough in. "Paper," she croaked. She cleared her throat. "For notes. I believe that one must always write down the important things to better remember them."

One of his dark brows rose. But he offered no comment and dropped his gaze to his papers again.

His lashes were so long and dark she was a bit envious. And his hair, a rich, coffee brown, was quite thick and curled loosely around his ears. She would be thrilled to have that sort of hair. She was suddenly struck with the image of running her fingers through his. *Oh, Hattie.*

"I have pencil and paper for you," he said.

"Pardon?" His accent was so cool and sleek that it was a moment before she realized he was responding to her reason for having paper. "Oh! I, ah… I thought you might. But I wanted to be certain I'd not miss a thing."

He frowned slightly. "What could you miss?"

"Well, hopefully, nothing. But it's better to be prepared than not." She felt an unconquerable need to explain herself, to fill the silence between them. "It's a habit I developed at school. I had an instructor who was very detailed with his remarks. I couldn't possibly commit them all to memory, so I began to write everything down. Remarkably, it worked rather well."

"I see."

Was she talking too much? Flora had once told her she talked too much. *You're always explaining things*, she'd complained. That had been a very long time ago, but still, she would do well not to review her school years or deliver more trite sayings. She would wait silently. She'd sit on the edge of this chair with her mouth closed and await his instructions. A proper correspondent.

She took in the room, noting the books stacked on the table next to an armchair. She couldn't make the titles out from here. One of the windows was open, and from her vantage point, she could see what looked like a lovely garden surrounded by high stone walls. The other two windows faced the opposite direction—the street, she assumed. Those windows were not open, which accounted for how deathly quiet it was in this room. She could practically hear each breath she took. She could hear each breath *he* took.

And the more she thought about how she could hear her breath, the louder it seemed to get. She tried holding it, but that wasn't advisable. She wondered if it would be considered rude to stand up and walk to the window and gulp in some air. Quietly.

She was half out of her seat when Lord Abbott abruptly stood, startling her. She fell back into her seat with a slight grunt. He looked at her strangely, then took two steps in her direction and held out a paper. At arm's length. "I should like to reply that the offer is unacceptable."

"Ah…" Hattie reached forward to take the paper, but as she did, the viscount was handing her another paper.

"The invitation to dine conflicts with a previous engagement."

She took that one, too, but in her effort to juggle her pencil and paper and the letters all at once, she dropped her paper, and the sheets spilled around her feet. She quickly dipped down to pick them up, managing to bend the letters he'd given her in her lap when she did.

She could feel his gaze on her, could feel the heat rising in her cheeks. "I'm not usually so clumsy." Her voice sounded loud and brash, like her mother's. That was enough to send her into a panic.

She managed to gather everything up and settle it all in her lap. He was watching her closely. He probably wondered if he'd somehow managed to employ a clumsy fool. She certainly hoped not, but at the moment, she felt like she had only thumbs for fingers. "I'm generally very steady on my feet, if you're wondering."

"No," he said.

No? No, as in she wasn't steady on her feet? Or no, he wasn't wondering?

"I'm really rather organized."

He didn't respond.

"And I'm quite ready, whenever you are."

He waited a moment. "Is there more?"

"More?"

"More you'd like to announce."

She was making a complete cake of herself. She could feel the heat in her cheeks as a tide of embarrassment rushed through her. "I think that will do."

He looked unconvinced, but he gave her a curt nod and walked to a small writing desk in front of the window open to the garden. He pulled out the chair, turned to her, and said, "You may sit here. I will tell you what to write, *si*?"

Of course! No wonder he'd been staring at her—how could she possibly expect to write a letter on her lap? She could kick herself for not having noticed the writing desk and going to it straightaway. She stood up with all her things. "Thank you, my lord. I am certain that my penmanship would not recommend itself if I were to compose a letter on my lap." She chuckled softly. He did not.

He waited for her to settle, which naturally took a long moment, as the writing desk was quite small. But when she had arranged everything, she picked up the pen, glanced over her shoulder and smiled. "There we are. Ready when you are."

"I've been ready," he said. "To Señor Carmichael."

Hattie hesitated only briefly.

"What? Why do you look like this?" he asked, gesturing to her face.

"Would you like to address it to Mr. Carmichael? I don't know who he is, but he might not understand the salutation."

"Ah. To Mr. Carmichael," he amended.

Thank goodness. She wrote that down.

The viscount put his hands in his pockets and strolled to the window. "Say I have reviewed the offer of purchase he made and my grandfather accepted, but that I find it so low as to be insulting."

That sounded intriguing. The sale of what, she wondered. Shouldn't she reference it?

"As for the invitation, please decline it. Say all the things in English one does when declining."

"Oh, umm…" She paused, wondering if she ought to say anything at all, or simply write exactly what he'd dictated.

He was already on his way back to his seat on the sofa, but he paused and turned his head and looked at her. As long as she lived, she would not forget those hazel eyes.

"Sí?" he asked when she didn't speak.

Hattie was generally a confident woman and, in most cases, unafraid to be heard. But the viscount was looking at her as if he was annoyed, and she didn't want to lose this position. In her hesitation, he turned, as if dismissing her. She suddenly remembered her promise to herself—to never again be demure and do what she thought someone wanted her to do. A man in this position would simply ask the question. So she stood. "If I may?"

He paused and slowly turned around. He gestured for her to continue.

"When you say to 'decline as one would in English.' Do you mean such as…sincerely? Or regrettably?"

"Pardon?"

"I suppose it depends on your feelings about the invitation."

"My *feelings*?"

"Do you regret that you can't attend? Or are you simply responding?"

To his credit, he looked away for a moment, seeming to contemplate it. "I don't regret it. But I am quite sincere." He waved a hand in the direction of her paper. "Write what you think is best."

Hattie preened on the inside—she'd done it, she'd spoken up like a man. She imagined their relationship blossoming into something entirely indispensable for him. Her, asking questions to clarify his thoughts; him, realizing how invaluable she was. As long as she was here…

"And the first one, my lord? Should I not mention what he offered to purchase?"

His lordship didn't even pause to think about it. "A carriage." He returned to the sofa, picked up the leather folder, and went back to his reading.

Hattie sat at the writing desk. There was thick cream paper embossed with the viscount's seal. She began to write.

To Mr. Carmichael,

Sir:
Having recently acceded to the title of viscount, I have had opportunity to review the purchase offer of a carriage you had previously made to my late grandfather, and for which you received a favorable reply from him. I regretfully inform you that I find the offer to be too low and cannot honor the terms.
Yours, Viscount Abbott

She laid the letter aside and carried on to the next.

Dear Mrs. Whitsun...

Who was Mrs. Whitsun? Hattie had never heard of her. Which hardly meant anything, but still, she wondered if Mrs. Whitsun had a daughter she was eager for the viscount to meet. Queenie said when gentlemen such as the viscount were on the marriage mart, women came out of the walls like rats. Hattie pictured Mrs. Whitsun with a rat face.

Anyway.

Please accept my kindest regards and thanks for the invitation to dine Thursday evening. Regrettably, I am otherwise engaged.
Sincerely, V. A.

Was V. A. the right way to sign the letter? After several moments of pondering and coming up with a different answer each time, she turned in her chair. He didn't look up. She cleared her throat.

"Sí?" he drawled, without even raising his eyes.

"Would you care to read what I've written?"

He held out his hand.

Hattie picked up the two letters and crossed the room to put them in his hand. He added them to the stack of letters. What was he doing? Wasn't he going to read them? Was she supposed to stand there? Was she supposed to return to the desk?

She stood.

And stood.

Why didn't he read them? And how long did one remain standing under such circumstances? She felt a bit like she was hovering over him, but he didn't seem to mind or even notice her. She would guess a man in his position would have servants hovering over him quite a lot. It must be second nature to him; he must be immune to the presence of another. She didn't mind standing there—she very much liked to look at him. Really, the only criticism she had of this glorious man was that his style of communicating was rather painful. His style being none at all.

He looked up and seemed startled to see her. She felt that spark of something delicious in her again. She smiled. "Miss Woodchurch?"

Oh. He didn't know what she wanted. "I, ah… I thought you might want to look at the letters I wrote for you. Perhaps there is something you'd like to see changed? In my experience, sometimes I am quite satisfied with the first letter I write, but other times, I must attempt it twice or even three times to get it right."

He seemed confused by this. He glanced at the letters on top of his stack. "I will review them in due course."

"All right." She remained standing, not certain what to do with herself.

He frowned. "You may take tea now."

Yes! A perfect solution and something to do with her hands, which she happened to be gripping at her waist as if hanging on for dear life. She glanced around for the tea service. "Where…?"

"In the kitchen."

The *kitchen*? But of course. Her fantasy of a partnership notwithstanding, she was in his *employ*. He was not going to send for tea or ask after her day. He expected her to do what he'd asked and then make herself invisible, like any good servant. She debated asking if he would like her to send for tea for himself, but he had that look of concentration directed at his papers again.

"You may go, Miss Woodchurch," he muttered.

Well, then. She'd been dismissed. And if she wasn't certain of it, he made a gesture to the door, indicating she should scurry along.

Hattie scurried, all right, her face flaming as she went.

It was a miracle that she found the kitchen, as confusing as she found this grand house. But there was a portrait of a woman who had caught her eye the first time through. She was wearing pink silk and panniers, and her hair was styled two feet high. She had a bit of a smile on her lips, as if she could see that Hattie was out of her depth here.

"No need to laugh," Hattie muttered as she walked by the portrait.

The staff dining room was empty. No one about at all, save two young women in the kitchen, preparing for the evening meal. They both looked surprised when she walked into the kitchen. "Umm… His lordship said I should take tea."

The two looked at each other. One of them spoke to the other in Spanish. That one wiped her hands on her apron. She left the kitchen through another door and the first girl went back to work, scrubbing potatoes.

A moment later the girl returned with a gentleman Hattie recalled was the butler. He had a linen napkin stuck in his collar—she had clearly interrupted a meal. Was she meant to do everything wrong today?

He seemed terribly confused by her. "Miss Woodchurch?"

"I beg your pardon, Mr.…"

"Borerro."

"Mr. Borerro. The viscount has employed me to do some corresponding for him. In English. I don't speak Spanish. That might be obvious, but in case you were wondering."

Mr. Borerro exchanged a look with the two women.

"He said I should go to the kitchen and have some tea. I'm sorry to have disturbed you."

"Ah, is that it? Come." He gestured for her to follow, escorting her to the staff dining room. "Please, take a seat."

"I don't want to be any trouble," she said as she walked to the table. "I don't really need tea, but the—" She turned back to the door and found that Mr. Borerro had disappeared. "But the viscount told me to," she muttered as she took a seat.

She could hear Mr. Borerro's deep voice speaking in Spanish in the kitchen. Moments later, one of the girls came in with tea and tiny little pastries. She set the tray in front of Hattie. "Thank you," Hattie said.

The girl responded with more Spanish than seemed necessary, smiled and went out of the room.

Hattie poured tea into a cup and examined the pastries.

They were flaky and delicate, and when she bit into one, she almost moaned with delight. The pastry was filled with a sweet cream as light as air. She ate all three of them, then licked her fingers.

She drank her tea and waited until she thought a suitable amount of time had passed. She'd been sitting here a quarter of an hour. How long should tea for one take? At home, she rarely took tea with her parents, because that was the time they most liked to argue with each other. But a quarter of an hour felt unpardonably short.

But she couldn't sit here. She collected her tea service and returned to the kitchen. The two women stopped what they were doing and stared at her. She placed the tea service on the center kitchen table. She smiled. "It's dreadful to take tea alone. It would be much better with a friend."

They continued to stare at her, not understanding the language. But as it was the only language she knew besides a bit of schoolhouse French, she carried on, certain that people could find a way to communicate if they desired it. "How do you find London? Was it what you expected?"

Somehow, a half hour of their attempts to communicate passed. Hattie decided that was enough time for tea, wished the women good afternoon—*buenas tardes*—and returned to the study. It was easier to find her way this time, as her smirking friend with the tall white hair sort of pointed the way.

But the viscount was gone from the study when she entered. So was his big folder of papers.

She walked to the small writing desk and found there the two letters she had written. They'd been signed, his signature made with thick black strokes and a flourish. Beside the letters was another piece of paper. He'd attached a square of a note onto which he'd printed, *What it says.*

Hattie looked at the paper beneath the note. The writing was so small it was nearly impossible to decipher. Why would anyone develop such obnoxious handwriting? She sat down and puzzled out the tiny cursive letters and finally thought she had it. At the bottom of the note he'd left her, she wrote, very plainly, in legible print: *The amount paid to Mr. Ed Moore for making of a coffin for Mrs. Crump, deceased*—Hattie certainly hoped Mrs. Crump was deceased at the time of the making of the coffin—*shall be six pounds forty pence, and the payment to be made by the fifteenth day of the month following interment.*

There was nothing else on the desk for her. She stood up and wandered around the room. She looked at the books on the table next to the armchair. All were in French.

On his desk was a stack of ledgers and some unopened letters.

Hattie went to the sofa where he'd been sitting and sat in the very same spot. She spread her hands over the chintz upholstery and found it cool to the touch. She imagined herself filling the contours his body had made. She stood up from there and wandered to the window to have a look at the garden. She glanced down—and quickly hopped backward and out of sight. The viscount was there! In the garden!

She pressed a hand to her racing heart to quell the surprise of spotting him, unnerved by the idea that he might have seen her and would assume she was spying. But her heart slowed, and she cautiously leaned forward to have a peek.

The viscount was seated on a bench next to a small fountain. The elderly lady who'd nearly doused Hattie with mop water was seated next to him. Between them on the bench was something…a plate? Hattie couldn't make out what was on the plate, but the two of them kept bending over it, picking something up and putting it in their mouths. They were tasting something.

And then, the biggest surprise of all—the viscount laughed. He *laughed*. He had a charming laugh, deep and gentle. Hattie drifted closer to the window, watching the two of them, and remaining there until the elderly woman stood.

Lord Abbott reached out a hand to steady her. Then he stood, too, picked up the plate, and offered an arm to her. The two of them casually strolled across the garden, toward the house, chatting in Spanish that drifted up and through the open window.

But he did not return to the study.

At half past five, Hattie packed her things, took her bag, and left the way she'd come. Down one long hall, lifting her hand in silent salute to the woman with tall hair as she passed. She ran down the servants' stairs, and carried on, passing through the kitchen, wishing the two women a good day and receiving the same, she thought, in Spanish. Then retraced her steps down the tiled hall. She went out the servants' door and into the alley and wended around the house to the street.

What a curious occupation this was. What a mysterious man he was.

She couldn't wait to come again.

CHAPTER SEVEN

THAT MISS WOODCHURCH could make out what looked like barnyard chicken scratch was astounding to Mateo. Even if he could read English fluently, he'd not be able to make out a single word of his grandfather's handwriting.

He discovered that the word which had given him the most grief was *coffin*. Coffin!

The first week of Miss Woodchurch's employment had gone along like that, her deciphering words and letters he'd nearly thrown into the fire. She was punctual, which Mateo greatly appreciated. She wrote a perfectly fine letter, stating politely what he said in his rough, more direct way. Her penmanship, as promised, was very good. And when he read what she'd written, the language seemed to flow in a way that he envied.

He found he didn't need her services for as long every day as Beck had suggested, and while he still wasn't entirely comfortable having this young woman in his sphere for hours on end, he kept thinking back to what Beck had said: that she needed this position. He didn't know why she needed it, but he liked her, and he didn't want to send her away if that was the case. So, he sent her for tea. Every day, dismissing her when the work was done to take her tea.

There was something else about Miss Woodchurch that stood out to him in that first week—she was very much at ease in his company and seemed to grow more so every day. She talked freely and she talked a *lot*. *Muy habladora.*

Moreover, from what he'd gathered, she was doing quite a lot of talking during tea, too.

Twice this week, he'd passed by the hallway leading to the staff section of the house and heard laughter. And then her voice, lifting above Borerro's deep rumble, followed by the kitchen girls' high-pitched voices.

One afternoon, it rained. When he went to the window to close it, he saw the lower half of her beneath the portico over the terrace. There was a man leaning against the column, smoking a cheroot. He recognized the man at once as Pacheco, his manservant. Miss Woodchurch was carrying on a conversation with Pacheco, and that stoic old Santiavan was laughing.

Even more surprising, Pacheco hadn't mentioned making her acquaintance.

He wondered what they could possibly find to talk about. The curiosity began to eat at him.

One morning, Borerro brought him the post. Mateo noticed that he had a small pin affixed to his lapel. He leaned forward, peering at it. *"Qué es eso?"*

Borerro glanced down. "A Tudor rose, *mi señor.* Miss Woodchurch gifted this to me."

"She *gifted* it to you?" he asked in Spanish. "Why?"

"I said I admired the roses I've seen about the town. They are everywhere. Its effect is pleasing."

This was the first Mateo was hearing that something had actually pleased Borerro. "You discussed roses with Miss Woodchurch?"

The gentleman colored a bit under his suntanned skin. "Briefly."

Miss Woodchurch had been in his employ for a week,

and she and Borerro were talking about roses and she was making Pacheco laugh? And just like that, his world had turned a bit topsy-turvy.

There was another thing about Miss Woodchurch that he found a little unnerving—moments when he would happen to look up, only to discover her staring at him. She would quickly look away with a blush, and she'd make a sudden show of appearing *quite* busy, which couldn't be possible, given the amount of work he had for her.

The first time, he was naturally inclined to wonder if there was something peculiar about him and self-consciously dragged his fingers through his hair, then rubbed his chin, thinking perhaps his emerging beard had already started to darken. But when it happened again and again, he began to suspect that perhaps she was a bit infatuated with him. It wouldn't be the first time a young woman had looked at him in that way—wealth and titles could make even a goat appealing.

But somehow, the idea that she was attracted to his titles and wealth did not seem to fit with the woman who sat at the small writing desk each day. But what did fit her? His curiosity about her was growing. Personally, he didn't speak to her about anything but the correspondence. His mistrust of people in general made it difficult for him. And really, what was there to speak of? Should he ask how she'd made Pacheco laugh?

He remembered something about his brother. One morning, they were riding along the shore, having spent the previous night in the company of a dozen or more of Roberto's friends. Roberto remarked that Mateo hadn't said much throughout the evening. "You appear aloof to others," he'd said.

"I am aloof," Mateo said. "Not by desire, but by circumstance." He never intended to be haughty, but his reticence was a result of having been endlessly corrected and chastised by his father. How to change was beyond his comprehension. "What would I have said?" Mateo had asked. "I've nothing in common with any of them."

Roberto had looked at him with exasperation. "They are people, Teo, just like you. Of course you've something in common with them."

It was a fair point—they were all human beings, fueled by the same base desires and wants and social mores. But even so, it wasn't easy for him. Roberto's charm came so naturally—Mateo envied his easy way with people. Roberto could look at someone like Miss Woodchurch and strike up a conversation, whereas Mateo couldn't think of a single thing to say that he thought she would find interesting, or a single question that would not seem invasive.

So he said nothing.

Mateo went about his day as he always did—mostly in silence. Sometimes he would sit at his desk, his gaze on the window, and it would inevitably trail over to where Miss Woodchurch was bent over her writing, her brow furrowed, a soft ringlet of brown hair brushing against her nape. He would study the curve of her neck, the swanlike bend to it, and how luminous her skin looked in the afternoon light. Why hadn't she married? How was it acceptable to her family that she secured employment? What was the word in English for the blue color of her eyes? In Spanish, it was *azur*.

At the start of the second week of her employ, Miss Woodchurch arrived with a small vase of roses. Red and white, he noticed, not unlike the small pin Borerro was wearing.

"Good morning, my lord," she said cheerily, and dipped into her perfect curtsy.

"*Buenos días*, Miss Woodchurch."

She held out the flowers for him to see. "Aren't they lovely? They come from Mary's garden."

Mary. Who was Mary?

"She's the new scullery maid," she said, as if reading his mind. "I hope you won't mind, but Mr. Borerro asked if I might know of anyone and it so happens I did. She was once in my family's employ and I was terribly fond of her. I don't know how they manage in the kitchens, not speaking a word of the same language. It's remarkable, isn't it, when people want to communicate, they will find a way? Oh, the flowers. Mary has a small garden at home—she has quite the talent with roses, doesn't she?"

Miss Woodchurch had brought them a scullery maid? He hadn't known they needed one.

She was still holding out the flowers, clearly awaiting his response. "What's your favorite flower?"

"Qué?"

"Everyone has a favorite flower, don't they? Is it a rose? I do adore roses. But I think everyone must, as they grow in abundance here. I also quite like daffodils. Did you know they are the Welsh national flower? Oh, of course not," she said, and laughed. "Why on earth would you have reason to know that?"

He blinked at her.

"Do you like peonies? I think they may be the grandest flower on earth. They are not yet in season, but when they are, I'll bring some."

He had never in his life heard so many opinions about flowers. He didn't have a favorite flower. He'd have to consult a botany text, have a look at them all before he committed to a *favorite*. "Ah… We have work to do, Miss Woodchurch."

"Then we should be about it, shouldn't we?" She went to her desk and placed the flowers, stood back to study them, then moved them to the other side of the desk. After another moment of study, she moved them back to her original placement. Apparently satisfied, she took her seat and picked up her pen. She looked at him. "Ready, my lord."

What an unusual creature she was.

The post was unusually heavy this week, several letters having to do with the business of the estate. One had perplexed him and then had annoyed him. It had come from Mr. Callum, who had returned to the country and Harrington Hall, Mateo's Essex country seat. The majordomo had written to inquire what Mateo would like to do with fifty goats that had been delivered in error. For a second time. Mr. Callum had attached the invoice.

Mateo had stared at the letter for a very long time. What was the matter with Mr. Feathers, the man who kept herding goats over to his property? Was it possible that the word *goat* had more than one meaning in English? The language was so damn confounding! He'd specifically sought the purchase of fifty *sheep.* And when he'd sent the goats back the first time, he thought he'd made it quite clear in his letter that what he wanted was sheep. For the wool, obviously.

"Miss Woodchurch."

She looked up.

He held out the letter. "Read it, please."

Miss Woodchurch took the letter and read it, then looked at the request for payment beneath it, which clearly detailed the delivery of goats. Or, at least, Mateo thought it did. Miss Woodchurch's brow furrowed with confusion.

"Please, have I confused the words *goat* and *sheep*? You may tell me that I'm in error, but for the life of me, I can't determine what I've done wrong."

"You've not confused any words that I can see."

"Is there any reason of which you are aware a man might deliver goats in error, not once, but twice?"

She bit her lower lip, her gaze still on the letter. "Not that I am aware." She peeked up at him, and he realized she was trying to hide a smile.

"Are you laughing at this?" he asked sternly.

"Oh, my lord!" she said, and he anticipated a profuse apology. "Only a little, really. Don't you find it amusing?"

"I am too exasperated to be amused." He gestured to her desk. "Please. To Mr. Callum." He rethought that. It was possible Callum was the problem. "No. Send directly to Mr. Feathers."

She jotted that down.

Mateo put his hands to his waist. "Sir: I thought I was perfectly clear in my last letter that I wanted sheep. Not goats. How one might confuse the two is impossible to imagine."

Something that sounded a bit like a strangled cough came from Miss Woodchurch, and Mateo glanced at her. She was bent over her paper, her pen moving across it.

He faced the window and continued. "I am confounded, sir, that I must again ask that you collect the goats and deliver the sheep."

Miss Woodchurch made another strange sound. Mateo turned back to her. "Is something the matter, Miss Woodchurch? Are you unwell?"

She shook her head.

He continued. "If you cannot distinguish between—"

Another strangled sound from Miss Woodchurch, but this time, she put down her pen, crossed her arms tightly across her middle, and laughed. The woman *laughed*. With glee, with abandon—she didn't seem to care that he was being made a fool.

"Miss Woodchurch!"

Tears of laughter sparkled in her eyes. She tried to calm herself, but it was pointless—another peal of laughter burst from her lips, followed by more laughter. "I beg your pardon, I do," she said, wheezing a little, "but who could possibly mistake goats for sheep twice over?" Her laughter again was uncontrollable. "What are we to think? That he's grown too fond of the sheep and can't bear to part with them? Or he is absentminded, and keeps forgetting that he's sold sheep, and not goats? Or that he is losing his sight and they look the same?" She suddenly gasped. "What if he means to vex you?" She squealed with delight at this suggestion, and bent over with laughter.

It was hard not to laugh, too, and despite his exasperation with Mr. Feathers, Mateo smiled.

"I don't truly believe he means to vex you, my lord," she said, gathering herself. "That's quite a lot of trouble to go to in the hopes of earning a laugh, isn't it?"

"One would think," he said. He pointed to the paper. "Shall we finish the letter?"

"Of course." She sat up, touched her fingertips to the skin beneath her eyes to dab away any tears of laughter, but she was still smiling broadly when she picked up the pen and began to write again.

Mateo returned to his desk, her smile shining in his mind's eye. He liked happy people. He liked being near them. He wondered what it would be like, to have the ability and the lack of self-consciousness to laugh with abandon like she had.

After a quarter of an hour, she stood up and walked to his desk, and handed him the letter she'd written.

To Mr. Feathers,

Sir:
*I have received your invoice as well as your delivery
and find myself quite at a loss. I have ordered sheep
twice now, and on both occasions, you have delivered
goats. I trust that you are aware of the difference in
the two animals, but in the event you are not, and are
sending herds of whatever sort of livestock you find
milling about your grounds, I offer you these render-
ings to assist.*

Just below, she'd drawn a crude sheep and goat. She
had written the names of the species above each drawing.

*I request that you correct your mistake without
delay.*
V. A.

It was a jest. She was smiling, clearly pleased with herself for it.

This was hardly proper, and Mateo wondered what he
would think if Pacheco or Borerro had made a joke of it.
What would he think if one of those two men suddenly
burst into laughter? He would smile, surely. He would join
in the jest.

Mateo picked up a pen from his desk and added a beard
to the goat and handed the letter back to her.

Miss Woodchurch laughed with delight. "He'll have absolutely no excuse for it now." She was still grinning when
she handed him another letter, this one more somber in
tone, asking Mr. Feathers to correct his mistake at once,

and if he did not, that he would instruct the majordomo to cancel the purchase.

A perfect letter for this strange circumstance. Beautifully written and presented.

But Mateo liked the first one better. He kept it on his desk. "Thank you, Miss Woodchurch."

"You are most welcome, my lord. What would you like me to do now?"

"You may take tea."

Her smile faded. She seemed to reluctantly make her way to the door. She paused there and looked back at him, and he sensed she wanted to speak. But all she said was, "Thank you," and left the room.

What had she meant to say? He realized he was very curious about what she meant to say and regretted not asking her.

He regretted sending her away at all.

CHAPTER EIGHT

WHEN MISS WOODCHURCH returned from tea, she was bearing a plate of madeleine pastries. Mateo looked with confusion at them, then at her.

"It is not my place, I know, but you really must try one." She held out the plate. "They're delicious. They are almost as good as Mrs. O'Malley's."

Mateo and Rosa had made the sweets just last night. And who was Mrs. O'Malley?

"I've never known anyone who can bake delights like Mrs. O'Malley. Until now, that is." She held the plate a little closer to him. He reluctantly took one.

"Thank you."

She took the plate to the small writing desk to put aside, then returned to his desk for instructions. He gestured to the chair. "I'll have a few things for you in a moment."

Miss Woodchurch did as he asked. She sat on the edge of the seat, her back straight, her hands politely folded. He looked at the work before him on the desk. He'd been working so long that the figures were beginning to swim. He put down his pencil and rubbed his temples.

"The weather has been fine, hasn't it?" she said. "I walked in Hyde Park this morning—it was lovely. Have you been?"

Mateo sighed softly.

"You really should, you know. Not that I would presume

to tell you what to do. But if you like to ride, Rotten Row is where all the fashionable people go to ride and be seen. It's quite crowded in the afternoons, but in the mornings it's a wonderful respite. If the sun is shining, of course."

He gave her a curt nod and picked up his pencil.

"Or, you can walk alongside the row. Or take a carriage if you like. Really, there is any number of ways you might enjoy the park."

He couldn't think.

"But I think the park is best enjoyed—"

"Miss Woodchurch."

"Yes?"

There was no delicate way to say it. "Madam…you talk too much."

She stared at him. "Pardon?"

"You *talk* too much. It is impossible to think with so many words flying about." It really was impossible, but… at the same time, he instantly regretted his words.

"Ah." She looked stricken and lowered her gaze to her lap. "I apologize."

He felt like an ass. "It's quite—"

"It's a terrible habit I have when I am in the company of someone who speaks not at all," she said, and lifted her gaze.

It took him a moment to realize she was criticizing him. "I beg your pardon?"

"I have noticed about you the very thing you have noticed about me."

"What do you mean?"

"I'm not being clear, which is another bad habit of mine, I will admit. But what I'm trying to say is that it's difficult to converse when someone doesn't speak at all, my lord. You're a very quiet person. And I have an unfortunate tendency to fill the silence when others won't speak. At the Iddesleigh School for Exceptional Girls, I was forever speaking for the girls who didn't want to or weren't confident to speak, until my friend took me aside and told me I was explaining too many things. I do thank you for the reminder that I should not."

He stared at her, uncertain if she was arguing with him or not. It didn't seem so. It seemed more like she was... speaking her mind? Without the slightest bit of hesitation. Extraordinary. He could name on one hand the people who easily spoke their mind in his presence, and they were mostly related to him. He put down his pencil and leaned back in his chair, his gaze fixed on her.

"But I won't utter another word," she said, and with that, she mimed locking her lips and flicking away a key. And then she smiled.

His gaze narrowed. "You won't be able to keep it locked."

Her eyes widened slightly. But then she shrugged.

"You are right, Miss Woodchurch, I do not speak often. And you speak all the time. Your tendency is to fill the room with more words and mine is to fill them with fewer."

She smiled but uttered not a word.

He picked up his pencil. But he stole a glance at her. She had turned her attention to the books on his table. She was craning her neck one way to read the spines. With a finger, she moved the book on top, angling it a little away from her to better read it. She was frowning, as if trying to make out the words in French.

"Le vicomte de Bragelonne: ou, dix ans plus tard," he said. "By Alexandre Dumas. In English, it is *The Viscount of Bragelonne: Or, Ten Years Later.*"

"Really?" She looked up with surprise. "One of my favorite books!" She suddenly gasped and put her hand over her mouth. "Lord, there I go again, talking." But then her gaze narrowed. "Did you trick me?"

"Tricking you is unnecessary. The odds were strongly in my favor."

"Touché." She smiled, pleased.

And surprisingly, he smiled, too. With his chin, he indicated the book. "You've read the work?"

"I have indeed. In English, of course. My favorite part is *The Man in the Iron Mask*. Did you know that there really was such a prisoner?"

Now this woman had his undivided attention. "I'm reading that part now. *L'homme au masque du fer*."

"I envy anyone who has the capacity to speak different languages. Imagine, to read a book in French! I only speak one language, and, as I am given to understand, I speak quite a lot of it."

His smile deepened. "You're quite...*cheeky*." That was a word he'd learned since coming to London. "It's common in Santiava to speak both Spanish and French, given our proximity to both countries. And my mother, as you know, is English."

"I still maintain it's remarkable," she said. "It would take me *ages* to read an entire book in another language, no matter how proficient I was."

Mateo realized that he enjoyed the way she spoke so freely to him. It was as if he was speaking to his sister, or a cousin. So many women he met in the course of his everyday life spoke only when spoken to. It made for some awkwardly long pauses, being who he was. "What did you think of the book?"

"I was captivated. Quite a lot of intrigue, wasn't it? And what an unbearable existence the poor man suffered. It was weeks before I could keep from dwelling on his plight, a life spent inside an iron mask. Who was he really, do you think?"

"You don't believe it was the king's brother?" Alexandre Dumas, the author who had fictionalized the tale of the mysterious prisoner, had presented the man as the identical twin brother of Louis XIV, imprisoned so as not to challenge the king's throne.

"I don't," Miss Woodchurch said firmly. "History would have revealed if Louis XIV had a twin brother."

"I agree. But the prisoner was obviously an influential man. What other reason would one have to go to such lengths of imprisonment?"

"Why must it have been so cruel?"

The conversation was remarkable—no one in Mateo's small circle of family and friends read as voraciously as he did. "I believe the author made the mask an iron one to add the dramatic to his story. But the real mask was made of fabric that was far more comfortable."

"Fabric? What was it?"

"I don't know the word in English," he said apologetically. *"Terciopelo."* He looked around the room and pointed at the drapes.

"Velvet," she supplied.

Velvet. Like her laugh.

"How lonely he must have been," she mused. "How cruel to live a life without anyone knowing you." She shivered slightly, as if the thought revolted her.

Mateo could well imagine living a life without anyone knowing him. Sometimes he felt as if he was living it now. He had siblings, a mother, and Rosa, of course...but he'd kept to himself for the most part, and it had felt very lonely at times. He was, in some ways, a man behind a mask.

"Are you an avid reader, Miss Woodchurch?"

"*Very* much. My favorite thing to do on a dark, cold day is settle in before the fire with a good book."

That was a great pleasure of his, too. "And what do you like to read?"

"Novels, mostly," she said. "Love stories. I do quite like a mystery set in a gloomy castle, too. Lately, I've been reading an atlas."

He didn't understand. "Forgive my English, but I thought one consulted an atlas."

"One does." She laughed. "I like to look at places then read the little details about them. Do you know the longest river in the world?"

"The Nile. My brother and I traveled to Egypt on expedition a few years ago."

"An expedition!" She sounded truly delighted. "Now I'm *terribly* envious. I've never been as far as even Ireland or France. I am desperately curious to see the world. Including Santiava, of course. What's it like?"

He didn't know where to begin to describe his homeland. For one, he'd never had to. And since arriving in London, he couldn't think of a single person who'd asked him about the duchy. He assumed Santiava was too small and too far away to care about.

He thought about the land he loved—the beauty of it, certainly. And the people—he firmly believed there was not a country whose people were more generous than the Santiavans. "The duchy is small," he said. "But powerful. We've had to fight for our independence throughout our history—first from the Spaniards, then the French, and only fifty or so years ago, from the Weslorians."

"The Weslorians! But Wesloria is so far from Santiava. The Duchess of Marley is a Weslorian, did you know? What does it look like? Santiava, I mean."

"The landscape is extraordinary. On the one hand, you have the crystal waters of the sea. The *palacio real*, the ducal palace, is on a cliff overlooking the sea. It's quite grand, with several loggias facing the sea. The views are stunning." He thought of how the sunlight sparkled like jewels on the surface. They would leave the veranda doors open most days to pull in the sea breeze. The breeze brought the scent of the honeysuckle and roses that twined around the veranda columns. The terra-cotta tile was cool beneath one's feet—Mateo still went barefoot in the palace, even as the leader of that small duchy.

"What's a loggia?"

Mateo gestured her forward, and on a piece of paper, he sketched the sort of covered terrace the palace sported.

Miss Woodchurch did not stand on the other side of his desk and view his rendering upside down. Oh no—this woman, who was so at ease with him, came around behind the desk and leaned over him. He was fully aware of her nearness, of how much smaller she seemed standing next to him.

"Oh, I see. It must be beautiful."

"We've another home. Castillo Estrella is in the mountains. We call it the Castle in the Stars."

"How terribly romantic," she said, and moved away from him, strolling to the window.

The Castle in the Stars was quite different from the palace. From those windows, one looked out over mountains that wore fat white clouds like hats. The lake near the castle reflected the blue of the sky above so perfectly that it looked like a mirror. The land around was lush and green, the air clear and scented with pine. The floors were polished wood, the walls dotted with tapestries to keep out the winter winds. "One can leave the mountains and reach the sea within two hours. Mountains to seaside…that's a beauty I find difficult to describe." What he loved about Santiava was that no matter where he was, he had a view that looked like a glimpse of heaven. To him, there was no place quite like it.

In contrast, London was cold and gray and too crowded. He sighed, rubbed his temples. He'd turned into a *casscarrabias*, a curmudgeon, and he wasn't even thirty years old.

"It sounds divine," Miss Woodchurch said.

Mateo had allowed himself to drift too far away. "I am, admittedly, biased…but I think it is. Here now, I have work for you." He handed her some papers and turned his attention to the work at hand.

In the remaining hour of her time, Miss Woodchurch deciphered more of his grandfather's writing and penned responses to two invitations. He was surprised when it was time for her to go—it seemed as if the afternoon had passed more quickly than usual.

When Miss Woodchurch took her leave, and wished him a good day, he went to the window for some air. He must have stood there for longer than he'd meant—his thoughts had drifted back to Santiava again, to a pair of hunting dogs he'd left safe in the hands of his staff but missed nonetheless—and happened to see Miss Woodchurch and one of the kitchen workers, Aurelia, emerge from the servants' entrance. He watched them walk to the end of the house together, then turn to the street and disappear from his view.

As far as he knew, Aurelia spoke not a word of English. But the two of them walked along as if they were friends.

Miss Woodchurch was so…*unexpected*. She was the only person in London who had caught his attention in any meaningful way. She was educated, she had a wide range of interests, apparently, and was not the least bit reserved.

He felt different with her. He never knew if the inability to know someone was because of his position as duke in Santiava, or because of his stoic nature. Whatever the reason, he tended to feel an invisible wall between him and people he met. Particularly women.

The existence of the wall was entirely his fault. He could never think of what to say that didn't sound either condescending, or worse—disinterested. With Miss Woodchurch, the conversation had been much easier because of her easy nature.

And he was not disinterested. No...if anything, his interest was growing.

CHAPTER NINE

THE VISCOUNT WAS the most remarkable man Hattie had ever met. She couldn't quite understand him, really—he was so reserved as to be detached, so cool in his response as to be at times unpleasant. A vexing man, indeed. And yet, she was fascinated by him. She had the impression that she annoyed him from time to time, but that didn't keep her from speaking up.

And then, somehow, she'd cracked his stoic facade. After she'd done all the talking for days on end, with no hope of ever receiving more than a word or two in response, the moment she noticed his book everything had changed. That was the only time she'd thought him truly interested in anything she had to say. In fairness, she said quite a lot of things that no one was interested in, and really, what did possess her to sing the virtues of Hyde Park, as if she were the mayor of London?

Still, she was very happy to have found a sliver of common ground with him. Reading was one of her favorite things, and she was thrilled the subject had moved him to speak. She wanted to find if there were more.

In the meantime, there wasn't a soul in Hattie's life who wasn't eager to know at least *something* about the new viscount. They asked questions about him they had no business asking, but asked anyway: Why was he not in society more? What did he say, eat, drink, smoke? Who called on him? Where did he dine? Was something the matter with him? Had he looked for a spouse? Did he have a secret lover? The last question had come from Mrs. O'Malley.

Hattie avoided answering, but the questions kept coming. The silent, brooding Santiavan viscount was an enigma to everyone. Even the newspapers didn't seem to know what to make of him, calling him a recluse, locked away in his grandfather's home. They complained he'd been rumored to make a match, and yet, no one could report any news on that front. Some speculated that the negotiations for a bride would begin in earnest with the start of the Season. Others speculated he had no intention of marrying an English woman, and any assumptions toward that end were wishful thinking. Hattie certainly didn't know.

Her family was especially curious about the viscount. For reasons Hattie could not fathom, her parents seemed to despise him based on his title alone. They would practically lie in wait for her when she came home, pouncing on her the moment she walked in the door with their questions.

Queenie and Flora were hardly any better. Queenie in particular pressed Hattie for even the smallest tidbit she might use as leverage in gossiping around town. Oh, but Queenie swore she wouldn't say a *word*. Hattie knew better and took her vow to keep the viscount's affairs confidential much to heart. She didn't tell anyone what she heard or what he said—which wasn't much at all, except when it came to the dispute about goats and sheep, which aggravated him into actually speaking. Or when he talked about the book he was reading.

She did, however, leave one small truth for everyone to gnaw on—the viscount often left the room while she worked. That news was disappointing to all.

"How *tedious* this position of yours appears to be,"

Queenie complained after Hattie had fended off a series of questions with *"I don't know, I hardly know."*

On this particular afternoon when Flora and Hattie called, Queenie was stretched across the chaise in her enormous bedroom, eating from a bowl of sweets like a Greek goddess. "What do you do, then, just *write* all day? Lord, Hattie—what do you find appealing about that sort of work? You put to mind the image of a monk copying ancient texts, stuffed away in some dusty attic with only the light of a single candle."

Hattie laughed at the image. She would have thought it was obvious what appealed to her. The money, certainly, although Queenie clearly had no understanding of that. From the look of it, she had everything she could possibly want. But then the chance to be near a very handsome man was rather exhilarating, too. That, she was certain Queenie could appreciate. It wasn't every day that any of them found themselves in such company. As if Queenie wouldn't leap at the chance to write a few letters for the opportunity to ingratiate herself to Lord Abbott.

"There is *nothing* you can tell us?" Queenie pressed, sounding suspicious. "He's not been seen anywhere for more than a fortnight! Everyone wonders if something is amiss. The only thing anyone knows is that he's to dine at the Forsythe house, and that's not until the end of the week. We shouldn't have to rely on Flora for news."

"Me?" Flora blinked. "I'm sure I won't speak to him more than a moment. Everyone will be vying for his attention. He won't even notice me."

"Then you'll have to try harder, Flora," Queenie said. She sighed and turned back to Hattie. "I have a theory about your secret."

"I don't have a secret," Hattie said.

"He's ill, isn't he? *That's* why he hasn't been seen about. That's why you won't breathe a word."

Hattie nearly choked. "He looks the picture of health!" Remarkably so, she thought—virile, all muscle and sinew, a broad back and strong hands. "I think it's simply a matter of a lot of work to settle his grandfather's estates. I can't imagine he has time to make calls and whatnot."

"The Quality always has time to make calls," Queenie scoffed. "It's a waste having you there, Hattie. It should have been Flora."

"*I'm* not meant to work," Flora scoffed, as if she believed Queenie was suggesting she dig a few ditches.

"It was a jest, darling!" Queenie said. "As if you'd ever be forced into labor."

Flora and Queenie laughed with Hattie sitting right there, obviously forced into labor. Flora was the one who came to her senses first and apparently remembered Hattie's lot in life. "Not that I would mind," she hastened to assure her.

"Oh, I think you would," Hattie said. "Work is not for everyone."

Flora's cheeks flushed and she looked around the room, as if trying to find something to speak about that would lead away from this uncomfortable part of the conversation. Queenie did it for her by asking what she intended to wear to the Forsythe dinner and then reminding her whatever she chose must be stunning, because Christiana Porter would be in attendance.

This piece of news clearly unnerved Flora. Hattie suspected she knew why—Christiana Porter was a woman of considerable beauty, with hair the color of cotton and enticingly plump lips. It was a mystery to Hattie why she'd not secured a match before now—her name seemed to be on everyone's lips. Flora would never admit it, but she was intimidated—she'd said enough over the last two years for Hattie to know that Flora didn't consider herself to be in the same constellation as Miss Porter.

"Oh. How wonderful for her," Flora said in an unusually high voice.

"Everyone assumes she will be the one to attract the viscount's eye, of course," Queenie continued, her gaze on Flora. Hattie didn't like this side of Queenie—the needling, poking side. It was a game she played from time to time, trying to rile her friend. She was unkind for sport.

"I'm certain of it," Flora said.

"It's no wonder, really," Queenie said. "She's so beautiful."

Hattie didn't want to hear more and moved to Queenie's dressing table.

Queenie's nudging worked—Flora suddenly blurted, "I'm not saying it should be *me*, I'm truly not, but why must everyone always assume that Christiana Porter will be the most sought-after lady?"

Queenie giggled, delighted by Flora's rare pique. "Darling! You are everything she is and more, dearest. As to why everyone always assumes her? Well…you'll explain it to us after you've dined at the Forsythes'. Tell us everything that happens, and we'll make sense of it."

With her back to them, Hattie rolled her eyes.

When she and Flora finally took their leave of Queenie—and not a moment too soon as far as Hattie was concerned—she returned home to find her family was overly occupied with her position in the viscount's office, too.

The subject came up at supper. While her brothers ate like demons, and her father nursed a whisky while he read the newspaper, Hattie's mother stroked a cat in her lap and studied her daughter across the table, her eyes narrowed.

Hattie hated when her mother got like this, too observant, trying to find fault. She continued her meal, her gaze on her plate.

At last her mother made her announcement. "You're smiling too much, Harriet."

Hattie looked around, confused. "I'm smiling too *much*?"

"Yes. It makes you look overly eager."

Hattie hadn't even been aware she was smiling. She wasn't overly eager about anything. Certainly not this meal.

"That's because she's very pleased with her occupation, Mama," Perry said. "Everyone can see it." He leaned over the arm of his chair, so that his face was directly in front of Hattie. "But it doesn't make you better than everyone else."

Hattie pushed him away. "I never said it did."

"Because you're not better than me," Perry added.

"But *I* am," Peter said, and threw a piece of bread across the table at his twin.

"Lads!" Hattie's father said without looking up from his newspaper.

"You shouldn't be too eager to work," Perry continued, as if, being nearly fourteen, he had even the slightest notion of how anything in this world worked. "It makes you seem desperate for attention. No one likes girls who want too much attention."

"For the love of God," Hattie muttered. "You know nothing, Perry. I'm *not* eager. But even if I were, why shouldn't I be enthusiastic about work?" Frankly, she couldn't wait to leave this house and go to Grosvenor Square on those days she was expected. "I wouldn't expect you to understand—you're too young." That would prick him. Peter and Perry hated to be reminded they were so much younger than Hattie and Daniel. "But some people are happy to *have* work."

"And thus I am reminded," her father said, lowering his paper at the end of the table, "when will I see payment for these *services rendered*?" He said it as if she was a dance hall girl.

With a groan, Hattie rested her head against the chairback and looked to the ceiling. Her family was impossible in every conceivable way. "I've received my first week's wages, Papa. I'll have the second week's wages tomorrow."

"Oh?" There was a new lilt in her father's voice. "You've received one week's wages? Did you forget our agreement?"

"It wasn't an agreement—it was a command."

"Call it what you like, I'll have my share."

"For God's sake," Daniel said. He'd remained silent through the talk, but now he put down the fork he'd been using to shovel lamb into his mouth as if the house was on fire and he only had seconds to spare. "This family is a bloody carnival show."

"Says you," Peter said.

"Yes, says I," he said. "I wonder, Hat, what your friends think of your position? They surely find your employment distasteful."

"If you are referring to Flora and Queenie, I don't know why you think so. They attended the Iddesleigh School for Exceptional Girls, too, you know. We were all trained for future employment. That was the point—leading the way to equality."

"Your—" Daniel started, but suddenly, several grandfather clocks began to chime, and for the space of a minute, no one spoke, as their voices wouldn't carry over the racket.

When they'd finished chiming, Daniel continued. "Your friends attended that school because their parents wanted to be rid of them. Not because they would *ever* be expected to work for wages. They're too upper-crust to dirty their hands."

"They aren't her friends," her mother said. The cat she was holding stood in her lap and stretched, and then gingerly stepped up on the table and began to weave through the plates, platters, and glassware.

"Of course they are my friends," Hattie said, and stood up from her seat, picked up the cat, and deposited it on the floor. "I've known them for ten years."

Her mother snorted. "Fancy Flora pays you, darling. You're not her friend."

"Mama!" Hattie exclaimed. But to be fair, that very thought had crossed her mind once or twice. Would Flora and Queenie want her to join them if she wasn't being paid to do so? She didn't want to risk discovering the answer because, really, they were the only friends she had.

"Especially the tall one," Daniel said.

Hattie frowned. "Do you mean Flora?"

Daniel shrugged. "How should I know her name? She is no one to me. Although I did see her in attendance at a concert in the Canterbury Music Hall. She's a bit overweening, isn't she?"

"You've clearly confused her with someone else. She's not at all overweening, she is very kind, and she happens to be my closest friend, Daniel. You shouldn't say such things—you don't even know her."

Daniel shrugged and pushed his clean plate away.

"She's the daughter of a viscount," Hattie's mother said, and for a moment, Hattie thought her mother meant to defend Flora. "They're all of them overweening, are they not?"

Daniel and her mother laughed loudly together.

Hattie put her napkin beside her plate. "Well, then. This has been..." She paused, trying to think of an appropriate word. "It's been what it usually is, disturbing and a little frightening. If you will all excuse me?" She stood to go.

"Don't forget my share!" her father called after her as she exited the room.

Hattie strode out of the dining room and down the crowded hallway, sidestepping packages, cats, clocks, dress forms and tea services. Oh yes, she was eager to work, all right, eager to do anything that would help her leave this damn house. And work seemed the only possibility she had that didn't include a pine box.

She sincerely hoped the pine box didn't come for her first.

THE NEXT AFTERNOON, Hattie paused in the foyer to put on a light cloak, as it had begun to rain. She had on her arm a basket full of gifts for everyone at the viscount's house. They'd all been quite pleased with the Tudor rose lapel pins she'd bought from Mrs. O'Malley for a half crown each. Today, Hattie had two linen handkerchiefs she'd embroidered with English ivy along the border, one for Aurelia and Yolanda, the women who worked in the kitchen. It was curious, she thought, how their friendships were forming. The two girls didn't speak English, and yet, the three of them had been making their way, mainly by teaching each other words as they went. Hattie would point to a dish, for example, and say, "Plate." Yolanda or Aurelia would respond with the Spanish version. *"Plato!"* Chicken was *pollo*. A potato was a *patata*. From Aurelia, Hattie learned that heart was *corazón*, which she'd learned after noticing Aurelia smiling shyly at one of the footmen.

She also had some tea cakes from Mrs. O'Malley's shop

for Mary, a salt shaker for Mr. Pacheco, after he'd marveled over one in the house, having never seen one before. In Santiava, she learned, they used saltcellars. She also had a cigar she'd stolen from her father's stack for Mr. Borerro, and a new deck of cards for the footmen, who played with a very worn deck.

And at the very bottom of the basket, covered by all the other things, she had something for his lordship, too. If she could find the courage to give it to him. She feared he might think her impertinent or too forward...but then again, did it matter? It wasn't as if she had anything to lose.

It was her much-loved copy of the book *Jane Eyre*. To her, it was the perfect novel-reading experience.

She was fastening her cloak when her mother appeared in the doorway of the drawing room, a cat in her arms, looking displeased.

"Good afternoon, Mama," Hattie said.

"Just look at you," her mother said darkly, her gaze critically sliding up and down Hattie. "Are you wearing *rouge*?"

"A bit," Hattie admitted. Her cheeks had seemed so pale to her when she was dressing earlier. She'd had the look of a wraith.

"You look like you've just lapped a bowl of cream, missy. You think you're one of the ladies in line to marry him?"

That was so outlandish that Hattie laughed. "No, Mama, I don't. I'm no one. I enjoy the work, that's all. Is that so strange? I've always kept myself busy, you know that."

Her mother came out of the drawing room. "Be careful, Harriet," she said darkly. "You're not one of them. Don't allow yourself to believe the ideas they put in your head."

Hattie's good humor cooled considerably. She was tempted to ask her mother just who *them* was, but deep down, she knew the answer. She preferred not to hear her mother say anything that would hurt her heart. Hattie knew she wasn't like Flora or Queenie—she didn't need her own mother to point it out. She knew she was not desirable, had nothing to recommend her, and really, had no chance of matrimony, thanks to this house and its inhabitants. And not to mention her broken engagement. "I have no idea what you mean," she said pertly. "I don't want to be late. Good afternoon, Mama." She opened the door and walked out into the rain, not even bothering to try and catch one of the cats that skittered out when she did.

She marched along, a bit miffed that her mother wanted her to feel shame for her work, for who she was. A bit miffed that her own mother would be the one to remind her that a man like Lord Abbott would never find anything about her to want. It hardly mattered that she was infatuated with the viscount—she was aware she was in no danger of that sentiment ever being returned or even noticed.

But as she marched along, she began to think that maybe her mother was right. She *had* allowed her imagination to get the best of her. She had imagined herself in Santiava. With him. Speaking Spanish fluently, delighting him, discussing books and all the interests they shared. It was a silly daydream. What was the harm?

She was convinced she had a gimlet eye as far as he was concerned—the man was aloof and distant! She'd thought at first that he didn't care for her, that he resented her presence, and was sending her off to tea just so that he wouldn't have to be near her. But when Pacheco or Borerro entered the room, he affected the same aloof manner with them. The only time she'd ever heard him laugh was through the window that first afternoon.

It wasn't until his lordship noticed her looking at his books that he had seemed to soften, if only a little. What had astonished her most about the entire exchange was that he seemed to be genuinely interested in what she thought of *The Viscount of Bragelonne.*

Her enthusiasm for bringing the gifts had been dampened by her mother's warning. She hoped she wasn't being foolish to bring him a gift. Well, it was too late now. No matter what happened, one day Hattie would look back fondly to the spring she wrote correspondence and read books with Viscount Abbott, the Duke of Santiava.

CHAPTER TEN

PACHECO WAS SPORTING a pin on his lapel that was the same red-and-white rose that Mateo had seen on Borerro and at least two footmen. He didn't understand the significance, really, but it was clear that Miss Woodchurch had used her wages to purchase lapel pins for his household.

Is that what she needed the position for? To purchase pins?

"You, too?" he accused his manservant as Pacheco held out Mateo's coat for him.

Pacheco had been his father's manservant and was a wise old soul. He not only understood what Mateo was talking about, but he steadily avoided his master's gaze as he brushed his hands across the tops of Mateo's shoulders, smoothing the fabric of his coat. Frankly, Pacheco's silence was one of the reasons Mateo got on with him as well as he did—the man didn't feel the need to respond to superfluous questions any more than he did.

And he did not respond to him now.

When he'd finished dressing, Mateo made his way downstairs. He intended to make his session with Miss Woodchurch quick today—he and Rosa were attempting to make a treacle tart before supper.

Miss Woodchurch was already in the study, standing at the window as she waited. She was wearing a soft pale yellow gown today that, with her blue eyes, reminded him of a bird that often visited the palace veranda in Valdonia.

"Good day, my lord!" she said brightly. "A bit of rain, but it looks as if the clouds will break."

This woman was always cheerful, no matter his mood. He appreciated that about her and wished he could affect even a bit of her good cheer. He wished he could walk into a room and shout out a good day to everyone. He could imagine the confusion if he did, how the people around him would faint away with it.

"Good day." He went to his desk and picked up a stack of papers that included some invoices to be sorted by property and asked her to do it.

They worked in silence for the first hour. When she had done all that he asked, they began to review the latest post. Most of it was invitations. It seemed to Mateo that all anyone did in London was host or attend one supper party after another.

The last was a letter from his mother. She wrote with news of her travels, listing the people she'd visited, the many invitations to dine—apparently all anyone did in Paris was attend supper parties, too—and a list of what she'd purchased that made his eyes gloss over. He had explained to her more than once that the duchy purse was not her personal financial reserve.

His mother closed the letter by asking him if he'd met with Lady Aleksander, and if he hadn't, when she might expect some news.

He handed the letter to Miss Woodchurch. "You may respond that all is well, etcetera and so forth."

"Etcetera and so forth?" She took his mother's letter and read it. Then she looked up at him.

"Is there a question?"

"No, my lord."

He turned back to the remaining stack.

"But then again..." She waited for him to look up. "Is that really all you wish to say?"

That was most certainly all he wished to say. To say any more would invite a host of questions and demands for answers from her. He drummed his fingers on the desk a moment. "You obviously think there should be more."

The slightest bit of blush crept up into her cheeks, and she brushed the back of her hand across one. "I wouldn't presume. And I'd not like to speak out of turn."

"Interesting that after these last two weeks you would fret about that now. But do go on, Miss Woodchurch. I would like to hear your thoughts."

She frowned a little. "She's your mother."

"I am aware."

"And you obviously enjoy her company."

"That is not at all obvious. Are you chastising me, Miss Woodchurch?"

"No!" she exclaimed. "I beg your pardon—I've offended you. Even though you did invite my opinion."

"I—"

"Heaven help me," she said, and threw up both hands. "You needn't say it. Once again, I am speaking when I have no business speaking. I—"

"Miss Woodchurch," he inserted calmly, before she spiraled off into an explanation he knew from experience would be lengthy. "I did invite your opinion."

"I don't want to give it."

"You clearly do."

"No," she said with a firm shake of her head. "I have said too much."

Now he was feeling a little stubborn about it. "Then perhaps you will tell me what you'd write if this letter had come from your mother?"

"*My* mother?"

"*Si, tu madre*. If she had written you from Paris with news of her friends and purchases, and asked only one question of you? Please, I should like to know how you would respond."

"Oh. I…" She uneasily tugged on her earlobe. "I would ask her what on earth she was doing in Paris, as she has never been. My mother is vastly different from yours."

"Interesting. How would you know?"

Her cheeks pinkened. Mateo was both amused by her chagrin and intrigued about why she was trying to avoid her mother. "My mother is…umm, she is…" Miss Wood-church looked up to the ceiling and sighed. "It's a bit tricky, isn't it? Our mothers bring us into this world, but as time goes on, one discovers that they…"

"Are meddlesome?" Mateo dryly finished for her.

"Precisely," she said with another sigh. "Sometimes it can be amusing, but sometimes not."

"I only find meddlesome mothers amusing if they are not my own. It would seem that perhaps our mothers are not so different. You must see my reluctance to write a lengthy response, which will only invite more scrutiny and more opinions."

"I understand. If I were to write my mother, I would natter on with details of things that would exhaust her or cause her to lose interest in any further interrogation of me." She shrugged. "One must resort to such methods."

"Natter on?"

"I mean…talk idly," she explained. "And at length."

"Ah, *charla*," he said.

"But I wouldn't recommend that for you, my lord. I'd guess that your mother is probably accustomed to very little from you, and if you were to natter on, it would arouse all her suspicions. If I may be so bold to say."

"You've already been so bold to say."

Her smile widened. "I suppose I have. I'm endeavoring to be bold in many things."

That proclamation only heightened his curiosity. She was endeavoring to be bold in what ways? How many ways? Endeavoring privately? Publicly? Did any of her endeavoring involve touching or flirting?

He glanced down at his desk, appalled that he'd just had that thought. But now that it was in his head, it wouldn't leave. He imagined Miss Woodchurch in bed, unafraid to speak. To act. He drew a breath. "If you would be so kind as to pen a response to my meddlesome mother and relay to her that all is well. If it pleases you, you may add that I wish her my sincerest hope she enjoys the rest of her stay."

Her smile was charming. "It pleases me. Thank you."

"And then you will refrain from offering more opinions or speaking for the sake of it, won't you? There is still quite a lot of work to be done today."

"Of course, my lord."

Miss Woodchurch returned to her desk. She made quick work of the correspondence as she always did. When she'd finished, she put the letters on the edge of his desk.

"Thank you. You may go now and have tea."

Miss Woodchurch didn't move.

He glanced up. "Allow me to guess—you have more opinions to offer and intend to carry on like a soldier."

"Oh no, I'm quite finished with any opinions, as you requested. But I must beg your indulgence as I speak without explicit invitation. Not simply for the sake of it, however."

He almost smiled. "Shall I rebuke you now, or wait until I've heard what you have to say?"

"Perhaps a stern warning not to forget myself before I begin?"

He smiled. "Consider yourself sternly warned, then." He gestured for her to continue, acutely aware that he was enjoying this banter with her this afternoon. He was enchanted with the sparkle in her blue eyes and the way her skin flushed pink at the slightest provocation.

"I've brought you a gift. Of sorts."

A *gift*? He was a bit flattered. But then he realized what it must be and smiled. "A pin for the lapel."

She laughed with delight. "You've noticed! I would not have guessed that the Tudor rose pins would be in high demand at Grosvenor Square, but there you are. I should be delighted to bring you one, my lord, and will do so with all due haste. But that's not the gift I have for you. I have a book." She dipped down to the floor, and when she stood again, she was indeed holding a book. She held it out to him, her smile luminous.

He eyed the book, wondering if he ought to accept it.

"The title is *Jane Eyre*, by the incomparable Charlotte Brontë, an English author. I thought… Well, you said you'd never read such a novel, and I thought perhaps you might want to try one. It is romantic and mysterious, and the setting is wonderfully gloomy."

"Gloomy?"

"Dark and foreboding," she clarified.

He looked at the book.

"I see where that might sound less than appealing, but I assure you it adds to the story's atmosphere. I wager you won't be able to stop reading once you've begun."

Mateo opened the book and read the first line a bit slowly. "'There was no possibility of taking a walk that day…'" He closed the book and set it aside. He didn't know what to think of this gift. He was intrigued, he was confused, and he was strangely grateful that it was not a lapel pin. "What would you wager?"

"Pardon?"

"You said you'd wager I won't be able to stop once I begin. What wager would you make, Miss Woodchurch?"

"Ah…" She glanced around the room.

There were any number of things he would like to wager. He'd like to touch the soft hollow of her throat. Brush that stubborn bit of hair that always came loose from her coif back into place. He'd like to sweep his thumb across her bottom lip. "We'll think of something," he said. "*Gracias*. Thank you."

"I hope you don't think me too forward—"

"Not at all. Please don't make too much of it, Miss Woodchurch. It's a book, not an invitation to dinner."

Her cheeks colored almost instantly, and he winced inwardly at how that must have sounded. This was precisely the thing that Roberto had pointed out to him.

"Miss Woodchurch, don't," he said, waving a hand at her. "Don't rile yourself up to a speech to excuse my poor choice of words. I spoke clumsily. Forgive me."

"Of course."

He felt terribly conspicuous. He rubbed his nape. "Would you like to take your tea now?"

She didn't seem as if she wanted to, but she nodded and retrieved her bag. "Please excuse me."

When she'd left, he picked up the book and opened it again. He began the laborious task of reading in English. But the print was legible, and he was intrigued by Jane Eyre and her dreary, rainy day.

But as he read, his thoughts kept straying to Miss Woodchurch. Her happy mien. Her fierce confidence. Her unwillingness to be intimidated by him. Her absolute dedication to speaking up.

And her very blue eyes.

What was the matter with him? It was almost as if he was making a...*friend*. A friend he wanted to touch. Was that even possible? He had so few friends he couldn't even be sure.

But he was so fascinated by the idea and by the book that he was, quite uncharacteristically, late for his meeting with Rosa.

CHAPTER ELEVEN

LILA ALEKSANDER HAD encountered some difficult subjects in her thirty years in the profession of matchmaking and did not view the viscount's disinclination to meet privately with her as a challenge. At least not at first.

When she'd first been introduced to him, in the garden at Grosvenor Square, she'd been surprised at how taciturn he was. Most people, when faced with the choice of a mate with whom they would spend the rest of their lives, had quite a lot to say. This man had hardly anything to say on the matter.

Lila had known quiet people. Her own mother had been notoriously closemouthed—Lila could scarcely recall more than a handful of things her mother had said to her. She thought that probably had more to do with her father's over-bearing control of his wife than her mother's true nature, and was genuinely sorry that she would never know.

Occasionally, Lila would encounter someone who spared so few words that it was impossible to know them. She hoped the viscount wasn't that—it would make her task all the more difficult.

His mother, Elizabeth, had warned Lila that her son would be a troublesome subject. *My son would marry a book if it were allowed*, she'd complained when she'd met with Lila a few weeks ago.

Elizabeth Abbott Vincente and Lila had known each

other many, many years ago, both of them debuting the same year when their waistlines were smaller and their visions of the future rosy. Then Elizabeth had married the handsome Santiavan duke and moved far away. And shortly after that, Lila's hopes for an offer had been destroyed by her father's terrible bribery scandal. She and Elizabeth had moved in opposite directions, out of England, and they'd lost touch through the years.

Lord Iddesleigh was the one to reunite them, by way of his good friend the Duchess of Marley, nee Princess Amelia of Wesloria. It so happened that Amelia was one of Lila's former clients—a decade or so ago, Lila had achieved the unimaginable by matching the outspoken Amelia with the grieving Joshua Parker, the Duke of Marley. She was delighted by them now—four children, marital bliss by all accounts, and friends from all walks of life.

Amelia had invited Elizabeth and Lila for tea at Beck's request. She said she'd met the current duke of Santiava a time or two at prestigious occasions in Europe, and she was more than happy to host a meeting of the minds.

The three women gathered at the grand Marley house in Mayfair. Lila and Elizabeth warmly greeted each other, caught up on all the news, then got down to the business of finding her reserved son a suitable wife.

"He's quite shy," Elizabeth said. "Or perhaps he is merely quiet. I confess I've never been able to distinguish which. His father was terribly hard on him, and I think Mateo learned to keep his thoughts to himself, lest he be criticized. My son Roberto, now there is a man who can charm a lady to her toes. But Mateo?" She sighed. "He really doesn't say much at all."

"Maybe because your other son says much," Amelia said as she stirred her tea. "I only mention it because my

sister, Justine—she's the queen of Wesloria, you know—
she was always rather reluctant to speak in public, and I
really rather thought it was because I spoke so much. I've
never had the slightest hesitation to speak in public, and in
fact, my mother often complained that I was always talking
about anything you like. Name the subject, she said, and
off I'd go. Now, of course, I don't talk as much, because
my children do all the talking. And mostly at once. Have
you ever noticed how children talk as if they are the only
ones in the room? They don't hear any voice but their own."

Amelia happened to look up then and noticed the two
women were politely waiting for her to finish talking.
"There, you see?" she asked, flicking a wrist. "I've proved
my point." She gestured for Elizabeth to continue.

"Mateo and Roberto are not together for public outings,
so I don't think his silence is a result of being overshad-
owed," Elizabeth said. "But his quiet nature vexed my husband terribly. He was gregarious—you may remember, Lila.
I believe you danced with him at the last ball the Season
of our debut? He used to complain to me that he couldn't
understand how his firstborn and heir could be the apple
to fall from his tree and roll so far away."

Lila did remember the duke and had thought him more
bombastic and pompous than gregarious. "In my experience, the quiet ones are always the reasoned ones," she said.
"The thinkers, if you will."

"Yes, well, my husband was convinced there wasn't
much thinking going on in Mateo's head. Honestly, I don't
know what to do with him," Elizabeth said. "On my word,
he wouldn't even come down from the mountains if I didn't
press the issue."

"So he is content to be alone," Lila offered, and jotted
down a quick note on her little notepad.

"Is he?" Elizabeth mused. "I wouldn't know. He hardly speaks to me, either."

Lila glanced up.

"That's what I've been trying to convey, Lila. He hardly speaks to *anyone*."

That might very well be true, but Lila wouldn't be surprised if Elizabeth's son simply didn't trust his mother. Funny how people preferred to make a match based on their own desires and not those of their parents.

"You mustn't fret, Elizabeth. I will get to the bottom of his likes and dislikes, I assure you. Is there anything or anyone you would deem unacceptable for your family or the duchy?"

"Unacceptable?" Elizabeth pondered. She shook her head. "I only want my son to be happy."

That was one small victory, at least, but Lila didn't believe her. Generally, she was up against parental demands that the person be well-connected or come with a sizable dowry, or bear a title that was impossible to find and match. "Wonderful! I think I have all that I need."

"Lila." Elizabeth leaned forward and placed her hand on Lila's knee to gain her attention. "My son will need a woman who does all the talking. That's the only way it will ever work—he must have someone who hardly cares if he speaks or not."

"I understand." But was that really what the poor man needed? Lila's guess was that, like everyone, he needed someone who understood he was thoughtful and wouldn't expect a response to everything she uttered. She also truly believed that when he found someone he loved and trusted, the words would come. Trust was such a grave issue with people in powerful positions.

For all couples, really.

The thing made most clear at that tea was that Elizabeth really didn't know her son very well at all. Lila would have to rely on the viscount himself, which, naturally, she would have done under any circumstance. But it always helped to have another eye or opinion.

In the days that followed she'd tried to gain entry into the Abbott house on Grosvenor Square. Unfortunately, the viscount made that nearly impossible. He was too occupied, or had engagements across town, or was simply unavailable. Lila wasn't entirely surprised—she'd suspected he might try and stonewall her after their initial meeting with Beck and his mother. His displeasure at being introduced to her by complete surprise in the garden was evident.

Still, he'd agreed to the matchmaking. Lila had even cornered Mr. Callum on his way out of the residence one evening, asking him to put her on his calendar.

"And jeopardize my position with the Abbott estate?" Mr. Callum had exclaimed. "I think not. I hardly know what he thinks of me as it is."

Lila had been forced to call on Beck and ask him to intervene.

"Ah, the new Viscount Abbott," Beck had mused when Lila had presented the reason for her call.

"Who, Papa?" The question had come from one of his middle daughters, Lady Margaret, who was lounging on the settee in the drawing room, idly separating strands of her long hair.

"Lord Abbott. You remember him, darling. I asked if you'd like to marry him."

Lady Margaret wrinkled her nose. "He's so old."

Lila blinked. "He's eight and twenty."

"Ugh," said Lady Margaret.

"You see?" Beck had asked, gesturing to his daughter, who was now gliding out of the room. "I won't be able to marry off a single one of them. Their mother has spoiled them terribly."

Lila knew who had done the spoiling, and it wasn't Blythe.

In the end, it wasn't Beck who gained her the meeting. It was Donovan, the mysterious servant or friend or uncle to the Iddesleigh household. He'd been present, too, standing at the hearth. Lila had never been certain of exactly what the relationship was between Mr. Donovan and the Hawke family, but he was ever-present. He was an astonishingly handsome man, had never married, and was, Lila knew, partial to gentlemen.

But he was clearly an important part of this large family. "I'll do it," he'd said with a shrug.

"Do what?" Beck had asked.

"Get Lady Aleksander in the door at Grosvenor Square." He smiled. "Leave it to me."

"You heard the man. Leave it to Donovan, Lila," Beck had said, happy to be rid of the responsibility.

Lila didn't know how Donovan had done it, and she dared not ask. All she knew was that today, at long last, she had an invitation to meet with the viscount at three o'clock.

"You'll not have much time," Donovan said. "The gent doesn't care for empty talk. My advice to you, madam, is to get straight to the point."

Lila assured him she would. She was certain the next meeting with the stubborn viscount would be doubly difficult. Which meant she had an awful lot of ground to cover. She was prepared. "I've dealt with clients like you," she'd muttered to her reflection as she fixed her bonnet to her head in her dressing room. "Don't underestimate me, sir. I will have what I want from you." She smiled at her reflection with confidence and went out.

CHAPTER TWELVE

MRS. O'MALLEY HAD perfected her brandy balls and was so pleased with the outcome she insisted on sending some to Grosvenor Square with Hattie.

In the kitchen, there was quite a lot of conversation about them in Spanish. In the end, having polished off two of the balls, Mr. Borerro said something to Yolanda which prompted her to find a dish and arrange three of the remaining balls on it. That left two, which one of the footmen swiped up and popped into his mouth, ignoring the cries of distress from the rest of them.

Mr. Borerro was quick thinking. He picked up the plate and left the room.

Hattie hung her cloak and paused to check her hair in the small mirror in the entry to the kitchen, then carried on down the narrow hall, up the stairs, past the portrait of the lady with the tall white hair, and on to the study. On her way, she passed one of the footmen and complimented him on his Tudor pin with the only word she knew in Spanish that would suffice. *"Hermoso!"* she said, pointing at it.

The footman grinned. For all Hattie knew, he thought she was calling him lovely instead of the pin.

When Hattie entered the study, Lord Abbott was standing at his desk, brushing his hands over the plate Borerro had brought. He was still chewing when he glanced up at her.

"Aren't they divine?" she asked as she curtsied. "I think they are the best I've ever tried."

The viscount swallowed. "Where did you get them?"

"From Mrs. O'Malley, the confectioner? I keep her books, you may recall."

"Yes." He reached for another one.

"I visit her once a week. And every week, she sends off a batch of her bestselling treats with me. I've been taking them home, but I've discovered they are more appreciated here."

He held up the plate. "May I offer you one?"

"Thank you." Hattie had several at Mrs. O'Malley's shop, but they were *so* very good, she couldn't resist. She crossed the room and took the last one from the plate and bit into it. "Goodness," she said. "It's even better than her last batch."

"If you would—" Whatever he was about to say, he was interrupted by Mr. Borerro entering the room. Lord Abbott put down the plate and walked out from behind the desk. *"Sí?"*

As they discussed whatever it was in Spanish, Hattie went to her desk to deposit her things. When Borerro stepped out of the room, Hattie turned back to the viscount. "You were going to ask—"

But his lordship moved to the middle of the room just as a woman strode inside.

"Madam," Lord Abbott said. *"Bienvenidas.* Welcome."

"Thank you!" The woman curtsied. "It's so good to see you again, my lord. I've been looking forward to our meeting—I have much to share with you."

"Please," he said, and gestured to the settee.

She was older than Lord Abbott by some years. She was pleasingly plump, with laugh lines around her eyes and a bag dangling from her arm out of which a leather-bound book was peeking. She sailed in, as if she'd been here dozens of times, talking as she went. "Have I said, I think your accent is lovely, and I can imagine the English ladies will find it quite charming. Thank you for agreeing to receive me—I thought I might have to resort to ambushing you on a walkabout!" She laughed at her jest, and when she did, so did Hattie, picturing this woman flying out of a bush somewhere to accost the viscount.

Her laugh clearly startled the woman, and her head jerked around to Hattie.

"Excuse me," Hattie said, and curtsied.

"Oh. Hello," the lady said. She looked…not entirely happy.

"May I present Miss Woodchurch," Lord Abbott said. "She is my scribe."

"Your scribe?" She looked so confused that Hattie thought perhaps she didn't know the meaning of the word. But then she nodded. "Yes, of course. A pleasure, Miss Woodchurch."

"And this is Lady Aleksander," the viscount said to Hattie. "She is…a friend of my mother's."

"How do you do," Hattie said.

"Very well, thank you," she answered. "Your mother's old friend, certainly. But I'm also here to provide some assistance."

Assistance? Hattie wondered what sort of service the lady provided. Lord Abbott did not agree that she was more than his mother's old acquaintance. He simply gestured to the settee. "Please," he said.

Hattie began to gather her paper and pen to leave them.

"Miss Woodchurch, you may stay," the viscount said.

Both Hattie and Lady Aleksander looked at him with surprise.

"You won't mind if Miss Woodchurch remains," he said to Lady Aleksander. "I might be required to write a letter of apology to some poor unsuspecting lady." He smiled as charmingly as Hattie had ever seen him smile.

It had the intended effect—Lady Aleksander almost blushed. "You're very amusing, my lord."

"I've never been accused of it."

"I sincerely doubt you'll be writing any letters of apology. You'll probably be fending off invitations like they were invading troops. Keep your nibs sharp, Miss Woodchurch."

What were they talking about? Hattie wasn't following the conversation exactly, but it was clear the lady didn't want her there.

As if to prove it, the lady said, "Are you certain you won't mind, my lord? This meeting could be delicate in nature. Most are generally held in the strictest of confidence."

Delicate in nature? Strictest of confidence? Was the lady a doctor? Highly unlikely but possible.

But the viscount chuckled darkly. "Madam…do you think there is anyone left in London who hasn't heard that I am in want of a wife?"

Hattie nearly gasped out loud. A *wife*? This woman had to do with him and a *wife*? She didn't want to hear about it. She didn't want to imagine it. She loved her position here and wanted nothing to ruin it for her. A potential wife absolutely would ruin it—she would probably shunt Hattie off to some attic office to do her work.

Hattie didn't know where to train her eyes. She feared meeting his gaze would betray her true feelings. She could feel her face heating with…what, exactly? She didn't understand herself at all—why should she be affected by any feelings whatsoever? It wasn't a wife or whatever they meant to discuss for *her*. And yet, she did not want to hear a word of this conversation—except for the part of her that wanted to hear every single word.

Lady Aleksander smiled thinly. "Probably not. However…" She moved a little closer and spoke low. But not low enough—Hattie could still hear her. "Some clients prefer to keep these meetings private, as the details are usually of a very personal nature?"

One of Lord Abbott's dark brows arched with amusement. "We'll be fine." He gestured to the settee. "Shall we sit?"

Some clients. What sort of clients?

"Thank you," Lady Aleksander said, and with a sigh of exasperation, she sank down onto the settee.

Hattie sat gingerly in her seat, then splayed her hands on her desk, uncertain what to do with them. Should she pick up a pen? Wait to be called? Try and fade into the drapery? Unfortunately, she was wearing her terrible purple dress today, so fading into anything would be impossible.

Lord Abbott took a seat in a chair across from the lady, crossing his legs casually. From her vantage point, Hattie could see them both quite clearly. They looked as if they were about to start a chess match, each eyeing the other with discernment.

"You are looking very well, my lord," Lady Aleksander said. "The London air agrees with you."

"I am surprised. The London air is not very good."

"It's not, is it? And yet, there is quite a lot more to recommend London, I'm sure you'd agree."

"Such as the custom of taking tea. I've taken the liberty of asking for it."

"Wonderful! I find a cup of tea tends to help move these meetings along." Lady Aleksander's gaze slid to Hattie.

What sort of meeting? Hattie wanted to shout. *What was this? What did this lady have to do with the viscount at all?*

"I find whisky helps even more," the viscount said, and stood up, went to the sideboard, and poured. "Lady Aleksander?"

"Oh dear, none for me, my lord. I think I'll need all my wits about me."

Lord Abbott looked at Hattie. "Miss Woodchurch? Whisky?"

She almost choked on her surprise. "No, thank you, my lord." She thought she might need all her wits about her, too. She picked up a pen, ready to write whatever she was instructed.

Lady Aleksander leaned down and retrieved a leather journal from her bag and set it on her lap. It looked worn, its edges discolored. Bits of paper had been stuck between various pages.

Lord Abbott returned to his seat, whisky in hand. "What's this?" he asked, nodding at her notebook.

The lady ran her hand lovingly over the cover that looked smoothed by age. "This book has been my companion for many years. It is a list of wonderful men and women, all desiring love and companionship, along with ticket stubs and embossed invitations, letters…all the keepsakes of successful matches I have made."

Matches. Hattie stopped breathing. This woman was a matchmaker. *A matchmaker!*

Carlos, one of the footmen, entered the room with the tea service on a rolling cart. He set it up on the table between his lordship and the lady. Blue china cups and saucers, cream and sugar, and a delicate platter filled with pastries. As Carlos arranged things and poured tea, Lady Aleksander said, "You didn't say, my lord, how you find London?"

"What I expected. It is as I recall it from my youth."

Lady Aleksander looked dissatisfied with that response. Hattie understood—his answers were often not very illuminating. "One can't help but wonder how you found it in your youth, then."

He ignored her and said to Carlos, "Miss Woodchurch will have tea."

Carlos brought her a cup of tea and winked at her. She wanted to shove him out of the way—she didn't want to miss a moment of this exchange between Lady Aleksander and Lord Abbott now that she knew the landscape.

"But I rather imagine it is hard to form an opinion when one is mired in the review of an estate," the lady continued. "Your mother said that the records are quite detailed."

"Quite."

"Then I will send a prayer that your work concludes soon and you might have some time to see a bit of our glorious old London."

"Miss Woodchurch tells me that Hyde Park is worth the walk, if one arrives early."

Hattie nearly spit out the tea she'd just sipped, and somehow managed to put the cup down. She could feel Lady Aleksander's eyes on her.

"It certainly is," Lady Aleksander said. "Now then. The Season begins this weekend with the highly anticipated Forsythe dinner. You may or may not be aware that the Forsythes are dedicated to the arts and bringing people together. Many years ago, I had the pleasure of dining at their residence with a Russian opera singer and the Raj of India."

The viscount nodded but did not seem moved by this bit

of information. Hattie was, however. How exciting to dine with opera singers and a raj, whatever that meant.

Lady Aleksander was clearly expecting more of a conversation. When his lordship didn't respond to her dining experience, the lady glanced at Hattie, then back at her journal. "Well. Enough of the small talk, then. Shall we get down to the meat of it?"

"By all means."

"I like to begin with some personal inquiries, my lord. Your answers will assist me in finding a perfect match."

"Is that possible?"

Yes, is that possible? Hattie desperately wanted to know.

"Well. As close to perfect as we might hope."

"Hmm," the viscount said. He sipped his whisky.

Lady Aleksander opened her journal. "I'd like to begin with your likes and dislikes in a potential spouse. For example, you may prefer a wife who is a companion in all things. Or you may prefer one who keeps her own calendar."

How interesting! Hattie had never thought about marriage in that way. When she'd thought about marrying Rupert, she'd thought of the meals they would take, the children they would raise, the work they would do side by side in his store. She thought only about how she loved him and couldn't wait to embark on that life with him.

Her stomach soured at the thought of him. How he'd disappointed her.

And then her stomach twisted again. She didn't want to hear the viscount's likes and dislikes. What if his list of dislikes described someone who was just like her?

Lady Aleksander leaned slightly forward. "I know it's not the easiest thing to do, presenting your private desires for me to see."

Certainly not! Hattie wanted to shout at her.

"It must feel daunting to enumerate what we need or want without thinking of a particular person."

Hattie looked at the viscount and wondered if he was thinking of someone specific.

"But I'm rather good at my profession. It is a point of great pride that I've put people together for companionship and love, and not just a formidable alliance. I can do that with just a few details."

"A formidable alliance? That sounds like war—not marriage," he said.

"A good marriage should be both, in my humble opinion."

"Dios mío," he muttered, and glanced down at his glass.

"Surely you've thought about what you would like in a wife. Isn't it natural to do so?"

"Miss Woodchurch," he said, without looking up from his glass. "What is your opinion?"

Hattie was so stunned by his question that she couldn't move her lips to form words. "Umm…" He lifted his gaze. He thought she would deny it. He was looking for an ally. But she couldn't agree with him. "It, umm…it seems natural to think of it."

"Oh?" He looked at her with more interest. "And what is it you would like to see in a husband?"

"Oh, well, that…that is personal," she said, thinking of Rupert. In hindsight, she would have wanted someone with a spine. "But generally speaking, someone whom you may trust to be the person they present themselves to be."

"How astute of you, Miss Woodchurch," Lady Aleksander said. "Then again, perhaps by necessity, women give more thought to it than men. We are, after all, entirely dependent on our husbands. And if it weren't for my careful consideration, my lord, it would be easy to match you with just about any woman because of that fact."

Hattie didn't know if Lady Aleksander meant to look at her, or if it was inadvertent, but she couldn't help but wonder if Lady Aleksander viewed her as "just about anyone." She dropped her gaze and drew a stick figure on the paper kicking another stick figure.

"I am here to ensure you are not taken advantage of."

"I understand your role," he said. "I am being unnecessarily difficult. Please continue."

Lady Aleksander picked up a pastry and bit into it. "Goodness. This is *delicious*." She put aside the uneaten portion. "Let's begin with something simple. What pastimes do you particularly enjoy?"

"Military history. Astronomy."

Hattie made a mental note.

"Is there a more active diversion you enjoy? Perhaps you like to ride. Are you particularly adept at gardening? Or do you have a passion for entertaining friends?"

Lord Abbott cocked his head to one side, as if he found this line of question slightly confusing. Or annoying. It was so hard to tell with him.

Lady Aleksander waited a long moment for him to answer. "What about strong dislikes?"

"Charla." He looked at Hattie.

"Oh," she said, realizing he was seeking the word in English. "Nattering on. He doesn't care for it."

"Doesn't he," Lady Aleksander drawled. "Perhaps something more concrete? For example, you might despise fishing."

"I like to fish."

"I mean it only as an example. Do you dislike having tea, or—"

"I'm here now, having tea with you. Therefore, it stands to reason that I like it at least a little."

Hattie blinked. What was that she saw in his eyes? Amusement? Was he *toying* with Lady Aleksander?

"Again, it was only an example," Lady Aleksander said, her tone betraying her impatience. "Surely there is *something* you can think of that you strongly dislike, or like, that you'd like to see, or not, in a potential spouse."

The viscount studied the lady for a moment. And then he suddenly leaned forward. "May I speak frankly, Lady Aleksander?"

"Please!"

"I understand the necessity for seeking introductions. But I do not believe that based on some vague likes and dislikes a near perfect match can be made. What I like and dislike changes with the company and the location and, sometimes, even something as simple as the weather. Perhaps it would be best for us both if you contained your services to introductions and allow me to carry on from there."

Hattie had to hand it to Lady Aleksander—she remained perfectly composed. If she was ruffled, she gave no hint of it. "That's certainly one way to go about it. But in my vast experience, these things can be done expeditiously with just a bit of information. Sometimes a person doesn't know himself as well as he might think. Sometimes a person may not know how to glean useful information from a potential match. *Sometimes* it is *quite* helpful to have assistance in such an important decision."

"I don't accept your premise," the viscount said. "How can a man of eight and twenty not know himself?"

"You'd be surprised," Lady Aleksander said pertly. "But if this is your desire, so be it." She opened her book. "Shall we continue? I've arranged for three introductions to occur at the Forsythe dinner party on Saturday. Please do tell me if you hear anything that would not suit you. *If* you are able to determine it would not suit you, knowing yourself as well as you do."

Lord Abbott chuckled.

Lady Aleksander looked down at her notes. "Miss Dahlia Cupperson is twenty-two years of age."

Hattie had to stifle a squeal of surprise—Dahlia was smart and accomplished but had an unfortunate equine face. Queenie said she looked as if she ought to be stabled every night. Queenie could be very unkind for wont of a laugh.

"She is the daughter of Sir William Cupperson, whose fortune derives from mining." Lady Aleksander looked up. "It is a *substantial* fortune, my lord, as is her dowry. And, Miss Cupperson has had the pleasure of traveling to Spain."

"Spain? Not Santiava?"

"Nevertheless, she has been closer to the duchy than most."

The viscount quirked a brow. "I shall consider close proximity a point in her favor, then."

Lady Aleksander's smile was very tight. "Have I said anything about Miss Cupperson and her background you think you might find objectionable?"

"You've said very little—what would I possibly object to?"

The lady sighed. She looked at her journal again. "Miss Christiana Porter is considered one of the *ton*'s beauties. Her family's wealth is considerable, and her father manages an estate nearly as vast as your own. She has a lovely singing voice and is often called upon to lend her talents to suppers across town. She is nineteen years old."

To hear Queenie tell it, Christiana's mother had put that

notion of talent into everyone's head when, really, a lot of begging went into allowing Christiana to perform.

The viscount said, "I shall look forward to her performance."

Lady Aleksander returned to her notes. Then she glanced up at him and smiled. "The next young lady is, I think, perhaps the best option for you in London. She is educated, well-liked, and her father is a respected viscount. He happens to have the ear of the prime minister. Apparently, they attended Eton together. His daughter is quite charming and speaks both English and French. She is two and twenty."

Hattie's heart began to pound—she knew someone who fit that description perfectly. She was—

"Miss Flora Raney."

Hattie coughed on a swell of shock, drawing the viscount's and Lady Aleksander's attention to her. Hattie waved her hand. "Beg your pardon," she said hoarsely. "I must have swallowed a gnat."

"The window is not open," the viscount pointed out.

Hattie coughed and, red-faced, stood up and walked stiffly to the sideboard. She poured water into a glass and downed it, put the glass down, and then shouted an internal chastisement at herself. *What was wrong with you?* Of course Flora would be in the running! Queenie had said it that day in the dress shop. Had there ever been any question? Flora was perfect in every way.

But Hattie wanted this man for herself. Not as a husband, obviously—she wasn't delusional. But her work, her time with him—

She was being ridiculous. Hattie dug into her bank of mental fortitude and forced herself to get a grip. She swallowed and slowly turned to see them both still watching her. "All better," she said, and went back to her seat and picked up her pen. *Flora. The best of the lot.*

"As I was saying," Lady Aleksander continued, "I would consider Flora Raney a near perfect match for someone in your position."

The viscount nodded. He stood. "Thank you, Lady Aleksander. They all sound perfectly reasonable."

She looked at him. Then at the pastries. "You must have at least a few questions?"

He shook his head.

"Wouldn't you like to know their—"

"I would like to discover their particular qualities on my own."

Lady Aleksander looked as if she was desperate to say more. But she pressed her lips together and slowly closed her book. She picked up a pastry from the table and gained her feet. "I sincerely hope you do discover them on your own, my lord, but if you should need any assistance, I am here to help, my services commissioned by the duchy. I know you wouldn't want to see those funds go to waste. Shall I come around next Monday and review the selections?"

"By all means. Please do help yourself to more of the chocolatines. They were made especially for you."

"Thank you, but this one will do," Lady Aleksander said pertly. As she made a move to leave, she happened to look at the table next to his chair. *"Jane Eyre!"* She smiled with delight. "You're a reader, then?"

"One could say."

"What an interesting choice. This is hardly military history or astronomy. How did you find it?"

"Miss Woodchurch has lent it to me," he said. "From one booklover to another."

Lady Aleksander's gaze snapped to Hattie so quickly

that Hattie thought she must have done something wrong. "It is very good," she said in her defense. "Have you read it?"

"I have." Lady Aleksander hoisted the bag over her shoulder. "I certainly have, Miss Woodchurch." She smiled, and that smile, Hattie thought, seemed too...personal. As if Lady Aleksander had seen some side of her that Hattie hadn't intended to show. A blush crept up her neck.

"Good day, my lord! Miss Woodchurch!" She walked out of the room as if she'd never been vexed, as if the meeting had gone just as she'd planned, when it clearly had not.

When she had left, Hattie drew a deep breath. She hadn't realized how tense she'd been. She shyly shifted her gaze to the viscount.

He was looking at her. "You must think this all absurd. I know that I do."

"Not at all."

"Mmm," he said, not believing her. "There are times my title brings with it necessities that I find...maddening."

"I can only imagine."

"I hope that you can't. What do you think, Miss Woodchurch? Shall I find my perfect match in that book of hers?"

She sincerely hoped not. He was better than Dahlia and Christiana and maybe even...

No. She wouldn't do that. Flora deserved happiness. But the tendril of jealousy was taking root. Flora could very well be the one to look at this man every day for the rest of her life. "I think you will!" she said brightly.

He snorted. "Would you happen to know the ladies mentioned?"

She quickly debated how much to say. That the world of the very privileged in London was quite small, and everyone knew everyone? That the only reason she knew any of them at all was a great act of kindness showed her by Lord Iddesleigh ten years ago, which had put her in a boarding school with so many of them? But she didn't really *know* them. She would never live a life like theirs. "I am acquainted. A little."

"Does your acquaintance lend itself to any wisdom for me?"

Why not? She had nothing to lose by offering what bit of insight she might have. "I would… I beg your pardon for what I am about to say—"

"Sounds *ominosa*. Go on."

"If you were to speak a little more when you meet them? To, ah…promote conversation, as it were. So that you might better acquaint yourself with them, as you said."

He stared at her in a way that made Hattie think she'd crossed a line. But then he grinned. "*Sí, sí*, I've been told this all my life. Speak more, Teo. *Habla más, Teo.* Unfortunately, it is not my nature."

Teo. They called him Teo. Hattie tucked that away in a little pocket in her heart. "Then I hope whoever you meet will do the speaking," Hattie said. "It's a pity, isn't it, that most of them are not like me in that regard?"

He chuckled. "It is indeed."

Hattie beamed inwardly.

"I wonder why, Miss Woodchurch, you may speak so freely when other ladies will not?"

"I think because I'm not afraid of you."

That certainly caught his attention. "And you think these ladies are?"

"You're an important man. One misstep could ruin their Season."

He frowned. "That's absurd. What of your Season? You don't fear a misstep."

Her Season? She didn't have a Season. She had a spring, a stretch of three months where she hoped to earn enough to leave her abominable family and home life—which he would never encounter, thank the heavens. "It's not the same for me. I am not expected to marry a viscount." She wasn't expected to marry anyone. Not anymore. Not since Rupert had ended things. "I think you will find a good match here. I really do." He would. It would be Flora.

He gazed at her a little longer. "Perhaps," he said, and returned to his desk.

Hattie already knew how she would instruct Flora to speak with him. She just had to do it with the utmost discretion.

CHAPTER THIRTEEN

HATTIE WAS FINISHING dressing for the evening—she was to accompany Flora to call on her cousin Moses—when Daniel sauntered into her room. She turned from her mirror to look at him with confusion as he surveyed her furnishings. "Quite tidy in here."

Daniel never came into her room. In fact, Hattie saw her brother rarely in the course of any week—occasionally at a family meal or passing as one came and the other left. Like her, Daniel seemed to prefer to stay as far from Portman Square as possible.

She folded her arms. "What are you doing?"

"I should ask the same of you." He moved deeper into her room, his hands clasped casually behind his back. "Just what *have* you been doing, Harriet Woodchurch?"

Hattie sighed. "I don't know what game you are playing, but I haven't time for it. I'm expected at a friend's house." She turned back to the mirror to attach her earrings.

"Something came for you today."

"What?" she asked without looking at him. Where her brothers were concerned, there was always some trick waiting for her she would not find amusing.

"It's an invitation."

Hattie hesitated. She didn't believe him, but still, she turned to look. Daniel held up a cream-colored folded piece of vellum between two fingers. It did indeed look like an invitation. "It's for me?"

"See for yourself." He held it out to her, but when Hattie reached for it, he jerked it out of her reach.

Hattie groaned. "Daniel, please. Is it addressed to me or not?"

"It is." He flipped the vellum in his fingers again.

"The seal is broken!" she cried. "How dare you read something addressed to me." She tried to grab it from him again, but with a laugh, Daniel held it overhead, just out of her reach.

"Give it here," she insisted. "You've sorely abused my privacy."

"Calm yourself, Hat. I broke the seal because…" He flipped the vellum around again and held it out so she could see what was written on it. "It is addressed to us both."

Hattie stopped moving and stared at their names, written very clearly on the envelope. There was simply no universe in which she and Daniel would be invited to any function together. If at all. Whatever that was, Hattie wanted it, and she lunged for it. This time, she successfully nabbed the invitation, then turned away from her brother to open it.

Her eyes scanned the words, but she couldn't believe what she was reading. The invitation, addressed to Mr. Daniel Woodchurch and Miss Harriet Woodchurch, was to dine with Mr. and Mrs. Forsythe and guests Saturday evening. The opening event for the social Season. The same dinner where all the Quality would gather to admire themselves.

"What in heaven? Is this some sort of trick?" It had to be. Her brother was trying to make her look foolish. She tossed the invitation at him. "Do you honestly expect me to fall for it? Is this your idea of a jest?"

She had to hand it to him—he looked astounded by the accusation. *"Me?"* He dipped down to pick up the invitation. "I am demanding an answer from you, Hattie! What is this about? And why must I be dragged into whatever it is?"

She was confused. She'd never met a Forsythe before. "It's not real," she insisted.

"It's real," he said, and forced her to take the invitation again. "Look at the seal."

Hattie looked at the red wax seal and the indentation of a signet. "This is not your doing?"

"My doing? I wouldn't know a Forsythe if I ran them over with my mount. You're the only one in this house pretending to be part of the *ton*."

"No, I don't know them, either." She held it up between them. "Do you know what this is? This dinner…this dinner is the one everyone in town is talking about."

"I'm not talking about it."

"I'm quite serious, Daniel! Their special guest of honor is Lord Abbott. He's to meet potential matches at this dinner."

"What?" Daniel asked with confusion. But then he looked at Hattie…and burst into laughter. "Surely no one thinks that *you*…" He laughed louder.

"All right," she said, frowning. "It's not possible, I understand."

"I *knew* it had to do with him! You're right, this is some sort of trick. For God's sake, Hat, what have you gotten yourself into?"

"Nothing!" she insisted. "I can't imagine why I should be invited. I can't imagine why *you* should be invited."

"Why me indeed," he scoffed. "Isn't it obvious?"

"No. Why?"

Daniel sighed and rolled his eyes. "Think about it, Hat.

You can't traipse off to a fancy dinner without an escort or companion. *That's* why me—because you're not married and have no prospects for marriage, so your dear old brother has been invited to do the deed."

He was right, of course. But who would see her invited only to humiliate her?

"It's just as well. I don't care to attend anything quite as fussy as I'm sure that will be," Daniel said. He picked up a bottle of perfume from her vanity and sniffed it before putting it down.

It was a trick, but what Hattie wouldn't give to have even a glimpse inside the event of the Season. Her heart began to pound with excitement or fear or something she didn't quite understand. She had an invitation into a rarified world, and suddenly she was desperately curious. "Daniel! We can't turn down an invitation like this!"

"Oh, but we can. What do you care for a lot of hobnobbing? Sounds like a bore."

"Flora has been invited. I can help her. She's one of the ladies being considered for a match."

He snorted. "Help her what?"

"Charm the viscount, obviously. Don't you see? That's what this is all about."

Something in Daniel's countenance shifted slightly. "What do you mean?"

"I told you—this dinner is so that he might be introduced to ladies who are a potential match for him."

"Your friend? The haughty one? She's no more of a match for him than you are," he scoffed.

Hattie clucked her tongue. "You don't know anything. She is the daughter of an influential viscount. Of course she's a match for him."

Daniel put his hands on his waist. "Are you saying that

there will be young women there, and not spinsters and hags?"

Hattie gave him a withering look.

"You know what I mean."

"I certainly know how you think." Another thought occurred to her—she had nothing to wear to something as fancy as this dinner would be.

"Have a care, Hat. You'll need me if you want to attend." He strolled to the door. "I don't see why you'd want to, but all the same, you can't go without me." He walked out of her room.

Hattie looked again at the invitation. Then she looked at her wardrobe, where her few serviceable gowns hung next to her new one that had the distinctive smell. Daniel was right—why would she want to attend? She was not one of them, as her mother had so bluntly pointed out. She *wanted* to be there—what person in their right mind would turn down such an invitation?

She didn't care to think of herself as the laughingstock of all the *haute ton*, but with her wardrobe and her family situation, she didn't see how she could be anything but that.

AT THE RANEY HOUSEHOLD, a maid showed Hattie to Flora's suite of rooms. She could hear Flora muttering to herself before she stepped foot into the room. "Flora?"

Flora appeared in the doorway between her bedroom and dressing room, her hair down her back, clad in only a chemise and a petticoat. "Hattie!" she exclaimed, as if Hattie's appearance was a complete surprise. But she was expected. "Come, come," she said, and hurried across the room, grabbed Hattie's hand, and pulled her into the dressing room. "Look!"

Hattie looked. There were at least two dozen gowns of various hues hanging along the wall. "What?"

"I don't know what to *wear*!" Flora cried, using both hands to indicate all the gowns.

"To dine with Moses?" Hattie couldn't recall a single time Flora had felt the slightest concern for her appearance for an evening with her cousin.

"Not *Moses*. The Forsythe dinner! It's two days away and I have absolutely nothing suitable to wear! And my father won't allow a new gown. He said I had so many I couldn't possibly wear them all in my lifetime, which is *patently* untrue."

Maybe not her entire lifetime, but Flora did possess a *lot* of gowns. And they were all beautiful, made by the best dressmakers, expertly embroidered and fitted. "Any of them would do. *Any* one of them, Flora. You will be the envy of every woman in attendance at the dinner."

"You're so kind," Flora said sweetly.

She wasn't kind, she was practical. She'd give anything to have even one of these gowns to wear.

Flora suddenly sank onto the lone chair in her dressing room. "I don't know what is the matter with me. I'm so *anxious* about this dinner."

"But why?" Hattie said, her voice light. "You've been to scores of such dinners."

"Yes, but…" She looked to the open door of her dressing room. She hopped up and hurried to close it, then turned back to Hattie. "What I'm about to say, you mustn't tell *anyone*, Hattie. Do you swear it?"

"Never," Hattie agreed. Who would she tell?

Flora got very close to Hattie, looked her in the eye and whispered, "Mama has heard that I'm considered one of the top potential matches for the viscount." Her eyes went wide. She bit her lower lip. She hugged herself tightly. She looked as if this was the worst news she could have possibly received.

"That's *wonderful*, Flora," Hattie insisted.

Flora was already shaking her head. "No, no, no, it's not. I don't know what to say or do! I'll make a cake of myself!"

"What do you mean? You're so elegant—"

"I'm not! You know how I am, how my words get twisted and I can't think properly."

"In all the years I've known you, I've never once heard you get your words twisted. You mustn't fret so—you'll know what to say when the time comes, I'm certain of it."

Flora did not look convinced. She fell back into the chair, her head resting against the back, her eyes closed.

"Flora! I've never seen you so wrought over the prospect of attention from a handsome man. You love that sort of thing."

"I do," Flora agreed. She opened her eyes and idly picked at a string that had come loose in the arm of the chair. "But this is different. He's so desirable, and everyone is watching to see who he admires. Everyone there will be at their best. How am I to compete with that? How am I to compete with Christiana Porter?"

So that was the real angst—Flora was at sixes and sevens because she was afraid of how she would compare to Miss Porter. "Shall I tell you something that no one else knows about him?"

Flora looked up. "What?"

"He likes to read. And he reads in French."

Flora's brow knit. "What has that to do with anything?"

"It's an interest of his that you can mention. No one else knows he likes to read. And you speak French. And you must like to read. You'll have something in common with him before he even knows Miss Porter's name."

"I don't like to read," Flora said, confused by Hattie's assertion.

How could anyone not like to read? Of all the girls at school, Hattie had been the most fond of reading. Any book she could get her hands on, she read. "It doesn't matter— you could say that you do," she insisted. "You could say something poetic about reading, how it opens your mind to the larger world."

For a moment, Flora looked as if she might agree...but then her expression fell. "But what if he asks me about a book?"

Hattie thought the odds of that were quite low, given how taciturn he was. "Mention one you've read. He won't have read the same thing."

Flora pondered this. "I suppose not. Oh, Hattie...I wish you would be there. I need your encouragement so desperately."

"Yes, well...that's the most amazing thing."

"What?"

"Something truly astounding has happened." She opened her reticule and withdrew the invitation and handed it to Flora.

Flora gasped. "*Hattie!* This is wonderful! But how did you manage it?"

"I haven't the slightest idea! No one is more astounded than me. But I can't go."

"What? Why?" Flora had come alive now, hopping up from the armchair. "You must! I won't accept any other answer."

"I can't."

"Why not?" Flora demanded.

She felt ashamed to admit the truth, but Flora was her friend. "Because I haven't anything suitable to wear."

Flora stared at her. She didn't dispute Hattie. She frowned and planted her hands on her waist. "Then you'll wear one of mine."

Hattie laughed. "I couldn't possibly!"

"Why not?"

"For the most obvious reason—you're smaller than me. And because it's a terrible imposition."

"It's not an imposition at all, and that's what corsets are for." She marched to her line of gowns hanging in the open wardrobe. She sorted through them, holding one up, then the next, finally deciding on a pale blue silk with silver trim. She turned around and held it up to Hattie. "Try it on." Hattie opened her mouth to speak, but Flora pushed the gown at her. "Don't be quarrelsome, Hattie. Go," she said, gesturing to the screen behind which Hattie could change.

Hattie went. And when she emerged, the back of the gown not fastened, as it would not close, Flora—who was now wearing a gold gown—nodded approvingly. "It's perfect."

"It's unfastened."

"We'll change that." She turned to the mirror. "What do you think of this?" she asked as she admired herself.

"It's beautiful," Hattie said, but really, she was looking at her own reflection, a sliver of which she could see from behind Flora. She'd never worn anything as fine as this, and she loved it. She loved the way it almost fit, the way the expensive fabric felt against her skin. And she resolved then and there to work for the viscount as long as she possibly could so that she could have gowns like this.

"Yes, I think I'll wear this one," Flora said. She turned from the window and took Hattie's hand. "Oh, Hattie. I'll feel so much better with you there. You always know how to encourage me. Do you remember when we were away at school, and Ellen Comstock was determined to make me cry?"

Hattie's brow furrowed. "You mean after you hit her?"

Flora waved a hand. "That had nothing to do with the other. But you were the one who told me that no matter what she said, I was beautiful and kind, and I should remember that Ellen only aspired to be all those things, and hence her disdain of me."

Hattie suppressed a small gasp. What *she* remembered was that Ellen called Flora a horrible, awful person after Flora had hit her, and Flora had felt such embarrassment that she'd burst into tears and fled to her room. Hattie had been very honest with Flora that striking anyone was wrong, but that punch was particularly mean, given that it was over the perceived affections of a boy. And that Ellen very much admired Flora made it even more egregious.

It was not the first time Flora had misconstrued what Hattie had said.

But she didn't think about that now. Right now, she was thinking about the beautiful gown she was wearing and hoping that someone could fasten her into it.

CHAPTER FOURTEEN

EVERYONE IN LONDON knew that thirty lucky souls had been invited to Mr. and Mrs. Forsythe's supper. For days, there was great speculation as to who the illustrious thirty might be. But on the day of the supper, when places in the formal dining room were set for thirty-*two*, tongues began to wag. Who had garnered the additional two invitations, and why?

Naturally, everyone believed it must be more young women to be introduced to the new Viscount Abbott. But in fact, it was two people who were never on any invitation list and likely would hardly be noticed at all.

One of those mysterious invitees was Hattie. She did, miraculously, manage to get into the dress she'd borrowed from Flora with the help of her mother's part-time lady's maid—but her corset was cinched so tight she could hardly breathe. She decided that breath was an unnecessary luxury, because she looked absolutely stunning in the dress. *Stunning!* Who knew such fine clothes could completely transform a person?

She was fastening a bracelet when Daniel strode into her room for a second time. Hattie's eyes rounded with surprise when she saw her brother—he looked quite dashing in his formal suit of clothing. His hair had been trimmed and he'd fastened his neck cloth with a diamond pin—she wondered where that had come from—and the result was a very handsome, trim man.

He, too, looked a little taken aback as he surveyed her. But the surprise quickly turned to a smirk. "And where did you get that fine frock?"

"I borrowed it. Where did you get such a fine suit of clothing?"

"I bought it." He straightened the cuffs of his shirt. "I can't believe you've convinced me to go along with this charade."

She hadn't convinced him of a thing. He'd simply announced he must go to accompany her. He wouldn't admit it, but he *wanted* to go. Daniel sometimes adopted their parents' disdain of the Quality, but really, who wouldn't want to mingle with them? To have a chance to see what it was like on the other side of the door?

"Come on, then. Better this is over and done." And then, quite unlike his usual self, he held out his arm for her.

"Daniel Woodchurch. Have you been a gentleman all along and are only now revealing yourself?"

"No. But I won't embarrass you before your important friends. I reckon you will do that all on your own." He smiled.

Hattie took his arm. "They're not my friends. I'm going to gawk at them just like you."

They began to make their way down the stairs, scattering cats as they went.

In the foyer, their father was pacing as best he could, but the grandfather clocks took up quite a lot of space. He eyed both of his children suspiciously as Hattie donned a cloak and Daniel picked up his hat. "Just where'd you get that invitation, Harriet?" he demanded. "And that gown? How'd you pay for it?"

God forbid she have a new gown to wear to a nice dinner. "The invitation to me and Daniel came from Mr. and Mrs. Forsythe, Papa, as you know. And the gown is borrowed."

He scowled at the two of them. "I don't like it. Something not right about it—why would they want you?"

"Perhaps because we are more charming than you," Daniel suggested.

Another surprise from her brother—he didn't typically stand up for her. And neither did he typically argue with her father. There was no need—their father reserved his criticism for Hattie and the twins.

"Come on, Hat. We'll be late." Daniel smoothly guided her past their father, ignoring his grumbles that he didn't like this, didn't like it at all.

Neither Hattie nor Daniel cared why their father felt as he did—as long as she could remember, he'd been suspicious of the *haute ton* on all counts and, at the same time, obsessed with news of it. He was suspicious of everyone, really, convinced the world was trying to cheat him out of the pounds he held with a tight fist.

Once outside, Hattie pulled the hood over her hair and the elegant headpiece she'd splurged on, adorned with silver and blue silk flowers, the same color as her dress. She'd fretted over spending the money for it, but when the woman in the shop showed her how it would be worn in upswept hair, Hattie couldn't resist. It seemed almost to change the color of her drab brown hair into a richer shade of tobacco.

She anticipated a long walk to the address on George Street, as there was no carriage waiting for them. There never was—carriages existed for paying customers, not family.

"When one's father owns most of the public transport in London, one might wonder why a transport is unavailable to his children," Daniel mused, apparently thinking the same thing as Hattie.

"I've long since ceased to wonder," Hattie said. "I consider it a fact of life, as immutable as I am a woman, and ducks quack."

"Fret not, Harriet Woodchurch," Daniel said as they walked to the end of the square. "Some things appear more immutable than they are." At the corner, he paused to consult his pocket watch.

Hattie stepped off the curb to carry on, not wanting to be late for this dinner. But Daniel grasped her elbow and pulled her back.

"What are you doing?"

"Be patient," he said. And then, like a bit of magic, a carriage came round the corner and pulled up beside them. The coachman climbed down and opened the door to the interior. "After you, madam," Daniel said.

Hattie gasped with delight. "How did you manage it?"

"I've a few tricks up my sleeve," he said. "We are not going to arrive at a fancy address like a pair of beggars. Up you go."

Up she went. She grinned all the way across town.

The Forsythe mansion was quite large, the result of combining three townhomes to make one very grand one. Carriages slowly passed the house, belching people out of their interiors and then sliding on.

Hattie clutched their invitation in something close to a death grip. She was certain that the only way into that magnificent house with all those magnificent people was the single piece of paper she held in her hand, and if she didn't present it, she and Daniel would be turned away as a pair of tricksters. She wouldn't be surprised if there was some sort of interrogation at the door. "*Who* are you? *How* did you gain an invite?"

But Hattie could not have been more wrong. It seemed anyone might have walked up to the house and sailed inside. Daniel gave the butler their names, and the gentleman asked no questions—he turned and announced them loudly to anyone close enough to hear. There were, in fact, several people close enough to hear, and when they realized the Woodchurches were no one important, they turned away.

A footman took Hattie's cloak and directed them to a line of people waiting to meet their hosts.

"Calm down," Daniel muttered to her as they inched forward.

"What are you talking about? I'm fine."

"You're shaking. You look as if you've come to steal something and are alarmed to find the home attended."

All right, her nerves had gotten the best of her. She was acutely aware she lacked a place in society that entitled her to this invitation, and even though she was dressed as if she were one of them, the farther into the house they went, the more painfully aware she became that she was not one of them.

Just as her mother had warned her.

When they reached the Forsythes, Hattie was momentarily blinded by the glint of light against the gold of Mrs. Forsythe's tiara. Daniel extended his hand too forcefully and thanked the couple for their generous invitation to him and his sister. Mr. and Mrs. Forsythe looked a bit confused, which came as no surprise, as the four of them had never met. But Mrs. Forsythe quickly ended the awkward exchange by inviting them to please enjoy the evening and ushered them along.

With that, Hattie and Daniel went into the grand salon with pink silk wallpaper and soaring ceilings and fine art and porcelain china bric-a-brac, brass candelabras, and floral paintings above the doors. The room was as grand as Lord Abbott's home on Grosvenor Square, but even larger.

Hattie understood that Mr. Forsythe had made his fortune in the railroad. She tried to imagine how many grandfather clocks could be stored here.

There were dozens of people milling about, in addition to a pair of footmen who wandered the room carrying silver trays, offering wine and spirits to the guests. Hattie didn't know who anyone was, but judging by their dress and jewels, she knew them to be among London's finest. She could hardly breathe, either from the excitement or the tightness of her corset.

"I'm having a drink," Daniel said, and before she could stop him, he wandered away, weaving into the crowd. "Daniel!" she whispered hotly after him, but it was no use—he left her standing alone in the middle of that grand room.

She was uncertain what to do. She pasted a thin smile on her face and looked around her, wondering if it was de rigueur to introduce herself to other guests? Or was she to wait to be introduced? Her etiquette classes at the Iddesleigh School for Exceptional Girls had not included invitations to dinner parties one had no business attending.

Where was the guest of honor? Was he here? Was Flora? Was Hattie supposed to greet Lord Abbott or wait until he acknowledged her? And why in heaven hadn't she asked Flora or Queenie any of these important questions before tonight?

Just when she thought she was in danger of launching herself at the nearest person, she heard her name. She jerked around in gratitude, eager to greet whoever had come to her rescue and, in her haste, very nearly knocked a drink from Lady Aleksander's hand. "Oh dear! I beg your pardon, madam," she said, and put a hand to Lady Aleksander's arm to steady her.

The lady laughed and shook a few droplets of champagne from her finger. "It's my fault—I startled you. It's good to see you, Miss Woodchurch. My, how beautiful you look." She smiled warmly.

Hattie could feel herself color—she wasn't used to compliments of any kind, and the last she'd seen Lady Aleksander, she'd seemed perturbed with her. "Thank you. I... wasn't sure you would recognize me."

"Well, of course I do!" She frowned a little and leaned forward. "I arranged your invitation!"

The bottom fell out of Hattie's stomach. "What?" She could think of only one reason that Lady Aleksander would arrange an invitation for her. She didn't seriously believe Hattie could be a potential match for the viscount?

Lady Aleksander leaned closer. "Are you all right? You look a little pale."

"Do I?" Hattie's gloved hand went instantly to her face.

"I know what you need." She turned and raised her fan, and just like that, a footman appeared with his silver tray as if summoned from clouds. Lady Aleksander took a glass of wine from it and handed it to Hattie. "This will calm any nerves."

"Oh, ah... Thank you." Her heart was fluttering—she could hardly seem to catch her breath. "I, ah... Why did you arrange an invitation?"

"Why?" She shrugged. "I thought you might enjoy it. And maybe...you'll help me a little."

"Help you?"

"You may have noticed that Lord Abbott is not one to share his feelings. Since you know him, I thought perhaps you might understand what he likes."

Hattie's heart sank like a rock. There for a moment, she'd thought maybe she... But that was so absurd. "Oh, I don't know." She could feel a bit of perspiration at her hairline.

She laughed a little. "I'm not generally plagued with nerves, but I've never been to a dinner as fine as this."

"I think you will quickly find that it's just a dinner, like any other. Have you come alone?"

"Oh no. I came with my brother. He is…" She paused, glancing around the room for him. And then she spotted him…*talking to Flora. Oh no.* She inwardly cringed and sent up a silent prayer that he'd not said anything offensive. Flora was Hattie's friend, but she was also her benefactor. "I, ah… I really should—"

"As I live and breathe, is that Miss Woodchurch?"

Hattie recognized Lord Iddesleigh's voice, and turned with Lady Aleksander to greet Lord and Lady Iddesleigh.

Lady Iddesleigh had gotten a bit heavier than the last time Hattie had seen her—the extra weight had softened her features. She smiled. When Hattie was a student, Lady Iddesleigh didn't smile much at all. Then again, she'd had five young daughters to contend with and it had seemed one of them was always quite unmoored.

"Look at this, little Harriet Woodchurch, all grown up," Lady Iddesleigh said with delight. "I understand you've come into a very important occupation."

"I don't think it's *very* important—"

"Nonsense, it is! It was obvious to me that his lordship relies on your counsel," Lady Aleksander said.

"No," Hattie exclaimed, alarmed. She could imagine the rumors that would swirl about her, the girl who thought she might counsel a viscount. "I think the circumstances were a bit unusual the day you called, but generally speaking, *no.*"

"Miss Woodchurch, you shouldn't have the slightest hesitation in stating your worth," Lord Iddesleigh said.

"I don't. I'm—"

"And where is our new viscount?" Lord Iddesleigh said, looking around the room. "I haven't missed him, have I? I daresay I'm the only friend he's got. Besides our own Miss Woodchurch, that is."

"I'm not his friend," Hattie pleaded.

"He's not come yet, Beck," Lady Aleksander said, ignoring Hattie. As was Lord Iddesleigh. "You may trust that you won't miss his entrance—every woman in this room will be attracted to him like flies to cake."

"He's probably waiting in the crush outside," Lady Iddesleigh said. "It was terrible, really."

"Miss Woodchurch," Lord Iddesleigh said. "Regale us with how you find your position with his lordship. He's not very forthcoming, is he?"

Of all the things she'd imagined for this evening, this had not been it. She looked around for Daniel. For Flora. Anyone to save her from this.

"She's given him a book to read," Lady Aleksander offered.

The Iddesleighs looked at her with shock. Hattie shrugged sheepishly. "He likes to read."

"Interesting," Lord Iddesleigh said. "One never knows what might arise in the administration of an estate. But, Miss Woodchurch, no one cares about his reading habits. What we want to know is, what does our young bachelor think of the prospects he is to meet tonight?"

The question mortified Hattie—her cheeks flooded with heat. "I beg your pardon, my lord, I would *never* inquire about such a thing."

"Never?" he asked.

"Beck, darling!" his wife exclaimed. "Don't tease her. Look, you're making her skin mottle. She's surely been sworn to secrecy! And here you have Lila, who has arranged for introductions to be made this evening. Why don't you inquire of her who that is?"

"Everyone is here to meet him," Lady Aleksander said breezily. "But in particular, Miss Christiana Porter—"

"There you are, an easy favorite," Lady Iddesleigh said. "Miss Dahlia Cupperson—"

"Rich," Lord Iddesleigh mused.

"And Miss Flora Raney," Lady Aleksander finished.

Lord and Lady Iddesleigh looked at each other. Lady Iddesleigh shrugged a little and Lord Iddesleigh said, "My wife thinks our Tilly should be considered if that's the best you've got. But I think she is—"

"There he is now!" Lady Aleksander suddenly sang out, ending any further conversation about Mathilda Hawke as a potential bride for the viscount, and all four of them turned at once toward the entrance.

There was a commotion at the entrance to the salon, as people closed ranks around the Forsythes and their special guest. It was a moment or two before Lord Abbott stepped into view, and when he did, it felt to Hattie as if the air changed, and her heart began to sputter along. He always looked quite handsome to her, but tonight, he looked divine. His hair was neatly combed, his beard closely trimmed. His suit of clothing—black, with a gold brocade waistcoat—was tailored to perfection against his frame. On his chest, he wore a red badge that dripped a gold star, which, she surmised, was a symbol of the Santiavan duchy.

She realized that someone in the crowd was speaking Spanish, and Abbott responded in kind, his voice deep and soothing, his Spanish sounding a bit like a song. In the next breath, in response to a question put to him by someone else, he effortlessly shifted to English. He said only a few words, but he clearly said enough. People were smiling and nodding along as if he was delivering a sermon of good cheer.

Mr. and Mrs. Forsythe proudly escorted him around the room, almost as if they were showing off a new horse to their friends. Trot this way and make an introduction. Trot that way and make another.

Lord Abbott strolled along, his hands at his back, nodding and responding as he greeted the other guests. Hattie glanced over her shoulder to where Flora and Daniel had been standing. Daniel had disappeared—probably in search of another drink—but Flora was in the same spot, now in the company of her parents. Even from here, she looked pale.

"Excuse me," Hattie said, and slipped away from the Iddesleighs and Lady Aleksander. No one noticed her departure. Lord Iddesleigh was complaining that the Forsythes seemed to be showing some favoritism in their introductions.

Hattie moved through the crowd to Flora's side and touched her arm, startling her. "Hattie!" she cried. "Thank goodness you are here. Your brother said you hadn't come."

"What?" Hattie almost rolled her eyes. "Pay him no mind, Flora. You shouldn't even talk to him, really." She paused. "How is it that you've made his acquaintance?"

"I don't recall." Flora suddenly gripped Hattie's hand. "How do I look?"

"Beautiful. More beautiful than anyone here." It was true—Flora looked like a princess in her pale gold gown with a cascade of red blooms down the bustled train.

Flora smiled, but her gaze trailed anxiously in the direction of the viscount. She did not comment on Hattie's appearance. She didn't tease her about how she'd had to squeeze into her gown or admire the new headdress Hattie had bought. Hattie didn't take it personally—she understood how anxious her friend was about meeting the viscount.

Flora leaned close and whispered, "Christiana has been at the door all night, just so she'd be the first to be introduced."

"Oh. Well, really, we're all by the door."

Flora suddenly gasped. "He's coming this way!" she hissed. Her grip of Hattie's hand tightened and she turned to the side, drawing deep breaths. "This is a disaster. A disaster! What will I say?"

"Flora, darling?" Her mother moved to her daughter's side. "Oh, Miss Woodchurch. I didn't expect to see you here."

No one had expected to see her here, herself included. "Good evening, Lady Raney," she said with a curtsy. Lady Raney looked at her daughter, then at Hattie. "What's the matter?" she asked. "Stand up straight, dear." She fussed with Flora's pearl necklace. "You look like you might be ill."

"I might," Flora said, and swallowed thickly.

"Nonsense! Put your shoulders back and lift your chin. Viscount Abbott is nearly upon us."

Flora did as her mother instructed, swallowing hard, then stepped up to stand beside her parents as Lord Abbott and his hosts approached them. Hattie didn't know where to stand, so she remained a foot or so behind her friend. There really ought to be instructions issued with invitations to fancy dinners.

Mrs. Forsythe made the introductions. Hattie couldn't hear what the Raneys said, but Lord Abbott smiled and nodded and said yes, he did find London to his liking. And no, he hadn't yet had opportunity to travel to his Essex estate, Harrington Hall, but that he hoped to do so soon.

Lady Raney then turned slightly in Flora's direction and said, "May I introduce our daughter?" And like she'd been trained, Flora sank into a perfect curtsy. When she did, Lord Abbott saw Hattie standing behind her. His brows dipped with confusion. "Miss Woodchurch?" he said, ignoring Flora for the moment.

Hattie dipped into a curtsy. "Good evening, my lord."

The Raneys, almost as one, turned to look at her, their expressions showing various stages of confusion.

"I didn't expect to see you here," he said, obviously trying to sort it out.

Perhaps she should have come with a sign—*I was not expected!* "Surprise?" she said weakly, as if she'd come as a lark.

He arched a brow, which made him look as if he wanted to ask what she was doing here.

Flora's parents were glaring at her. And Flora seemed absolutely gobsmacked that the viscount was speaking to Hattie. But she suddenly remembered herself and turned her attention to the viscount. "It…it is my distinct pleasure to make your acquaintance, my lord."

Lord Abbott likewise turned his attention to Flora and smiled warmly. "Thank you. But the pleasure is certainly mine."

And then Flora's father stepped in, keen to have a word. The two gentlemen stepped away. Hattie risked a look at Flora. She stared back at Hattie with confusion that felt wildly personal—it seemed almost as if she was hurt that Lord Abbott had acknowledged Hattie at all. "Hattie? Is there—"

Hattie was saved from hearing her question by Mrs. Forsythe's announcement that supper was served. The words set everyone into motion, and the promenade to the dining room was arranged. As Lord Abbott moved to the front of the line, he glanced at Hattie, a question still in his eyes.

She could feel a warmth spreading through her, a familiarity with him that she realized she was not supposed to have. She smiled and shrugged, then stepped back, letting the important people go in as they ought. She looked around for Daniel to escort her, but he was nowhere to be found... until the last possible moment when she spotted him with his arm out to escort Flora. *What in blazes was he doing?*

Moreover, there was no one left to escort her into the dining room. Hattie was forced to follow along like a forgotten duck at the very tail of the promenade.

She was seated next to Lord Iddesleigh, who leaned over to whisper, "Your friend has caught the interest of the viscount, I'm certain of it." He smiled and waggled his brows at her, as if they had conspired together to bring this about.

She thought she ought to be terribly pleased by the news, overcome with happiness for Flora...but the declaration and the evening thus far left her feeling uncomfortably sad.

CHAPTER FIFTEEN

THE DINING ROOM in the Forsythe home was one of the largest Mateo had ever seen in a house, and yet, it wasn't large enough to comfortably seat thirty-two people. They were crammed together, elbows brushing elbows.

Mateo was spared the worst of it, as he was seated next to Mr. Forsythe, who sat at the head of the table. Mateo recalled that once, when he'd just assumed the title of duke, he'd been feted at the palace in Valdonia. He'd been seated at the head of the table, and the doors behind him had been opened to the sea. He remembered the feel of the sea breeze on his back, the sweep of fresh air through the room. He wished for an open window in this room, but the London air was thick with smoke and unpleasant.

What a morose dinner guest he was.

Unfortunately, from his vantage point he couldn't see many of the other guests. He was curious about where Miss Woodchurch had been seated. He was even more curious to know why she was here. Had Beck brought her? That didn't make sense to him—why would Beck want to have her dine here? Was she a member of the working class or a member of this society? Was it possible to be both? In Santiava, at least, those two worlds did not intersect.

No matter what had brought her here, he'd been surprisingly pleased to see her face in this crowd.

He would have thought that, as the guest of honor, he

would have been seated in the middle of the table. But Mr. Forsythe made it clear why he had not been before the first course was served. Mr. Forsythe had an interest in a new rail line in Europe that he hoped to bring into Valdonia. "Can you imagine the amount of wool we might ship with a new rail?" he asked, almost gleefully.

Mateo listened, but he was distracted by the many conversations around him. He was not sure how much he wanted to say about rail service in the middle of a social evening, and he was more interested in the snippets of conversation he kept hearing to his right—something about someone with extensive gambling debts and no way to pay them.

None of the young ladies he was to assess for a potential mate were seated anywhere near him. Contrary to what his mother or Lady Aleksander believed, he was looking forward to meeting them. He just wished it was under different, less fanfare-ish circumstances. He would have preferred a private stroll with each of them or, at the very least, a smaller dinner gathering where the conversation included everyone.

He focused on his meal, which was well done, centering around a delectable piece of lamb. But the best part of the meal was the dessert. The woman beside him called it a sponge cake.

"Sponge cake?" he repeated.

"It's a favorite of Queen Victoria."

He would ask Rosa to find the recipe for it.

After the dessert dishes had been cleared, Mateo participated as best he could in the obligatory social exchanges about the weather and admitted that spring in London was too cold for his tastes. He nodded along as another gentleman waxed philosophically about the chances of an education bill to pass Parliament. When asked about the Abbott estate—everyone seemed to know something about it—he was forced to admit he hadn't known his grandfather well, but had learned a lot about him in the course of reviewing the records.

And so it went.

After dinner, the ladies retired to the salon, and he remained behind with the gentlemen to sip brandy and smoke cigars, because it was the polite thing to do. But the custom—which had been imported to Santiava—felt a bit archaic to him. Why shouldn't they all, ladies included, enjoy brandy and a cigar, if it was so desirable? Why was it always necessary to separate the sexes? Why did society make so many blasted rules?

Alas, as there would be no social revolution this evening—more was the pity, as that at least would be entertaining—Mateo sipped his brandy. Eventually, Mr. Forsythe proclaimed the male portion of the evening had concluded and led the way to rejoin the ladies.

They returned to the large drawing room, and there Mateo was served more port he didn't want. Lady Aleksander descended on him like a heron descending to the shore, talons thrust forward, wings outstretched. "My lord, I found you! May I introduce you to a friend of mine?"

That friend, as it happened, was Miss Christiana Porter. Mateo had made her acquaintance briefly when he'd arrived, and as promised, she was indeed quite beautiful. Her skin was creamy and smooth like porcelain, and she had hair the color of corn silk that made her pale blue eyes stand out. He thought them a bit lighter than Miss Woodchurch's, whose eyes were the color of a spring sky.

He was admiring Miss Porter's fine looks as she ran through her litany of proper things to say to him: How delighted she was to make his acquaintance. How wonderful he had joined them this evening. Didn't he think the lamb was delicious?

The conversation suited Mateo, as it required very little from him.

But then something terrible happened—Miss Porter asked him where Santiava was and then proceeded to demonstrate her utter ignorance of European geography. Mateo didn't know if it was more startling that a young woman born into privilege and with a proper education would have no notion of where countries such as Spain and France were, or that he cared. But he discovered in those few moments that he did, indeed, very much care. How could he entertain the thought of marrying someone who hadn't the slightest idea of what country was across a narrow sea from the one she inhabited?

He was relieved when the heron descended again, this time whisking him away to converse with Miss Cupperson.

Miss Cupperson was the opposite of Miss Porter both in looks and knowledge of the world. In fact, she was so knowledgeable that she was determined to regale him with all that she'd learned about Santiava. She even threw in a few obscure tidbits about Spain, lest he think she not know where Santiava was. The woman rattled off so many facts that there ceased to be any semblance of conversation at all. He felt as if he was sitting before his tutor, receiving a lesson he'd already heard. Did he know, for example, that Santiava exported animal skins, spices, and olive oil?

He never had to admit that he did, because she moved on quickly to Santiava's history as a seafaring nation.

When Miss Cupperson had exhausted all the things she'd learned for the occasion, Lady Aleksander was on hand to bring him to the third lady of the evening.

Miss Flora Raney was standing in a group of people that included her parents and two others whose names Mateo had already forgotten. He also noticed that very nearby, standing with her back turned to Miss Raney, as if she were waiting for someone else to come, was Miss Woodchurch.

Mateo greeted her parents and then Miss Raney. She curtsied and smiled. He asked how she'd found the evening thus far—the dullest of questions, for what could she possibly say? It had been miserable thus far? That the lamb was tough, the wine sour? Of course not. She said it was lovely—no more, no less.

Which, unlike the previous young lady, left Mateo with the burden of carrying on the conversation. Not his forte. He remembered Sofia had once told him that young women were taught not to say too much lest they say the wrong thing. He understood that—as a boy, he'd lived in constant fear of saying the wrong thing and being publicly humiliated for it. But how could a woman like Miss Raney say the wrong thing? It was only for him to hear, and he was too polite to contradict her. People were entitled to their opinions—men certainly offered theirs without thought or invitation.

He liked that Miss Raney was attractive. Not remarkably so, not like Miss Porter, but very appealing all the same. She was petite, and her hands so small they looked almost fragile. Mateo tried to picture her fingers kneading dough and couldn't. She seemed a bit anxious, and he assumed it was because of him—it was beyond his comprehension why he could never seem to put anyone at ease. But he would try, for her sake.

He asked in what part of town she resided. She rallied— she said where she lived then asked him how he liked Grosvenor Square and before he could answer, reported that she had a very good friend who lived across the square from him, and that they liked to stroll through from time to time. He said that he found the square pleasant, which wasn't entirely true. He rarely stepped foot into the square, preferring his own private garden. And he'd given very little thought to its ambiance when he did.

Miss Raney bit her lower lip as she tried to think of what to say next. This was the point of any given acquaintance where Mateo struggled, as he was likewise trying to find something that two complete strangers might discuss.

He was grateful to Lady Raney for turning to them when she did and asking if he'd seen the art exhibit at the Royal Hall.

"I have not," he said.

"It's a wonderful exhibit, isn't it, darling?" she asked Miss Raney. "You really must see it, my lord. Flora, tell him your favorite," she instructed.

Miss Raney dutifully agreed that the art was lovely, and that she very much liked the paintings of landscapes. She said it reminded her of the country where they went to summer. Mateo asked if she had a particular interest in art. She said she liked art, but it wasn't a particular interest, really. He asked what her interests were. Miss Raney looked almost confused by the question, as if she'd never put any thought to it.

"Well, I *like* art," she said, as if he'd somehow misunderstood her. "And music."

Art and music, standard fare. Show him a person who did not list art and music as their interests and he'd show you someone who lived in a cave. He'd hoped for something a bit more interesting, something he might find a response to. Or something entirely unexpected, like an interest in the Sahara Desert. Maybe he should ask if she'd ever met a Spaniard or Santiavan, or if her education had extended to geography of the world.

He was contemplating any number of ways to take this conversation and happened to glance at his hand. Miss Raney apparently interpreted it as a sign of disinterest and blurted, "Do you?"

He lifted his gaze to her. "Do I...?"

"Care for art and music."

"Ah. *Sí*, I like both very much." He winced inwardly. Now he was the one who was uninteresting. "And the Sahara Desert." He didn't know why he said it, other than to see what sort of response it might prompt.

Miss Raney's expression conveyed confusion and then what Mateo could only think was horror. Who could blame her? What would anyone say to that? Besides Miss Woodchurch, who would probably agree that she liked it, too, in theory, and launch into some tale she'd heard that it was quite beautiful in the morning but hot in the afternoon and had studied it in her atlas.

Miss Raney's panic was reflected in her eyes, and he could imagine her searching her memory for even one mention of that desert. He was constructing an excuse to step away, to relieve the poor girl, when Lady Raney turned again and asked Mateo when his mother might return to London.

He didn't remember mentioning his mother had left London. "Ah...a fortnight. Perhaps longer. She very much enjoys Paris."

"Paris is *lovely* in the spring," Lady Raney said approvingly. Her daughter, Mateo noticed, was speaking to Miss Woodchurch over her shoulder. "London can be so soggy in the spring, wouldn't you agree? But Paris? The sun seems to shine on that city."

"Indeed," he said.

Her daughter had turned back to him, fully recovered. She was even smiling. Mateo wondered if it was possible to have a whisky brought to him. "I like to read," Miss Raney blurted, as if the thought had just come to her. Lady Raney smiled thinly and turned away.

"Ah." And she mentioned this...why?

"Very much."

All right. If she wanted to talk about reading, he would need a little more than that. "History? Philosophy?"

"Novels."

"You are the second person who has said as much this week. Is there a favorite you would recommend?"

She straightened her shoulders. "Well, I, ah... I recently read *Honorine* by Monsieur de Balzac."

Mateo smiled with surprise. *"Est-ce un roman Fran-çais?"*

She blinked. "A French novel, yes."

Now he was getting somewhere with Miss Raney. She understood French, which would, of course, recommend her to a small, dual-language duchy.

"What drew you to a French novel?"

Miss Raney blinked again. "Umm...I think that I, ah... I enjoy reading about other places."

She thought she did? Did she not know? Why did it sound as if she didn't know anything about the book or what had drawn her to it? Had he phrased his question in a confusing way? It wouldn't be the first time. He tried again. "What did you think of it?"

"The book?"

"The book."

"It was...interesting."

She hadn't read it, he was certain of it. "What was it about?"

Before she could answer, a footman appeared and held out a tray with glasses of port. Mateo shook his head. The footman offered the tray to Miss Raney, but she was speaking over her shoulder to Miss Woodchurch again. When the footman moved to Miss Woodchurch, she took a glass from the tray and handed it to Miss Raney, then took another one and turned away before Mateo could catch her eye. He had the distinct impression that she was trying to avoid him.

Miss Raney shifted back to him, all smiles, the port in hand. "I beg your pardon, my lord. You were saying?"

"I asked what the book was about."

"Yes, of course. Unrequited love."

That was...odd. "A curious and perhaps distressing subject."

"Well," she said, with a bit of a shrug. "Really, it is more about marriage."

He was certain he wasn't understanding her. The book was about unrequited love and marriage? "One would assume in a marriage all love is requited."

She had to think about that. "I suppose," she said after a beat or two.

Now he wasn't certain this book even existed, but he had to admire Miss Raney's approach. He could confidently say no one had ever made up a book or claimed to be fond of reading to impress him. "I will take this as a recommendation to read the book."

She smiled, clearly delighted. "I do hope you enjoy it."

"My lord?"

Mateo turned. Mrs. Forsythe was at his side. "For your pleasure, Miss Porter has offered to sing for us this evening. Shall we retire to the music room?"

He agreed that they should, and away the guests trooped to the music room across the hall.

That room was painted yellow and white. A piano was angled before chairs that had been arranged in rows. It was crowded, and there were not enough seats for the number of people who wanted to hear Miss Porter's musical performance. Mateo was given a seat at the front of the room beside the Forsythes and Lord and Lady Iddesleigh, which unnerved him. He didn't like the idea of everyone watching him watch Miss Porter. "Really, I can stand—"

"I wouldn't hear of it," Mrs. Forsythe insisted. "You are our honored guest."

He reluctantly sat. There was quite a lot of shuffling about as more people entered, and then Miss Porter came to the front of the room in the company of the pianist. Mateo considered her fine looks once again. Maybe he'd been too hasty in his mental dismissal of her for not knowing geography. He was only human—a dimpled smile could make him forget that the woman didn't know that France was just across the Channel.

The pianist sat and played a chord or two, but before Miss Porter could begin, an elderly woman wandered to the front of the room in search of a seat. Mateo saw his opportunity and immediately stood and helped her into his, ignoring Mrs. Forsythe's loudly whispered protests, then quickly made his way to the back of the room to stand with those who had not been lucky enough to find a seat.

Miss Porter began to sing. The man standing next to Mateo slinked away, and when he did, Mateo found himself standing next to Miss Woodchurch.

She glanced at him from the corner of her eye and smiled wryly.

He whispered, "Fancy meeting you here. You didn't mention you'd be in attendance this evening."

Miss Porter's first high note was a bit of a screech that caused them both to recoil slightly.

"My invitation came quite late," she whispered in return.

"Are you enjoying the evening?" he whispered as Miss Porter fixed her gaze at some point above everyone's heads.

"Not particularly," she whispered back.

Just then, the music swelled and Miss Porter's singing grew louder. Not in the style of opera, which one might expect from such an open mouth and earnest look. But more in the style of a hyena.

The song, from what Mateo was able to understand, was about a soldier returning from war, whose love had abandoned him. Another case of unrequited love? Whatever the lyrics meant to convey, Mateo was too distracted to notice or care, because the woman continued to sing off-key, screeching the high notes. He wanted to throw his hands over his ears and spare them, but of course, he had to bear it like every other poor soul in the room.

If anyone else noticed how horribly the woman sang, they did not show it. There was no looking about, no one trying to pull her off the stage. Mateo glanced at Miss Woodchurch. She glanced back with dismay. Mateo couldn't help himself—he bit his lower lip and feigned concern that something was terribly amiss.

She tried to suppress a smile, but she was unsuccessful. So she looked down, hiding her expression from anyone who happened to look in their direction. Anyone looking would still be able to see the slight tremor to her shoulders as she swallowed down her laughter.

The song finished on a very high and long note that got sharper and sharper with the duration. When Miss Porter was done, she smiled brilliantly, and the room applauded, and Mateo and Miss Woodchurch looked at each other with wonder.

"I'm so happy I've had the opportunity to hear your future wife sing."

Mateo choked back a laugh. "You've confused me with another future husband."

The music began again and Miss Porter settled in for another shrieking, and Mateo and Miss Woodchurch leaned back in unison, trying to escape it.

The second song was decidedly worse than the first.

When the young woman had taken her last bow, Mr. Forsythe came for him directly, and Mateo lost Miss Woodchurch in the crowd. After a time, when he couldn't possibly think of another thing to say, and Lady Aleksander was having a brandy and talking loudly with two women, he thanked his hosts and bid them all a good night, then walked directly to the door to escape before Lady Aleksander could accost him.

On his way out, he spotted Miss Woodchurch standing off to one side by herself. He thought she looked quite lovely in a silky blue gown.

CHAPTER SIXTEEN

ONCE LORD ABBOTT took his leave, others began to leave, too, probably rushing home to put a compress on their ears. Hattie was eager to make her exit as well—she desperately needed some air. She was grateful for the experience, she truly was…but as the evening had gone on, she'd realized with increasing urgency that she was out of place in this house. Hardly anyone but Lord and Lady Iddesleigh had spoken to her. Gazes moved past her like she was invisible to the eye. No one knew her, and no one cared to know her, obviously.

Daniel, on the other hand, had attracted many pairs of eyes as he'd sauntered around the salon, introducing himself to women as if he was a prince here, and not the pauper he truly was. The men looked at him askance, the women looked at him with interest. His saving grace was that he was a man, and a handsome one at that.

Hattie had no saving graces.

She thought she'd at least been helpful to Flora. It had been terribly uncomfortable watching her friend squirm in the presence of Lord Abbott. And it was so unlike Flora— she'd always been self-assured and confident. But Lord Abbott's hazel gaze had somehow reduced her to ash.

When Mrs. Forsythe had asked everyone to repair to the music room, Flora had grabbed Hattie's elbow, squeezing so hard she'd probably left a bruise. "How *could* you?"

she whispered hotly as Daniel joined them, another port in hand.

"How could I what?" Hattie asked, confused, pulling her glove up from where it had slipped with Flora's rough handling.

"*You* told me to say *Honorine*. Unrequited love, Hattie? I sounded like a fool."

Daniel laughed with surprise at Flora's pique.

"What are you laughing at?" Flora hissed.

"Your charming self," Daniel said with a bow.

"Daniel!" Hattie pulled Flora away from him. "I'm so sorry, Flora. It was a very interesting book and I thought—"

"*Interesting!* What is the matter with you? I don't want *interesting*, I want charming! You ruined everything!" She flounced off to rejoin her parents.

Hattie rubbed her elbow. "You'll cost me my position," she said as Daniel sidled up to her.

"What sort of position is it that requires you to take such condescension? You're better than that." But his words belied the curious look of amusement in his eyes as he smiled after Flora. "That one's easily riled, isn't she?"

Hattie stepped in front of him so that he'd have to look at her instead of Flora. "You may think the position beneath me, but it's the only way I have of leaving our father's house. Please don't ruin it for me."

Daniel rolled his eyes. "I haven't done anything." He walked away from her, following Miss Cupperson across the room.

Hattie didn't see her brother again after that, and neither had she wanted to. But now that the guests were beginning to disperse, she was looking everywhere for him. She could imagine nothing worse than a pair of Woodchurch siblings being the last people to leave, especially when Mrs. Forsythe kept looking at her as if she was some misplaced poor relation she ought to know.

Where *was* he?

As one of the last few carriages pulled away from the curb, Hattie finally had to accept that he'd left without her. She was seething with fury, but she painted a smile on her face and thanked the hosts. She avoided Lord and Lady Iddesleigh as she collected her cloak, intending to march home while wildly hoping she was not accosted or harmed. How *dare* he care so little for her safety?

She began striding down the street, too embarrassed to be seen lingering like a beggar as the last carriages departed. But before she reached the corner, she heard a whistle. That was followed by her brother calling her name. She stopped walking and turned around. There was a hansom cab just down the street. Daniel was standing on the running board, hanging on with one hand to the carriage. "Hat! Over here!" he shouted at her, waving his arm overhead, as if they were at a country fair and the swine show was about to start.

She debated for a moment if she would even deign to answer his bray. But the thought of walking across London at this time of night was too fright inducing to be borne. Her cheeks were burning with indignation, but she held her head high, and walked to the waiting cab.

But as she neared it, she realized her brother was not alone. Two of his companions—where had *they* come from?—were squeezed into an interior meant only for two. She thought surely they would disembark, but no, they eyed her like hungry wolves, laughing together as if this were all some sort of jest.

"What are you doing here?" she demanded.

"What do you mean? I've come to fetch you home, obviously," Daniel said. He patted his lap. "You didn't think I'd leave you in that pit of vipers, did you?"

"It was not a pit of vipers. You can't deny it was a lovely evening."

One of Daniel's companions, whom her brother had yet to introduce, snickered.

"I tolerated it. Come on," Daniel said. He patted his lap again.

She gaped at him. "You can't be serious."

"I apologize for having left the gold carriage at home, but unless you have another conveyance, come on board. *Now*, Hat."

"A gold carriage," one of the men scoffed as he eyed Hattie closely.

They were drunk. Somewhere in the space of the past hour or so, Daniel had left a respectable evening and returned with two drunken mates. Why had fate put her in this family?

"We haven't got all night," Daniel snapped, and leaned forward, his hand outstretched to her.

Hattie was humiliated. She was supposed to ride off like some night flower with them? But what choice did she have? It was far worse to walk home and have strange men assume she was a three-penny upright looking to pay her rent, wasn't it? When Daniel impatiently wiggled his fingers at her, she put her hand in his and allowed him to haul her up to sit in his lap.

And then she tried to hide her face beneath her hood, lest anyone from the Forsythe party see her.

They clattered along, passing the Forsythe house and disappearing into poorly lit London streets as Hattie bounced along uncomfortably on her brother's knee.

"What's it like up in that house?" one of Daniel's friends asked.

Hattie ignored him. The cab made a sharp left, and she fell into the wall. When she did, her hood fell away from her hair.

"Hey," said one of the men. "I know you, don't I? You were engaged to Rupert Masterson."

The second man leaned forward to have a look at her. "Blimey, it is." He burst into laughter. "What'd you do to make the lad cry off? He—"

"Shut up," Daniel growled.

"*Och*, Dan, we didn't say any—"

"Shut your mouth," Daniel said more forcefully, jerking toward his friends and very nearly dislodging Hattie in the process.

Hattie said nothing. She was dying a thousand small deaths, mortified that one of those men had recognized her as Rupert's fiancée. Is that who she was in this town now? Rupert Masterson's jilted fiancée? The truth, which Rupert had so gallantly said he meant to conceal, was apparently out there.

When the cab pulled to the curb on the north end of Portman Square, Hattie leaped from it, stumbling and landing on all fours when she hit the hard pavement. She heard the rip of fabric and felt the pain in one knee. She heard them laugh, heard Daniel direct the driver as she ran down the sidewalk, away from them and their leering faces.

She slipped into the house, relieved to find no one awake. She found a butt of a candle by groping around an entry console and made her way upstairs through the shadows of grandfather clocks and dress forms. She found two cats curled on the foot of her bed, but Hattie was so exhausted she didn't make them leave.

She looked down at her borrowed gown. She'd torn a

hole in the knee, all right. She fell, with despair, facedown onto the bed and let her shame sink into her.

She'd thought mixing with the Quality would be fun. She'd thought that's what she wanted from life. But now that she'd done it, she only felt empty. She was not of that world.

But neither was she part of this one.

Where did that leave her? What world did she belong to? Was she to be an island of a woman, moving through various parts of society, belonging to no one but herself?

One of the cats began to purr and flex its claws against her arm.

Hattie rolled onto her back and stared at the ceiling overhead, stained from a leak in the roof that her father had left unrepaired for too long. In the vague outline of the stain, her mind's eye saw Lord Abbott.

He'd looked so striking in his formal suit of clothing. Virile and worldly and mysterious. She'd tried not to ogle him, but that had proved more difficult than she would have guessed. He'd said very little to her, other than to express his surprise that she was there. And then to exchange a look or two when Miss Porter sang.

She'd watched him speak to the three women Lady Aleksander had deemed worthy of his consideration, obviously making an effort to know them, just as he'd said he would do. She'd yearned to know what he said, what he asked, but except for Flora's conversation, that had been impossible. She wondered if he wanted to be married. Maybe he was one of those gentlemen who would prefer to remain a bachelor all his life, but fate had intervened.

Then again, perhaps he saw marriage as something to aspire to—a state of being that was more blissful than his solitude.

What if his marriage was to Flora? Hattie tried to imagine her friend as the duchess of Santiava. Flora was naturally gregarious and liked to have her friends around her. She would want to host parties and suppers and patronize her favorite charities. But how would she cope if her husband hardly said two words to her every day? She couldn't imagine it—Flora thrived on companionship.

Christiana? No. After this evening's disastrous performance, during which the viscount had had to bite his lip to keep from laughing or crying—it was hard to know which was more appropriate—she guessed that Christiana would not be his choice.

Dahlia Cupperson? Hattie had always liked Dahlia and found her to be curious about any number of topics. A match with Dahlia was possible, she supposed. She pictured the two of them, bent over their books, discussing things like…math. Dahlia had always struck her as smart and clever in that way.

The vision of the two of them made her feel a little queasy.

Hattie pressed a hand to her forehead. She could feel a headache coming on, probably from lack of sleep. Or the tension that came with feeling less than. She didn't have the ingredients to be considered for a marriage with the viscount. And she didn't have the qualities necessary to suit someone as pedestrian as Rupert Masterson.

She hated feeling like this, despairing and hopeless. She resolved to not allow herself to feel this way.

If only she knew how.

CHAPTER SEVENTEEN

MRS. O'MALLEY WAS desperate for details of the fancy supper Hattie had attended, and as she boxed up some whisky bonbons for Hattie to take to Grosvenor Square, she pelted Hattie with one question after another. Who was in attendance? What did they serve for the meal? What did the ladies wear? How did the viscount seem? Which young lady did he like the best?

Hattie laughed as she put away Mrs. O'Malley's ledgers. "I think he liked them all, really. Or maybe he liked them not at all. I'm sure I'll be the last to know."

"If you ask me, he ought to look no further than you, Hattie Woodchurch. You're the best of the lot."

Hattie smiled warmly. "You're very kind, Mrs. O'Malley. But you've not seen the ladies he is considering. If you had, your opinion would be much changed."

"Rubbish," she said with a cluck of her tongue.

"I'm very sure of it," Hattie said laughingly. "I'm not cut from the right cloth. He'll marry someone with proper connections and a pedigree he'll need for his heirs."

"Oh, those people," Mrs. O'Malley scoffed. "They value the wrong things! They ought to search for compatibility and a return of affection. Mr. O'Malley didn't care a whit that my father was a poor farmer—he loved me for who I am, and we were happily married for twenty-eight years before he died." Mrs. O'Malley paused a moment and looked misty-eyed into the distance.

Hattie smiled. "He must have been a wonderful man."

"Aye." Mrs. O'Malley dabbed at her eyes with the corner of her apron. "Never you mind those toffs, Miss Woodchurch. You'll want someone who loves you for who you are, not for the size of your purse."

"That is the hope," Hattie agreed. She slung her bag over her shoulder and took the bundle of bonbons. "Good day, Mrs. O'Malley!"

She walked across town to Grosvenor Square, her pace a jaunty one. The self-doubt she'd directed at herself Saturday night had vanished in the sunlight. She knew who she was. She knew what to expect from her life. She would have to make her own place to belong—life was not going to simply hand it to her.

She also knew she only had a limited time with the most handsome viscount in England. She intended to make the most of it. It might very well be one of the high points of her life.

At Grosvenor Square, she entered through the servants' door as she always did, arriving in the kitchen with her basket of treats from Mrs. O'Malley. Everyone gathered around to see what she'd brought. "Bonbons," she announced as she held the basket out for everyone to see.

"Ooh, *bonbons*," they repeated in awed unison.

The two kitchen ladies, the footmen, and Mr. Pacheco were on hand to sample them. As they did, exclaiming in Spanish, Hattie went round the room and asked after everyone with the bit of Spanish she had learned. *"Cómo está?"*

They smiled with delight at her attempt. Yolanda said loudly, *"Muy bien!"* But then, Mr. Pacheco spoke to her in Spanish, and she said again, much more softly, *"Muy bien."* Aurelia and one of the footmen attempted to respond in English, but it made no sense to Hattie. Although Mr. Pacheco spoke both English and Spanish, he was not inclined to translate. For one, he was stuffing bonbons into his mouth. For another, he claimed translating one language to another gave him a headache.

But Hattie understood them well enough. In a very short time, she had come to consider these people her friends. When she asked Aurelia how she fared, the girl blushed furiously. Yolanda spread some flour on the table, picked up a wooden spoon and, with the handle, drew the rudimentary shapes of a woman and man. Aurelia let off a string of very heated Spanish, and Carlos quietly left the room. Yolanda laughed until Mr. Pacheco said something that made both ladies stop talking altogether.

Mr. Pacheco shook his head. "These girls, they fill their heads with silliness." He held out his hand, palm up. "Berries," he said to Hattie. "I found them growing wild, in the park." He picked one off his hand and tossed it in his mouth.

Hattie laughed. "Those are rose hips, Mr. Pacheco. Not berries."

"No?" He shrugged and thrust his hand a little closer. "Try."

"No, thank you. Once, when I was a girl, I made myself ill with rose hips." She hung up her bonnet and her wrap, smoothed the lap of her gown. "Have a care you don't eat too many in one sitting."

"Och," he said with a wave of his hand. "I've a stomach forged from iron."

She wouldn't be surprised if he did.

Hattie wished the staff a good day and, with her bag, began to make her way to the study.

The viscount wasn't there when she entered. Hattie went

to her desk, assuming he'd left work for her, but found nothing. She put down her things and moved to the window, expecting to see him in the garden. But a light rain had begun to fall, and no one was outside. Restless, she moved around the room, looking at the paintings and knickknacks. At the hearth, she spotted a small painting she hadn't noticed before. It was on a tiny easel, and as she leaned in to have a closer look, she realized it was the viscount at the center of the portrait, flanked by a man and a woman who resembled him.

"My brother and sister."

Hattie started with surprise—she hadn't heard anyone enter the room. She whirled around as he strolled toward her, smiling a little. He was dressed in riding clothes and had discarded his coat and rolled up his sleeves above the elbows. His trousers were splattered with mud. "My apologies for startling you." He moved to stand beside her. She detected a scent of rain and dirt, but there was also something distinctly masculine about it. She had a sudden image of him taking her in his arms, pressing her against his body, her head against his chest, just so that she could inhale him.

"Roberto and Sofia."

She mentally shook herself. "Do you miss them?"

"*Sí*, I do. Do you have siblings, Miss Woodchurch?"

"Three brothers. All of whom enjoy tormenting their sister."

"Ah. At one time, Sofia would have accused Roberto and me of the same." He moved away from her, his woodsy essence trailing behind him. Hattie closed her eyes a moment and imagined having that scent to accompany her through life. How safe she would feel. How aroused.

"Your brothers, they are in London?" he asked.

She opened her eyes and turned around. "They are. My

younger brothers—twins—are presently in school here in London. My older brother is here, too. You might have seen him—he was my escort to the Forsythe dinner."

This seemed to interest him; the viscount glanced up from his perusal of the documents on his desk. His gaze casually moved over her, a little more intently than usual. Or maybe she felt it more intently than usual, but it felt as if his gaze was actually touching her, stroking across the bare skin of her neck and her arm. "You didn't have a suitor to squire you there?"

Her pulse ticked up a little. "No."

He smiled. "I don't believe I made your brother's acquaintance. I'm certain I would have remembered a Mr. Woodchurch."

"I'm certain of it, too," she said with a near snort. "But I rather doubt anyone would have made the introduction."

"Why not?"

She would think it was obvious. "We are…unknown in the Forsythes' circle of friends." The Woodchurch name was not exactly a sought-after introduction in this town.

Lord Abbott's gaze moved over her again, and she resisted the urge to put a hand to her throat.

"How did you find the evening?" he asked.

Evening? What evening? She was feeling an electric thrumming through her. "Umm…" She glanced toward the window for a slender moment to gather herself. She would say it was lovely or some such. But her tongue moved ahead of her brain. "It was not what I expected."

Lord Abbott chuckled. "It was exactly what I expected. How do you mean?"

She'd expected to be swept away by the grandeur of the sort of party that went on behind the polished oak doors of a house like that. To meet a tall, strikingly handsome and wealthy man who would fall in love with her. To breathe the same air as the Quality, have them laugh at her wit and hang on her every word. Or, at the very least, enjoy herself instead of worrying about where she stood and whom to speak to. "I thought it would be more…interesting." She didn't think that was precisely the right word. She didn't know the right word.

"I have long hoped that dinners such as that will be interesting, but they rarely are. However, there was a musical performance to liven things, no?"

There was laughter dancing in his eyes, and Hattie couldn't keep herself from laughing out loud. "I most certainly was not expecting that."

He grinned. "Neither was I."

"I hope you won't think me the worst sort of friend to Miss Porter, but I fully expected someone would help end the agony! Then again, I suppose she must have worked hard to prepare, and it wouldn't be fair."

"We should have worked as hard to prepare to hear it."

Hattie laughed. The viscount smiled at her laughter, and somehow, their gazes held. She felt something shift between them. She was mad to think it, but in that moment, she believed that she and his lordship understood each other completely. There was an easiness to them. An agreement about the world that tethered them together.

"I must admit, Miss Woodchurch, you intrigue me. You're quite unexpected."

A lightness was filling her chest. "I am?"

"I wonder why you don't follow the well-trod path of privileged ladies."

"Privileged?" She laughed at that notion. "I am not privileged, my lord. But I gather that the well-trod path you are referring to is marriage? You are wondering why I haven't entered that holy state."

His smile was slow and a little sultry. "You understand me well. *Sí*, I have wondered why you are not. It is unusual at your age, no?"

"I suppose." The entire world wanted to put women into two categories: Married or Not Married. As if that was all there was to their lives! "I was engaged once." Regrettably, she sounded unintentionally defiant.

He merely held her gaze, waiting for her to fill in the rest. "But I cried off."

He nodded. He very politely did not ask why. But Hattie didn't want him to assume there was anything wrong with her, so she clarified, "He was perfectly fine, but my father is…particular."

She could feel a blush of shame creeping into her cheeks. There were many words to describe her father, but *particular* was not the best one. He was unreasonable, tight-fisted, surly, suspicious… She could think of any number of ways to describe him, but settled on the vague, "He's inexplicable, really."

The viscount steadily held her gaze, and Hattie's heart skipped a beat or two. "I understand—my father was inexplicable, too."

"I hope you're not saying so to be kind. Was he really?"

"He was. Does your father have an occupation?"

His occupation was lying in wait for her to come home every day. "He owns most of the public cabs around town. Hansoms and Clarence cabs. Horse busses."

"A lucrative endeavor in a town the size of London."

"One might assume, but I assure you my father would insist otherwise."

"Men and their money," he muttered. He glanced at his

desk, as if the conversation was over, but Hattie thought that it was only fair that he answer her burning question.

"Why have you never?"

He looked up. "Married? A personal question, Miss Woodchurch."

"So was yours."

He laughed lightly, and the sound of it was a caress. "That it was. *Dios mío*, Miss Woodchurch, how unguarded you are."

"I see no reason to be guarded—I trust you."

His smile faded. He seemed to take that information and tuck it away, his eyes wandering over her, leaving a warm trail across her body. "I've lived a solitary life, as you know. I suppose that is the reason why I've not yet married. I prefer the Castillo Estrella to the Valdonia palace. But I would wager you've deduced that much about me."

She hadn't deduced any such thing. "Have you lived that way by choice?"

"By choice. And by necessity."

What did *that* mean?

"Have you any more questions for me, Miss Woodchurch?"

He meant to end this inquiry, but Hattie had one last question. "Do you want to be married?"

He frowned with confusion. "*Sí*, I do. I'm no different from most in that I would like a family."

That was something, at least. Flora might be happy at the Castle in the Stars. But Hattie worried the "solitary" part of his life might be problematic for Flora—she liked to be surrounded by friends and family. To Hattie, it sounded like heaven.

"Now I must ask you, Miss Woodchurch—do you wish to be married?"

Since her engagement to Rupert had ended, Hattie hadn't

had the courage to ask herself that question. She didn't know the answer anymore. "I did."

His brows dipped into a slight frown of concern. "It saddens me to hear it. It saddens me to think a gentleman has hurt you so."

A rush of warmth spread through her and centered in her chest. No one, not a single person, had paid any heed to her after she ended her engagement to Rupert. As if her crying off had said all there was to say about it. Everyone around her seemed to believe she ought to be relieved it was over.

But nothing could have been further from the truth—she'd mourned Rupert. And then she'd despised him and everything he'd represented to her.

Mr. Borerro suddenly came into the room, interrupting the closeness she felt between them. "Lady Aleksander calling."

The viscount stood up from the desk. "Show her in. I'll join her in a few moments." He smiled sadly at Hattie and strode across the room.

And then he was gone.

CHAPTER EIGHTEEN

MR. BORERRO GREETED Lila at the door and took her umbrella and cloak. He asked her to wait and disappeared down the hall. Lila paused to pat her hair and make sure everything was in place. When Mr. Borerro returned, she happened to catch sight of a pin on Mr. Borerro's lapel in the mirror. She turned around. "Are you wearing a Tudor rose, sir?" she asked, peering at the pin on his lapel.

"*Sí.*"

"You're a student of English history! Where on earth did you find it?"

"It was a gift. Please follow me." He turned and began to walk.

Santiavans, Lila thought. They were so terribly reticent about every little thing. How did they survive the winters, gathered around the hearth, no one uttering a word? No wonder Elizabeth was so frequently in Madrid or Paris.

He escorted her to the study, where she was fully prepared to find another reticent Santiavan but, instead, found Miss Woodchurch. Alone. The young woman stood up from her desk when Lila entered and curtsied.

Lila could not have been more delighted. For the first time in many years, she'd been dreading a meeting with a client—she was certain she wouldn't get a thing out of Lord Abbott, and the only thing she knew about the Forsythe dinner was that she'd arranged to have three perfectly suitable women introduced to him, and he'd left with no clear, discernible interest in any of them.

His demeanor all evening had been reserved. The only time he seemed to have enjoyed himself was when he stood in the back of the music room next to his scribe.

"Miss Woodchurch!" she trilled.

The young woman was dressed in a drab gray gown, worn at the hem and cuffs of the sleeves. Her hair was done up in a pleasing fashion, but a tendril had escaped and drifted down one side of her face. She had pretty blue eyes, which Lila had admired before, and a healthy glow to her skin. Miss Woodchurch was attractive, really, if one looked closely enough. What was it Beck had said about her? Lila tried to pull the nugget of memory to the forefront.

"I must say you're looking well rested from the weekend! I hardly left my bed Sunday, I was so exhausted," Lila said.

Miss Woodchurch eyed her warily.

Lila took a seat on the settee and set her bag aside. "Just between us chicks, have you seen the viscount today?"

"Briefly."

Lila looked around the room. No tea or pastries, she was sorry to see. She didn't know what magic was working in the kitchens here, but they had the best pastries in town. She leaned back and fixed her gaze on Miss Woodchurch, who was still standing. "What did you think of the Forsythe dinner? Was it to your liking?"

"Yes," she said. "It was lovely. Thank you for arranging the invitation."

"It *was* lovely, wasn't it? Although I am not as fond of lamb as others. Do you like lamb? And the sponge cake I thought a bit dry. Tell me, darling, what did you think of the ladies his lordship met?"

"Pardon?"

"You must have some opinions, and don't you dare tell me you don't, as *everyone* has an opinion on most things."

Miss Woodchurch smiled nervously. "I thought the sponge cake was very good."

"But what about the ladies?"

She looked toward the door, as if she hoped that the viscount would enter and save her. "Really, I... No one cares what I think."

"Au contraire, my dear. I do, or I wouldn't have asked. You were there. You saw them. By your own admission, you know them."

"Yes, but I don't—"

"Whatever you say will be kept in the strictest confidence." Lila suddenly stood and moved to stand before Miss Woodchurch. She glanced over her shoulder at the door, and said softly, "You may have noticed that his lordship is not exactly keen on sharing his views. That is so typical of men—they seem to think it too revealing to state their likes and dislikes. You understand me, don't you?"

"I don't think so," Miss Woodchurch said, and took a step back.

Lila matched her by stepping forward. "I only want to make the best match for the viscount, as I'm sure you do, too. You admire him, don't you?"

"Yes, but—"

"I'm only asking for your opinion on who you think might suit him, as you know him better than anyone."

"No," Miss Woodchurch said emphatically. She stepped back again. "You really must stop saying that. You have mistaken me, Lady Aleksander. I don't know him at all, really."

Again, Lila matched her by stepping forward. "Please call me Lila. And what do your friends call you?"

Miss Woodchurch stared at her.

"Harriet, isn't it?"

"Hattie."

"Hattie! What a lovely name. All right, Hattie, let's start with Miss Porter, the renowned beauty."

Miss Woodchurch squared her shoulders. "I don't know, *Lila*," she said firmly.

Lila liked this girl. "Did you enjoy her performance?"

Hattie blinked.

"Oh dear."

"I didn't say anything!"

"But you're thinking it."

Hattie sighed. She glanced over Lila's shoulder to the door, then whispered, "Did *anyone* enjoy her performance? I daresay her own mother was dismayed."

"It was *wretched*," Lila agreed. "Who has allowed that poor dear to believe her singing voice is to be admired? I thought my ears would bleed. I assume his lordship thought it untenable, too."

"I didn't say that," Hattie said again.

"You didn't have to. I saw the two of you at the back of the room."

Hattie pressed her lips together and glared at Lila.

"What of Miss Cupperson?"

Hattie folded her arms across her middle. "I know what you're doing."

"Of course you do, because you're a clever young woman. What of Miss Cupperson?"

"Dahlia Cupperson is practical and dependable and has many admirable qualities. Frankly, I wish I were even half as practical and dependable—"

"But she's not very attractive, is she," Lila said, wincing a little.

Hattie's eyes rounded.

"I know, you didn't say that. I said it. I realized it myself Saturday evening when I saw her with the viscount. They did not make a handsome couple."

Hattie's mouth gaped open with shock.

"Darling, I *must* think of these things. For the rest of the world, it is the compatibility of souls that matter. But for this lot…" She shrugged. "And the red dress did not suit her. Which brings us to Miss Raney."

Hattie blushed almost instantly. "She likes to read, and so does his lordship."

"Interesting," Lila said, eyeing Hattie shrewdly. "Her love of reading did not come up when I interviewed her. But that is a point in her favor, isn't it?"

"Miss Raney is a good person."

"Of course she is, or she would not be on my list." Lila smiled. "There, you see? That wasn't so bad." She turned and went back to the settee. This was perfect—having Miss Woodchurch in close proximity to the viscount was exactly the sort of help she needed. "You know, Hattie, we could be a team."

Hattie snorted.

An idea came to Lila as she resumed her seat on the settee. "The commission for a successful match is very generous," she said. "I would be willing to share a percentage of it in exchange for a little help."

Hattie looked aghast. "I beg your pardon?"

"Good Lord, I'm not suggesting anything criminal. Close your mouth and listen—I'm asking for assistance and I am willing to pay you a fair wage for it. With a bit of information from you, I can help guide the viscount to a successful match."

But Hattie continued to look at her agape. *"No."*

"I very much like that about you," Lila said breezily. "You have principles. But have a think."

And she would, too. There was something niggling at Lila. Hattie was an employee of the viscount and, by that fact alone, entirely unsuitable as a potential match. Not to mention the thing Beck had brought up about Hattie that Lila was trying to recall. And yet, after refining her list for the viscount to include London's most eligible ladies, Lila couldn't dismiss the feeling that the best match for the viscount might be in this room right now.

"Lady Aleksander."

They both turned to the door as Lord Abbott strode in, looking handsome and aloof and clean. He was carrying a sheath of papers, which he handed to Hattie.

Lila knew of only one other man who was handsome in a way that could startle, and that was Mr. Donovan. She couldn't even say her own beloved husband, Valentin, was as handsome as this one. He reminded her of a lion—beautiful, and quietly observant, his hazel eyes following her every move. From the lift of her hand to tuck back a wisp of hair, to the way she sank into a curtsy. It seemed almost criminal that his eyelashes were so dark and long when women her age mixed cream and soot to darken theirs.

He bowed. "Welcome."

"Thank you for receiving me, my lord. Hattie and I were just discussing the Forsythe dinner."

"Hattie?" he said, and glanced at Miss Woodchurch, who looked wide-eyed with panic.

"She enjoyed the evening," Lila said. "Did you?"

"It was perfectly fine." His voice was flat. He had not enjoyed it—as if she'd needed to be told that.

"I won't take up much of your time, my lord. I think we

can agree that perhaps Miss Porter, despite her beauty, is probably not suited for a life in Santiava."

To her surprise, the viscount looked almost relieved. "We can agree."

"You spoke at some length with Miss Cupperson. Should I assume there is some interest there?"

"On the contrary—Miss Cupperson spoke at some length as I listened. She is a new and enthusiastic student of Santiava."

Lila chuckled. "You can't fault a lady for preparing."

He said nothing. Bloody *hell*, this man was difficult. "And Miss Raney?" she asked.

He clasped his hands behind his back. He nodded curtly. "She spoke about a book she'd read. Something to do with unrequited love."

"Unrequited love!" Lila exclaimed. "That seems rather a gloomy subject, doesn't it?"

The viscount smiled. "Perhaps as gloomy as keeping one's mad wife in the attic."

"Oh!" Hattie said, smiling. "You read *Jane Eyre*!"

"I have begun to read it. Tell me, Miss Woodchurch, why are English ladies drawn to such dark tales of love?"

She laughed. "We are drawn to tales of love in its many forms, I suppose. But if I may, *Honorine* is really more about the state of a marriage. Not unrequited love, precisely."

Surprised, Lila and the viscount looked at her. "You've read this book?" the viscount asked.

"Yes. We all did. It was assigned in school."

"Then perhaps you will be kind enough to explain it to me. How can it be about unrequited love and marriage in the same breath?"

"It's about a wife who was unhappy in her marriage. And

a husband determined to do whatever he could to prove to her that she was not."

"Really? Why, because he knew her feelings better than she did?" Lila drawled.

"I think because he so desperately wanted it to be so," Hattie said. "Desperate desire can cause people to do desperate things."

Both the viscount and Lila looked once again at Hattie with some surprise.

Hattie shrugged. "That was my reading of it, anyway. I beg your pardon, I'm speaking out of turn."

"Not at all," the viscount said. "I welcome your viewpoint."

Hattie blushed.

That was the moment Lila realized these two were speaking another language altogether, and not about books. "It would appear we have a reading club!" she said grandly. "If you will allow me to pass on an invitation, my lord, I shall take my leave."

He gestured for her to continue.

"Lord and Lady Iddesleigh are hosting a garden tea later this week. Lord and Lady Raney and their lovely daughter will be in attendance."

Lord Abbott said nothing. He had retreated back behind his private internal screen. Frankly, Lila had never seen him come out from behind that screen except to speak to Hattie. How very interesting.

"In addition, Lady Mabel Stanhope, the daughter of the Earl of Stanhope, will be in attendance. She has thirty thousand pounds a year from an inheritance."

"A king's ransom," the viscount said dryly, and looked at Hattie. "Are you acquainted with Lady Mabel Stanhope?"

"No, my lord. I know her only by name."

He shifted his gaze to Lila.

"There will be others in attendance as well, including myself."

"I'd be astonished if you were not, Lady Aleksander."

Lila smiled thinly. "I will take that as your express desire to have me on hand," she said airily. "And, Miss Woodchurch, I think you ought to come, too."

"What? Why?"

"Why not? Lord Iddesleigh is quite fond of you and will be delighted to see you."

"I don't think… I'm sure he's seen quite enough of me."

"You wouldn't mind, would you, my lord, if your scribe was in attendance?"

His gaze narrowed slightly. "Not at all, madam."

Oh, but he was a difficult, *difficult* client. But she would not be beaten at this game.

He glanced at his pocket watch. "I beg your pardon, but I am expected across town."

Lila stood up. "That's all I have. Thank you for your time, my lord. I look forward to the garden tea." She swept out of the room, her mind already racing ahead.

She suddenly had a new mission, and that was to find out everything she could about one Miss Harriet Woodchurch.

CHAPTER NINETEEN

BETWEEN THE WORK for Mrs. O'Malley, Flora's increasingly hectic engagement calendar, and her work for Lord Abbott, every day was ending in something of a blur for Hattie.

Her days that week with Lord Abbott were a bit longer than normal. They were talking more—the stoic, reticent man she'd first encountered in this study was slowly coming around to it.

One afternoon, after he'd given her the work he had for her, she'd started for her desk. "Miss Woodchurch."

She paused and turned back. "Yes, my lord?"

"Your book. It was quite…" He paused, frowning a little. "Romantic?"

He looked at her aghast. *"Horrifying."*

"Horrifying?"

"The man imprisoned his wife in an attic."

Hattie smiled wryly. "Well, yes…but in his defense, she was mad."

"You don't honestly believe—"

"No!" she exclaimed with a laugh. "But wouldn't you agree that in a work of fiction, certain liberties are allowed?"

"That's quite the liberty," he said.

They spent the afternoon debating on and off if the tale of Jane Eyre was one of an immoral affair or a passionate love story.

And then when a letter came from Harrington Hall, they laughed with bafflement to discover that the sheep had at long last been delivered...along with fourteen head of cattle.

He told her the next dreary afternoon that he missed seeing the stars, that the sky was too dense over London. He said he was an amateur astronomer. "When I was a child, my uncle gave me a telescope. Have you ever looked at the stars through a telescope?"

She shook her head. "The lights and smoke obscure the night sky in London."

"In Santiava, you can see them clearly. But the telescope... it opened a new world for me. I became very interested in stars. Unfortunately, my tutors knew very little, and my father thought it a waste of my time. When I became duke, I was successful in bringing a famous astronomer to teach at our university in Valdonia."

She imagined him as a boy, looking through a telescope to a world far away from this one.

One thing Lord Abbott did not talk about was the young women he was supposed to be considering. Hattie had penned replies to invitations and knew he'd been to dine at some very elegant homes. Lady Aleksander came only once more that week, and when Lord Abbott refused to say much, she'd left with a huff of exasperation. When she'd gone, he looked at Hattie and smiled. "I don't think the lady cares for me."

"Oh, I think she hates you," Hattie said, and he had chuckled.

Every day that passed, she felt his presence pressing against her, wrapping around her like a blanket. She thought she'd never been as happy as she was those afternoons in his study. But in the end, he always sent her for tea, and when she returned with the pastry of the day, he was already gone.

But on this particular afternoon, he was waiting for her when she returned from tea with two petit fours. He asked her if she would retrieve some papers from Mr. Callum's office. "If you will allow me to impose on you," he said. "I generally send Señor Pacheco, but he is indisposed."

Mr. Pacheco had been eating rose hips all week. "I warned him about those rose hips," she murmured.

"Pardon?"

"I'd be happy to retrieve them, my lord." She set the petit fours on the corner of his desk.

The viscount didn't seem to notice them; he dragged his fingers through his hair and looked at her in such a way she knew he wanted to say more. Anticipation was rising in her—she couldn't imagine what he would say, but she sensed it was something personal. His gaze floated over her, settling on her lips, sparking a slow burn in her groin. It was that look he'd given her more than once in the past few days, a gaze with a bit of heat behind it. And maybe a question mark. Whatever it was, it made her heart pick up steam, made her feel a little dizzy.

But he pressed his lips together and looked down. "That will be all for today."

Disappointment settled on her. She wanted more. It felt as if they'd become friends in a way, but it wasn't enough. Hattie wanted to find all the reasons to stay and talk to him. She wanted to ask him what his greatest fear was, what his greatest love was. She wanted to know everything about him, no matter how inappropriate.

She walked to the door. *Call me back. Call me back!*

He did not call her back.

In the hall, Hattie drew some very deep breaths to rid herself of the dizziness. She didn't understand what was happening between them. Were they becoming friends?

Because she never felt short of breath with friends. Did he ever feel short of breath? Did he believe them to be friends? It was entirely possible that he felt nothing about her, nothing at all. That made the most sense, really—she was as unsuitable for him as Yolanda or Aurelia.

He was being kind to her, and she was lusting after him. She couldn't help herself.

RAIN WAS POURING from the skies when Hattie arrived at Mr. Callum's office. She shook her umbrella out, smoothed her cloak, and walked down the hall to where a bronze plaque proclaimed Mr. Callum could be found within that room. She rapped on the door.

A moment later it swung open, and the portly estate agent eyed her suspiciously. "His lordship sent you," he stated disapprovingly.

Hattie lifted her chin. "It's certainly not a social call."

He snorted. He turned and walked into his cluttered office. He didn't invite Hattie to follow, but she did anyway. He often had the look of someone who wanted to slam a door in her face. She had no idea what had caused his animosity toward her—she guessed it had everything to do with her being a woman and working for her livelihood. She was aware how many people viewed that with disdain.

Mr. Callum went to his desk and rummaged through some papers, then found a packet. He held it against his chest. "You're not to look at the contents. You're to take it straightaway to the viscount. I'll know if you haven't, so don't you dare try and fool me."

What could she possibly want with the contents of that packet? "What is it? A king's ransom?"

"You should watch your mouth," he said, and held out the packet.

Hattie reached for it with a forefinger and thumb and extracted it like it was dripping with poison. "You have no cause for concern, Mr. Callum. I know my responsibilities and what I stand to lose by ignoring them."

"*Do* you," he said with a sneer. "I have never cared for immodest women."

Immodest! "I can't imagine they have cared for you, either, sir. Good day." She turned and walked out of his office, wild with fury. He had taken an instant dislike to her from the moment he'd laid eyes on her. What was it to him what she did with her life? Why did so many people in the world believe they had a say in any woman's life?

But Hattie was proud of herself as she snapped open her umbrella. There had been a time she would have crumbled had a man spoken to her in that way. She would have blamed herself for it, would have thought she was too forward, too unladylike. But when one suffered a broken engagement for no good reason, one tended to look at some men with suspicion.

She supposed she could thank Rupert for that, at least—he'd made it easier for her to respond to the foolishness of men like Mr. Callum.

Frankly, he'd made it easier to cease caring what anyone thought of her.

It was still pouring rain when she reached Grosvenor Square with the packet. It was well past teatime, and the lamplighters were already out, moving down the street to each lamppost. Hattie entered through the servants' entrance as she normally did, dropped her umbrella, and removed her cloak. It was soaked through. She decided to take it to the kitchen and let it dry by the hearth before she started home. She could probably persuade Yolanda to give her something to eat. Maybe there were still some petit fours.

She walked into the kitchen with her cloak over one arm, Mr. Callum's packet in her other hand…but it wasn't Yolanda behind the rough-hewn kitchen table. It was Lord Abbott. And he was wearing an apron. And there was a dash of flour on his cheek.

Hattie froze in place, trying to make sense of the scene before her. He was with the older woman who'd accidentally splashed her with mop water her first day here. She couldn't help but gape at them both.

Lord Abbott looked mortified. "Ah…" He looked around him, grabbed a towel, and began to wipe his hands. The woman, however, smiled as if she'd been expecting Hattie. She said something to him in Spanish.

The viscount shot a look of exasperation at the older woman. "Miss Woodchurch, what are you doing here at this hour?"

"I brought the packet from Mr. Callum?" She held it up so he could see.

"Yes, of course." He frowned. "You walked here in the rain?"

"Yes, my lord." She set the packet on the end of the kitchen table. And when she did, she noticed the several balls of dough spaced apart on the table. Was he—she was surely mistaken—but was Lord Abbott *baking*? He had to be. The apron, the flour on his cheek!

The woman noticed her gaze and spoke again to the viscount, who responded softly, almost in a whisper. The woman put her hand on his arm and spoke again. There was a familiarity between them that made Hattie think she must be his grandmother. Now, whatever Hattie thought she knew about aristocracy was evaporating. Would the Duke of Santiava and his duchess grandmother enter a kitchen, much less prepare food? Lord, her parents only aspired to such lofty titles, and *they* never entered a kitchen.

Lord Abbott sighed. "Señora de Leon would have me beg you forgive her for not speaking English. But I will tell you she understands English perfectly well. She doesn't speak it as well as she would like." He shot the woman a look. "Nevertheless, she wishes to make your acquaintance. Properly."

"Oh." Hattie swept a bit of rain from her cheek. "Of course."

"May I present Señora de Leon," he said. "She has been with my family for all my life."

Apparently not his grandmother, then.

To the lady, he said, "Miss Woodchurch, my study assistant."

Hattie curtsied. "A pleasure, madam."

The señora smiled and said to Hattie, "Miss Woodchurch, please." She gestured Hattie to come to the table.

"Oh no, please—I wouldn't dream of interrupting your..." She gestured to the balls of dough. "Evening."

"She would like to show you," Lord Abbott said. "Please," he added.

Hattie draped her cloak over a chair near the hearth, tried to smooth her hair made curly by the damp, and then very hesitantly came forward, as if she was being asked to view some strange creature children had found swimming about in the Thames. It was only balls of dough, but the atmosphere was strangely intimate, and she couldn't quite grasp what role the viscount was playing here.

The woman touched his arm and spoke again. The viscount sighed to the rafters then said, "As you can see...we are making empanadas."

"Empanadas," Hattie repeated. *We*, she thought.

Señora de Leon picked up a rolling pin and began to roll out one of the balls of dough. When it was flattened, she picked up a bowl and spooned out a mixture of meat, onions, and mushrooms onto half the dough. She folded the other half over the mixture, then crimped the dough together to form a seal, creating a bun of sorts. She basted both sides with egg.

She narrated as she went—in Spanish, of course. Hattie had no idea what she was saying. And the viscount did not translate. He was watching Hattie, his expression sheepish but curious.

Señora de Leon went on to do three more just like the first, then moved to the oven, and pulled out a sheet with several of the cooked buns. Lord Abbott placed them on a plate, and Señora de Leon cut one into small triangles. She and Lord Abbott each forked a triangle and sampled it. They looked at each other, nodding, discussing it with a few words, but clearly agreeing.

Señora de Leon picked up the plate and held it out to Hattie for a sample. The viscount handed her a fork.

Hattie hadn't eaten all day, and the smell alone was enough for her to abandon all good graces. *"Gracias,"* she said, to the delight of Señora de Leon, forked the piece, and bit into it.

It was scrumptious. The burst of flavors was spicy and salty and with a hint of something she'd never tasted in her life. "Oh *my*," she said. "Oh my, this is so *good*."

Señora de Leon laughed. She spoke again to the viscount, pointing at various things on the table and in the kitchen, then removed her apron. To Hattie she said, "Good evening."

Hattie, still chewing, watched her go, then turned to the viscount in confusion. "Where is she going?"

"She is retiring for the evening. She's left it to me."

"You?"

"Is it shocking that I enjoy baking?"

"Yes!" Hattie said emphatically.

He gave her a lopsided smile. "I won't defend myself against my hobby."

His hobby? Something clicked in Hattie's brain. "I beg your pardon, but…are *you* the cook behind the wonderful pastries served with tea?"

His smile deepened. "Not always. But *sí*, sometimes."

Hattie laughed with delight. "You never said! How did you let me bring them to you to try?"

"I'm not above a bit of flattery, Miss Woodchurch. You've been an enthusiastic admirer of my attempts and I didn't want to risk your praise revealing my secret. But it's true—I very much like to bake. There is something satisfying in it. Will you help me finish?" He gestured to the many balls of dough still left to bake. "We meant to make enough for the week."

Hattie didn't hesitate. "I would." She went to the pump and washed her hands, then returned to his side of the table. He held out an apron. "May I?" He stepped behind her and wrapped the apron around her waist, tying it off in the small of her back. When he'd finished, he put his hands on her shoulders and turned her around to face the table.

And just like that, her breath left her. It was the lightest of touches, but her shoulders were tingling where his hands had been. And now she was standing so close to him she was certain the warmth she felt was the heat of his body. Her heart was racing, her pulse fluttering, and when she glanced up, she discovered he was looking at her, his eyes shining with pleasure.

There was that spark again. That low burn of want in

her body. This man had the capacity to turn her to a heap of ash if she looked too long.

"Do you bake, Miss Woodchurch?"

"Not at all," she confessed. "How long have you?"

"A few years. Since the time I was small, I desired to learn to create the pastries that are common in Santiava. But my father...he would not have liked it. After he died, Rosa—Señora de Leon—began to teach me." He poured flour into a bowl, along with butter, eggs, milk, and salt. He handed her the bowl and a wooden spoon. "Please, will you blend it together?"

She began to mix the ingredients. He rolled out some of the balls of dough as Señora de Leon had, and filled them as she had. "Are you Hattie, then, in your family's home?" he asked.

She smiled. "I'm Hattie everywhere, really. My parents call me by my given name, Harriet. But everyone else calls me Hattie."

"I like it, this name. Hattie," he said, as if trying it on. "It suits you."

She was ridiculously pleased that he liked it. "What does Señora de Leon call you?"

He hesitated briefly. "Teo. My family calls me Teo. Only my father used my given name, Mateo."

Teo. Hattie imagined whispering his name in his ear. "I like it, this name. Teo," she said, mimicking what he'd said about her name. "It suits you." She peeked at him from the corner of her eye.

He smiled. "Then you have my leave to address me by that name. And I shall call you Hattie."

"Really?"

"Why not? We are too much together to be so formal."

"But...does the rest of the staff call you Teo?"

"No," he said emphatically, but his eyes crinkled with his smile. "It's different with you, is it not? You're not a servant."

She was relieved and flattered that he didn't think of her as a servant. But it begged the question of how he did think of her. "Then what am I?" she asked.

"My scribe."

Of course. She glanced down, disappointed by his answer. She didn't know what he'd say, but she'd certainly hoped for better. Friend, at least.

He continued to roll the balls of dough. "She likes you. I can see it—Rosa likes you very much."

"She was being kind. How could she possibly have formed any opinion of me after such a short meeting?"

"Most people form opinions quickly, no? She likes the look of you," he said. "Have you mixed it?" He leaned over to have a look at her bowl. He *tsked* at what he saw and took the bowl and spoon from her, then vigorously mixed the contents before handing it back to her. "Now then," he said. He sprinkled some flour on the table. "Empty the contents here."

"Onto the table?"

"Sí."

Hattie did as he instructed, then watched as he showed her how to turn and knead the mixture with her hands. Hattie shoved her fingers into the dough, but it kept sticking to her. "No, no," he said. "You must find a rhythm. May I?" he asked, but he was already at her back. And now he was reaching around her.

"Oh," Hattie murmured. Her heart began to race again. She felt too warm, and yet, not warm enough.

"Are you uncomfortable?" he asked into her ear.

Only if one considered it uncomfortable when one's

blood turned to fire. She shook her head. She was something else—alert. Sensitive. And definitely not a scribe.

"Like this," he said softly, and covered her hands with his, his fingers twining with hers to knead the dough.

Hattie could feel his hard chest at her back. She could detect his cologne. She wanted nothing more than to lean back into him and close her eyes, feel his arms encircle her.

"Do you feel it?" he asked, his voice softer still. "How the dough yields to the pressure of your fingers?"

When he spoke to her like that, with his lovely accent, she thought she would do anything he asked. She was hardly conscious of what he was doing, really—the feel of his body so close to hers and the desire creeping up her spine made it impossible to think. His hands moved alongside hers, turning and kneading, pushing the dough with the flat of his hand, then squeezing it with his fingers. "I feel…everything." Words had deserted her. She felt hot, as if steam was rising out from the neck of her gown. Her heart fluttered madly, trying to find a beat that would allow her to keep standing and not implode.

But then he asked her, "I should like to know what it means, desperate desire."

Had she said that out loud? Or had he felt her heart racing, heard her tortured breath? "Pardon?"

"You said it about the book."

Ah, of course. She'd said it about *Honorine*.

"I meant only a desire for something that you'd move heaven and earth to have, only to discover they can't be moved. It would make one frantic."

He stopped kneading the dough but kept his hands on hers. "Have you ever felt a desire so desperate?"

She immediately thought of Rupert. That had been another kind of desire. That had been a desire for respectability. For a life outside her family. But it had not been *desperate* desire—it had not made her ache with longing.

"I don't think so." She drew a breath. "Have you?"

"Until this moment," he said, his breath warm on her neck, "I have never wanted for anything."

Her breath deserted her. She turned her head slightly, to see him, but he was behind her, and she couldn't see his face. But she could feel him, hard against her back, his chest broad, his body lean, his arms pure strength. She flushed from the feel of him, from the desire that was surging through her, turning desperate. From the magnetism of this beautiful man that was making her forget her own name.

She turned so that she was facing him, still trapped between his arms and the table. She couldn't look away from his hazel eyes—she was mesmerized. She couldn't stop her mind from racing, couldn't stop her heart from urging her to live life, to experience it.

His gaze moved down her face, to her mouth, to her bodice. She felt something stirring in her, and it felt like... *love*. She was falling in love with the viscount. "Until this moment, neither have I."

His gaze turned smoldering. He reached up and touched a stubborn tendril of her hair that always worked its way free of her coif and tucked it behind her ear. Hattie still couldn't seem to find her breath. With his knuckle, he traced her jaw, then touched the tip of his finger to her bottom lip. It had come to this—in what felt like a fleeting moment, she'd gone from scribe to this, and she looked at his mouth, at his plush, full lips, and she'd never wanted to be kissed so badly in her life. "My lord—"

"Teo," he said, and lowered his head to hers.

Oh, but he kissed her. Not chastely, not in a way that

could confuse a woman as to his intent. It was a real kiss, one that was full of a man's desire, full of an understanding that they both wanted this to happen. His lips were succulent, the tip of his tongue playful. His teeth grazed her bottom lip, his lips moved against hers. He cupped her face, angling it just so, and just when she thought she could bear it no longer…she could feel the heat of his body, felt as if she ought to rip her gown apart for air as he leaned against her, his body hard and lean and pulsing.

He kissed her and she kissed him back, wrapping her arms around his neck, pressing back against him. She felt fluid, molding to him everyplace they touched.

But then he lifted his head. A lock of hair had fallen over one of his eyes, his gaze full of want. But he pushed back from the table.

"That was badly done," he said. "I should not have taken such liberty."

She couldn't do anything but stare at the very handsome face that had just kissed her.

"I do beg your pardon."

"Please don't."

He wiped his hand on his apron and pushed the tendril of hair behind his ear. "I lost myself in a moment, and that is unfair to you."

"What? Why?" How could it be unfair? Before there was ever a Rupert, Hattie would have demurred, would have allowed him to have the last say. But she wasn't that person any longer. "I disagree."

Teo looked at her with such sorrow. In that look he conveyed it all—she was beneath him, she could never be his. She was an employee that he'd dallied with and now he regretted it. She felt indignant. And hurt. She would not be another man's regret.

Hattie picked up a towel and wiped her hands. She walked around the table to the hearth and picked up her cloak, aware that he was watching her. She donned her cloak and pulled the hood over her head.

"Hattie...you're leaving?"

"I am," she said. She felt calm. Unnaturally calm.

"I'll have someone drive you—"

"I prefer to walk." She didn't sound angry, she hoped. She wasn't angry, precisely. She was frustrated. Not by him—well, a little by him—but really, the rules of society. He was doing what a gentleman ought to do—extracting himself from a situation that had no end. Apologizing for acting on his desires.

She braced her hand against the kitchen table across from him, wanting to convey her frustration but feeling out of place. She drew a breath. "A kiss can only be unfair if just one party wanted it. But when two people are both lost in a moment and desire it, I don't see how it can be viewed as anything but fair."

"By virtue of my position in this house. In life," he said earnestly. "I took unfair advantage of you, Hattie. You must see that. Please accept my apology."

"I won't," she said back to him. "You can't take advantage of me when I understand my own actions. I may be a lowly scribe in your house, but I am fully aware of myself and the consequences of what I do. I wish you a good night." She turned and started out of the kitchen, back out into what was now night.

"Hattie! Will I see you Wednesday?"

"Of course!" she called back, a little more sternly than she would have liked. As if one kiss would chase her from a position she sorely needed. Men were such fools.

She found her umbrella and fled into the wet night of London.

She grew increasingly agitated as she sloshed through the streets. She was furious with herself for falling in love with that man. It made her furious because she was *not* a fool. She knew in her heart that he didn't view her as a prospective match, and really, how could he? Even if she was so lucky to have the most handsome man in Europe fall in love with her, there would be the issue of her place in society with no connections, and worse, her family.

Her wholly unacceptable, greedy family.

No, a match between them was out of the question. But that didn't mean she would shove her feelings down into a dark hole and bury them, as much as she would like to. Time on this earth was precious, and in some ways, time was for her even more precious. She was young yet, but she wouldn't be forever. She was not far from being a spinster that no one would care about.

She would make the most of this opportunity while she could.

She would *not* shy away from it or her feelings. Because deep in her soul, Hattie knew she would probably never feel this way again.

CHAPTER TWENTY

FLORA WAS RIFLING through her wardrobe in search of something to wear to the garden party. She'd already tried on several beautiful dresses while Hattie and Queenie watched, but nothing suited her.

"Are those new?" Queenie asked, surveying the gowns Flora had discarded onto her bed.

"Yes," Flora said absently and held up a pale yellow gown to her body in the mirror. "I told my mother the yellow makes me look sallow." She whirled from the mirror. "Do I look sallow?"

"You look beautiful," Hattie said.

"Perhaps a bit sallow," Queenie added.

With a huff, Flora tossed the gown aside and returned to the wardrobe, and Hattie shot Queenie a look that Queenie very much ignored.

"I don't know why you're in such a dither," Queenie said. "Christiana Porter has removed herself from consideration. She said she found him boring. She said he hardly spoke at all."

"It is far more likely that he found her singing intolerable," Flora said. "I thought you said her singing was passable, Queenie. It was wretched."

"How should I know?" Queenie asked. "I only know what people tell me."

Hattie had to stifle a snort at that one. Queenie said

whatever she wished to be true, and quite often without any evidence at all.

"Dahlia Cupperson is still considered a potential match. Her family means to host a ball in his honor."

"A *ball*?" Flora looked helplessly at them.

"What?" Queenie asked. "Why do you look at me like that?"

"My father refuses to host the viscount at all. He said it isn't our place to create opportunities to see him, not unless his intentions are better known. Really, what's the use of all this—the viscount will never find anything to recommend me, and I hardly care. I don't want to live in Santiava, anyway."

"You may not want to live in Santiava, but you do want to be rich, darling," Queenie said. "Once you've married him and given him his heirs, you can return to London and lord it over all of us. Oh! Did I tell you? Mabel Stanhope has been invited to the Iddesleigh tea."

"Stanhope?" With a groan, Flora sank to the floor and folded over her knees. "I don't want to go."

"Nonsense. You must go so that you can tell me everything," Queenie said gaily.

A maid appeared at the door. "Miss Rodham, a carriage has arrived for you."

"Already!" Queenie complained. She slowly stood up, then stretched her arms high overhead. "Don't worry, Flora, darling. You're every bit as desirable as anyone else. Not as rich, mind, but still desirable. I'll see you tomorrow?"

Flora nodded, and Queenie went out of the room. Somehow, Hattie managed to not kick her in the rump when she passed by.

"Oh, Hattie," Flora moaned. "You understand me. What

am I even doing? My parents are over the moon for this man. But I couldn't think of a single thing to say to him! And don't you dare suggest I talk to him about a *book*. I know you were trying to help me, but really, Hattie. No *books*."

"No books. I understand," Hattie said patiently.

"But do you really?" she asked mournfully. Flora could get petulant when she was distressed. "I'm not good enough for him. It's so obvious!"

"Nothing could be further from the truth!"

"I swear it is. The man is intelligent and kind, and he's handsome, and he's a duke and a viscount and he doesn't belong with someone like *me*. What have I got to entice him? I'm not a beauty like Christiana or a brain like Dahlia, or even a kind spirit like Mabel."

Hattie moved to sit beside her friend on the floor. "You're better than all of them. You're kind, too, and smart, and you're as worthy as anyone in all of England. Moreover, *I* think he rather likes you."

"Why?" She pinned Hattie with a look. "Did he *say* so? Has he told you something?"

"No, no—but I could see it. The way he looked at you. It was quite clear."

Flora rubbed her nose. "Do you really think so?" she asked meekly.

"I do."

Flora managed a bit of a smile and sat up from her slump. "But what do I *say*? I'm so flustered when I'm near him and I turn into a cake."

"Well," Hattie said, crisscrossing her legs beneath her skirt, "he likes the study of stars. And history. Although I think he is more inclined to military history than any other."

She glanced away, thinking of what else she knew

about him. But when she looked back, Flora was eyeing her strangely.

"What?"

"You seem to know a lot about him for someone who is stuck in a closet, writing letters."

Hattie could feel a bit of heat in her cheeks. She felt conspicuous, almost as if her lips were still swollen from that kiss. It suddenly occurred to her that Flora might discover one day, after she was married and a duchess and a mother, that Hattie had once kissed her husband. She felt a little sick.

Flora was still watching her, so Hattie forced a smile. "I work in the same room as him. But…they are only things I've heard from the other servants."

The *other* servants? Had she reduced herself to a servant? What else could she be?

Flora suddenly laughed and reached across the space between them, giving Hattie's arm an affectionate squeeze. "For a moment, I let my imagination run wild. I can't help imagining that *everyone* in London is better suited for him than I am." She laughed again and shook her head, as if marveling over the fact that for a moment, she'd been so ridiculous to think that even Hattie Woodchurch was better suited to a match with Lord Abbott than her.

Hattie swallowed down the hurt.

"All right, tell me again what he likes," Flora said, her enthusiasm renewed, and settled back, ready to be tutored.

So Hattie did. She told her the subjects she might broach, and how to discuss them. She said to mention the stars in a way that suggested she found them romantic. To indicate her interest in him as something other than a friend. And by all means, to ask him about Santiava.

And while she talked, her stomach twisted into a knot

of despair and anger. Was it really so impossible to believe that she might be suited to Lord Abbott? All her life, she'd been viewed as second best. A different class. Someone to be befriended, but never taken seriously.

She was sick to death of it.

CHAPTER TWENTY-ONE

AT THE IDDESLEIGH mansion in Mayfair, Lila was shown to the grand salon. She could hear the voices coming from that room as she followed the butler down the hall, and when she stepped inside, it seemed as if everyone was in the process of dismantling the room. Balls of yarn, needles, and embroidery patterns were strewn about. Papers and books, cloaks and hats, all looked as if they'd been joyously blasted into the air by cannon and then left where they'd landed.

The other thing she noticed was that there were a *lot* of females. They were literally everywhere! The entire Hawke family was gathered in the salon on that dreary gray afternoon, including three small dogs. It was a madhouse.

Maisie, the middle child, scarcely looked at Lila, as she was in the middle of arguing with her mother about her desire to call on someone. Lady Iddesleigh—or Blythe, as Lila knew her now—wouldn't hear of it. She said it was too damp, and that she would not risk her daughter catching her death.

"We're *prisoners* here!" Maisie exclaimed with theatrical flair.

Beck was at a writing desk, randomly barking at everyone to "keep quiet, a man can hardly hear himself think!" as he apparently struggled to finish writing something.

Donovan was sitting in an armchair and reading a newspaper, as if he were in a park on a sunny afternoon, oblivious to the commotion around him.

Maren, the second oldest, who Lila considered to be the quiet one—if any of these people could be considered quiet, which was debatable—was in the corner of the room with a book. Margaret, one of the youngest, whom they called Peg-leg Meg despite her having two fully functioning legs, was playing the piano. Birdie, the youngest at thirteen years, was on the floor, playing with a pair of rambunctious puppies that would streak away from her and tumble over each other across the floor. Lila watched Donovan lift his legs to allow the puppies to pass without looking up from his newspaper.

And the oldest daughter, Mathilda, or Tilly as she was called, was lurking in front of the large street-facing windows, her arms crossed, her gaze fixed outside. She looked terribly bored.

Blythe was sitting in an armchair next to Donovan, a small Pomeranian dog on her lap, resting its head on the arm of the chair.

"Lady Aleksander," the butler intoned.

Beck jerked around at his desk. "Lila!" he practically shouted. Meg had not heard the announcement of a visitor and continued to play the piano. "So good of you to come. Please, come in, come in."

"Thank you for seeing me on such short—"

"What's that?" Beck shouted, rising to his feet and cupping his hand around his ear. "I can't hear you over the piano!"

I said thank you for—"

"Meg!" Tilly shouted. "Will you *stop*? My ears are ringing and no one can hear a thing!"

Meg stopped and looked up with surprise. "Why didn't you say?"

"I just did. We have a guest," Tilly said, gesturing half-heartedly to Lila.

Meg stood up to look across the piano at Lila. "Oh."

Now all of them were looking at Lila. Even the dogs. "Good afternoon," she said.

"You all remember Lady Aleksander?" Beck asked.

"Isn't she the matchmaker?" Maren asked.

"What's a matchmaker?" Birdie inquired.

"She's not here for *me*, is she, Papa?" Tilly demanded. "I swear I—"

"She is not here for you, love," Beck said. "At least, I don't think she is." He looked to Lila for confirmation.

"No, no," Lila said.

But her quick answer caused Tilly to gasp with affront. "Why *not* me?"

"Tilly, another time!" Blythe complained.

"That's what you always say, Mama," Tilly said, and turned back to the window. "I'm twenty years old! Does no one care?"

"I do, Tilly, darling," Beck assured her. "I care very much. Now then, Lila, what can we do for you?"

Lila looked around the room. She'd really hoped for a little privacy. "I need a smidge of information."

"Ah. Splendid." He stood there expectantly, waiting for her to ask. They all looked at her expectantly, in fact.

"Oh. I see. I think it's a private matter," Blythe said.

"Yes, thank you. It is," Lila agreed.

"And by *private*, you mean you wish my many offspring were not present to hear it?" Beck asked. "I assure you, they listen to no one."

"Beck!" Blythe said. "She means to speak to you privately. She looks very serious just now."

Donovan, bless him, understood the obstacles Lila faced with this family. He unfurled himself from the armchair, then sauntered over to Lila with a smile. He reached for her hand and brought it to his lips, kissing her knuckles with a twinkle in his eye. He was, Lila thought, as gorgeous as he was the first day she'd ever laid eyes on him all those years ago. She wondered if he was still involved with the "valet," or if he'd taken a new lover.

"Subtlety does not live in this house, madam," he said. "Everything must be spelled out in the most basic of terms. Leave that to me." He dropped her hand and turned. "Ladies, you will come with me."

"Why? Where are we going?" Birdie demanded.

"Lady Marley has requested your presence," Donovan said.

"She *has*?" Blythe asked disbelievingly.

"She will," Donovan said confidently.

"Really?" Beck asked. "She seemed rather annoyed the last time."

"She was *quite* annoyed last time," Donovan agreed. "But her husband was delighted."

"Marley does love children," Blythe mused.

"I am not a child," Tilly reminded them.

"Yes, darling, you have just turned twenty years. You remind us frequently," Beck said. "A grand idea, Donovan. Come along, my loves, accompany your uncle Donovan to visit Marley. Birdie, you are not to slip off to see the horses this time, do you understand? We had the whole of London in search of you."

"I won't," Birdie promised breezily as she walked to the door.

The rest of them followed along, Tilly with a heavy sigh, Maren with her book clutched to her chest, Maisie muttering under her breath, and Meg carrying one of the dogs, the other one trotting after her.

Donovan bowed to Lila, then followed the girls like the grand goose of the flock.

That left Blythe and the Pomeranian. Lila looked at Beck. He looked at his wife. "Darling?"

"What?"

"You were right—Lila would like a private audience."

"But does that mean me?" Blythe asked, surprised. "She knows I won't say a word. You do, don't you, Lila?"

Beck shook his head. Blythe clucked her tongue at him and hoisted herself up, dumping the dog from her lap. "I don't know why I must always be excluded," she said to him on her way out.

"Don't mind her," Beck said after his wife had gone. He fell onto his back on the settee, his feet propped on the arm, and folded his arms behind his head to form a pillow. "Do you have any idea how often I am alone? I'll tell you— *never*. There is a female underfoot at all times. If she's not complaining, she's eating all the food I've paid for. It's exhausting, living with them all."

"I can well imagine," Lila drawled. She sat in the chair Donovan had vacated.

"All right, Lila, you have me on tenterhooks. What information are you looking for now?"

"I need to know more about Miss Woodchurch."

"Why? What's she done?"

Lila laughed. "She hasn't done anything. I want to know where she comes from, her family, that sort of thing."

Beck frowned. He propped himself up on one elbow. *"Why?"*

"I remember you said something about her when you were advocating for her to Lord Abbott."

"Did I?" He thought about it. "I said she needed the position."

"Yes, that's it. Why would a young woman from a prosperous family need an occupation?"

He fell back onto the settee again. "Because her father is a miserly, unpleasant bastard, that's why. Can you imagine having a daughter as bright and cheerful and *industrious* as Hattie Woodchurch and seeing nothing more than livestock?"

"What?" That description was appalling.

"Let me tell you about Miss Woodchurch. On the occasion of Marley's oldest daughter's first birthday, when was that, eight or nine years ago, possibly more, we were gathered to celebrate when Marley's butler announced Miss Harriet Woodchurch had come to call. No one knew who she was but I, and that was only by chance. I'd had a dispute with a transportation company—her father, if you want to get to the nub of it—and had met her in the course of that exchange, when her father had forced her to mind the door like a watchdog as we discussed my complaint. Which, I can say, was never resolved to my satisfaction."

"What has that to do with the birthday party?"

"She didn't know it was a birthday, but she had knocked on Marley's door, no more than fourteen years, looking for work. She had in mind a secretarial position. Can you believe it? Naturally, she was turned away. But I had an inkling why she'd come, and later that week, I went round to call on her father. I suggested his daughter be allowed to attend the Iddesleigh School for Exceptional Girls. He said he saw no reason to educate a girl past a certain point, and certainly not paying for the privilege. I told him she would be allowed in on scholarship. I could go on, but I had quite a row with the bastard, and in the end, I was so incensed that Lady Marley and I joined together and ended up paying *him* to send his daughter to our school."

Lila was shocked. "You didn't."

"Oh, but I did. How could I leave her in such a situation! And her mother! You've never seen a house like that one on Portman Square, Lila. She's filled the house with clocks and whatnot."

"With what?"

"Clocks and cats and tea services and I don't know what all," he said with a flick of his wrist. "So many of them that one can't walk through the hall without stepping over one thing and squeezing in behind another. Miss Woodchurch has three brothers who are just as unrefined as their parents. Terrible home, I tell you. But it is her father's parsimonious ways that create the problem. He won't even keep her fully clothed."

"What do you mean?"

"I mean he won't buy her as much as a frock. Blythe tells me her dresses are secondhand." He sat up again, his gaze narrowing on Lila. "So why, exactly, are you asking about Miss Woodchurch?"

"Curiosity," she said with a shrug.

"Curiosity my arse, if you will pardon me for saying so. What are you about?" His expression said he already knew.

"All right," she conceded. "I think she might be perfectly suited to the worst client I've ever had in my life."

"What? Who?" He suddenly smiled. "You have someone in mind for her? I'd be overjoyed to see her matched with someone who could remove her from that house."

Lila hesitated.

Beck's smile faded. "Oh no."

"Lord Abbott."

"Lila!" Beck kicked himself up so quickly his feet hit the ground with a thud. "You can't be serious."

"I am."

"No, no, you can't be. Please explain yourself."

So Lila did. She told him how the viscount didn't really speak to anyone, but he did speak to Hattie. How they apparently liked similar things and how he'd even looked to Hattie for advice about the matches she was proposing. And there was more, the way the two of them looked at each other, which, of course, she didn't say to Beck. She didn't expect him to understand.

"I feel these things in my gut, Beck, and I feel this is an excellent match between two like souls."

"Perhaps between two like souls, but not two like families, Lila." He shook his head. "You don't know what you're up against, and I won't allow you to get Hattie's hopes up, do you hear me? She's already suffered one broken engagement because of her wretched family, and *that* gentleman was no one of import. She would be humiliated! Abbott would never settle on her! Her family would bleed him dry."

"That's a *terrible* thing to say," Lila said, alarmed by Beck's stark opinion.

"Nevertheless it is true. This is trouble, Lila, and you are best to leave well enough alone."

"Have you no faith in my abilities?"

"Not in this. You've always put together people of common backgrounds and experiences. But this? Her father is the worst sort of opportunist. Not only will he find any reason to keep her dowry for himself, he'll create as many obstacles as he can in hopes of being paid to remove them.

He lacks even the most basic of scruples. He's a Midas and wants it all for himself. Listen to me, Lila, for Hattie's sake."

"I understand," Lila said. And while she did understand, she didn't agree with him. Beck was a good man and wanted to save this young woman from her father. What better way to do it than see her married to a viscount? She stood up. "You'll keep this between us?"

"Of course."

"Thank you, Beck." She began to walk to the door, but she paused and turned back. "By the bye, I'll need an invitation extended to Hattie and her brother for your garden tea."

"Lila, for God's sake," Beck said, and groaned. "Have you heard nothing I've said?"

"I heard every word. But what if I'm right? What if I can manage it?" She smiled.

Beck sighed and shook his head. He didn't give her an answer, but Lila was certain an invitation would be sent. If there was one thing about Beckett Hawke that everyone in London knew—he could not say no to a female.

CHAPTER TWENTY-TWO

MATEO HAD BEEN in something of a strange fog since he'd kissed Hattie in the kitchen. He couldn't work out what all, exactly, had possessed him. He brooded on it to the extent that by the time he arrived at the Iddesleigh garden tea party, he was fully morose.

On the surface, there was no mystery. Hattie was a woman, and he was a man. And she wasn't any woman, she was Hattie of the sunny disposition and like interests. But he might as well have kissed Yolanda. This wasn't very different—both women were in his employ.

He had his own personal code of honor, beliefs about what was right and what was wrong, and he'd ignored them all. It was so unlike him—he was so circumspect, so careful to say or do nothing that could draw rebuke. How strange and distressing it was that even as a grown man, he could still hear his father's voice, belittling him for being so stupid, so rash.

And yet, he could not ignore or avoid the fight against the wave of desire that had flooded him and had not left him yet. Hattie Woodchurch was so unlike the women he'd been around most of his life.

He didn't want to lose her as his scribe, although he understood she'd be well within her rights to leave his employ. Imagine, after all the opinions he'd voiced regarding Mr. Rochester's behavior in the novel *Jane Eyre*, after complaining that the man had taken advantage of his governess, had treated his mad wife unfairly, had given another woman every reason to believe he loved her, to turn around and do what he'd done in the kitchen? Preposterous.

Now his imagination was running wild. He imagined that Hattie despised him. Or worse, believed his kiss to be some sort of promise. No, no, she was too smart, too shrewd to think that. As she said, she understood the rules of engagement.

Whatever she thought of him now, he hoped to find out at the Iddesleigh soiree this afternoon. He would find a moment to speak to her. To explain himself.

As if he had a suitable explanation.

Beck was on hand to greet him when he arrived. "Welcome, my friend, my lord! We are positively bursting with excitement. Come with me," he said, already moving ahead before Mateo could discard his hat.

He followed Beck through the large house to the back terrace. Luck was shining on Iddesleigh and his family, as the day was a glorious blue, with white puffy clouds skittering across the sky. The garden, which was a small park in size, had been done up in spectacular fashion. On the terrace, there were six tables set with fine china. Two giant-sized topiary teapots had a cascade of fresh flowers pouring from their spouts to the ground. The lawn had been set with croquet pickets and lawn bowling, and there was even a small petting zoo for the children. It was the most opulent garden tea Mateo had ever seen.

Beck was eager to drag him around to his many guests, introducing him as his "very good friend," even though they'd only met a handful of times. As usual, Mateo was met with "welcome to England" and "how do you find London" and "how long will you be with us." He answered the questions by rote, like a schoolboy reciting his facts. The women—all of them pleasing—made no real impression on him, but then again, his thoughts were elsewhere today.

Lady Aleksander arrived in a sky blue frock, waving a fan at her face. "So good to see you, my lord!" she said cheerfully. "I've someone I should very much like you to meet." She spirited him away from the couple who were explaining to him how they rarely came to town but had come to see the London Zoo's elephant. She introduced him to their daughter, Lady Mabel Stanhope.

Lady Mabel had dark hair and eyes and an easy smile, but she was hardly bigger than a child. Mateo liked her at once—she pointed out a pair of puppies on the lawn, romping among the children. They were two fat balls of fur tumbling over each other and the feet of the guests, colliding with more than one pair of legs. And as he and Lady Mabel watched, one of them stopped running to lie on its belly and nap.

"I think all garden teas should have puppies, don't you?" she asked.

"It should be the law of the land. And there should be more than two. A dozen is a good number, is it not?"

Lady Mabel laughed, and Mateo escorted her down the stairs to the lawn. He squatted and attempted to entice one of the puppies to come to them. *"Ven, cachorro, ven,"* he called, his hand outstretched, luring the puppy their way. The fattest of the two eventually waddled over. Lady Mabel cooed over it until it tried wiggling its way out of Mateo's arms.

Mateo bent down to set it free, and when he did, he heard a familiar laugh. He straightened and looked around for Hattie, but his gaze fell on Miss Raney. She smiled at him and lifted her hand in greeting before dipping under a parasol. She was speaking to a tall gentleman.

"I have monopolized your time," Lady Mabel said, following the direction of his gaze.

"Not at all," he insisted.

"I should say hello to Mrs. Barron," she said, and excused herself. He watched her make her way up the terrace steps. Mateo tried to think of something to say to call her back—but he could think of nothing, as he really had no desire to call her back. Lady Mabel was lovely. But she was not the one.

He turned away from her departure and started—Lady Raney was standing before him. "Good afternoon, my lord!" she said with great enthusiasm, and her gaze trailed over his shoulder to where Lady Mabel was still climbing the second set of steps to the main terrace level. "My Flora is looking forward to greeting you again. She very much enjoyed your company."

"As I enjoyed hers."

The lady held out her hand. "Would you mind terribly? I'm so clumsy with so many steps."

He suppressed a sigh. She would put herself on his arm to claim him, thereby ensuring he wasn't waylaid on their way to speak to her daughter. He offered his arm, and the two of them ascended the steps to her daughter, who had yet to lower her parasol or acknowledge their approach.

"Darling, look who has come!" her mother trilled loudly.

Miss Raney dropped her parasol and whirled around, her eyes wide. "My lord," she said, and dipped into a curtsy. "A great pleasure to see you again. I hope the day finds you well?"

"I am indeed, thank you." The man she'd been talking to eyed Mateo with a look of disdain. "A fine day for the tea," he added.

"Isn't it? And after all that terrible rain. Have you had the pleasure of meeting Mr. Daniel Woodchurch?"

Woodchurch? Mateo looked at the man with renewed interest. Of course...he could see a vague resemblance around the eyes. "A pleasure, sir. You must be Miss Woodchurch's brother."

"Yes." The distrustful look he gave Mateo made him think that perhaps Hattie had told him what had transpired between them. He prepared himself to be challenged to a duel of satisfaction—he'd heard the English were particularly eager for them—and squared his shoulders. But in the next moment he remembered what Hattie had said about her brothers vexing her and wondered if she would really share something so personal. That, and the fact that her brother had not yet demanded satisfaction.

"Has your sister joined you here today?" he asked, glancing around them.

"She's here somewhere," Mr. Woodchurch said. "Why? What do you want with her?"

Miss Raney gasped at the bluntness of his question.

"To greet her," Mateo said, and steadily held Mr. Woodchurch's gaze until the man looked away.

"There are so many people here," Miss Raney said.

Yes, London was far too crowded, Mateo silently agreed.

"She must be here somewhere, in the crowd," Miss Raney said, glancing around them.

"It's too warm, really," Mr. Woodchurch complained. "Perhaps you'd like something to drink, Miss Raney." He held out his arm.

"*I* certainly would," Lady Raney said. "Thank you, Mr. Woodchurch." She edged her daughter aside and put her hand on Mr. Woodchurch's arm. The man looked so astounded he didn't know what to say, and with a look at

Miss Raney, he smiled thinly and escorted her mother away. Mateo had to admire the woman's mastery of putting her daughter in his company.

Speaking of her daughter, Miss Raney looked at Mateo and smiled sheepishly.

Mateo returned her smile. He knew what it was like to have a mother who was a force to be reckoned with—Lady Raney was not going to allow anything or anyone to come between her daughter and the eligible viscount. "I best sweep you away while I have the chance. Shall we walk?"

"Please." She opened her parasol, and together they strolled across the lawn in the direction of a fountain.

They strolled in silence for a few moments until Miss Raney spoke. "It's really very nice to have such a large garden in town. One can see the stars very clearly with so much space."

Mateo instinctively looked up at the blue patch overhead. *"Sí,"* he said.

"I prefer the night," she said. "There is something so magical about it. The sky looks like black velvet, dotted with crystal stars. It's as if we're all looking into another world."

He glanced at her. Her love of stars sounded a bit…stiff. "But it's difficult to see the stars from London."

"Oh, it is. I'll show you the best place to see them." She pointed to the back wall of the garden and hurried ahead, checking over her shoulder to see if he followed. When she reached the high stone wall, she said, "Help me up?" and pointed to a bench. She braced herself against his arm and stepped up, then beckoned him up beside her. On the other side of the stone wall, the ground sloped away and into a larger park.

"I was raised with Lord Iddesleigh's daughters. We spent

many evenings looking over the wall." She smiled up at him prettily, and for a moment, he imagined her smiling at him like that in Santiava.

But then, annoyingly, the image of Hattie flashed in his mind's eye.

"I heard a secret about you," she said, a smile playing on her lips.

The kiss. But no, no… Miss Raney was smiling with delight, and she would not be delighted if he'd kissed his scribe. Bloody hell, he was plagued by that single kiss. "About me? I can't think of one." He stepped off the bench, then helped her down.

"I've heard you are an excellent horseman."

What in hell? He laughed with surprise. "I am not an excellent horseman. Who has said it?"

"Lady Aleksander."

Mateo resisted a roll of his eyes—of course she had. She probably attributed all sorts of talents to him that he didn't possess. "She's generous in her praise. Do you ride, Miss Raney?"

"I do. I *adore* it. We keep dozens of horses in the country. My father likes to put them in races."

A point in the lady's favor—Mateo enjoyed a good horse race. "There is a race in Spain, the *Carreras de Caballos de Sanlúcar*," he said. "The horses race alongside the Mediterranean Sea." It was a spectacular setting, and the memory of horses racing on the packed sand, the sea sparkling in the background, made him a bit homesick.

"That sounds lovely." She smiled. But her smile seemed strained. Almost forced. Unlike Hattie's, whose smile always appeared naturally easy.

What the hell was he doing? What was the matter with him that he kept thinking of Hattie Woodchurch?

"Perhaps we ought to return," he said. "It looks like they are preparing to serve tea."

They strolled back across the lawn, and just as they reached the terrace steps, Mr. Woodchurch appeared again. He ignored Mateo completely and said to Miss Raney, "How are you at croquet, Miss Raney? I'd like to invite you to partner with me when play begins. That is, if you are free." He looked at Mateo.

"I, ah…" Miss Raney glanced nervously at Mateo.

"By all means," Mateo said.

Mr. Woodchurch smirked. Mateo wondered why he felt such animosity from the gentleman.

"Wonderful," Mr. Woodchurch said.

Miss Raney looked again at Mateo, and he bowed, setting her free. Mr. Woodchurch seized the opportunity and offered his arm to her. With a last look for Mateo, she carried on with Mr. Woodchurch.

Mateo watched them go. He was already wishing the afternoon would end. Apparently, after tea, he would be forced to play croquet.

And really, where was Hattie? He craned his neck, looking for her in that crowd of too many people.

CHAPTER TWENTY-THREE

HATTIE WAS IN the miserable thick of the garden party. It was nothing as she'd expected, which was a small crowd, one or two tables, and polite conversation. But no, this garden party was crowded in between enormous floral teapots and lawn games. Men in morning coats that were quickly discarded due to the heat, women in fancy hats, liveried footmen dashing about, and children. *Squads* of children.

The moment Hattie arrived, Lady Iddesleigh said she was very happy to see her, and then immediately pressed her into service that Hattie didn't know how to refuse. "You'll help me, won't you, dear?" Lady Iddesleigh had asked frantically. "Mrs. Hughes has fallen ill and Donovan is nowhere to be found. There isn't anyone to help with the children. There are simply too many of them! Do you see them? Look, they're all there at the table under the maple tree," she said, gesturing to a table where several kids were chasing each other. "Will you mind them for a few moments? I'll be forever in your debt. *Thank* you," she said, and turned away before Hattie could object.

Daniel—who had of course protested about another invitation to a hoity-toity gathering, but then had been ready a full half hour before Hattie—laughed. *"You'll help me, won't you, dear?"* he mimicked Lady Iddesleigh, and set off, leaving Hattie to fend for herself. She felt she had no choice but to walk over to the children's table.

Lady Margaret Hawke, the Iddesleigh daughter known as Meg, was at the table. She'd been a girl the last time Hattie had seen her. Her youthful face was the same, but she was clearly disgruntled. She sat on a chair with her chin propped on her fist, looking morose. She hardly glanced up when Hattie took a seat next to her. "I don't know why I must sit here," she complained. "Birdie is almost as old as I am—why can't she watch them?" She looked curiously at Hattie. "Oh! Are you the governess, then?"

"The gov… No," Hattie said uncertainly. "I'm a guest." She supposed she couldn't blame Lady Margaret for thinking she was—she'd tried her best to update the old gown she'd stolen from her mother's closet. "I'm Harriet Woodchurch. You may remember when I was a student at the Iddesleigh School?"

"Oh. No," Lady Margaret said, and sank back into her despondency just as two boys raced by so fast that they nearly knocked Hattie's hat from her head.

She sighed. It was like being surrounded by a dozen Peter and Perrys.

She tried to ignore the children racing around the table and kept her gaze on the adults milling about on the terrace above. She spotted Teo once, and her heart leaped in her chest…until she realized he was speaking to Lady Mabel Stanhope. Mabel had always had the privilege of looking quite charming no matter the circumstance, and today was no exception. What did Teo think of her?

She lost sight of him in the crowd and didn't spot him again until it came time for everyone to be seated for tea. Hattie assumed her watch was over and rose from the table. But a footman intercepted her on her way back up the stairs with the message she was seated with the children. She bristled; there was nothing in the invitation she'd received to suggest she was the help. But she did as she was asked, then listened to Lady Margaret's heavy sighs while the Duke of Marley's two youngest, Annika and Bredon, argued over the toffee candies.

Hattie was hot in her gown, her hair sticky beneath her hat. It was too warm, and really, why had she come? Did she really think these invitations meant anything other than people saw her as useful? What could possibly come of it? She would never feel anything other than a poor relation or a servant.

She sat at the table with the unruly children and watched Lord Iddesleigh escort Teo to a table with him and his wife, and Lord and Lady Marley. The other tables quickly filled, but there were so many people that there weren't enough places for them all to sit. She realized that some of the unseated guests were eyeing the children's table and talking amongst themselves, as if plotting a coup.

Hattie sat back, her arms crossed over her middle, bored and angry and feeling inferior.

She didn't know how long she sat stewing, but eventually, people began to rise from the tea tables and more people took their places. Hattie stood from the children's table, having decided she was making it worse by obeying. But as she started up the steps, she saw Teo speaking with Lady Mabel again.

She turned and walked away from the steps, toward the fountain, completely disheartened. That was where Flora caught up to her, breathless and giddy. "I've looked all over for you!" She latched on to Hattie's arm and glanced up at her hat. "Where did you get *that*?"

Hattie self-consciously touched the brim. "Umm...it was my mother's."

"Hattie, you won't believe it—I talked to him about the stars!" she whispered excitedly.

"You did?"

"And *he* told *me* about a horse race on the beach in Spain. I don't know, but I feel like it's going very well."

Hattie's heart sank a little. He hadn't told her about a horse race in Spain. But what was she thinking? She'd hoped he would take interest in Flora. If he was going to marry someone, it should be her.

"What should I say next? We're all playing croquet."

"We all...?"

"I wish I had your talent for it. You know me, knocking the balls hither and yon." She laughed.

"You'll do well, I'm sure of it."

"And there is lawn bowling. He might ask me to bowl with him. Remind me how to play?"

How lovely for Flora. And now Hattie would very much like to hurl a ball at the stone wall. "It's easy—you just roll the ball toward the smaller one."

"But what should I say?" Flora asked. "You know him so well."

"I don't," Hattie insisted. She was beginning to believe she didn't know him at all. All the things she'd imagined she knew... Did she really?

"Hattie," Flora whined. "Don't fail me now."

Fail her? She'd done everything she possibly could to prepare her! She had bolstered her confidence, told her what to talk about! "Compliment him," she said. The good Lord knew that her father responded to flattery. "Mention that he's naturally athletic and how strong he is when he strikes his ball."

"Compliments," Flora repeated solemnly. "What else?"

Could she really think of *nothing* to say to that beautiful man? "Admire his intellect. Or his prowess when determining which shot to make."

Flora was nodding along. "I knew you'd think of something," she said. "Now if only your brother doesn't interfere," she added with a roll of her eyes.

"My brother?" Hattie frowned with confusion. "He won't. He can hardly abide these gatherings."

Flora blinked. "Really?"

She couldn't really be concerned about Daniel. Hattie shrugged. "I'll make sure he doesn't interfere."

"I don't think you can."

"Oh, I can," Hattie assured her.

And yet, Flora's smile seemed doubtful. "Thank you, Hattie."

Hattie did as she promised. As the teams were being picked and she saw Daniel lurking around Flora, she enlisted the unwitting help of the ten-year-old Marley twins. She knew of twin boys, knew how persuadable and ridiculous they could be. And she knew they'd respond to a challenge.

She bet one of them that he couldn't reach a particular hedge where Daniel was standing before the other one. The two boys bolted before she even got the words out. Daniel was confused by the sudden rush of boys and didn't know which way to move. One of the boys slammed into him, the other one reached the end and shouted, "Free!"

Daniel tried not to curse, but it was beyond his ability to control. Lord Iddesleigh, alarmed by the language, drew Daniel away to have a word. And amid it all, Flora was teamed with the viscount and Lady Mabel was teamed with Sir Richard Canton, a wealthy bachelor.

Other teams were selected until there were no more mallets. No one glanced in Hattie's direction. No one asked if she would like to play or offered to partner with her. She was hardly surprised. She leaned against a post, her arms folded, her disposition turning darker. As the game progressed, and the players laughed and carried on, she moved farther away, into the shade. She wished she'd worn something lighter, like muslin. And the hat! She felt as if she was wearing a beaver pelt on her head, she was so hot. She was considering she'd never been quite so miserable in all her life when a croquet ball came skidding across the grass and stopped at her foot.

She looked up to see who had such a spectacularly bad shot, and who should come striding along, a mallet resting on his shoulder, but Teo. He'd discarded his coat and neck cloth and looked very much at home. When he saw her standing there, he stopped walking and looked at her with surprise.

Neither of them spoke at first.

"Miss Woodchurch," he said.

"My lord."

He glanced over his shoulder, and seeing no one, came closer. "I had hoped for an opportunity to speak to you today."

"Did you? Well, if you mean to speak, you best do it before Lady Iddesleigh finds me. Apparently, I was invited to look after children."

"What?"

"Pay me no heed," she grumbled, and sighed. It was not like her to be so cross.

He stepped closer. "This is hardly the place, but I should like—"

"No, thank you," she said crisply.

Teo frowned. "Pardon?"

She'd had enough of being made to feel inferior. By men,

by countesses, by her own family—and she wouldn't be made to feel like someone's lapse of judgment now. "I beg your pardon, but I can guess what you would say. And before you say it, I would like to say that what happened, happened. My opinion of it hasn't changed. And that I refuse to tread on eggs because of it. I don't have designs on you, my lord. I am painfully aware that we are from vastly different corners of this life. But neither am I going to pretend I don't esteem you or wish that I mattered to you. There, I've said it. If you want to let me go from my position, I understand. But I won't apologize for what I've said or accept your apologies for having dared to touch me."

He stared at her as if he couldn't believe what he was hearing. He stared long enough that she began to feel a tiny bit remorseful for having spouted off. She folded her arms defensively across her middle. "I...I do beg your pardon if I've been unkind or otherwise perturbed you."

He shook his head. He let his mallet drop from his shoulder. But he didn't speak.

Hattie moaned. "What? What are you thinking? You can't remain silent after that."

"No, I can't remain silent after that. I am thinking I know you better after that speech."

She was expecting a rebuke or an apology. She was expecting something that made sense. That did not make sense.

"And I would never ask you to change a single thing about yourself."

But? "Wonderful. Then...then who—"

Lady Birdie suddenly ran up to them. "Did you find it?" she asked breathlessly.

Teo bent down to pick up the croquet ball and handed it to her.

"Thank you!" Lady Birdie looked at Hattie. "Miss Wood-church! You'll partner with me, won't you? No one will partner with me."

"Of course," Hattie said. She looked at Teo. Her question—who were they now?—died on her tongue. She followed Lady Birdie out to the croquet ground, only to find that a separate game had been set up for the children. She would be playing with the children, not the adults.

This day would never end.

For the remainder of the afternoon, she tried not to look for Teo at every opportunity, but it was impossible. The few times she did, she would see him smiling with Flora, or leaning close to hear what Lady Mabel was saying. He looked unconcerned. As if nothing had happened.

She wondered what he thought of her now. He hadn't told her not to come back to his employ, but she supposed he would come next week. *I beg your pardon, but it is entirely necessary—I can't be kissing the help.*

She knocked her ball too hard and it rolled into the shrubbery. When she went to fetch it, she saw Teo and Flora wandering away from the croquet field, chatting like a pair of lovers. But before her eyes clouded with tears of frustration, she realized someone else had seen them, too: Lady Mabel. The poor young woman looked crushed.

Yes, well, try spending afternoons in his presence and then having him kiss you and then act as if nothing happened and see how crushed you feel.

At long last, when the garden tea party was at its end, Hattie found her brother with a full glass of wine in his hand. As they were leaving, prepared to walk to Portman Square, they happened on Flora. She was waiting in the foyer for a carriage to be brought round. Her mother was nearby, speaking to Lady Iddesleigh.

"Did you enjoy the afternoon?" Hattie asked as she jabbed her hands into her ill-fitting gloves.

"Hattie..." Flora grasped her arm. She shot a look at Daniel and leaned close to whisper, *"I think he esteems me."*

She didn't whisper softly enough—Daniel heard her. He snorted loudly. "He esteems every woman he meets." With his chin, he indicated something over Hattie's shoulder. She and Flora looked back and saw the viscount standing with the Stanhopes. Lady Mabel's face radiated hope.

"That's because he is very polite," Flora said. "Something you could stand to learn, sir." And with that, she skipped off to join her parents.

Hattie looked at her brother as they started for the street. "Why do you hate him?"

"Hate who?" Daniel asked, looking away from her.

"Lord Abbott, obviously."

"*Hate* him?" Daniel scoffed. "I don't care about him, Hat—I don't think of him at all. A better question is, why do you care so much about him?"

Had he seen her looking at him today? Hattie blushed with self-consciousness. "I don't."

"Hat," Daniel said. "It's obvious you do. I can see it just here," he said, and with his forefinger, made a circle in the air just in front of her face.

She pushed his hand away. "You have no idea what you're talking about."

"Don't I? Well, here's a bit of brotherly advice—keep your desire to yourself. Hidden, in fact. Our father would make your life quite miserable if he suspected there was something to be gained."

"I have nothing to hide," Hattie said curtly. But her gut was sinking because Daniel was right. Her father would ruin everything if he suspected her true feelings.

CHAPTER TWENTY-FOUR

TWO DAYS LATER, Mateo returned from a meeting at the bank, and Borerro informed him Lady Aleksander was waiting for him in the drawing room.

"Maldición," Mateo cursed softly as he removed his gloves. He detested the meetings with the matchmaker.

"And Doña Vincente," Borerro added.

Mateo's head snapped up. He hadn't expected his mother.

"She returned this morning," Borerro said to his unspoken question. "They are at tea in the drawing room."

Bloody hell. He had enough on his mind without having to deal with his mother. He handed Borerro his hat and gloves and walked on to the drawing room.

The two women didn't notice him at first; they had their heads close together, talking softly, as if they were afraid the footman attending them would overhear. "Mami," he said, and the two of them snapped away from each other.

They were discussing him, apparently. Mateo crossed the room to kiss his mother's cheek. "I wasn't expecting you for another fortnight," he said.

"I hadn't planned to come back so soon, but a little bird told me that you might need a little help settling on a match."

Mateo turned a cool gaze to Lady Aleksander, who studiously avoided eye contact by examining the finger sandwiches on the tray between her and his mother. "The little bird is mistaken," he said. "I am not in need of any help."

"Perhaps just a little, *mijo*," his mother said. "I understand you've had the opportunity to meet some lovely young women."

He was going to need some fortification for this talk. *"Sí."* He walked to the sideboard, poured a whisky, and tossed it down his throat. Then he poured another one. "I have spoken to every woman Lady Aleksander has put in my path." He turned back to them.

"And it has been a *delight*," Lady Aleksander said, which prompted both Mateo and his mother to look at her with suspicion. There was no one in this room that thought he was a delight in any sense of the word.

"What?" Lady Aleksander asked innocently. She put a lady finger on her plate and picked up her fork.

Mateo took a seat across from his mother. "You enjoyed Paris, I take it?"

"Immensely, darling! It's so lovely this time of year. I sent for your sister, but she's with child! Isn't that exciting?"

"Wonderful," Mateo said. "You should go to her. Things are progressing here."

"Are they?" she asked dubiously, and helped herself to a pair of petit fours.

Unexpectedly, the door opened, and Hattie's head popped in. "I beg your pardon," she said, and tried to back away, but Mateo was immediately on his feet. "Come in, Miss Woodchurch. I'd like to introduce you to my mother." He did not miss the look his mother and Lady Aleksander exchanged, and he detested them for it.

He put down his glass and walked to the door, pulling it open. Hattie gave him a look of apprehension, but he smiled at her. "Come in. She won't bite."

"Mateo!" his mother said behind him.

Hattie hesitantly stepped through the door and curtsied deeply to the two women.

"My mother, the Duchess of Santiava," he said. "Mami, allow me to introduce Miss Woodchurch, who has proven invaluable to me here in London. She is my scribe."

"Your *scribe*?" his mother said, without acknowledging Hattie. "I thought you'd have some old gentleman like Mr. Callum. Really, why is it *not* Mr. Callum?"

"I think you meant to welcome Miss Woodchurch?"

His mother looked at Hattie, but her gaze glossed over her. "A pleasure, Miss Woodchurch." She turned back to her plate.

"The pleasure is mine, madam," Hattie said.

His mother did not respond. Mateo was greatly irritated by her behavior—she could be so condescending and superior at times. He wanted to remind her they were all God's creatures and she was not, by virtue of some bloody title, better than anyone else in this room. He could feel the stiffness in Hattie, could sense the desire to be anywhere but here. He touched her elbow. "I'll join you in the study shortly. My mother has only just arrived from Paris."

She nodded and quickly disappeared.

Mateo reluctantly returned to the tea. He could feel Lady Aleksander's eyes on him, but that was nothing new. He could feel his mother's indifference to anything that wasn't of interest to her, and that was also nothing new. He tried to make small talk—he asked if there was any news from Roberto. When Sofia expected her third child. He listened to her recount all that she'd bought in Paris, and wondered if the list was intended as a boast before Lady Aleksander. Frankly, her talk made him a little ill—his mother had a habit of treating the duchy as a bottomless well of funds.

Lady Aleksander must have also grown bored of the

recitation of purchases, because in the slender moment his mother took a breath, she said, "I haven't had the chance to speak with you since the tea, my lord. What did you think of Lady Mabel Stanhope?"

Dios mío. He hated these interviews, hated the whole idea of being matched. He hated everything about this room, this tea, about London. "A bit too young."

"Oh?" Lady Aleksander seemed surprised, probably because he'd actually responded to her question. "And Miss Raney? You spoke to her at some length at the garden tea."

"Miss Raney is the same as she was the last time you asked, madam. Perfectly fine."

Lady Aleksander put down her cup and saucer with a clank. "Do you think that Miss Raney might be the perfect match for you? I only ask because you don't seem to enjoy the process, and you've had an opportunity to assess compatibility with her."

His mother's gaze turned sharp as a hawk and fixed on him. He didn't answer straightaway. Miss Raney was a good match for him, in theory. And yet…he couldn't agree to it. "It is possible."

He expected Lady Aleksander to do some cartwheels or clap her hands with delight, but she nodded and said, "If I may tell your mother a little about her?"

He nodded, then listened impassively as Lady Aleksander ran through Miss Raney's list of attributes—she was pretty. Her family rich. Her father well-connected.

His mother's eyes kept darting between him and Lady Aleksander as the latter exalted Miss Raney.

When Lady Aleksander had finished, his mother cocked her head coyly to one side. "Well, darling? How do you feel about Miss Raney?"

"It is impossible to know how I *feel* about anyone after a few short, superficial conversations."

"Then did you find anything to put you off of her after your one or two conversations?"

Mateo laughed sourly. He was beginning to feel a bit like a trapped animal. "I haven't found anything objectionable about anyone. They have all been pleasant, pretty women."

Her gaze narrowed and she leaned forward like she would when he was a boy to scold him. "Why do I feel you're not sharing your true feelings?"

Oh, perhaps because he'd been berated for sharing his opinions all his life. But there was no point in denying it. He was not one to dissemble. Or to charm his way out of this conversation. "I have no objection to Miss Raney. And neither do I have any esteem for her. I don't know her well enough to know if I want to spend the rest of my life with her."

"Teo." His mother sighed.

Mateo stood up. "Would you like me to marry for the mere sake of it, Mami?"

"Well...*yes*," she said. "That is the point of this endeavor."

"I am not *propiedad*," he bit out, losing some of his English in the moment to his anger.

"You're not the duchy's property, if that's what you mean." His mother stood up and stepped forward, forcing him to look at her. "But you are the duke of a duchy with no heir. You really have no time for a long courtship or the development of feelings, *mi amor.* Your parliament is anxious to secure a succession because we all know what can happen when there is no heir. The clock is ticking."

Mateo fisted one hand to control himself from exploding and saying something he would sorely regret.

"I have an idea," she continued. "We'll have a ball here and invite all the ladies on Lila's list."

"No," he said firmly.

"And Lila might invite any other lady she would like you to meet," she said, as if he hadn't spoken. "You may talk to them all night, Teo, but you'll have to *talk*. We really must conclude this business."

"Are you mad? You can't produce a ball in a matter of days."

"Oh, but I can," she said, and her voice was made of steel. "Ten days is all I need."

He could imagine it—she'd call on every trade in this town and would have what she wanted by the end of the week. He wanted to argue. To explain to her he'd been to enough balls, had met enough ladies. But he said nothing because he feared the explosion that would come if he opened his mouth.

He turned and walked out of the room. He heard her calling for Borerro the moment he stepped into the hall. Not a moment to waste, was there?

The trouble was, he didn't know how to stop her. He could, of course, instruct that no ball would be hosted here. But his mother was tenacious—she would hound him, follow him like a cat, complaining and carrying on. She would assume the role of his father, berating him for being stubborn or indecisive.

Moreover—and this infuriated him—his mother was right. The clock was ticking. But so was his heart, for the one woman in London that was not on Lady Aleksander's damnable list.

Speaking of that woman… Hattie was at the window when he walked into the study. She didn't hear him at first—she was laughing.

"Hattie?"

She gasped and whirled around. "Oh! I didn't hear you."

"What has amused you?"

She pointed to the window. "Him," she said.

Mateo joined her at the window and looked down. Hattie leaned over the sill, smiling as she pointed to a gentleman and his dog on the street.

His head filled with the scent of her perfume. Her hand was pressed against a pane as she leaned forward, and he wanted to take it in his, press it against his heart.

"Do you see?"

He mentally shook his head clear and glanced down.

"He's been attempting to teach the dog to roll over."

"To what?"

"Roll over," she said, and demonstrated by flipping her hand.

Mateo watched as the old man mimicked the act of rolling over, but the brown dog circled instead, its tail wagging with excitement. The man tried again, this time by putting his hand on the walk and "rolling" it. The dog stretched its body and sniffed the man's hand.

Hattie giggled. She covered her mouth with her hand, trying not to laugh out loud...but her eyes were brimming with amusement. "He's tried absolutely everything."

Mateo wanted to kiss her. He wanted to take her in his arms and lay her down on the settee and make her his. But as with everything in his life, he did nothing. He sank into the habits of a young boy. He hated himself for it.

Then the man and the dog walked on, the dog's tail wagging enthusiastically, and the man looking rather dejected.

Hattie instantly moved away from the window and went to her desk. "My apologies. I opened the window for a bit of air and—"

"No apology necessary." He watched her rearrange some things on her desk. Her levity had disappeared, and strangely, he could sense some tension in her. Was he the cause of it? If so, he hated himself for it. "Are you all right?"

"Estoy bien," she said.

He arched a brow—someone had been teaching her Spanish. She said she was fine. He didn't believe it, but he was not going to make the situation worse by interrogating her.

"Actually," she said, "I'm not *fine*. I'm more... Well, I'm probably fine. But I think it's a bit too early to say."

She was confusing him. "What?"

"I thought that..." She stood up from her desk and clasped her hands together at her waist. "I thought that perhaps I might have said to you what I did—at the garden party, I mean, at which, I'm sure you recall, I really was quite awful—that I might have said the same in a less agitated manner."

He'd thought her agitation was deserved. "You made your point very well. You said you'd not tread on eggs around me but it seems...it seems like perhaps you are, still?"

She stared at him. "I am, aren't I?" Her shoulders sagged. "I don't want to, but neither do I want to vex you."

"On the contrary—I think I am the one vexing you. I don't think you could ever be vexing, Hattie."

She smiled wryly. "Oh, I think I could." She pushed a stray tendril of hair from her face as she gazed at him. "Is it possible, do you think...that we might be friends?"

Friends. It was the last thing he wanted—or rather the first thing he wanted—but he wanted so much more. He thought of his mother, of his parliamentary council. He thought of every conceivable angle, but as no other option presented itself, he would cling to this notion. "Friends," he reluctantly agreed.

She smiled. She extended her hand. He shook it. The agreement was made.

Hattie returned to her desk. But Mateo stood there, unmoving, for a long moment. *Friends* left a sour feeling in the pit of his stomach. It was wrong, all wrong. He was the duke, he had responsibilities—but he was also a man.

An image of his father's unsmiling face suddenly loomed.

"My lord?"

Borerro's voice cut through the silence in the room. Mateo turned to the door where his butler had come in with the day's post. Mateo walked across the room to receive it, and Borerro went out, leaving the door open behind him.

Mateo looked at Hattie. He couldn't stand there like this, dithering about feelings that were too complicated to sort. He decided he would test their friendship. "May I ask you something? As a friend?"

"Of course." She put down her pen and turned in her seat.

"What do you think of Miss Raney? As a match?"

Hattie blinked her perfectly blue eyes. "I, ah…"

"Forgive me. I shouldn't have asked." What a ridiculous thing to have done. He was trying to douse his feelings with stupid questions. He turned back to his desk.

"She's a good person, Teo," Hattie said. He paused. "She always means well, and she always tries her best."

He glanced at Hattie over his shoulder. "I see."

"You can't possibly see, not really."

He turned to face her. "I can't?"

She shook her head. "That's the problem with our society, isn't it? We're hardly able to know anyone before we're engaged." She glanced away from him, and he assumed she was thinking of her broken engagement. "Flora is my friend. We attended school together. She is kind, and she can make me laugh. And I think she is a good friend. I never told anyone this," she said quietly, "but it was Flora who told me what no one else would. That my fiancé's feelings had changed."

He sank onto the arm of the settee. "That must have been difficult to hear."

"It was, indeed. But…but my point is that she would be a good match for you. She has many admirable qualities."

But could he ever love her?

Hattie looked at her lap. "Are you close to making an offer?"

Mateo sighed. Was he? "I don't believe I will have the option to leave England without a match. Not if I want peace with my family. Or with my duchy. Or with my parliament."

She nodded. "Then I think she would make you an excellent match. You couldn't possibly do better."

Oh, but he could do better. For himself, he could do so much better. He'd never contemplated having to choose between his heart and his duty—he'd always assumed the two would align.

His father had once called him naive. Maybe he was.

But what Mateo knew was that the best match for him—here, in Santiava, in the world—was this woman. Hattie was refreshingly honest. And fascinating. She was attractive and alluring, her disposition nearly perfect. He had never in his life been so enchanted by a woman as he was by her. He thought about their kiss often. He thought about how much more he wanted from her.

He looked at his post, forcing himself to turn his attention. Because his mind was busily listing all the reasons it could not be her, and he didn't want to hear them.

LILA WAS NOT above eavesdropping, particularly when the opportunity fell into her lap. What was she supposed to do? The door was open, she'd heard them talking, and she'd heard them laughing. *Laughing.* She'd never heard that dour, unhappy man laugh. He'd sounded like a completely different person, and of course her interest had been piqued.

So she'd paused, had leaned against the wall, and she'd listened. Her husband, Valentin, would tell her she was being rude. She certainly was being rude. But she was also trying to divine her way out of a terrible problem. It was becoming increasingly clear that Lord Abbott was in love with Miss Woodchurch. He wanted the woman who could offer nothing but her love and affection. Lila was all for that sort of match, but Elizabeth, well…she would not be happy.

It was a terribly difficult problem and one that required finesse to solve. But that's what Lila loved about her services. She relished the challenge of turning things around for the viscount. He needed love, and he needed to laugh. Miss Woodchurch needed a safe harbor in this world. Those two were perfect for each other and she was giddy with the prospect of making it happen.

CHAPTER TWENTY-FIVE

THE INVITATION TO the Abbott ball came while the Wood-churches were at their lunch—the twins, Daniel, Hattie, her parents, and an assortment of cats, all gathered in the dining room.

Her father, having eaten his meal before everyone was served, was picking his teeth with a knife as he squinted at each letter in his post. Hattie was trying to force down a bite or two of mutton. They'd lost another cook this week, the third this year. Imagine, a woman who refused to make large meals while surrounded by dress forms, loud clocks, and cats.

Her father paused his teeth picking and squinted at one of the envelopes, then dropped the knife and held the envelope overhead. "Take a look at what we have here, lads," he said loudly, gaining the attention of all.

"What?" asked Peter.

"An invitation for Miss Harriet Woodchurch, that's what."

Hattie certainly hoped it wasn't for another garden party.

"What's it for?" her father asked her, waving the thing at her across the table.

"I don't know, Papa. I've not seen the invitation."

"You don't *know*," he mimicked. He lowered the envelope, picked up the knife he'd used to pick his teeth, and opened it.

"Papa! That's addressed to me!" she protested.

He ignored her and read the card. *"Fancy,"* he sneered, then tossed the card in her direction. It skidded across the table and landed with one corner in the gravy. Perry grabbed it before anyone moved and licked the gravy from the envelope.

"Disgusting!" Peter cried, and then howled with laughter.

"Give it to me, Perry," Hattie insisted.

"It's a ball," her father said, settling back in his chair. "Your fancy viscount is hosting a bloody *ball*."

She'd heard some rumblings about a ball but had no idea when it was planned or who was invited. She certainly didn't expect to be. She grabbed Perry's wrist and squeezed. He cried out as if he was in pain, but then dropped the invitation on her plate, on top of her uneaten mutton.

"Mama!" Hattie exclaimed. "Can't you do something?"

"They're boys, Harriet," she said, and bent down to pick up a cat.

Dear God, this family. How much more could she endure?

"It's obscene that all of London is so eager to meet this man," Daniel said. "What's so bloody special about him, really?"

"Please," Hattie's mother said, and for a moment, she thought her mother meant to help her. But no. "It's his money, quite obviously."

"We have money and they aren't lining up to meet us," Daniel pointed out.

"What do you mean?" her father said to his oldest son. "*You* haven't got any money."

Daniel ignored him and looked at Hattie. "I heard he's unbearably rude."

An interesting criticism from someone who was, in fact, unbearably rude. Her first instinct was to defend Teo, but she knew what her brother was doing. He wanted to rile her, to put her back on her heels.

"Isn't that so, Hat?" Daniel pushed. "Aloof and superior and disdainful to us poor, simple Englishmen."

Hattie shrugged. "I don't know how he is to poor, simple Englishmen." She was not going to share Teo with her family. She was not going to give them the satisfaction of finding reasons to belittle him to her. She had one blessed thing that they hadn't yet destroyed, and that was her days with him.

She could not wait to leave this house for good, one way or another.

"It's absurd, these invitations you're getting," her mother complained. "Why are they sending them? Just what are you promising for them?"

"I beg your pardon?" Hattie exclaimed, greatly affronted. "Nothing!"

"Leave her be, woman," her father said to her mother. "This might all lead to something."

That struck fear in Hattie, and she slowly turned her gaze to her father. "What do you mean?"

"I mean, keep your ears and eyes open for opportunity, Harriet." He pointed at his own ear.

"You've got nothing to wear to a posh ball," her mother said.

"Yes. Papa… May I buy a ball gown? I need one."

"You don't need one," he said dismissively. "An expensive frock to wear a single night? No." He returned his attention to the post.

Hattie rubbed her temples. She was giving him fifteen percent of her wages. He couldn't allow one gown?

"I might have one or two," her mother said with a sniff. "I was quite remarked for my clothes when I was young."

A ball gown from twenty years ago, Hattie thought gloomily. She'd be the one everyone talked about. And not in a complimentary way.

THAT AFTERNOON, Hattie accompanied Flora and Queenie to a fitting of their many ball gowns. How ironic that today, of all days, she would be forced to look at all the beautiful clothes the two of them had purchased.

When Flora stepped behind a screen to don the first gown, Queenie sat beside Hattie on the small settee and smiled in a manner that made Hattie immediately suspicious.

"Tell me, Hattie," Queenie said, her voice low. "Flora believes she has all but secured the viscount's proposal. Is that *true*?"

"Queenie, I never said that," Flora protested from behind the privacy screen.

"Perhaps not, darling, but you're thinking it," Queenie said back.

Flora stepped out from behind the screen and presented her back to the attendant to fasten the hooks. "What do you think, Hattie, really?" she asked.

"It's beautiful," Hattie said, admiring the yellow-and-white silk gown.

"Not the clothes, goose. *Him.* I truly don't know what he thinks of me. And I feel as if I talked and talked to the point of being overbearing and insufferable."

"Men don't like women who talk too much," Queenie said.

Hattie shot Queenie a look. "You did wonderfully, Flora."

"Did I, really?"

"You were the picture of elegance and confidence."

Flora beamed. Queenie rolled her eyes.

"But...has he said anything about me?" Flora asked.

Hattie's heart pinched. She swallowed. "Not to me," she lied.

Queenie smiled as if that answer pleased her. "Has he said anything about anyone?"

"No."

Queenie snorted. "Really, Flora, why do you bother? She never knows anything."

It felt like Queenie was judging their friendship based on what gossip Hattie was able to provide. It left her feeling indignant, and she said, "I heard him speak to his mother, however."

Flora gasped and jerked around, causing the attendant to stumble. "And?" she asked, wide-eyed.

"And...he esteems you."

"What?" Queenie looked at Flora. "He esteems her? And no one else? Are you certain he didn't mention anyone else?"

"Queenie!" Flora complained.

Hattie looked Queenie directly in the eye and said, "No, Queenie, no one else. I heard him speak only of Flora."

Queenie sank back into the settee with a look of disappointment. Another attendant appeared. "Miss Rodham, we are ready to help you into one of your gowns."

"Fine," Queenie said, and hauled herself up and disappeared behind another screen.

Hattie stood and moved to Flora's side. *"Flora,"* she whispered. "The viscount truly esteems you."

Flora frowned at her. "You said you didn't know."

"I don't." Hattie winced, annoyed that she was already

tangled up in her lie. "But…but I know the sort of person he likes."

"How? Does he discuss it with you?"

"Not…not like that." Why had she opened her mouth? "Really, it's more of a feeling I have. Based on a few things I've heard him say about acquaintances here and there."

Flora looked dubious. She returned her gaze to her reflection in the mirror.

Hattie inwardly groaned. "He… I think he really does admire you, but I can't say more than that. I mean, I don't *know* more than that. But…I know him a bit better than Queenie. After all, I see him several times a week."

"You do, don't you?" Flora said. She gave Hattie a look, then turned to the attendant. "This one seems fine. Shall we go to the next?"

As the attendant went behind the screen to prepare the next gown, Flora smiled at Hattie. But her smile didn't feel genuine. "Thank you, Hattie. You're so good to me." She followed the attendant behind the screen.

An hour later, when Flora and Queenie had tried on their gowns and had them fitted—five for Flora, seven for Queenie—the three of them left the shop. They stood on the corner of Bond Street for a few moments—Queenie had a carriage to ferry her off and was taking her time in saying her goodbyes. "Hattie, dearest," she said just before she climbed into the carriage. "You really should be more helpful to Flora. I think you could if you only put your mind to it."

Hattie smiled thinly. "I will do my best." She was really beginning to despise Queenie.

She and Flora turned in the opposite direction. Flora wasn't very talkative as they walked—she seemed lost in thought. And because Hattie was desperately wondering if she'd offended her somehow, she missed Daniel completely. The two of them almost plowed into him. Where had he come from? He just seemed to appear.

"Well, well," he said, his gaze on Flora. "What a fortunate day for me." He tipped his hat.

"Mr. Woodchurch," Flora said stiffly. "Fancy meeting you on Bond Street."

"What's the matter, love? Think I don't belong here?"

Hattie gasped at the cavalier way he spoke to Flora.

"I didn't say that, did I?" Flora shot back, and Daniel chuckled darkly.

"What are you doing here, Daniel?" Hattie demanded.

"That's none of your affair, sister. But I'm not spending my father's money," he said, his gaze sliding back to Flora.

Flora lifted her chin. "That's perhaps because *my* father is very generous with his money."

"Oh my—" Hattie started, but Daniel had leaned in close to Flora. "I don't care."

"Daniel!" Hattie cried. "Please, not another word. Go! Leave us be, please!"

Daniel laughed. He smiled and winked at Flora, then tipped his hat again. "Good day, ladies." And with his hands clasped behind his back, he strolled on.

Flora watched him go, her expression growing darker. "I'm so sorry, Hattie."

"What? Why? I should apologize to you."

"Yes, you should. But that doesn't make me any less sorry that he is your brother. He has the *worst* of reputations, you know."

Hattie frowned. "It's not the best, I know…but the worst?"

Flora turned to her and put a hand on her arm. "I mean, dearest, the Woodchurch name in general."

Hattie recoiled with a surprise that felt terrible.

"I'm so sorry, but it's true. Your family... Everyone knows your brother is a rake, your father notoriously cheap, and you, working for a bachelor."

Hattie was so stunned she couldn't speak. That was all true, but it was still her family Flora was casually disparaging. She didn't know if she ought to defend them or even if she could.

"I mean, no one thinks ill of *you*, of course. Everyone knows you've been pushed into work."

"You...you don't need to say more," Hattie said shakily. "I'm aware of—"

"Mr. Masterson didn't cry off because of you, remember that. It was because of your brother and the rest of them."

Hattie felt strangely floaty, as if she was leaving her body. And she didn't know what to do with her hands. Because they desperately wanted to go around Flora's neck.

"I'm so sorry. I'm being insensitive," Flora said with a wince.

"Yes, you are," Hattie agreed. And *cruel*.

"I do beg your pardon, but seeing your brother reminds me that you're *so much* better than the rest of them." She linked her arm through Hattie's and began to walk. "I wish we could have you all to ourselves." And she continued to stroll along as if she'd said nothing wrong.

Hattie couldn't shake the confusion over why Flora would speak to her like that. Or the feeling of disloyalty for not standing up for her family—even when she had no desire to because they were awful. She felt caught in a vise, not knowing which way to turn.

But there was something else leaving her feeling terribly uncomfortable. This was not the first time Flora had mentioned her family, and Daniel in particular.

CHAPTER TWENTY-SIX

MRS. O'MALLEY WAS practically levitating with excitement—she'd been commissioned to make bonbons and *two* four-tiered marzipan cakes for the Abbott ball.

"That's wonderful!" Hattie exclaimed.

"You must tell me everyone's opinion. Even if the opinions aren't flattering, you must tell me."

Hattie put her things on the little desk. "I would, but I won't be attending."

"What? *Why?*" Mrs. O'Malley cried. "But you must! Weren't you invited?"

"Yes, but—"

"Then you must go! You can't decline an invitation like that."

Hattie winced. "I've nothing to wear, Mrs. O'Malley. You've seen my gowns."

Mrs. O'Malley blinked. "Is *that* all?"

Hattie laughed. "It seems an insurmountable obstacle to me."

But Mrs. O'Malley was shaking her head. "You leave that to me, Miss Woodchurch."

Hattie smiled gratefully. "That's very kind, but—"

"Trust me." She put her hands on Hattie's shoulders and turned back to her work. "Come round tomorrow, and you'll see."

Hattie thought she'd come round tomorrow and see

something much like what was in her mother's wardrobe. But she promised she would return the next day.

When she'd finished her work for Mrs. O'Malley, Hattie carried on to Grosvenor Square. Teo was not in his study, but he'd left some things for her to decipher and to write. She was in the middle of writing a reply to a letter when she heard the door open. She turned, smiling, expecting Teo.

It was not Teo. It was his mother. She strolled into the study and looked around the room before allowing her gaze to settle on Hattie. "My son has gone to Harrington Hall today. Were you not informed?"

Hattie gained her feet and curtsied. "Good afternoon, your grace. No, I wasn't aware."

"Hmm," she said, and her gaze flicked over Hattie as if she suspected her of something. She then moved a little deeper into the study. "I wouldn't think your services would be required if the viscount is not present."

"Ah…he left three letters to respond to."

The duchess took another step closer, and her eyes narrowed. "Who are your people, if I may?"

Hattie blinked. "My people?"

"Your parents," the duchess said impatiently.

Why did the duchess want to know? The question made Hattie anxious. "Hugh and Theodora Woodchurch."

The duchess frowned. "I've not heard of them."

"I would think not," Hattie agreed.

The duchess looked her over again. Hattie couldn't fathom why the woman was looking at her like she was. As if she thought Hattie was up to no good.

But she turned and started for the door without another word. At the open door, she paused and looked back at Hattie. "You best be about finding someone else to write letters for, Miss Woodchurch. My son will be leaving London very soon and will have no need of your services."

The tone with which she said *services* made Hattie's skin heat. It sounded untoward. But Hattie couldn't help herself. "He's leaving?"

"Of course. I expect he will leave soon after the ball. Are you surprised, Miss Woodchurch? Did you think he'd be here always, needing letters written?"

"No, I—"

"Because he is the duke of Santiava. A *sovereign* duke. Not a man sitting at a desk dictating letters." And with that, the duchess walked out of the study.

Hattie waited until she was certain she was gone before she turned and sank into her chair. She pressed a hand to her heart, it was beating so wildly. Not because the duchess had been so terribly rude. But because he was leaving soon.

HATTIE RETURNED TO Mrs. O'Malley's shop the next day, as promised. Mrs. O'Malley grinned when she came in, and wiped her hands on her apron. "I knew you'd come."

"I said I would," Hattie replied, and smiled. She really had no intention of attending the Abbott ball. She didn't belong there, and she didn't care to see Teo courting Flora. But when his mother had said he was leaving... Well, Hattie had changed her mind.

"Come with me," Mrs. O'Malley said. "Molly, darling, you'll keep an eye on things here, won't you?" she called to one of her daughters, then took Hattie by the hand and pulled her into the small office in the back where Hattie usually worked. And there, hanging on a cooling rack, was a dark green dress over a pale gold petticoat with what looked like a daring neckline. The petticoat was ruffled, and a velvet band wrapped around the waist. Hattie was awed by it. "Oh my. It's *beautiful*."

"Isn't it?" Mrs. O'Malley went to the gown and removed it. There was another gown behind it, black and white.

"Mrs. O'Malley! Wherever did you get them?" Hattie exclaimed as she ran her hand over the green velvet.

"My sister. She married Mr. Colin Pearce, who serves on the King's Bench. There was a time they were invited to every drawing room. But she's had two children in quick succession, and she's gotten fat." She laughed. "She and Mr. Pearce do not attend balls as they once did. She sent three gowns, in fact—two evening and one day." She lifted the black-and-white one to reveal a deep sea-blue gown with a pale blue petticoat peeking out beneath. Hattie stared at them in shock.

"She has made a gift of them to you."

"No!" Hattie exclaimed. "I can't possibly accept such a generous gift."

"Of course you can, Miss Woodchurch. My sister is as grateful to you as I am for creating this opportunity for me. And she's thrilled that her gowns could be worn to something as fancy as the Abbott ball. Come, let's try them on. Estella!" She called for another one of her daughters. "Estella is quick with a needle and thread."

Hattie could hardly see because of the tears in her eyes. How could she be so fortunate?

"Now, you send your favorable reply for the ball, love," Mrs. O'Malley said. "And listen carefully to what is said of my bonbons."

Hattie laughed. "I can never repay your kindness."

"Darling, you already have."

CHAPTER TWENTY-SEVEN

THE TRIP TO Essex and Harrington Hall had left Mateo feeling out of sorts. For one, the estate was so large he couldn't imagine what he would do with it. For two—and this one shocked him, as he did not consider himself a sentimental man—he had gone the day without seeing Hattie.

He could feel the tides shifting in him. He'd begun to feel a gnawing sense of time slipping away. It wouldn't be long before he would bid farewell to his friend and leave England.

His *friend*. The word, both in English and Spanish, felt inadequate to describe how he felt about Hattie Woodchurch.

He watched the clock on his study mantel slowly tick, counting the minutes until she appeared with her bag and her pen, ready to write. And when at last she did arrive, she was wearing a deep blue gown that shone in her eyes—they seemed to leap from her face.

He stood up. "Good afternoon. You look lovely."

She smiled with delight. "Thank you."

"I went to Harrington Hall yesterday, in Essex," he said. He felt an urgent need to tell her why he'd been absent.

She brightened. "How did you find it? Was it terribly grand? I've heard it's as big as Buckingham Palace."

"It's unconscionably big," he agreed. "I couldn't help but

wonder what my grandfather thought the point of it was for one man."

"For his heirs," Hattie said. "It's always for the heirs, isn't it?" She walked across the room and held out her hand. He realized he'd been holding some work for her. He reluctantly handed it to her. He watched her go to her desk. He watched her sit and arrange paper and pen and the small vase of flowers someone had placed on her desk. He sat at his desk, too, and tried to concentrate, but he found all he could do was watch her. There were so many emotions stirring in his chest and his head. He had terribly mixed emotions. He was ready to leave England—he missed Santiava—but obviously not ready to leave some things behind.

He didn't realize just how unsettled he was until his mother swept in with the list of replies to the ball. He looked at the list of attendees. His mother had taken it upon herself to underline the names of those women that were unmarried and suitable for a match. He ignored those; he was looking for another name. And it wasn't there.

He glanced up at Hattie, hard at work at her desk. She had not replied.

"Thank you," he said to his mother, and handed her back the list. "If you will excuse me, I've a matter to attend to."

"Where are you going?" his mother demanded, and followed him out of the study, the list in her hand.

"Out," he said curtly. In the foyer, he took his hat and struck out, his destination unknown.

Mateo walked to think. He walked to Hyde Park, and through it. Then on to Green Park. He walked up and down Piccadilly, trying to make sense of his life.

When at last he'd had enough walking, he returned to Grosvenor Square. His mother had flitted off to somewhere, and Hattie was just finishing up for the day. She'd wrapped her long shawl around her shoulders and was rummaging through her bag when he walked in.

"Hattie," he said. "You're for home?"

"I am." She hoisted the bag onto her shoulder.

"I, ah… I don't mean to impose, but I…"

He dragged his fingers through his hair. He was unnervingly anxious. "I have some work to do on the accounts from Harrington Hall, and I thought, perhaps…you might stay past tea and help me? I…I would compensate you, of course."

She stared at him for a long moment, and he thought she meant to decline, and he thought if she did, he would excuse himself, walk out to the garden, and scream into the hedge.

"I should be delighted to help, of course. But I don't want compensation for it." She smiled.

He felt ridiculous for having offered it. "Thank you. I… If you don't mind, I'll ask Yolanda for a light supper. But only if you…want." He knew he was blathering.

Her smile widened. She put down her bag. "I *do* want. I hope it's something deliciously Santiavan. Will I need a pen?"

"A pen?"

"For the work," she said.

"Ah, of course. But I think not." Because he had no work for her. It was all a made-up, preposterous pretense, because he had nothing but a desire to be with her and didn't know how to ask that of her. He rang for Borerro, and told him, in Spanish, that he and Miss Woodchurch would be finishing up this evening, and he would like Yolanda to prepare the paella she'd made.

When Borerro went out, Mateo directed Hattie to the

settee and took a chair across from her. "May I ask a question?" he asked.

"Of course."

"Why have you not replied to the invitation to the ball?"

She looked a bit taken aback. "Oh. I only just decided. I'll bring my reply tomorrow, if I may."

"Of course." Why had she only just decided? "Did something give you pause?"

She shrugged lightly. "It's simple, really. I don't belong there. Your ball is for the Quality."

He was surprised by her response—she didn't strike him as someone concerned about that sort of thing. At least, she hadn't thus far. "That's not so. I didn't see to it that an invitation was issued to you so that you might look after children."

She grinned. "Well, thank you for that, at least. Why did you invite me?"

She had to ask? "Hattie...you belong. You're my friend and I wish to have you there. I expect to be accosted by eager mothers and their daughters. What if I'm dragged onto the dance floor and made to choose before God and everyone? Who will avenge my demise?"

"Oh, Teo," she said sweetly. "I believe with all my heart that your mother would avenge you. I think she would relish the challenge."

He couldn't help but laugh. "So you have taken my mother's measure. But you are mistaken—she will lead me to my demise. I don't mean to impose on our friendship, but you've surely noticed by now that I'm not particularly affable or easy around people. And that is not from a lack of want."

"I haven't noticed any such thing."

He gave her a knowing smile. "Hattie."

"I haven't!" she insisted. "What I've noticed is that you are reserved. Many people are reserved. In school, there was a girl, Mary Collins, who could hardly utter her own name out loud. We thought something quite wrong with her, that she suffered from a shyness so profound as to render her a mute. But when Jenny kicked Sarah, Mary intervened and knocked Jenny to the ground."

"Dios mío," Mateo said, surprised and amused by the turn in her story.

"It was a bit violent, but the point is, Mary was reserved—until she needed not to be. So are you."

"No, I am..." He tried to think of the proper English word. *"Timidez."*

"Timid?"

"Something like that. My father was very hard on me as his heir and future head of the duchy. He wanted to discipline and teach me and mold me into his image. He attempted to do so by finding fault in most everything I did or said, and as a result, I learned to say very little and believed everyone who looked in my direction was eyeing me critically."

"How awful for you. And your mother?"

"My mother kept my father happy and didn't burden herself with her children—Rosa has been more of a mother to me than the duchess."

"Teo, goodness," she said softly. "That must have been difficult for you."

He smiled ruefully. His childhood had not been a storybook, and for better or worse, it had shaped who he was today. "I was privileged in many other ways."

"Mine was a bit difficult, too—until Lord Iddesleigh saved me."

Mateo frowned. *"Saved* you?"

"He did, truly. He managed to convince my parents that I should attend his school. I don't know how he managed, as they can rarely be convinced of anything other than what serves their interests, and my father...my father does not like to part with his money. But had it not been for Lord Iddesleigh and the school, I don't think I'd have the confidence to seek work and make my own way. I owe him a debt of gratitude."

"Then I owe him one, too," Mateo said.

Hattie grinned, and the warmth of it sank into his marrow. He imagined how rejuvenating it would be to see such a smile every day.

A knock at the door; one of the footmen wheeled in a cart with two platters covered with domes. Mateo instructed him to place the food on the small table nearby, then invited Hattie to sit there.

The footman uncovered the platters and spooned paella into bowls. She looked on with interest, asking about the ingredients. When the footman had finished, Mateo invited her to have a bite.

She closed her eyes. "It's divine," she proclaimed it. "I could eat the entire pan of it." She opened her eyes. "But I will share with you."

He laughed.

She asked him, as they dined, about his life growing up among the stars. Mateo told her as best he could—he found it difficult to describe the splendor of those mountains in English. Somehow, he got around to his hunting dogs. She said she'd always been fond of dogs, but that her mother preferred cats, and she'd not been allowed to have one.

From there, they moved to topics that had no bearing on anything. Games they played as children. People they'd met as adults who'd baffled them for various reasons—such as a woman Mateo had heard of who'd left her wealthy husband for a farmer. Or the gentleman Hattie knew who gave all his riches to a slum and then lived in the slum himself.

They chatted like old friends. Or better yet, old lovers. Mateo didn't want the conversation or evening to end—he couldn't remember the last time he'd been so at ease over dinner, so compatible with another person at his table.

She asked about Harrington Hall, and he told her that it was really more of a palace. There were so many rooms, all of them furnished, with paintings and porcelain and gold and fine rugs. It seemed too much, as if his grandfather's wealth had been used not for the greater good of the estate, or to improve wages, or to help the poor…but to feed his ego.

He told her that from one end of the ballroom there was a stunning view of the sea. That French doors in the morning room opened onto a terrace and below that, an amazing topiary that seemed to stretch for a mile.

"It sounds astonishingly beautiful," she said wistfully. "What a blessing it would be to live in such a place."

And Mateo wanted, more than anything, for her to live in a place like that.

When the meal was finished, and the footman had taken it away, Hattie sat back in her chair, folded her hands in her lap and smiled wryly. "We've spent the entire evening talking. You've not yet asked me to do anything for you."

He'd forgotten about that. He smiled a little, too. "I want you to look at something for me."

"Of course."

"Not in here."

Her brows dipped. "Where?"

"Come with me." He stood up and held out his hand.

Hattie didn't leap to her feet. She looked warily at his hand. "Come where?"

"You are suspicious. Please, just come."

Her eyes locked with his. He saw that light of warmth in them, of affection. Of…friendship or camaraderie, or affinity. Or rather, what he supposed those things must look like. But he felt them at his core, and when she smiled, and slipped her hand into his, and allowed him to pull her to her feet, he felt as if he'd won a very long race. She was standing just before him, and an ocean of regard began to rise between them.

Her gaze narrowed playfully. "Are you quite certain? Because you look a tiny bit unsure of yourself, Teo."

"The only thing I'm unsure about is if you can see in the dark. Come," he said, and led her out of the room.

In the hallway, he looked around to assure himself no one was watching, then put his hand on the small of her back and hurried her along to the servants' staircase. Up they went, him putting a finger to his lips, her giggling. At the very top of the stairs was a hatch door onto the roof. He opened it, climbed to the top, then helped her up.

They were standing on top of his house. London was below them, chimneys at eye level, and the night sky spread above them. "Oh," she said, looking up. "The whole night is on top of us."

It was a clear, cool night, and the stars glittered overhead, sometimes obscured by a trail of smoke from a chimney. Mateo stepped behind her and pointed. "Do you see an oval shape? It should look a bit fuzzy."

"Where?"

He moved closer, his front against her back, and slipped his arm around her waist and pulled her into his chest. She didn't resist him; he felt a slight tremble run through her that matched the shiver of desire that shimmied down his spine. He leaned over her shoulder. "It looks as if someone pressed their thumb against the night."

She leaned her head against his shoulder as she looked up. With his hand, he lifted her arm and pointed her fingers directly at the star. "Now do you see it?"

"I—I think so," she said.

"That is Andromeda. Do you know her story?"

Hattie shook her head.

He lowered her arm and wrapped his hand around hers. "She was the daughter of a king who chained her to a rock to appease a sea monster."

"A sea monster! That sounds wretched. Was she forced to spend her life in chains?"

"Until Perseus saved her."

"Good for Perseus! I hope he didn't make her wait too long for rescue."

He leaned down and kissed the curve of Hattie's neck— she sucked in a breath and shivered against him. "You need a Perseus, I think," he murmured, and kissed her neck again.

Hattie leaned her head to one side, to allow him access. He moved a hand to her neck and her chest, felt the inevitable sweep into desire and lust—

Hattie pushed his hand down and stepped away.

He was stunned at first, rudely ejected from that feeling of bliss.

"We are friends," she said. "Because there is no other option for us."

"There must be," he said, and dragged his fingers through his hair. "There must be a way."

"But there isn't," she said. It was dark, and the moonlight shimmered in her eyes like light on a dark sea, and he couldn't be certain, but he thought that maybe her eyes had filled with tears. "I must go," Hattie said. "Now. It's time for me to go."

"Don't. Not yet. We—"

"Now. Please, Mateo."

He reluctantly nodded and helped her down the narrow steps. When they returned to the study, she collected her things. She paused to look at him before she went out, her expression full of the same longing he felt in his breast. Mateo sent Carlos after her, to see her home. "She'll refuse you," he said in Spanish, "and if you can't convince her, follow at a distance. But see her home."

The footman nodded and ran out to catch Hattie.

Mateo stood in the open doorway, staring out at the square and the sky above. Hattie was Andromeda, sparkling above him. Or maybe he was Andromeda, as he felt the invisible chains trapping him. But he was determined to be Perseus and save them both.

If only he knew how.

CHAPTER TWENTY-EIGHT

IF HATTIE HAD any doubts about attending the ball—and she had many in the next few days—it was Daniel who in the end convinced her by appealing to her vanity. "Might as well attend if you've this to wear," he said as he held up her gown to his body and studied it in the mirror in Hattie's room. "You'll not have many opportunities to wear something as fine as this, will you?"

He was never one to blunt his opinion. Hattie eyed him with suspicion. "You have never cared before what gowns I have or where I might wear them."

He shrugged. "Seems like a waste to let this one go."

He was right. She wanted Teo to see her in that gown. She was as drawn to him as she had been the first time she'd laid eyes on him; she was in love with him. But she was also exasperatingly practical, and in spite of anything Teo or Daniel had said, she knew she didn't belong in that crowd.

Still, Teo was leaving soon—how many more times would she see him?

Not enough. Not nearly enough.

So it was the night of the Abbott ball she found herself in the ballroom, a room she had not seen in all her time at Grosvenor Square. Teo's mother had outdone herself. There were performers in the garden, one of them swallowing fire while another one walked a high wire strung between the garden walls. There were torch lights all around, and it made the garden seem to glitter.

Inside, a twelve-piece string orchestra played from an alcove above the ballroom, and floral displays were hung from the ceiling to create the illusion of dancing in a garden.

Daniel had abandoned her the moment they'd entered, as usual, so Hattie was standing in the back, admiring it all, as well as her lovely dress, and sipping a glass of punch when Mateo entered the ballroom.

His entrance was a grand one—he looked magnificent, handsome and proud, tall and assured. He was dressed in a formal black suit, a riband across his chest bearing the many medals of Santiava. His dark hair was brushed back, his beard neatly trimmed. He hardly stepped foot into the ballroom before he was accosted by guests.

Just seeing him gave her a bit of a shiver. His lips had been on hers. They'd been on her neck. And in her dreams, they'd been everywhere else.

There was one thing she could say for herself—she was not the least bit shy about torturing herself.

She had hoped to catch his eye, to show him that she had come. But Lady Aleksander quickly intercepted him and began to introduce him to ladies. It looked as if he didn't have a moment to breathe, much less look around.

She wondered what it was like for him, to be the fish in the bowl, given what he'd told her about his childhood. She imagined herself in another life, at his side, soothing him with her presence. She would be the one to do all the talking, for which she knew he'd be grateful. The thought made her smile.

"What are you smiling at?"

Hattie jumped at the sound of Queenie's voice. "Oh, just…everything."

"Hmm," Queenie said, and looked across the room to where Teo was talking to a lady.

"Have you seen Flora?"

"She's in the retiring room, letting her nerves get the best of her," Queenie said. "Look, the dancing is about to begin. I overheard two ladies placing a small wager on who he'd start the dance with. Who do you suppose they said?"

"Flora?"

"Flora, yes…and Christiana Porter." She rolled her eyes. "Looks always win over anything else when it comes to gentlemen. I won't be the least surprised when he offers for her. It's simply biology."

The small orchestra began to play a waltz.

"There's Flora," Queenie said, and moved away from Hattie, presumably to be on hand for the moment Teo asked Flora to dance. She would probably claim she'd arranged it or knew in advance.

Teo walked deeper into the room, his gaze scanning the crowd. Everyone was watching him, to see how he'd start the dance. His mother was talking to him, leaning into him with a possessive tilt of her body. But Teo ignored her and began to cross the dance floor.

The crowd murmured, looking around them, trying to see who the lucky lady was. And then the crowd was parting. And *then*, as if Hattie was in a dream, Teo walked up to her. He bowed.

Hattie's mouth gaped open. She quickly glanced around, almost certain someone would leap out of the drapes or the flowers to haul her away. "Miss Woodchurch, good evening."

"What— Good evening," she said, remembering herself, and curtsied.

"May I say, you look…*beautiful*. I hope that you will do me the honor of the first dance."

He was mad! *"Me?"*

"I would be my great pleasure."

"I don't... I have—"

He smoothly took the glass from her hand and held it out without taking his gaze from her. A footman appeared from the ether and took the glass from him. Teo held up his arm.

She looked at it.

"Just put your hand on it," he murmured.

She numbly placed her hand on his arm.

He led her onto the dance floor and smiled down at her. "*Dios mío*, I hope you know how to dance," he whispered. He took her hand and held it out, then put his hand on her back.

She stared at him, still shocked this was happening. She couldn't seem to move properly, but somehow managed to put her hand on his shoulder.

He stepped into the rhythm of the waltz.

She followed without stumbling, her gaze fixed on a point over his shoulder.

"Is something the matter?" he asked as he moved her around the floor, drawing her closer.

"Are you mad?" she whispered hotly. "I shouldn't be your first dance. The first dance sends a message to the world about your intentions."

"Does it?"

He sounded almost cavalier. More people joined them, and Hattie risked looking at him, half fearful she would melt with want, half fearful she would scold him. "You are singling me out. People will make something of it."

"Let them," he said, and pulled her closer. "You are my friend, aren't you? I need you now. I need a Perseus, and you have spared me the choosing of someone else."

"But I haven't been spared," she told him. "They will all hate me."

He smiled at her.

"Stop smiling at me like that."

"I can't help it. I've never seen you afraid."

"I'm *not* afraid, I'm—"

"It's a dance, Hattie. A single dance," he said soothingly. "No one will remember it by the end of the evening, but at this moment, everyone is watching. Now, help me present a commanding presence and the air of someone who is confident and suave."

"You don't need me for that. You present a commanding presence no matter what you do. I will never forget the first time I saw you."

"Really?" he asked, interested. "And when was that?"

She felt herself smiling, too. "If you must know, it was through a shop window. And there you were, commanding and aloof and with a definite air of superiority."

He laughed and twirled her around. "I remember the first time I saw you, too. It was in my study, and I thought you average in looks and bearing, and with the confidence of a bloody mule."

Hattie snorted. "What a lovely compliment."

"But as the days went on, you became larger than anything else in that study, and more lovely every time I looked at you."

"Now you're making me blush."

"That's what friends are for," he said, and twirled her again.

Hattie smiled. "Is that what they are for? And to think that all this time, I've had it wrong."

His smile deepened, and Hattie felt something powerful pass between them. Something so familiar, yet so new. Something much bigger than her.

The dance was coming to an end. He let go of her, and

she instantly felt adrift. He led her off the dance floor. She curtsied.

He bowed. "Thank you. I hope we have an opportunity to speak again this evening." He walked away.

She watched his mother descend on him, clearly unhappy. And then Lady Sarah Grandview was on his arm.

Hattie turned and walked in the other direction, aware of the eyes on her, aware of the question on everyone's lips—who was she? And why had she garnered the first dance?

She kept her gaze down until she was away from those crowded around the dance floor, and only then did she look up—

And right into the eyes of Queenie Rodham. "Well, *well*," Queenie said. She was looking at Hattie like she'd never really seen her before now. "Why is it the viscount asked you to dance before anyone else, I wonder?"

Hattie tried to laugh as if it was a trifling thing, but sounded a bit like a horse. "Because he is acquainted with me, that's all."

"Not in that way," Queenie said, and Hattie knew what she meant—he was acquainted with her as help. Not a dance partner.

"Where did you get this dress?" Queenie demanded.

Hattie was about to tell her what she could do with her question when Flora appeared. She smiled. "You look beautiful, Hattie."

"Thank you."

Queenie frowned at Flora. "Where were you? I looked everywhere."

"Getting some air, Queenie. Hattie... Why did he dance with you?" Flora asked.

That seemed to be the burning question on everyone's mind. "I think because...he...didn't see you," she blurted.

Flora's expression flooded with relief. "Do you really think so?"

"I do. He as much as said he was looking for a familiar face."

Which could have been anyone, but Flora didn't know that. She smiled triumphantly at Queenie.

Queenie, however, was not fooled. "Then why isn't he looking for her now?"

"Why? Oh, he, ah—"

"Miss Raney?"

The three of them turned at once, surely all of them thinking it was him. But it wasn't him, it was another gentleman who asked if they might spare Flora for a dance. She accepted, and went off, leaving Queenie and Hattie once more.

Queenie was eyeing her closely.

Hattie sighed. "What, Queenie?"

"It doesn't add up, that's all. You're not...you're simply not—"

"You don't have to tell me my place in this world," Hattie interrupted.

"Well, I didn't mean *that*," Queenie insisted.

"I'm sure you didn't," Hattie said, and turned away from her, disappearing into the crowd. She was constantly reminded that she wasn't in her "place." But where was her place? What room, what house, what city was that? She would dearly love to know where it was quite all right with everyone that she simply be herself.

The evening dragged on as she knew it would. No one asked her to dance. No one introduced her, although she saw introductions being made all around her. She saw Daniel a few times, dancing with different women. She didn't know he knew how to dance or even liked it. It was so unfair—because he was a man with a handsome face, he was allowed to enter the private kingdom of the elite.

She tried desperately not to look for Teo every time she turned around, but her heart defied her head, and she kept seeing him in the company of attractive, wealthy women— blonde, brunette, ginger, it was all the same. They were women of privilege and standing, of child-bearing years, and she had no doubt any of them would make a fine duchess. And Teo? He played his part beautifully. He nodded at things they said, held their gaze when they talked. And he danced.

It was hard to imagine this regal man was the same one who had been mixing dough in the kitchen one night.

At long last, one gentleman introduced himself to Hattie. He was a captain in the navy, he said, and wore a worn coat. He was at least three decades older than her. She danced with him and listened politely as he complained about the closeness of the room and theorized why Lord Abbott had not hired a hall. She escaped him and retreated to the potted ferns with a glass of champagne.

That's when she saw Flora and Teo dancing. They were smiling at each other.

Her heart sank like it had been weighted with rocks. She wasn't surprised, and in a strange, impossible way, she was happy for them. They would make a lovely couple.

But at the same time, she felt sick. It was just her luck to have fallen in love with a man so far above her as to be on a cloud.

"Miss Woodchurch, you are quite far away to be admiring the dancing."

Hattie turned; a very handsome man smiled down at her. She knew him at once—he was Mr. Donovan from the Iddesleigh House. He used to come round to the school with tarts. "Mr. Donovan!" she cried, thrilled that there was someone here she knew.

"You look luscious, madam, if I may say. But a little forlorn. Now tell me, *why* are you hiding in a corner? Have your suitors exhausted you?"

Hattie laughed. "I have no suitors, Mr. Donovan."

"What?" He pressed a hand to his heart and pretended to be shocked. "Then how lucky I am. Will you do me the honor of this dance?"

"I certainly will," she said, and put down her glass.

Mr. Donovan led her onto the dance floor. They stepped into the music—he was very smooth, an excellent dancer. He asked after her, about her life and her work. He said she looked quite pretty, and the dark green suited her. She answered all his questions and responded to his compliments, but at the same time, she was surreptitiously looking for Teo.

"You esteem him," Mr. Donovan said. "Perhaps even more than esteem him."

Startled she was so terribly obvious, Hattie looked at him. "Pardon?"

His smile was a bit lopsided. "Lord Abbott, love. You esteem him."

"Well, of course. In a manner of speaking, I suppose. We are friends."

"Ah, *friends*," he said with a knowing smile. "Your secret is safe with me. In fact I will boast and tell you *all* secrets are safe with me."

Hattie blushed. "There is no secret," she said and tried to laugh. "I'm his scribe. I shouldn't even be here! He only invited me because he felt obliged."

Mr. Donovan clucked his tongue. "Obliged! Do you honestly think that Lord Abbott feels obliged to anyone? On my word, he does not."

Hattie frowned. That was probably true to a certain extent.

"Do you know what's wonderful about dancing?" Donovan asked.

She shook her head.

"When we step onto the floor, everyone is the same. We are either good or bad, but no one is above the other. There are no awards or titles or people too poor to dance."

Hattie smiled sheepishly.

"If I may offer some advice?"

"About dancing?"

"Not about dancing. Miss Woodchurch—*Hattie*, if I may—no one is above the other. No matter what the doyennes of society would have you believe, we are all the same. We all have hearts, we all have wants and a desire to be loved. The only thing that matters is that we remain true to ourselves."

He was confusing her. "I don't understand what you're trying to tell me."

"Don't you? My advice is to pursue what you want from this life and don't let anyone convince you that you shouldn't."

Hattie blinked. His point was well-taken. "How did we go from dancing to this?"

He laughed. "I had a pressing need to share. I was once like you in that I tried to fit inside the box that society said I ought to be in. And then one day, I realized I couldn't do it and live with myself. So I made my own box."

The music was coming to an end. "I'm not sure I understand," she said.

"I know." He smiled. "Just know that it's possible to chart your own course. I did. And so can you."

The music ended, and he stepped back and bowed. "The pleasure was mine." He held out his arm and led her from the dance floor.

Mystified, she watched him walk away, but his point was slowly sinking in. She turned, and almost slammed into Teo and Flora.

Flora was glowing. *"Haaaattie,"* she cried, her arms going around Hattie's shoulders. "His lordship and I mean to take some air. It's such a warm night, isn't it? Or maybe it's perfectly fine, but I've been dancing all evening." She fanned her face with her fingers. "I'm so warm." She turned to Teo, beaming.

"It's a beautiful night," Hattie agreed. She could feel Teo's eyes on her, but she kept her eyes fixed firmly on Flora. She wouldn't let him see how much she cared. She wouldn't let him know how her heart was breaking. What was the point? "If you will excuse me?" And then she walked away before she burst into tears.

She'd had enough of this night and went in search of her brother. She'd worn her fancy dress and had danced exactly three times and no matter what Mr. Donovan said, she would never, ever, have that Santiavan duke.

CHAPTER TWENTY-NINE

LILA HAD TO drag herself out of bed the next day for her call with Lord Abbott. She'd had a grand time at the ball, particularly after he'd exited the ballroom. When she was no longer required to make introductions or listen to Elizabeth complain, she'd danced. And drank. And ate. And availed herself of all the lovely things to do at the Abbott ball.

And now her head felt like lead and her belly felt queasy.

When she arrived at Grosvenor Square—only to discover half the hooks of her dress were not, in fact, hooked—Mr. Borerro directed her to the kitchen.

"The kitchen?" she asked, certain her heavy head had misheard.

"*Sí*, the kitchen. Follow me."

Off to the kitchen they went, Lila having to walk quickly to keep up through the maze of corridors. And when they arrived, she was astonished to see Lord Abbott at the center table, mixing something in a bowl.

He looked, she thought, rested and handsome. He glanced up. "Ah. Lady Aleksander. I was expecting you."

"My lord." She looked around the kitchen, certain that at any moment, some woman would appear and snatch the bowl from him, then stared in amazement when no one did. In fact, a young woman was sitting at a table in the corner, peeling potatoes, as if it were perfectly natural for the viscount to be wearing an apron and mixing something in a bowl.

"You've never seen a man bake," he said.

"No! There...there have been times that my husband and I attempted it, but... No, my lord. You are certainly the first." Why hadn't he told her this before? This was something she could have used, something that would have helped her find the perfect woman for him. At least it was interesting.

She walked into the kitchen, ducking under herbs hanging upside down to dry, as well as one chicken, also hanging upside down. "We had planned to meet today," she reminded him.

He didn't look up from his bowl. "We are meeting."

Well then, this was even more interesting. "And your scribe?"

He shot her a look. "She is not expected today."

"All right. Your mother said she would like—"

"She is visiting a sick friend. Shall we begin?"

She noticed something then—this wasn't his usual, gruff manner. He was different—he looked despondent. She glanced uneasily at the kitchen girl.

"Yolanda does not speak English. You may speak freely."

At the mention of her name, Yolanda looked up. Lord Abbott spoke to her in Spanish, and she returned to peeling potatoes, humming a little as she did. With his chin, his lordship gestured to a stool. "I apologize for not having something a little more comfortable for you."

"I don't mind a sturdy stool," Lila said, and sat across the table from him. "I must first congratulate you on a wonderful ball. Your mother is a wonder! I can't believe she was able to put it together so quickly."

"Sí," he said.

Chatty as always. "You met some new faces last night. What did you think?"

He glanced up at her as he sprinkled flour onto the table. "All quite lovely." He pushed a plate of gingersnaps toward her. "You must try one."

"I really couldn't," she said, and then helped herself to one. "Did anyone in particular stand out to you?"

He shook his head.

"No? I thought perhaps Miss Woodchurch stood out to you. You asked her for the first dance."

His head snapped up and his gaze sharpened. "And?"

She shrugged and nibbled the gingersnap. "It was an interesting choice."

"In what way?"

"Well, generally, we reserve the first dance for whoever is first on your list."

He began to roll dough. "So I've heard. Is this a rule set forth in English law? Or written on scrolls?"

Lila laughed, mostly with surprise that she'd hit a nerve. "Not that I'm aware. But it makes sense."

"Not to me."

"Wonderful!" She helped herself to another gingersnap. "Then shall I presume Miss Raney is first on your list?"

His jaw clenched. He kept his gaze on the dough he was rolling. Lila was fascinated by the scene. This man, this virile, handsome man, wearing an apron and rolling dough. "Of the ladies you have presented to me, I suppose she is. In theory."

"In *theory*? What does that mean?" Lila asked.

"It means, madam, that I don't know her well enough. It's impossible to assess our compatibility in the midst of a crowd."

She wanted to suggest he bring Miss Raney on as his

scribe, and then he'd be able to assess her compatibility. But he was not the only one who needed time. Lila needed it, too. She needed to learn even more about Hattie Woodchurch, because she had a feeling the viscount's internal dilemma was not going to work itself out.

She took another gingersnap. "It is my experience that 'in theory' works as well as anything in these cases," she said brightly. "I think the only thing left—before a declaration of feelings and a proposal—is to meet Miss Raney's family."

The viscount said nothing.

"That can all be arranged."

He still said nothing.

"I've an idea for an outing that might provide opportunities to speak with less of a crowd gathered, if you like."

He glanced up. "Whatever you need, Lady Aleksander."

She figured that was as good as she would get from the man and stood up from her stool. "Wonderful! I'll send details around." She picked up another gingersnap. "You said Miss Woodchurch is not expected today? I wanted to ask what she thought of the ball."

"She is not," he said tightly.

Lila smiled. "Good day, my lord." She headed out of the kitchen, but just before she stepped through the door, she happened to glance back. The viscount had stopped rolling his dough. His hands were braced against the table and he was staring into space, his jaw as tight as a drum.

Lila needed to learn exactly where Hattie Woodchurch stood. And she needed to do it posthaste.

CHAPTER THIRTY

LILA WAS FORTUNATE enough to catch Beck at home with only Donovan in attendance. His wife and daughters were out.

"Shopping," Beck said with a groan. "We'll be home to Devonshire soon, and apparently one cannot buy gowns or gloves or hats there. We were just about to have some port, Lila. Would you like some?"

"Please!" She took a seat on the settee.

Donovan poured the ports and handed them around. Beck sat in a chair, one leg crossed over the other. "Now then. What can I do for you?"

Lila sipped her port. "I have a problem."

"Another one? Darling, have you noticed you seem to have a lot of problems here of late?"

"I certainly have. But this time, my problem is that I think Lord Abbott is in love with Miss Woodchurch."

Beck waited a moment or two for a jest, and when it didn't come, he laughed. Donovan didn't. Beck looked at Donovan, then at Lila. "What?"

"I'm serious, Beck."

He uncrossed his legs and sat up. "Lila. I told you before that it's impossible. Impossible!"

"I know," she said. "But he loves her and I can't in good conscience ignore that and arrange a marriage with Flora Raney."

"You're too tenderhearted, and if I may say, you seem to get more tender the older you get. I've always supported you, but in this, I can't. There is no way we can overcome Miss Woodchurch's family. Can you imagine the Santiavan Parliament? They'd be apoplectic the first time they made the acquaintance of Mr. Hugh Woodchurch." He shuddered and set aside his port.

"But there must be a way," Lila insisted. "For the life of me, I can't see it, but there *must*."

"There is always a way," Donovan said. "Even in this."

Beck and Lila looked at him. "How?" Lila asked.

"We must legitimize her family in another way."

"How?" Lila and Beck said in unison.

"Through her brother, Mr. Woodchurch."

"Good Lord. The worst of the lot," Beck said with a flick of his wrist.

"Perhaps. But he is the one man besides the viscount who has caught the eye of the ladies. One in particular."

"Who?" Beck asked, casting his arms wide. "What woman in her right mind would want anything to do with him?"

Donovan chuckled. "Miss Flora Raney."

Lila gasped. "I thought he looked familiar! I've seen them together more than once!"

"There is an attraction there," Donovan said. "And I would think that Mr. Hugh Woodchurch would like to see his eldest son married into money. He might be more agreeable to terms with the Raney family than he would for a daughter he sees as nothing but a liability."

"That is a *horrible* thing to say," Lila exclaimed.

"Yes, but no less true," Beck said sadly.

"But how do we manage it?" Lila asked.

"We? I can't be party to this," Beck sniffed.

"It has to be made apparent to everyone," Donovan said.

The three of them looked at each other. Lila suddenly said, "Aha!"

"Aha?" Beck echoed.

"Jumbo the elephant."

"I beg your pardon?" Beck asked.

Lila was suddenly on her feet. "The elephant. He's to parade on Wednesday, and I thought it would be a perfect opportunity for the viscount and Miss Raney to spend a bit of time together. In the patronage box, of course."

"Excellent," Donovan said, and grinned.

"Excellent! Why is it excellent? Will someone please explain this to me?" Beck demanded.

"I will, I promise," Lila said, but she was already at the door. "But first, I must purchase some tickets and pay a call to Miss Woodchurch."

She could hear Beck shouting after her that she should *not* pay a call to Miss Woodchurch, but Lila was running out of time. Something had to give.

CHAPTER THIRTY-ONE

IN A BOX hidden in her wardrobe, Hattie kept her wages. On a dark and wet Sunday afternoon, she'd pulled the box out and was counting how much money she had. Thus far she'd saved twenty pounds, after paying her father and buying a few needed things. She figured she'd need at least forty pounds to rent a small cottage for a few months. Mrs. O'Malley told her that telegraph operators earned as much as six pounds a week—she was contemplating asking her father to help her find a position like that.

But asking him to help with anything would cost her.

And where was she going to go? She had in mind the country but wasn't certain what sort of work she might find in the country.

The door to her room suddenly swung open and Peter fell through her door, landing on one hand and knee before popping up.

"Peter! Does no one in this family think to knock?"

"You've a caller."

Her heart skipped. "I do?" She stood up and immediately regretted having donned her plain gray gown. Who could it be? No one had called for her since Rupert. It wasn't Teo, was it? *No.* He would never come here. Or rather, she prayed to high heaven he never would.

"It's a lady."

A *lady.* She instantly relaxed. "Young or old?"

"What do you mean?" Peter asked. "They're all old."

He headed for a small desk where she kept her journal. Hattie moved fast and reached it before he did. "Get out," she said, snatching it out of his reach.

"What? Why is it a secret?"

"Out, Peter!"

With a huff, her brother went out. Hattie waited until she was sure he was gone, then hid her journal from prying eyes. And her money. She didn't trust anyone in this house. Not even the cats.

She headed downstairs, and as she maneuvered through the hall, she could hear voices coming from the drawing room. As she got closer, she heard her father laugh in the snide way that he had. Her parents were "entertaining" whoever had come to call. She stepped around a dress form and over a tea service and walked into the room. Lady Aleksander—Lila—was seated on the settee. There was a cat in her lap and one next to her. She looked instantly relieved when she saw Hattie.

"Good morning, Miss Woodchurch! I hope you don't mind my unexpected call."

Hattie minded very much. She would rather die than have anyone see the chaos in which she lived. Not to mention Peter and Perry were there, playing a card game that had them flicking the cards against the wall. She could perish here and now from embarrassment. "Of course not," she said. "Welcome."

"We were just asking the lady why she called," her father said.

"Papa!" *Please, Jesus, take me.*

"Why not? No one comes calling for you, lassie. What's it all about?"

Lila lifted the cat from her lap and dropped it to the

floor. "I have called because Hattie and I have become friends. It's a lovely day and I hoped she would walk with me."

"It's raining!" Hattie's mother cried. "Walk where in this rain? Why is everyone always *walking*?"

Hattie opened her mouth to respond, but the hour struck and the grandfather clocks around the house began to chime in a terrible cacophony. Lila's eyes widened with shock. And just as the chiming stopped, they heard a door open and slam, followed by the sound of someone striding down the hall.

Daniel entered the room, pushed a cat out of the way with his boot, and tossed his hat on a console table before looking at anyone else in the room. He started at the sight of Lila.

"Hallo, who is this?"

"Daniel, this is Lady Aleksander. Madam, may I present my brother, Mr. Daniel Woodchurch."

Lila was staring at him, her eyes narrowed slightly as if she was trying to see him more clearly. "Mr. Woodchurch."

Daniel at least bowed. "Lady Aleksander," he said. "Have we met? You look familiar."

Lila smiled. "No, I don't think so."

"I'm certain I've seen you," Daniel said.

"Be that as it may, we're going out," Hattie said, and gestured for Lila to come. Lila didn't need to be asked twice. She stepped over a cat as she insisted it was her pleasure to make the acquaintance of Hattie's parents and brothers and wished them well.

Hattie hastily donned a cloak and found an umbrella. Lila already had hers in hand, and they burst outside together.

Once they were on the street, under their umbrellas,

Hattie looked back at her sad family home. "I am so sorry for it."

"For what?" Lila smiled.

"You're being kind, but you don't have to pretend. I am aware how my family and our house appear to the world. It's deplorable."

"*You're* not deplorable. Come, I know an art gallery not too far from here. We can talk there."

The gallery was quite small, and on a day like this one, crowded. Still, Lila and Hattie managed to squeeze in. "How did you enjoy the ball?" Lila asked as they gazed at a pastoral scene.

Hattie rolled her eyes. "Does it matter? Go on, Lila, I know what you want. Ask me. Ask me what he thought of the ladies."

"All right. What did he think of the ladies?"

"I can't say."

"Because you're his friend."

"Yes," Hattie said emphatically, and looked at Lila crossly. "I *am* his friend."

Lila smiled. "It's funny how I keep hearing that word."

Hattie frowned. "What word?"

"*Friend*, darling! But that's wonderful—it means he will be a friend to Miss Raney, too. My husband, Valentin, and I were friends before we were lovers. It makes for the best marriage, I think. We discuss everything."

"I don't know what you want me to say," Hattie said as they moved to the next painting. "Cheers?"

"Thank you," Lila said breezily. "Do you think the viscount is set on Miss Raney as a potential match?"

Hattie folded her arms tightly across her body. It was amazing how much it hurt to even hear the words spoken aloud. "I do."

"Wonderful. I think it's time he made a more intimate acquaintance with her family, don't you? Something to warm everyone up. A private supper. What do you think?"

Hattie felt her body stiffening. "How should I know? I'm not the matchmaker."

"No, you're not." Lila smiled enigmatically. They moved to the next painting. This one of a girl in a frilly frock surrounded by sheep.

"Have you heard of Jumbo?" Lila asked.

"Who?"

"Jumbo the elephant. He resides at the London Zoo. He's to be in a parade on Wednesday. People who attend will get the opportunity to touch him and children may ride him. Doesn't that sound like a grand outing for a pair of potential spouses?"

"Please stop asking me what I think. I hardly care."

"I've already arranged it." She glanced at Hattie. "I invited your family, too."

Hattie gasped. "You did *what*? Why?"

Lila shrugged. "Your younger brothers seemed very interested in Jumbo. Actually, your parents were excited, too, particularly when I told them the tickets I had were free."

"What are you doing?" Hattie demanded. "Why would you ever invite them anywhere?"

"Don't be angry, Hattie. I was fortunate enough to receive several tickets. I'm happy to be of service! Don't look like that—you might very much enjoy it. Oh, and I arranged for you and your older brother to be in the patron's box."

"The what?"

"It's like a grandstand for those who can afford it and don't want to be in the thick of a crowd. Think of it like a box at the theater."

Hattie gaped at Lila. "You are *using* me," she said. "I

refused your offer of payment, so you've come up with another way to use me."

Lila turned her back on the portrait of the girl surrounded by sheep. "I understand you are displeased, Hattie. But I am not using you. You'll just have to trust me when I say I am helping you."

"Dear God," Hattie muttered. "I don't see how. And even if I could, I beg of you, please don't help me, Lila."

She turned and walked on to the next portrait, seething.

And a little heartbroken, quite honestly. She'd allowed herself to be swept up to attend the ball, but she didn't think she could bear to see Teo with Flora one more time without her heart completely shattering.

WHILE HATTIE WAS suffering through an art gallery with Lady Aleksander, Mateo was suffering his mother. She was in a pique, annoyed with him for taking too long to choose a woman to be his wife. It baffled him that she seemed to think it was no harder than choosing a new hunting dog. Look them over, review their bloodlines, and voilà, here is the woman you will wake up next to for the rest of your life.

She was pacing before the hearth, her new petticoats rustling beneath her skirts. "Lila says you won't say much at all, Teo."

"What is there to say?" he asked her.

"There is everything to say! You could start by telling her which woman with whom you would like to begin negotiations!"

She made it sound so…transactional, as if he was buying a broodmare.

"Is it the Raney woman?"

Mateo looked at his mother. He could not finesse this like Sofia would, or please her like Roberto. But he could be honest. "It's Miss Woodchurch."

"Who?" she asked, before she realized who he meant.

"My scribe," he said, to erase any doubt.

She stared at him. And then she attempted to laugh in the vain hope it was a joke.

Mateo didn't laugh with her.

"Good God," she said. "Don't be ridiculous, Teo."

"Is it ridiculous to follow one's heart? Don't you want happiness for me, Mami?"

His mother's expression was turning a bit ashen. "She is no one."

"She is someone to me. And she is a fully formed person, like you."

"No, no, you won't shame me. Of course she's a person, and I'm sure she's lovely. But she is no one to Santiava. We are talking about the future of the duchy, *mijo*. We must consider a marriage with a certain amount of wealth and connection. You know all the reasons why. There are those in the duchy who would like to see us absorbed into Spain. If they perceive you as weak, they will push for it. This marriage must be a strong one."

He knew the reasons. But he was finding that he no longer cared. He could hear his father even now, after all this time, berating him for even entertaining such a pedestrian notion that he might marry for love. He stood and walked to the window. It was dark; he couldn't see much.

"Mateo." His mother came to the window. She put her arm around his waist and rested her head against his shoulder. "I understand you want to marry for love, but our reality is something completely different. Don't you think you could come to love Miss Raney?"

"I don't know," he said. "I suppose anything is possible. But I love Hattie."

His mother rubbed his back the way she used to do when

he was a child and fell ill. "Your position in this world is not easy, I know. You have enormous responsibilities."

"And I've met them all."

"You have, my love. But in this? This especially, you must choose carefully. Miss Raney's father is influential in the English Parliament. She would be an excellent choice for our corner of the world."

He said nothing. He knew what his mother thought. But he couldn't see the logic to why it should matter. He was the duke. He knew that having an heir was necessary, and that was another responsibility he would meet. But what difference would it make who he chose to fulfill that obligation?

"It will be better, *mijo*," she said. "You will have a wedding and you will have your bride. You will show her Santiava and delight in it, and then, when the children come, you can do as you please."

Mateo turned his head to look at her. "Is that what Papa did?"

His mother shrugged indifferently. "I didn't mind so much. I couldn't account for your father's whereabouts throughout our entire marriage, and I sincerely doubt he could account for mine. But we came together and had three beautiful children, and he gave me an extraordinary life. I don't think either of us had any complaints, and I don't think you will, either."

He didn't want to argue with her, but his life was vastly different than his father's, who, as far as Mateo could see, never cared for anyone or anything but himself. He didn't want that sort of life. If he was to take a bride to Santiava and have a family with her, he could not imagine seeking companionship anywhere else.

He wanted a family. He wanted to love a wife and his children. He did not want to marry the duchy. He wanted to marry who he loved.

Everything felt wrong. Being in London felt wrong. His feelings for and about Hattie felt all wrong, upside down, and turned around—they were too bloody *friendly*. That was not right.

What he was doing was not right.

CHAPTER THIRTY-TWO

FLORA'S CONFIDENCE HAD grown by leaps and bounds over the course of the week, chiefly because Queenie told her *everyone* was talking about her as the one who'd captured the Santiavan's heart. "If not his heart, at least his agreement," Queenie added slyly.

Hattie was walking with Flora and Queenie to the elephant exhibit at the zoo. Hattie didn't mention how she'd come by her ticket, and neither did anyone ask. For two women who could have whatever they wanted, how she had come by her ticket was of no consequence to them.

Hattie hadn't wanted to go, of course, but after a few rainy days, the day was so beautiful and bright, she was happy for an excuse to be in the sun.

An arena had been set up at the zoo, and a large railed-in grandstand—the patron's box, as Lila had called it—was set above the masses for people willing to pay to have a better view. It looked to hold about fifty in all, and there were already quite a lot of people in the box. It reminded Hattie of a stroll in Hyde Park in the morning—everyone who was anyone wanted to be seen.

Flora reported that her parents had come, too, and had invited Lord Abbott and his mother to join them.

"So brave of you, darling, to issue an invitation," Queenie said. "Did he reply?"

"Of course! Well, someone did. But he's coming."

They made their way to the box, where a steward directed them to seats. Flora moved to the front row to join her parents. She was wearing a white muslin and looked ethereal to Hattie. She couldn't deny that Flora would make a lovely duchess.

Queenie saw someone she knew and wandered off, leaving Hattie standing alone in the aisle. Someone knocked into her; she realized she had to take a seat because she was blocking the aisle. She took the closest one she could find—in the last row.

She watched as people filtered in to take their seats. She heard someone yelling her name and she looked over the side of the box. It was Daniel, of course. He and her entire family were in the crowd below. Even her mother, who swore her poor circulation made her ankles unusable and therefore rarely left the house.

Hattie ignored Daniel and sat up. Lady Aleksander had given her the only ticket for the box that she had left. The tickets for her family were general admission. She was excited to see this elephant without her family around her. Queenie said it performed tricks.

Most of the seats were taken when Lord Abbott entered the box with his mother. He didn't notice Hattie and led his mother to the front, where Lord Raney had saved them a pair of seats. He introduced his mother to them all, then took a seat next to Flora.

It was as good as done, Hattie guessed, and tried to ignore the painful squeeze of her heart.

At last, Jumbo appeared, laboring down a path. Six men were crowded into a box on his back. A fenced paddock of a sort had been assembled, and the crowd closed in around it to watch Jumbo walk in a circle. The men on his back—

acrobats—jumped down, then tumbled and twisted away from the elephant to the fence. One man placed a box in the middle of the paddock, then waved a baton at it. It seemed impossible that the elephant could understand what the man meant, much less fit himself on the box, but he did, balancing his great size on a surface that was hardly even the size of her writing desk.

Next, when the elephant had stepped down from the box, a dog appeared in the arena with a rope in its jaws. With its tail wagging, the dog dropped one end of the rope in front of Jumbo. The elephant picked up the rope with its trunk. The dog raced back to the man with the baton and gave the other end to him. The man and the elephant began to turn the rope, and the dog jumped. The crowd roared with delight.

Hattie couldn't help but watch Teo watching the elephant. She was at an angle, but it seemed to her his expression was stoic. Occasionally, Flora would lean close to say something, and he would nod or respond briefly. But he didn't appear to be enjoying the performance.

Jumbo went on to trumpet on command, and to back up, and to turn in a circle. The dog ran up his trunk and rode around the ring on his back. Each trick sent the crowd into more roars of approval. A brief intermission was announced, and someone brought Jumbo some hay. Hattie remained in her seat and watched a steady stream of people come to greet Flora and Teo. Flora was very proud—Hattie could tell from the way she smiled and greeted everyone in turn, and then made sure that they had been introduced to Teo.

The man with the baton was getting ready for the second act when Teo stood to stretch his back. That's when he saw Hattie. He smiled. She did, too. He said something to Flora, then began to make his way to the top of the box just as Jumbo returned, this time carrying children on his back. The crowd was delighted; several of them rushed the fence to have a turn.

Teo reached the back row and took the seat next to Hattie. One gentleman stopped to greet him, but when he left, Teo turned to her and smiled. "You've come to see Jumbo."

"He's huge. I've never seen anything so large."

Teo nodded. "He is the largest elephant I've ever seen."

Hattie laughed. "You've seen more than one?"

"I have. In Africa, with my brother. I saw the flying elephants there, too."

"The flying elephants," Hattie repeated uncertainly.

He nodded but kept his gaze straight ahead. "They are quite a bit smaller, but their ears have much greater wingspan. Quite impressive, really."

Hattie slowly smiled. "That may trick all of your potential brides, my lord, but I won't fall for it."

He turned his smile to her, his gaze falling to her lips. "You're certain?"

"Completely." She laughed. "What else did you see?"

"Tigers and wildebeests."

Hattie noticed Flora turn her head, looking around. She spotted them in the back row, and her gaze slid over them before facing forward again. Below, a line was forming to meet the elephant.

"What do you think of the dancing elephant?" Hattie asked.

"He has reminded me of my childhood."

"How?"

He shrugged. "In that when I was in public, I was always made to feel as if I was a trained monkey. Jumbo has a look in his eye that I understand."

Hattie looked at the elephant. People were crawling up a small ladder and then the elephant took them around in a circle. "He doesn't seem entirely happy, does he?"

Teo smiled ruefully at her. "Is anyone?"

"Sometimes most of us are. Sometimes not."

"I'm happy to see you here today. I'm happy to see you every time."

There was suddenly a cry of alarm—two people had jumped into the arena to pet Jumbo's trunk, and Hattie realized in a moment of horror it was Peter and Perry. Flora glanced over her shoulder at Hattie, her eyes wide. She was mortified for Hattie, but...but Flora knew the twins? How did she know them? When did she meet them?

She heard someone shout Flora's given name and realized with even more horror that it was Daniel. He was calling to her like she was part of the riffraff. He was standing on the railing of the paddock fence, pretending to be conducting the platform of rich people. Some people laughed at his antics. Others glared at him. One man shouted at him to get down and leave them be.

Just when Hattie thought her family couldn't possibly embarrass her more, they found a way. They were the true backwater cousins, terribly behaved and oblivious to the discomfort they caused.

Now Daniel was pretending to have a trunk of his own. And—it was beyond Hattie to grasp, but—Flora was laughing. She was *laughing at Daniel*.

Teo suddenly rose. "I should return to my mother before the crowd gets too out of hand," he said. "I'll see you soon?"

She nodded. Her face felt on fire from the heat of her shame. She didn't know how she would ever apologize to Flora.

As it seemed nothing was left of the show but rides for children, people began to leave the box. Hattie watched Teo speak to Flora's parents. And then, naturally, Lila appeared seemingly out of thin air, and the discussion turned livelier. At last, Teo bowed and held out his arm. His mother took it, and they began to climb the steps to the exit. Flora, Hattie noticed, had reunited with Queenie.

She struggled to get through the crowd to reach Flora and Queenie before they disappeared. She had to rush to catch them, and put her hand on Flora's arm to stop her.

Flora jerked around.

"Flora," Hattie said, breathlessly. "I must apologize for my brothers."

"What?"

"My brothers? And Daniel in particular—I'm so sorry for his behavior. I hope you weren't terribly offended."

"Of course I was," Flora said, and her cheeks flushed bright. "He's impossible, I've told you. He really ought to know his place."

"I agree!" Hattie said. "For some reason, he is desperate to impress you."

"Oh, Hattie," Flora said. She leaned forward and pinned her with a dark gaze. "I really don't care."

"Look, there's Lady Mabel!" Queenie exclaimed. "She's come after all. Shall we go and see her?"

"Yes," Flora said, and linked her arm through Queenie's. Hattie moved to keep in step with them, but Flora suddenly turned, jerking Queenie to a halt. "Hattie...you can make your way home, can't you? Your family is here. I'm sure you'll want to walk with them."

Hattie was dumbstruck. Flora had never dismissed her like this. She must have nodded or uttered a reply, because

Flora and Queenie were walking away, arm in arm. She looked around at all the people leaving the zoo. She didn't know where her family was. She didn't want to know where they were.

She wished the earth would open a hole and swallow her up.

CHAPTER THIRTY-THREE

LADY ALEKSANDER HAD finagled the invitation to dine at the Raney household in front of him and his mother at the elephant show, and then had delivered a formal invitation from Lord Raney so Mateo couldn't maneuver himself out of it. The woman was clever that way.

She'd reported to his mother that Lord Raney was over the moon about the prospect of an engagement for his daughter and was prepared to provide a generous dowry. His mother was eager to announce an engagement before he departed London. Mateo wondered if she intended to ask for Miss Raney's hand herself. Her plan, she informed him, was to sail in a fortnight, and return in a few months after that for a wedding. How convenient—his mother had mapped the most important decision of his life for him.

And she'd done it all while pretending she'd never heard him say that he was in love with Hattie.

He was waiting for Hattie when she arrived for work. He and Rosa had made another attempt at sponge cake. Hattie was delighted to sample it for him. They sat down on the settee together to taste it.

He watched her as she chewed. "Teo...this is *much* better."

"I thought so, too," he said.

She took another bite. "So *good*." She put her plate aside and smiled. "What do we have today?"

"Only a few things." He handed her the formal invitation to dine at the Raney house. "You may reply in the affirmative for both the duchess and myself."

She was still smiling when she looked at the invitation, but it quickly faded. "Ah," she said softly. "This must be important."

Mateo wanted to say how much he hated that this was happening, but the words sounded hollow and ridiculous in his head. Was he not a grown man? Was he really led by his mother?

Hattie forced a smile. "I'm happy for you, though."

She stood to go to her desk, but he caught her hand. "Hattie, I—"

She pulled her hand free and carried on to her desk. "When do you think the happy day will be?"

This was agony. "I don't know. I'm returning to Santiava."

That stopped her. She turned back. "When? If...if I may ask?"

"Ask me anything. I plan to depart in twelve days. There are matters at home that need my attention."

"Oh." She pressed a hand to her abdomen and bent over a little. *"Oh."*

"Hattie?" He leaped up from the couch and reached her in a couple of strides, his hand going around her back.

She pushed him away, hard. "Don't do that, please, don't do that. I understand, Teo. Do you think I don't understand? You're a duke and a viscount and I am no one—"

His mother had said that, and it made him irrationally angry. "That is not true."

"It is!" She dropped the Raney invitation on the floor. "I have always been very clear about who I am and where I'm from, Teo. I've enjoyed our friendship. I've enjoyed the work. I...I will miss you terribly, and I will never forget you, but I—"

He stopped her from saying another word with a kiss. He grasped her arms and pulled her to him and he kissed those words from her lips.

She didn't resist—she rose up on her toes and kissed him in return, with lips as soft as butter, her fingers like silk on his face. It was a sweet kiss—hardly a kiss at all, really—and yet his body felt as if a bomb had gone off in him. He was tumbling hard down a path of desire, and alarmed, he lifted his head, his eyes locked with hers. "I love you," he said. *"Te quiero mucho."*

She gasped. *"Never* say that again," she said, and cupped the back of his head and kissed him so violently that he stumbled back against her desk, knocking things to the floor.

She pressed her body against his, and he could feel every soft, pliant curve. He wrapped one arm around her possessively, caressed her face with his hand. He couldn't let her go. Given that they were in his study, with the door wide open, his mind shouted at him to let go, to get a hold of himself. But his body refused, and anchored her to him, pressing against the length of her. She responded with urgency, nipping at his lips, sweeping her tongue into his mouth, and shoving her fingers into his hair.

Mateo was dangerously aroused, his body hardening with want. He pressed a hand to her breast, filled his palm with it, and Hattie moaned.

That small moan crashed through the fog of desire and Mateo woke up. With a gasp, he shifted back, stumbling a step, his gaze locked on her.

Hattie blinked with surprise at the abrupt end of the kiss. She stared back at him, her eyes heavy with lust. She slowly ran the pad of her thumb across her lower lip. "We really must stop doing that," she said in a whisper. "I beg your pardon for my part."

She didn't look as if she wanted his pardon. She looked like she wanted to toss him on the rug and have her way with him. And he was a heartbeat away from doing it for her. She was the most unique woman Mateo had ever known—he was spellbound by her. But he knew one thing—he could not offer marriage to Miss Raney when he felt this strongly about Hattie Woodchurch.

"I don't want to stop doing this," he said. "I won't apologize for it."

"Teo! You are going to marry my *friend*. I can't...*you* can't." She bent down to pick up the dropped invitation. "This is madness—I should go."

"You don't have to go," he said, feeling frustrated now. "Stay. Let's talk—"

"About what?" She stood up and looked at him. The desire had been replaced with unshed tears. "What is there to say? You can't imagine how difficult this is for me."

"I can imagine very well. It's difficult for me."

"I really must go." She stepped around him, hurrying to the door before he could stop her.

Mateo let her go. This time. But he wouldn't let her go again.

CHAPTER THIRTY-FOUR

WELL, THAT WAS IT, then. She was desperately in love, but the clock was ticking—he was leaving, and she had only so many more opportunities to be with him.

She carried on the rest of that day in a terrible fog of uncertainty and poorly buried desire and hopelessness. Daniel said she looked like the walking dead.

The next day, Mrs. O'Malley remarked how sad Hattie looked. She wasn't sad, she was exhausted—she hadn't slept at all the night before. "I'm a bit under the weather, that's all." She managed a smile.

"Oh dear. Well, have some chocolate." Mrs. O'Malley handed her several pieces.

The chocolate did not help.

When she'd finished her work at Mrs. O'Malley's, she went to Flora's house. On Fridays, Flora liked to visit her cousin Moses.

But Flora wasn't there.

"Oh, Hattie," her mother said. "Flora's gone out. Didn't she send word?"

"No," Hattie said. "I thought…I thought we were going to visit Moses."

"Moses?" Her mother looked confused. "She and Queenie have gone for ices."

Ices? Hattie rubbed her temple. "Should I wait?" she asked, also confused.

"Perhaps a quarter of an hour? I'm not certain when

she'll be back. Have a seat in here," Lady Raney said, and directed Hattie into the formal parlor.

She sat on the edge of a chair, waiting. This was not like Flora. She was usually so eager to see Hattie that she came bounding down the stairs and made Hattie rush back up to her rooms with her.

She had a terrible sense of foreboding.

She'd waited a half hour when she heard Flora come in. She was laughing, and she told the butler a rain had started. Hattie stood up and walked to the door of the parlor.

"Oh. Hattie," Flora said, her voice cool and distant.

"Good afternoon. I thought we were to visit Moses today."

"Yes, well… I decided against it."

She was so cold. She stepped into the parlor, forcing Hattie to take a step backward.

"Actually, Hattie, I've decided a few things," Flora said. She glanced over her shoulder, then quietly shut the door.

"Are you all right?" Hattie asked. "Is something wrong?"

Flora rolled her eyes. "I think you know."

Hattie shook her head in confusion. "I don't know, I swear it. Did I forget something?"

"Honestly, Hattie! You're pretending to be innocent, but I know you're not. I don't need you anymore."

Hattie's mouth fell open. The news was a punch to her gut. Didn't *need* her anymore? "I don't understand, Flora. I thought we were friends—"

"Friends?" Flora laughed bitterly.

"Flora!"

"You think I haven't noticed, don't you?" Flora sneered. "You think I can't see that you're in love with Lord Abbott."

Hattie was stunned. Had she somehow hinted at it? But how… "I'm not!"

Flora laughed, and it sounded a bit wild. "Yes, you are, Hattie! I've seen it. *Queenie* has seen it! And we both think you are mad! Do you honestly think that he can look past your family? Your horrible brothers, your mad mother, your miserly father?"

Hattie recoiled like she'd been slapped. "How dare you," she said quietly.

"How dare *I*? All this time you pretended to be my friend, to *help* me, and really, it was just a reason to be close to him. But that's the saddest thing of all, because he will *never* consider you, Harriet Woodchurch. And if he has given you any reason to believe it, it's only so he might have his way with you."

Hattie was so appalled, she was shaking. She was horrified by the way Flora was speaking to her and impugning her character. It was especially devastating because Hattie had believed they were friends.

Somehow, she managed to dig deep enough to find her composure. She lifted her chin. "If you mean to hurt me, you can't. I have always known who I am. At Iddesleigh, you all made sure to remind me in every possible way— and you still do. I am keenly aware of how my family is perceived. But you know me, Flora. I thought I knew you, too. I thought you had compassion. Clearly, I was wrong." She brushed against Flora as she stepped around her to the door. "I have always tried to help you. Because I have always believed we were friends. Thank you for disabusing me of that notion. I wish you the best. Good day."

Flora snorted. And she did not call her back.

Hattie walked to the foyer. The rain was coming down in buckets. The butler took pity on Hattie and handed her an umbrella. But it was raining so hard that Hattie was still soaking wet by the time she got home, dragging herself in like a drowned rat.

Daniel stepped into the foyer as she removed her cloak and poked his head around the grandfather clocks. "Where have you been?" he asked her, eyeing her curiously.

"Out, obviously."

"You have a caller."

Her head jerked up. "I do? Is it Lady Aleksander?"

"No. Why? Are you still harboring some hope she'll put your name in the hat?"

Hattie closed her eyes and wished for strength. "Who is here, Daniel?"

"An *earl*," he sneered.

An *earl*? She pushed past him and hurried to the drawing room. Lord Iddesleigh was inside, looking very much trapped by her father.

"Look who washed up to our humble door," her father said, and with his chin, indicated Lord Iddesleigh.

"I didn't wash up to your door, sir, I came in a carriage. Miss Woodchurch, might I have a word?"

"I…" She looked down at herself. She was soaked from the knees down, and she could feel her hair frizzing.

"It won't take a moment," he said.

"Whatever you have to say to my daughter, you can say to me," her father said.

"Papa," Hattie said wearily. Was there no end to him? "Please, my lord," she said, and gestured to the hall.

"Harriet!" her father shouted. "You're not to receive him alone!"

Hattie ignored him and led the earl into a smaller sitting room. It was filled with dress forms and stacks of fabrics.

Iddesleigh held himself stiff as he looked around the room.

"My lord?"

"Yes." He shook his head as if trying to clear the image of this room from his sight. "I have a position that might interest you."

Hattie was too emotionally exhausted to even think.

"Abbott is leaving soon, as I understand it," he said. "Your position will come to an end. The widow Lady Bradenton could use some help in her house. Not as a maid, mind you, but as a secretary. It is a live-in position, and the compensation is quite good."

Hattie could hardly absorb this news. "What?"

"You would live there, Miss Woodchurch. I can't vouch for the accommodations, but she has a fine house in Belgravia. I think you will approve."

"I would live there?" she asked again, because it was impossible for her to grasp that she had a way out of this house. She wouldn't have to share her earnings with her father. She wouldn't have to even *see* her father.

"You would live there. Free of these," he said, pointing to a dress form. "Are you interested in the position?"

"Yes," she said. "When?"

"She would like someone as soon as possible. It seems the last person to serve as her secretary was a gentleman who made off with one of the maids, and I should warn you that you will have to hear about that at some length. Nevertheless, I asked if she might wait until you have completed your position with Abbott."

But if she took the position now, she would have a dignified exit from the world of Grosvenor Square that was causing her such sorrow. It was particularly unbearable now, knowing that he would offer for Flora. It was as if her entire world had collapsed in the space of an afternoon. But here was Lord Iddesleigh, her savior once again, offering her a way out.

"If you are agreeable," his lordship said, "we might go and make Lady Bradenton's acquaintance?"

"Now?" She looked down at herself.

"I can come and collect you in an hour, if you are not otherwise engaged."

She was supposed to have gone with Flora today. Her day had just exploded into endless possibilities without that commitment. "Yes, thank you, my lord," she said. "One hour."

"Wonderful." He smiled and started for the door. One of the cats darted out of the door before him, startling the earl, and he gave a small cry of alarm, followed by a breath of exasperation. "I don't know which is worse, Miss Woodchurch—too many cats? Or too many daughters?"

"My lord?" Hattie said before he could exit the room.

Lord Iddesleigh turned back. "Yes?"

"Why…why are you helping me?"

He seemed genuinely confused by her question. "Why wouldn't I help you? I like you. You remind me of my daughters. Frankly, all young women remind me of my daughters." He smiled with affection at the mention of them. "You deserve a happy life as much as anyone. I guess that's why." He went out.

Hattie sank onto a chair to collect her thoughts. A cat yelped; she stood, pushed the cat from the seat, and sat again.

Lord Iddesleigh was so kind. She wanted a happy life. She just hoped she could have a life where she didn't think of Teo and Flora every day.

LADY BRADENTON WAS an ancient woman who lived in widow's weeds because, she said, "the queen does." She lived quite alone in a large, beautiful house, full of expensive furnishings. But it was so quiet, one could hear a maid walk from one end of the house to the other.

Lady Bradenton eyed Hattie closely and without compunction. "You're young. I expected someone much older. Widowed. Why are you working for money?" She phrased the question as if the very idea revolted her.

"I only have myself to rely on," Hattie answered.

"Where's your family?"

"In town. But… They are not very helpful."

"Hmm." Lady Bradenton's eyes narrowed to slits. "Are you in any sort of trouble, girl?"

She was asking if Hattie was pregnant. *"No,"* Hattie said emphatically. "I am an honest woman and I am honestly working to provide for myself. I don't see anything to be suspicious about."

"Oh dear," Lord Iddesleigh muttered.

"I didn't say there was," Lady Bradenton said. "But I find it *odd.*"

"Yes, yes, odd and all that," Lord Iddesleigh chimed in. "But she's very good, madam, and as you explained to me, you need a good Christian woman to act as your secretary. Well, here is one. Will you employ her?"

"I don't care if she's Christian or not," Lady Bradenton said, sounding perturbed by the assumption. "I care that she doesn't steal from me."

That was enough. Hattie stood up. "Thank you for your time, my lady."

"Miss Woodchurch," Iddesleigh said, and then to Lady Bradenton, "Lady Bradenton, I must insist you show a bit of respect. She's given you no reason to suspect her, and I would not introduce a thief to you."

Lady Bradenton groaned, then waved a hand at Hattie. "Sit down, sit down." When Hattie didn't move, the old woman sighed. "I apologize. I am without companions and my mind has turned to dust. Of course I don't think you'd steal from me."

That was better, but still, Hattie hesitated. Lady Bradenton did not seem an easy woman. But what choice did she have? None. No choice at all. Still, she would not stand for this woman's disdain. She slowly sat. "Shall we begin again?"

The woman smiled a very little bit. "Yes, let's."

CHAPTER THIRTY-FIVE

THE DINNER WITH the Raneys went precisely as Mateo assumed it would. They put on quite a display for his benefit—liveried footmen, fine wine, a meal of soup, roasted stuffed goose, brussels sprouts, a Battenberg cake, and a selection of cheeses. The wine was French, Lord Raney said. "I tried to procure a bottle of Santiavan wine, but it is not readily available. Perhaps we can change that in the future." He winked at Mateo, as if they were already conspirators in the pursuit of profit.

His mother was alive this evening, undoubtedly smelling victory. She dominated the conversation, chatting about her many travels and engaging Miss Raney in talk of all the places she would like to visit one day.

Miss Raney was lovely. She was dressed in a soft green gown and had her hair done up with pearls. She said she would be honored to travel anywhere her future husband might like, but that Paris sounded divine. She was demure and polished, refined and cultured. A perfect candidate for duchess.

Mateo preferred a duchess who was not afraid to speak her true feelings.

Still, he studied her as surreptitiously as he could manage. She was a perfectly fine match...but he wasn't engaged. He wasn't curious at all. And he was certain he could not simply force himself to love a woman he felt nothing for.

When at long last he and his mother took their leave—

she tended to overstay her welcome—Lord Raney asked when he might see Mateo again. He was asking when Mateo would come and ask for his daughter's hand in marriage. "I will call this week," Mateo assured him.

"I should hope so, young man," his lordship said grandly, and clapped his hand on Mateo's shoulder. "I have a very good feeling about you." He and his wife were beaming. Flora was smiling, too, but her smile was different than her parents' smiles. She didn't seem as enthusiastic. If he had to guess, he would say that was because she couldn't make sense of him. He was used to that.

In the carriage home, his mother acted as if the offer had already been made and told him she was so very happy for him. "And so *proud, mijo.*"

"Proud?" he asked curiously. "Because I will offer marriage for a woman I have no attachment to and scarcely know?"

She clucked her tongue at him. "I don't know why you make things so difficult. You've *always* made everything so difficult!" she complained as they pulled up in front of the Abbott house on Grosvenor Square.

"It's interesting, isn't it, how two people can view the same thing and see something so vastly different. For me, it seems the other way around."

His mother gaped at him. "For the love of God, am I supposed to wait for you to come down off the mountain and open your mouth and speak to a woman? Your father always said there was something peculiar about you, and I am beginning to think he was right."

"I beg your pardon?"

"Well, what was he to think, Mateo? You never showed any interest in the fairer sex."

Mateo should have been stunned, but he wasn't, considering the low regard his father had had for him. "On the contrary, Mami—I have always had a very healthy interest in the fairer sex. But I had no interest at all in the meddlesome ways of my parents. I kept my thoughts to myself."

She gaped at him. "Mateo, darling!" she said, realizing she had offended him.

"Good night." He leaped from the carriage and strode inside, leaving Borerro to escort her in.

That night, Mateo tossed and turned. This was not what he wanted. He had no desire for Miss Raney. He hated that he had such difficulty saying what he wanted. How long would he be ruled by the vague fear of censure and criticism? He was a grown man, his father long gone. He was the bloody duke, for God's sake, and yet, he couldn't seem to find his voice. Was he content to spend his life in the mountains, away from the pressures of his title and fear of criticism? Was he content to be married to a woman he didn't love?

But now that his future had been seated across the table from him at supper, he felt the pressure to be himself, to be who he was. To be like Hattie, when he got right down to it. There was a woman who was unabashedly who she was. There was a woman who sparked his interest and enthusiasm and desire. *Desperate desire*, as she'd explained to him. She was far superior to any other person he had ever met, and yet, somehow, she was not up to the standards of the duchy. It was absurd.

He brooded all night.

The next morning, he and Rosa tackled the sponge cake once more—they had yet to discern the secret to the moistness. He took two pieces with him to the study—he and Hattie had made a habit of this lately: he brought what he'd baked, and she brought the latest confection from Mrs. O'Malley. They would taste and compare.

But when Hattie arrived that day, she looked a bit gray. And she was not carrying any pastries or sweets.

Mateo felt the change in her and stood at once. "What has happened?"

"What? Nothing has happened!" She brushed the hair from her face. "Except that something did happen. It wasn't a bad thing. I think it might have been good. That is, for me." She looked helplessly at him.

"What is the matter?" he asked, coming out from behind the desk. "You look stricken."

She answered him by thrusting an envelope at him. The post hadn't come, and it confused him—but when he saw his name in her handwriting, his stomach turned. "What is it?"

"Read it. Please, Teo."

He didn't want to touch that envelope. Whatever was in it would upend his world, he could feel it. But he made himself take it. He unfolded the note and read.

Please accept my resignation from the position of scribe. I have accepted employment elsewhere.
Sincerely,
Harriet Woodchurch

So formal. So dry. He looked up. "What is this?"

"Just as I said. I am leaving my position here."

"No," he said, the voice coming from somewhere deep inside him. "You can't. I won't allow it." He read the few words again. "Hattie...you can't."

"Of course I can," she said softly.

The world was closing in on Mateo. He was at a loss—

he couldn't let this happen. But how, exactly, did he stop it? He held out his hand to her. "*Ven aquí.* Come."

"Where?"

He reached for her hand, taking it. She allowed him to pull her to him, and together, they strode quickly down the corridor, past the woman with the tall hair, through a morning room, then out onto the terrace and into the garden. She didn't speak, didn't ask as he urged her to run across the grass to the arch that led to the private garden. Once there, he seated her on the bench and proceeded to pace. So many thoughts raced through his head—in Spanish, in English, jumbling together, incoherent.

Hattie watched him warily, her hands clasped in her lap.

Mateo managed to get a grip on his emotions and thought what he wanted to say. *How* to say it. "Forgive my English," he started.

"Your English is perfect."

"Not in this. Hattie, I—I never expected..." He paused and put his hands on his hips and looked skyward. He drew a breath to settle himself. "I never *wanted*..." No, that wasn't right, either. "I am...in love with you. *Te amo.* Do you understand?"

"I asked you never to say that again."

"Why?" he demanded. "I want to express to you my devotion—"

"Teo! I don't want to hear it because I love *you.* And it makes it all so unbearable!"

"*Qué?* That makes no sense. How does two people admitting love make anything unbearable?"

Hattie bowed her head with distress.

Mateo went down on one knee before her and took her hand. "Hattie, listen to me. You are my friend, my... *confidente.* You accept me as I am. You are the only one with whom I feel free to be exactly who I am. I have come to love you above all others."

"Are you *mad*?"

He took her face in his hands and kissed her. "Not mad. But desperate with desire."

She wrapped her hands around his wrists and pushed him back. "We can be seen from the window."

"I don't care." He kissed her again, dipping his tongue between her lips, sliding his hands over her arms, memorizing her body, imprinting her on his skin. "There is no one but you," he said, and Hattie arched into him, her arms going around his neck. He moved his hand to her breast, but this wasn't enough. He pulled her off the bench and fell onto his back in the grass, pulling Hattie on top of him. He devoured her lips, every patch of skin, the inside of her mouth and the curve of her neck at her shoulder.

Her hands were moving on him, arousing him to even greater desperation when she caressed his hardness. He rolled again so that he was on top of her. "I want only you, *mi amor*. No one but you."

"I want you, too, but I—"

He kissed her to keep words from drifting between them that would ruin this moment. *But, but, but...* There was no *but*, there was only the two of them, destined for each other, in love with each other, meant for each other.

He pressed his hard length against her thigh, and moved his hand down her leg, grabbing muslin and pushing it up and out of the way until his hand found her skin.

"Teo," she whispered.

He paused, waiting for her to tell him to stop. She didn't tell him to stop—she kissed his neck, curled her fingers in his hair. She nibbled his lobe, she pressed against him, and sighed longingly.

He moved his hand up her thigh, into her knickers. He dipped in and out of her crevices, swirling around, his fingers following the rhythm of his tongue. She clung to him, surprisingly strong, her breath quickening. It was a heady, frothy concoction of skin and lips and desire all mixing into one utterly explosive moment, and Mateo was moved. He was *moved*.

He caressed her, slow and fluid, his mouth on hers in one long, stupefyingly seductive kiss. Her body strained against him, her breath turned hot on his skin. And then she began to writhe. She bit his shoulder when her pleasure ignited, stifling her cry with a whimper into the fabric of his coat. He laced his fingers with hers, squeezing as her body shuddered through a climax.

Then she stilled. He withdrew his hand from her skirt. She lay back in the grass, one arm carelessly thrown over her eyes. "What have you done to me?"

"Loved you." He pulled her up. "I've let my heart sit in silence too long. I never doubted I would gain a wife in the manner anyone in my position might gain one. But I never dreamed I'd find you first."

"Teo." She took his hand into both of hers. "There is no hope for us."

"You're wrong, Hattie. I can offer you—"

"I don't want anything," she interrupted. "The only thing I want is you, and that is impossible."

"It's not impossible. I want you to be my duchess, Hattie—"

"Teo! Don't say it. I am begging you, don't make this any harder than it is," she implored him, her eyes filling with tears. "I'm sorry. I'm so very sorry. I can't be with you. I've given you my resignation and now I have to go." A tear slid down her cheek as she gained her feet.

Mateo was speechless. What could he do but beg? There ought to be something, some magic words, a touch, a promise—something that he wasn't grasping that could convince her to stay. But she kept walking, and he sat in the grass like a fool, and watched her flee his private garden, through the arch, and disappear from view.

CHAPTER THIRTY-SIX

LILA WAS NOT at all certain that Lord Abbott was going to follow his heart. Despite her machinations, she feared he might go through with the more expedient offer of marriage to Miss Raney. She did not doubt for a moment Elizabeth's actual influence over him.

She'd come to the Raney household today to speak to Miss Raney. Before any offer was made, she had to know what Lord and Lady Raney would accept as part of the dowry negotiations. They intended to be quite generous.

But as Lila prepared to leave, she looked again at Miss Raney, who seemed a bit cool to her. "Are you excited?" she asked.

Miss Raney looked at her without emotion. "As I've not received an offer, no."

It seemed an odd thing to say—the young woman knew one was coming.

The whole affair made Lila sad. What she most enjoyed about her profession was bringing together people who loved each other. She could make this sort of match every day of the week—a match made for the continuation of wealth and influence, with a duty of producing an heir. But it wasn't very satisfying. She thought back all those years ago when no one thought she was good enough for Valentin. Look how happy they'd been all this time! She missed her husband so—he would be in London next week.

She would like this business done so she could devote all her time and attention to him.

But there was something bothering her about this match. She couldn't help but think that Lord Abbott would not have a happy life if he was to marry Flora Raney.

When she arrived at Grosvenor Square, and Borerro invited her into the foyer, she was startled by the raised voices coming from down the hall. She looked curiously at the butler.

Borerro pretended he didn't hear it. "Would you care to leave your hat, *señora*?"

Lila handed him her hat. "Is everything all right?"

Borerro said nothing as he took her hat and set it aside. "If you will come with me, *por favor.*"

He led her down the hall and paused before the study, rapping loudly three times before opening the door and walking in to announce her. The voices fell silent. Lila stepped in behind him—Elizabeth and her son were in the room. He was leaning against his desk. She was pacing. "Enter at your own risk, Lila," Elizabeth said. "There may be blood spilled before the day is done."

"Goodness," Lila said. "May I be of assistance?"

"He won't listen to reason! He means to destroy the duchy."

"That is a terrible exaggeration, madam," the viscount said calmly. He looked at Lila. "My mother and I are in the midst of a disagreement, and much to her displeasure, for once I will not do the polite thing and remain silent."

"Polite!" Elizabeth shrieked. "Your silence is insulting! Why would you wait until *now*, when all the work has been done to arrange a marriage, to tell me how you truly feel?"

Lila's pulse began to race with excitement. "What is happening?"

"Tell her!" Elizabeth cried, and pointed at Lila.

"Perhaps you'd like to sit, Mami," he said, and pushed away from the desk. "Lady Aleksander, please forgive us— my mother is quite angry with me."

"Livid!" Elizabeth cried.

"Livid," he agreed. "Because I have told her I will not offer for Miss Raney. Or any of the other fine ladies you've introduced me to."

Lila's heart was pounding. He was speaking up when it mattered most. "What do you mean?" she asked, careful not to show any excitement. "I've worked so hard on your behalf." She had to feign indignation, of course.

"See?" Elizabeth ranted. "I told you if you'd just been clear with her in the beginning!"

"I can't disagree," he said. "It has taken me some time to learn how to do that. I beg your pardon, Lady Aleksander, but my affections lie elsewhere, and I cannot, in good conscience, offer marriage to a woman I will never love for the sake of the duchy."

Lila was so thrilled she feared she might faint. What was it that Valentin always said? When you least expect a miracle, one will come. But she needed Lord Abbott to tell her. "Who?" she asked. "Miss Porter?"

"Not Miss Porter. Hattie Woodchurch."

With a cry of distress, Elizabeth fell into a chair. "Your father would turn over in his grave! How could you possibly settle on the least acceptable woman?"

"I love her," he said simply.

"I love her, too," Lila said.

Elizabeth gasped with shock and stared wildly at Lila. "What are you doing?" she demanded.

"But it doesn't matter," Lord Abbott said. "Miss Woodchurch has refused me."

"What?" Lila exclaimed as Elizabeth shrieked again.

"Who would refuse you? Is she mad? Have you considered that she is quite possibly *mad*?"

"I think," Lila said, "that she has refused you because of her family, my lord."

That earned her a look. He frowned. "What of them?"

"Rather bluntly put, they are not the sort of people families like yours would want to associate with."

"I don't care about that," he said dismissively.

"Yes, you do!" his mother insisted desperately. "You are the duke of Santiava! You are Viscount Abbott!"

"Those are titles, Mami. I am a person."

"You're talking nonsense, Mateo. Why are you doing this to me?"

To that, he smiled wryly. "I'm not doing this to you, I am doing it for me. Because there is no time like the present. *Camarón que se duerme se lo lleva la corriente.*"

"What does that mean? No one knows what that means," Elizabeth snapped.

"It means, the shrimp that sleeps is taken by the current. I don't intend to sleep now. I've been asleep for too long." He shifted his gaze to Lila. "Tell me about them."

"That…is not easily explained," she said, holding up a hand. "But I may have a plan."

"What plan?" he asked.

"Lila! We don't need a plan, we need you to talk some sense into him," Elizabeth all but wailed.

Lila shook her head. "Elizabeth, love, I understand your concern. But in my experience, the heart will not stop loving on command. You are swimming upstream." She turned to the viscount. "I need to think through a few things. But I will figure it out. I always do." She had no real plan at all, really. The idea she had was not only improbable, it could be particularly disastrous for Miss Raney. But that was a problem for someone else. It was a fact that sometimes the execution of her services was not pleasant, but the aftermath could be so beautiful. Before she did anything, however, she needed to be assured that if she risked everything, Hattie Woodchurch would marry this man.

Now that Beck had given Hattie a way out of her family's house, there might be a solution.

CHAPTER THIRTY-SEVEN

HATTIE COULDN'T COMPLAIN about her situation at Lady Bradenton's house. She had her own room on the third floor. It was hot in the afternoons, but there were no cats. There was hardly any room at all for the dresses she'd managed to procure during her spring of trying to be someone, and she'd had to fold a few and put them away. Lady Bradenton had informed her that she would tolerate blue and gray in a dress, but nothing too cheerful or colorful. "Color is not appropriate for the sort of work you're doing."

Oh dear, God forbid she wear yellow while reading the Bible to the old woman.

That was the first thing she'd learned—she was to read scripture to Lady Bradenton every day over tea.

This was her second day of reading, but she didn't hear anything she was saying. She couldn't think about anything other than Teo. She couldn't see anything other than him. It was like her mind had divided itself between him and functioning.

She was just about finished with today's scripture reading when Lady Bradenton's ancient butler, Darwin, came into the parlor. "A caller, madam," he said with a bow, and proceeded to shuffle across the room carrying a silver tray with a calling card.

"A caller! But I'm not expecting anyone. Why must people call without giving some notice?" she complained.

"The caller is for Miss Woodchurch," he said, and held out the tray to Hattie.

"What?" Lady Bradenton exclaimed.

"What?" Hattie said at the same time. She took the card and suppressed a loud groan.

"Well, Darwin? Send them in, for heaven's sake," Lady Bradenton said.

A moment later, Lila swept into the room.

"Who, pray tell, are *you*?" Lady Bradenton demanded.

"You don't remember me? You were my mother's dear friend."

Lady Bradenton peered at her. "Lila?"

"The one and the same," Lila said. "So good to see you."

"What are you doing here?" Lady Bradenton asked.

"Oh, I just needed to speak with Miss Woodchurch. You don't mind, do you?"

"I do," Hattie said, but Lila already had her hand on her arm and squeezed it tightly. "We'll be but a moment." She pinched Hattie.

"Ouch!"

"Please," Lila said and smiled again at Lady Bradenton.

Hattie reluctantly followed her into the hall. "I am no longer employed by the viscount, Lila. I have nothing to say to you."

"Do you know that you and Lord Abbott are the two most intractable, *stubborn* people I have ever known? Hattie— do you love him?"

Hattie's mouth dropped open. She felt a wave of nausea roil through her. "What?"

"You heard me. Do you love him?"

She couldn't answer. Of course she loved him, more than anything—but love could not overcome her family. They were insurmountable. She wouldn't have a dowry, and she wasn't even sure she could gain her parents' blessing.

"Just tell me the truth, please. I'm trying desperately to help you both."

She wanted to dissemble, to make up some reason she did not. But she remembered she was not going to be demure, to say things people thought she ought to say instead of what she truly felt. She squared her shoulders. "Yes, Lila, I love him. With all my heart. More than I thought was even possible. Which is why I left! I can't bear to see him marry the person I thought was my friend. There you are—are you happy now?"

Lila clucked her tongue. "She was never your friend," she said. "Flora is in love with someone other than Lord Abbott."

Hattie gaped at her. "That's not true. She wants to marry Teo."

"Teo," Lila said with a smile. "I like that. And she may want to marry him for all the benefits that would bring, but trust me, she loves someone else."

Hattie was stunned. She thought back through all the times she and Flora had been together. She couldn't think of a single gentleman Flora might have mentioned or noticed. *"Who?"*

"That will come later. For now, I need to know if you love the viscount. If you want to be with him always. If you are willing to live in Santiava, away from your family."

Hattie laughed bitterly. "Of course I do. But it's impossible. You saw my home. You met my parents. My father would find a way to extort money from him. And if Teo ever were to meet my family? He would run, as anyone with half a brain would."

"Don't worry about that," Lila said airily.

"Rather easy for you to say."

Lila suddenly cupped her face. "Darling...you deserve love. You deserve happiness. Believe that, and it will come to you."

Tears suddenly sprang to Hattie's eyes, embarrassing her. "I don't trust anyone," she said. "Not anymore."

Lila smiled sadly and caressed her cheek. "You really are a dear. All right, at least trust that you will attend one last soiree."

Hattie shook her head.

"You will, because I hope that things will be made clear, for all parties involved." She reached into her reticule and withdrew an invitation. "It's a soiree. Have you ever heard the name Emma Clark?"

Hattie shook her head.

"Lady Dearborn rarely comes to London. But when she does, she hosts the most delightful parties." She winked. "I'll see you there. And now, I really must be off. I'm to meet Mr. Donovan shortly. We have some work to do." She turned and hurried down the hall.

Hattie watched her go, clutching that last invitation. She didn't want to get her hopes up just to see them dashed. Did she really deserve happiness?

"Miss Woodchurch!" Lady Bradenton called. "Where are you?"

Hattie slipped the invitation into her pocket with a sigh, then trudged back to the scriptures.

CHAPTER THIRTY-EIGHT

MATEO DID NOT want to attend this soiree with yet another roomful of people he didn't know and didn't want to know. He'd already received a note from Lord Raney asking him to call at his earliest convenience but had managed to put that off.

His decision had been made. The estate had been sorted, and he was prepared to leave it with the stodgy Mr. Callum. He was departing London without a bride or a marriage match. He would call on Lord Raney—he was not a coward—but he was putting it off as long as he might. The man would not be pleased to know he would not be making an offer.

Still, Lady Aleksander had insisted he come to one last event, that she thought the tables would turn in his favor. When he asked what that meant, she was elusive. But she said, "I think Hattie will be in attendance."

He went.

It was only nine o'clock, but the soiree was already at full bore—music spilled out the open windows of the town house onto the street. He could hear so many raised voices, all of them gay, laughing and hooraying at each other.

The door was opened by a butler who looked harried. Mateo handed him the invitation, but because it was so loud, the butler gestured for him to follow. Mateo quickly lost the butler in the crush. Still, he managed to find his way into a drawing room where dozens of people were crammed.

A woman with stunning auburn hair turned around when he entered. She had pretty green eyes and a warm smile and flushed cheeks. "Welcome!" she cried happily. "Welcome to England, to my home!"

Mateo bowed. "Lady Dearborn, I presume."

"Yes! But you must call me Emma. Everyone calls me Emma. And you must be Lord Abbott! I can tell. You have an air of sophistication about you. Do you like wine, Lord Abbott? We have quite a lot of it. And dancing in the dining room. We haven't a ballroom here, but we've moved the tables and chairs. Feeney, show him to the dining room! Do you like to dance? I hope you do, because I'd like to dance with you. I'll come in shortly."

The butler had returned to his side. Lady Dearborn turned away from him and resumed her conversation with two other gentlemen. It appeared that everyone in that room was drunk.

Mateo dutifully followed the butler to the dining room, past all the laughing, drunken people. As he looked through that crowded room for any sign of Hattie, he was accosted by Lord Iddesleigh.

"My lord! Wonderful to see you!" Beck said jovially, the scent of whisky heavy on his breath. "I said to Lila you'd not come, as you are preparing to leave soon. When do you leave?"

"Next week," Mateo answered.

"So soon? Before an offer is made? I happened to see Raney a day or so ago—between you and me, he's eager for your call."

"I understand," Mateo said.

"Good, good," Beck said, and clapped him on the back

too hard. "Wine? Emma has the best wine. Has it brought in from France in the middle of the night, if you take my meaning." He reached around Mateo and took a glass from a passing footman's tray and handed it to Mateo.

"Thank you." He sipped the wine, then glanced around the room…and found Hattie.

She was standing alone in the middle of the crowd, looking at him. She smiled. He did, too. He suddenly handed the wine back to Beck. "If you would be so kind," he mumbled, and Beck juggled his glass to take Mateo's.

He moved through the crowd to her, curtly greeting people who tried to intercept him as he went, his gaze locked on her. Hattie's eyes followed his progress, her smile one of amusement. People watched him, curious why he was pushing through as he was, some of them offering him a drink. He ignored them all.

When he finally reached her, having escaped the clutches of a woman whose hair was starting to fall out of her coif, he was a bit tongue-tied. "You are so beautiful."

She laughed. "And you are too kind."

"How… How are you? How do you find your new position?"

"Tedious," she said, and glanced past him. "I am forced to read aloud scripture. And there is not much actual writing, so my excellent penmanship is going to waste."

"A tragedy," he murmured as his eyes moved over her. Just looking at her made his heart feel full. He was a different man. A better man.

"And there are no pastries."

"I must ask—how have you kept from throwing your body from the roof?"

Her smiled broadened with delight. "It's been a terrible struggle."

He could feel a tether between them that felt like a lifetime of knowing her instead of a few short weeks. "I've missed you," he said.

"I've missed you," she whispered. "Everyone is looking at us. Have you made your offer?"

"Let them look, I don't care. And no, I have not."

"When will you?"

He very cavalierly tucked behind her ear the tendril of her hair that always fell, uncaring who saw him. "Dance?"

She shook her head.

"Walk in the garden?"

She smiled sadly.

"Then will you at least run away with me? We'll run upstairs first so I can make love to you."

She laughed, but her gaze moved past him.

"Then we'll take to the streets. We'll run until we find a stable where we can rest and decide what to do from there. Perhaps steal a horse."

"I don't ride."

"You'll ride with me."

One of her brows arched. "People will talk. They're already talking. If you turned around just now, you'd see dozens of eyes on us."

"They will talk no matter what, Hattie. They will be kind or cruel—it hardly matters what we do—so let us do what we want."

"Then may we just stand here?"

He dropped his hand and twined his fingers with hers. "It is not my preference, but for you, anything."

"Are you still leaving in a few days?"

He nodded.

"I will miss your baking terribly," she said. "Just when you discovered the secret to a moist sponge cake. Mrs.

O'Malley has been desperate to make your acquaintance. She'll be so disappointed."

"I will miss your long-winded tales."

She laughed and squeezed his fingers. "No, you won't."

"I will. I will be reminded of you every time the leaves of the trees rustle incessantly outside my window."

"I will miss you staring at me as if you don't speak a word of English."

Mateo laughed at that. "And I will miss...every bloody thing about you. Hattie." Emotion overcame him. "I need you to be my duchess. Will you marry me? Come with me? Be with me?"

"Teo," she said, and smiled. "Is this why Lady Aleksander insisted I come? To have my heart broken all over again?"

The spell was weakened for a moment. He paused and frowned. "She asked you to come this evening?" He was confused. Lady Aleksander said Hattie was coming, but she had not indicated she'd asked her to.

Hattie nodded.

"Why?"

"I don't know, exactly. She said it was important, and that all would be clear."

He didn't understand. "What will be clear?"

He never heard Hattie's answer—their not-so-private conversation was interrupted by a scream.

CHAPTER THIRTY-NINE

N<small>EITHER</small> L<small>ILA NOR</small> Beck dreamed it would go like this. The plan, which Donovan had devised, was to catch Miss Raney and Mr. Woodchurch together, and then make them an offer that they hoped neither would refuse for the sake of their reputations. But they didn't count on Lord Raney being on hand when they did.

That spun their plan wildly out of control.

It all happened so fast! Lila had been keeping an eye on Mr. Woodchurch, watching him saunter about the crowded house, whisky in hand, flirting with ladies, inserting himself into conversations, and smirking at everyone around him. It amazed her that no one ever turned a cold shoulder to him.

But then she saw a footman come out of a service door painted to look like the wall, and then watched Mr. Woodchurch go through it once he noticed it.

"Beck," she'd hissed, and hit him on the shoulder. Beck had been partaking of the whisky and appeared to be arguing with Lady Maisie. *"Ouch,"* he said, rubbing his shoulder.

"He just went through that servants' door."

"What servants' door?"

Lila had to point for him to see, and when she did, the door opened and Miss Raney slipped through. Beck gasped with shock like a young girl. "Come, come," he said.

"Where are we going?" Lady Maisie asked.

"You are staying right here, darling."

"No," she said, and stubbornly followed along as they made their way around the perimeter of the room and to the servants' door. But just as Lila was reaching for the door, she heard her name. Lord Raney was approaching, all smiles.

Beck instantly saw the conundrum. "Maisie, quick as a lark—make certain Lord Raney doesn't follow us," he said, and nudged his daughter forward.

"How am I to do that?" she asked.

Lila wasn't going to lose this moment. As Beck and his daughter sorted things out, she opened the servants' door and stepped through into a poorly lit, short hallway. At the end of it was another door. It was a passage for servants.

"Lady Aleksander?"

Lila whipped around—she couldn't believe it—Lord Raney had followed her through the servants' door. Where was Beck? "Oh, my lord!" She smiled. "You must forgive me. I was looking for the ladies' retiring room."

"I think you've gone the wrong way. I'm certain it's at the other end of the dining room. This is a service passage."

"Are you sure? I was positive it was this way," she said. "I'll just—"

Lord Raney was a gentleman. "Do you think so?" he said as he strode forward to push open the other door.

"What's happening?" Beck whispered loudly behind her, causing Lila to jump.

She glared at him. "Could you not have kept him from coming through?"

"Did you see how determined my daughter was?" he shot back. "And really—"

"What the bloody hell!" Lord Raney's voice thundered through the small hallway.

Lila and Beck looked at each other, then sprinted after him.

They burst into the room to find Flora Raney and Daniel Woodchurch standing guiltily together. Her face was red, his beard and hair were mussed. Her skirt was wrinkled where it had been bunched up around her waist. It was terribly obvious what had been happening in this room. Lila gasped. "Dear God! Miss Raney! Mr. Woodchurch!"

"I will kill you," Lord Raney shouted, and lunged for Mr. Woodchurch. Miss Raney shrieked and tried to throw herself in front of Mr. Woodchurch. Beck lunged for Lord Raney, stopping him before he could inflict bodily harm on anyone.

But the damage was done.

Lila, Donovan, and Beck had never meant to create a scandal. They'd only wanted to catch the lovers and threaten them in exchange for their cooperation. There was a lot of shouting and crying until Lila convinced Lord Raney and Mr. Woodchurch that the conversation should be had at the Woodchurch house on Portman Square. She went out to fetch Lady Raney, and they met the others through a back entrance to the mews.

But their attempts to keep it under wraps were pointless; whispers were already firing through the crowd. Apparently, they were not the only ones who had noticed the growing infatuation and absences surrounding Miss Raney and Mr. Woodchurch throughout the Season. If there was one thing the *ton* loved, it was a proper scandal.

THIS TIME, it was Queenie who told Hattie what no one else would. "You heard about Miss Raney, didn't you?" she asked at the buffet table.

"Miss Raney? Do you mean Flora?" Hattie laughed. "No, what?"

Queenie had a peculiar smile on her face. "She was caught in a compromising position with someone who is all wrong for her."

The bottom of Hattie's stomach dropped. "What do you mean, caught?"

"What do you think I mean, Hattie? And by her own father, too."

Hattie was shocked. Flora? "With *who*?"

Queenie laughed. "Really, you're no use to anyone, Harriet Woodchurch. Do you really expect me to believe you don't know who?"

"By God, Queenie, just tell me—"

"Your brother," she said, and smirked.

And still, Hattie did not understand. "My brother... what?"

Queenie rolled her eyes. "You should consider the theater—you are very good at deception. Your brother was kissing Flora and I don't know what else in a dark room and her father walked in. It's over. The whole Santiavan duchess thing is over. I *knew* it would never happen. I knew she'd sabotage it."

None of this made sense. Flora had been caught with *Daniel*? "You must be mistaken."

"I'm not. She's been toying with him for a while. If you don't believe me, go home. They've all gone there to set the matter to rights."

"This can't be true," Hattie insisted. "Flora hates my brother, and he's never said a kind word about her."

"Oh, Hattie. Sometimes attraction looks like hate."

Hattie felt sick to her stomach. She could be so stupid at times. And now they were going to her family's house? Lord Raney meant to demand satisfaction from her father?

She whirled around and began to push her way from

the room. She ran into the street and looked wildly about for a cab or conveyance. Why were there never any cabs?

"Hattie!"

She looked back—Teo was jogging out to her. "What are you doing? Where are you going?"

"Teo." Her voice was shaking. "I have to go."

"What's wrong?" he asked, catching her arm. "You're shaking."

"Something has happened. It's my brother, and I have to go home."

"I'll take you."

"No!" She shoved against his chest. "You can't come!"

He took her arm again. "Don't be ridiculous. My carriage is just here." He pointed. She looked at the carriage and imagined it rolling up to her home. She imagined how devastating it would be to watch Teo discover how her family lived.

She would rather die than have that happen. But she couldn't believe it—she chose her terrible, awful family over her pride. Swallowing hard, she said, "Let's go."

CHAPTER FORTY

HATTIE WAS FRANTIC. Mateo only got a bit of the crisis from her—a compromising situation between her brother and a woman, a fear of a duel or worse. When they reached the modest house near Portman Square, she tried to keep him from going inside. But Mateo refused. "You are wasting your breath. I will not allow you to face whatever is happening in there alone."

She looked crestfallen. "You'll never speak to me again," she said tearfully. And she ran inside.

Mateo went after her.

At first, he was confused as to where they were. He thought it was a warehouse of some sort. He didn't understand why there were so many grandfather clocks, so many tea services—on every surface. There were dress forms and hats and stacks of books he had to dodge as he made his way after Hattie. And *cats*. So many cats, a dozen if there was one.

He followed Hattie and the sound of angry voices down the hall, dipping and sidestepping and stumbling over something, until they entered a room where the hearth was blazing. But every bit of furniture had a cat, or a stack of newspapers, or a collection of needlepoints and books. He noticed in one corner there was a collection of spittoons.

The assembly of people included Lady Aleksander and Beck, Lord and Lady Raney, their daughter, Hattie's brother, and two teenaged boys, laughing as if they were at a public house.

There was a woman in a chair in her nightclothes. A small, mean-looking gentleman was perched on the edge of his seat, glaring at Lord Raney.

Lord Raney was shouting at Hattie's brother. He was rattling off so many things so quickly that Mateo had trouble following in English. But then the small man stood up with a roar. "You will leave my son be!"

Mateo unthinkingly stepped between the two men before it could come to blows, his arms stretched to keep them apart. "Gentlemen!"

"Please, everyone! If we could just take a deep breath, this can all be put to rights!" Lady Aleksander pleaded.

Everyone stopped talking. Lady Raney was weeping. The woman Mateo assumed was Mrs. Woodchurch was fuming. "How dare you come in here and make any demands!" she cried.

"Hush, Theodora," Mr. Woodchurch said, and glared at Lady Aleksander. "How? How do we put any of this to rights?"

"Quite clearly there are affections here," Lady Aleksander said coolly, gesturing to Hattie's brother and Miss Raney.

"There are?" Mateo asked in surprise.

"Who are *you*?" Mr. Woodchurch demanded of Mateo.

"May I introduce Lord Abbott," Beck said. "Or his grace, the Duke of Santiava. Really depends on where you are. You were saying, Lila?"

She smoothed her gown. "I was saying that clearly, Miss Raney has affection for Mr. Woodchurch. Isn't that so, Miss Raney?"

Miss Raney looked frightened. She looked at Hattie.

"Flora... If it's true, now is the time to say it," Hattie said carefully.

Miss Raney looked at Mateo. "I beg your pardon, my lord, but...it's true."

"Good *God*," Lord Raney cried. *"Him?"*

"And now that everyone in the *ton* knows about the, ah... the scene," Lady Aleksander said delicately, "then perhaps we ought to be about how to make this less odious than it is. What if... What if it was made known that Miss Raney never had any intentions of accepting the viscount's offer?"

Mateo blanched. "An offer has not been extended," he reminded her.

"Yes, yes, we all know that, but speculation has been wild. What if the rumor was that she never intended to accept it because she had already accepted an offer from Mr. Woodchurch?"

"Just like that?" Hattie's father said. "I don't know. Seems to me that some compensation—"

"Papa!" Hattie said sternly. "Now is not the time."

"Mr. Woodchurch," Lady Aleksander said, "a marriage to Miss Raney would lift the Woodchurch name in the eyes of society."

Hattie's father snorted. "I don't give a good goddamn what society thinks of me," he sneered. And then he paused. "Just how high would our name be lifted? Practically speaking?"

"Bloody *hell*, Flora!" Lord Raney cried. "Look what you've done." He gestured at Hattie's father.

"And then, so that everyone comes away with their reputations intact and no one the wiser," Lady Aleksander continued, speaking to Mr. Woodchurch, "you will accept an offer for your daughter's hand and, naturally, provide her an excellent dowry. Were it not for her, none of this would have happened."

"So she is who I have to thank?" Lord Raney said, eyeing Hattie.

"What?" Hattie exclaimed. "But I don't have an offer of—"

"You do, Hattie." Mateo felt a surge of gratitude for Lady Aleksander. "You've had the offer more than once. Mr. Woodchurch, I should like to ask for the hand of your daughter in marriage. That is, if she is willing."

"You want to marry *her*?" Mrs. Woodchurch blurted in surprise.

"I do," Mateo confirmed.

"Absolutely not," Mr. Woodchurch said.

"Absolutely *yes*!" Mrs. Woodchurch shouted. Dumping a cat off her lap, she came to her feet. "That's it, Hugh! I will not have you stand in the way of our daughter's good fortune! For once in your life, let loose the purse strings!"

"Let loose the purse strings?" he shouted back at her. "Woman, have a look at the number of clocks and tea services around you!"

She ignored him. "You have our blessing, Lord…or your grace."

Mr. Woodchurch did not contradict her, but he glared at Mateo.

Lady Raney began to sob. "How is this happening? It will never work! No one will ever believe I allowed my daughter to marry into this family!"

"Mama," Flora said and tried to smile. "I *love* Daniel!"

"You do?" the younger Mr. Woodchurch asked skeptically.

Miss Raney looked stunned by his doubt. "Of course I do. Don't you love me?"

"I mean…" Hattie's brother rubbed his nape. "I don't know if I'd say—"

"He loves you," Beck said, and clamped a hand down on the young man's shoulder. "He loves you, or he drags his family's name into ruin, and then there will be nothing left for him, so I think he will see that he loves you *very much*."

Miss Raney gaped at her love. Mr. Woodchurch looked nervously around the room. The two boys were laughing. "Shut up," he said to them. "Fine. Flora, I love you. I want to marry you." He turned woodenly to Lord Raney. "My lord, may I have Flora's hand," he said without enthusiasm.

"Yes," Lord Raney replied, and Lady Raney and Miss Raney began to cry in unison. "But don't expect a large dowry. You dragged us into this fiasco."

"How much?" the senior Mr. Woodchurch asked and seemed, incredibly, truly curious.

Just then, the grandfather clocks began to chime the eleventh hour, the sound of it as deafening as the people in the room who were wailing.

Mateo looked at Hattie. She looked at him. Her eyes were shining with love, with relief, with all the things he felt inside him. She began to laugh. Mateo did, too. He nudged two cats out of the way and embraced her. "I'm going to marry you," he said. "I'm going to take you to Santiava and away from this."

"Oh, Teo… When can we go?" She laughed again.

LILA WAS SPENT. She looked around that room, amazed that she was able to pull this off. Well—she and Beck and Donovan. There was still the problem of Elizabeth, who would wail just as loudly as Lady Raney. But Lila was pleased. She couldn't wait to tell this very strange story to Valentin.

She was the first to leave the Woodchurch house. She

returned to Emma Clark's party to say good-night to her. She was such a lively woman. She couldn't imagine why Emma's husband had left her for years to wander around Africa and the Sahara. She was the sort of woman who would be perfect for Lila's nephew. It was a pity she was married.

Ah well. So many people. So many love stories. She was eager to go to the next one.

EPILOGUE

Santiava, 1871

THEY WERE AT Castillo Estrella, on the roof. There was a blanket spread beneath them, as well as a stack of pillows and a selection of pastries. Next to Hattie was a bassinet. Their newborn, Luisa, was sleeping under the stars.

Luisa's parents had just made love and were happily stargazing. Teo complained they would be caught, bare as the day they were born, but Hattie laughed as she crawled on top of him. "Who in their right mind would come up on the roof to see what we are doing?"

"Rosa," he said. "She thinks Luisa is hers."

"She wouldn't dare climb all those stairs," Hattie said, and had unbuttoned his shirt.

It had gone from there, Hattie crying out so loudly that Mateo warned her she'd bring the household to the roof.

As they lay together under that warm summer night sky, Mateo began to tell her about the time he'd gone fox hunting with his brother. It was a long, detailed recounting. The duke talked. And he talked. And he talked. He did not leave out a single detail—even the color of the leaves was something he wanted to share.

Hattie had never believed she could be so happy. She didn't know this sort of happiness even existed. But she was, indelibly, indestructibly happy every single day.

She wrote her mother from time to time, but mostly, she heard about her family through Flora, who was not her friend, but was her sister-in-law, and wrote often to complain about her husband's bad habits. If Flora had asked her that spring the Santiavan duke had come to London, Hattie would have told her what no one else would: that Daniel would make a terrible husband.

The twins had been sent to boarding school—apparently, they'd become too obnoxious for even a mother to love. Speaking of her parents, they had been invited to a party or two, and always left early to get home to the cats. Queenie, Flora said, had latched on to Miss Porter and was hoping to marry her brother, who was just as handsome as Christiana was beautiful.

Mrs. O'Malley had been terribly sorry to see her go, but she'd had her wish before Hattie departed London—she'd met the baking viscount. And Teo and Rosa were still trying to perfect the sponge cake.

Mateo's mother hadn't quite accepted the fact that her son had married a nobody. But she'd been a little more forgiving once Luisa came into this world. So was the parliamentary council of advisors. When Mateo and Hattie had first come to Santiava—married, as they had thought they ought to straightaway, given the events in London—there had been some rumblings from those sympathetic to Spain. What better time than now, they asked, to unite with Spain? Look how the duke conducted himself. Look who he'd married! She was no one!

But the loyal Santiavans had not shunned her—they had welcomed her. And, when she became pregnant, well... everyone was suddenly determined to pass legislation allowing the firstborn of the duke to succeed him so that the duchy would carry on. One day, Luisa would be the sovereign duchess of Santiava.

Hattie was learning Spanish. Mateo helped her, and even wrote things for her in Spanish so she would learn how to write it properly.

He was still talking. God in heaven, did her husband talk. Once the gates of trust had been opened, words spilled out of him. Story after story, observations, quips. It was mostly to her, however—he was still rather shy in public. But his siblings came often, and he was beginning to talk with them, too. He could make Roberto laugh like no one else.

Hattie helped herself to a Santiavan tart. She was gaining weight but she didn't mind. This was what happiness did—it left you feeling full and satiated.

Mateo took Luisa out of her bassinet and laid her across his bare chest. "I wanted to name you Estrella," he said to the baby as he stroked her head. "Your mother said it was confusing, Estrella of Castillo Estrella."

"And Luisa is such a pretty name," Hattie said.

"Do you see this sky, Luisa?" Mateo asked. "I give it all to you. I will make this sky your sky. You will never want." He kissed the top of her head on a tuft of dark hair like her father's. She had her mother's blue eyes. Hattie leaned over and made sure the baby was covered, then curled against her husband.

"Do you know what I wish?" Mateo asked. "I wish that we will be like this, always. Just the three of us."

She stared up at the night sky and smiled. "I don't want it to be like this always."

"*Qué?* Why would you say that?"

"Because I want there to be more of us. Children and dogs. Eventually, grandchildren."

"All right. I will agree to it," he said, and kissed her temple.

Luisa stirred and began to cry. "Your baby is hungry, *mi amor*," he said, and handed their daughter to her. And as she nursed her child, Mateo fed Hattie pieces of tart and told her about his travel to the Sahara Desert. She didn't have the heart to tell him he'd already told her this story. It didn't matter—she'd listen to him tell the same story a thousand times and still be this content.

No, Hattie had never realized happiness could be this big and this wonderful.

* * * * *

Get 3 FREE REWARDS!

We'll send you 2 FREE Books plus a FREE Mystery Gift.

FREE
Value Over
$20

Both the **Romance** and **Suspense** collections feature compelling novels written by many of today's bestselling authors.

YES! Please send me 2 FREE novels from the Essential Romance or Essential Suspense Collection and my FREE gift (gift is worth about $10 retail). After receiving them, if I don't wish to receive any more books, I can return the shipping statement marked "cancel." If I don't cancel, I will receive 4 brand-new novels every month and be billed just $7.49 each in the U.S. or $7.74 each in Canada. That's a savings of at least 17% off the cover price. It's quite a bargain! Shipping and handling is just 50¢ per book in the U.S. and $1.25 per book in Canada.* I understand that accepting the 2 free books and gift places me under no obligation to buy anything. I can always return a shipment and cancel at any time by calling the number below. The free books and gift are mine to keep no matter what I decide.

Choose one: ☐ **Essential Romance** ☐ **Essential Suspense** ☐ **Or Try Both!**
(194/394 BPA GRNM) (191/391 BPA GRNM) (194/394 & 191/391 BPA GRQZ)

Name (please print)

Address _____ Apt. #

City _____ State/Province _____ Zip/Postal Code

Email: Please check this box ☐ if you would like to receive newsletters and promotional emails from Harlequin Enterprises ULC and its affiliates. You can unsubscribe anytime.

Mail to the **Harlequin Reader Service:**
IN U.S.A.: P.O. Box 1341, Buffalo, NY 14240-8531
IN CANADA: P.O. Box 603, Fort Erie, Ontario L2A 5X3

Want to try 2 free books from another series? Call 1-800-873-8635 or visit www.ReaderService.com.

STRSMAX23

HARLEQUIN
PLUS

Try the best multimedia subscription service for romance readers like you!

Read, Watch and Play.

Experience the easiest way to get the romance content you crave.

Start your **FREE TRIAL** at
<u>www.harlequinplus.com/freetrial</u>.